STRANGE PLAYGROUNDS

GEORGE DANIEL LEA

dark moon

LARGO, FLORIDA

DARK MOON BOOKS
an imprint of Stony Meadow Publishing
Largo, Florida

www.DarkMoonBooks.com

STRANGE PLAYGROUNDS

Cover art by

ISBN-13: 978-0-9894090-6-3

Printed in the United States of America

dark moon

DEDICATIONS

To Ray, without whom I wouldn't have had the courage, to Nick, without whom I wouldn't have had the scope, and to my parents, without whom I wouldn't have had the space or time. (You can find out more about Nick at https://www.facebook.com/NickHardyPhotography.)

Also, to everyone at Dark Moon Books who allowed me the opportunity.

FOREWORD

Done. *Done.* An intensely strange experience, hitting that last key, placing that last figure; a sense of goodbye, as with moving home or watching a child leave for their first day of school or work. I can barely recall where most of the stories in this collection originated; only that they span from when I was a very young—an intensely naïve, insular, ill-experienced young man, utterly consumed and obsessed by the absurdity in his own skull, and seeking a means of exorcising it, to a point barely two weeks before this moment, when the closing piece found itself scrawled in haphazard bits and pieces snatched between work, shopping, paying bills and whatever myriad mundane pursuits constitute my life off page.

So, what is this *thing,* exactly? For the most part, that's up to you to decide; as the stories themselves consistently assert, whatever significance I could enshrine or insist on will likely pale to whatever *you* find here and in whatever follows. I can tell you that it is an attempt . . . an attempt to explore certain obsessions and ideas; ideas concerning stories, their nature and relation to us; their creators and subjects. It is an attempt to delve into the essential metaphysics of what is generally corralled in the "horror" genre-stable; to surgically tear the subject's tongue from its cheek and explore its themes and subjects with a little earnestness; to appreciate the profundity of them. Beyond that, I sincerely hope that it's something that disturbs and distresses more than terrifies; I don't write fiction to "frighten;" I write to unseat, to allow us both a moment of removal from certainty, and in that removal, a place where we can regard ourselves and the playgrounds where we wander from a little distance.

That's the point, you see?; The essential conceit. Where it came from, I don't know; only that it featured in a far earlier incarnation of the title story, long since consigned to the folders of abandonment hidden like corpses in the walls throughout my apartment, the story itself a reaction to Edgar Allen Poe's classic *The Pit and the Pendulum,* an exercise in ineffable dread in which the protagonist describes experiences of horror and confusion in acute sensory detail, yet lacking any context for reason or explanation, at least until towards the closing portions of the tale. This is where I always felt it failed; through justification of its core circumstance. How much more terrifying if we never find out where, or how, or why! But we do, much to the tale's dilution.

As for the rest, they are a rag-doll, (post)modern Promethean bunch, very different in terms of tone and subject, but all related in terms of their core themes and significance. This didn't become apparent to me until I began reading through great wedges of what I'd written over the years of university and the period of unemployment that followed, patterns and unifying factors becoming clear with each tale added to the pile, arguably chief of which is that of *shedding;* of humanity as egg or chrysalis, the dry shell of old certainties waiting to be—often painfully—torn away by experience or revelation, resulting in the emergence of something new, often beautiful and horrifying in equal measure.

But whatever you happen to take away from here, whether it's the metaphysics I envisioned upon writing, or something entirely removed, I sincerely hope it's something cherished as well as something you might be unsettled by; something you might return to, when time and circumstance allow, and perhaps find yourself there, in your own playground, ready for a new game to begin.

George Lea

07/04/2013

CONTENTS

STRANGE PLAYGROUNDS

A vile waking, clawing up through layers of shifting sludge. The details weren't clear yet; his name, his nature; what manner of world he woke to. They came by and by, buzzing around his skull like flies in search of rot in which to lay their eggs.

It wasn't light he struggled towards, but a pin-prick of pulsing darkness; deeper and more absolute even than the species surrounding him. Pain waxed with every inch he crawled, but he couldn't stop. He had to be awake, and away from dreams.

*

The groan echoed, returning corrupt and distorted. He imagined unseen creatures in the darkness, mimicking, making mockery of his confusion like cruel school-yard children.

Pulsing pink fog filled his skull to capacity, thoughts blundering, groping blindly for one another. Fragments of memory tumbled behind his eyes; shards of broken mirror reflecting kaleidoscopic nonsense. The drink again? Or perhaps that beloved bitch opium had coaxed him back into her arms . . . ?

Too painful, the pieces scattering beneath his scrabbling fingers.

Only the *where* mattered, and the *how* that would lead him away.

Darkness so dense he couldn't see the hand he held up in front of his face. The ground where he'd made his bed was cold; uneven stone, worn smooth in places as if by water's passage. Nothing bruised or broken, insofar as he could tell.

What the *fuck* happened to his clothes?

A face wavered briefly through the fog: a boy, *beautiful;* features deeply shadowed by evening glow.

Then nothing.

Had he gotten lucky last night?

His legs trembled like a newborn foal's. He was going to vomit . . . maybe faint, the surrounding darkness shifting, whirling.

He closed his eyes, breathing slow and deep 'til the nausea subsided.

Wier. Anthony Wier. The name meant something. Was it his? Maybe, though he had an inkling it wasn't his first.

Anthony Wier, *Anthony Wier.* He liked it. It'd suffice, for now.

Rising from his squat, he extended his arms, testing the floor with experimental taps of his feet. *Vast chasms yawning, waiting for him to trip, tumble down, down* . . . The ground seemed solid enough, despite imagination's masochism. Inching forward, he inhaled sharply, his palms brushing fractured stone. A wall, irregular, coruscated with cracks and fissures.

Logic dictated that if he'd blundered in, there *must* be a way he could blunder *back out*; all he had to do was follow the wall, and he'd find it eventually. But which way?

Splaying out across the wall like some vast, hairless spider, he let his hands wander, testing the quality of stone to either side. The right found itself bruised and grazed by various edges and outcroppings, the left sliding, slipping across a smoother surface; slime slicked stone giving way to soft, mossy masses and fungal growths.

Lacking any more rational criteria, he opted for the left; at least that way he wouldn't bruise and slash himself to ribbons for want of liberation.

*

The plant life grew denser the further he progressed, feathery fronds licking his face and torso, a sharp, green scent filling his nostrils, dispelling some of the fog clouding his thoughts:

Anthony Wier. His name. He'd chosen it; found it on a gravestone, obscured by a tangled growth of weeds and white flowers.

His wandering fingers found strange configurations; fluted forms of cold, weeping flesh that quivered; blossoming or receding to the touch. *What else might be down here*?; Blind cave things, adapted to living off of the weird vegetation; eyeless, silvery spiders, spinning webs in cracks and fissures, translucent bodies pulsing with alien inner workings . . .

Feathery caresses at his groin, phantom fingers stroking him to semi-hardness. Imagination had him buried up to the hilt in lichen cushioned stone, some accommodating crack or fissure accepting him more readily than any ass-hole he'd ever pierced. What weird children might result from the union? Flesh and stone troll-things, the fauna of twisted fairy-tales . . .

He stopped dead, breath abruptly snaring. What was that?

His heart's frantic hammer, silence chattering, hissing . . .

Nothing. Daring to breathe again, he resumed his blind scramble, progressing no more than a few inches when his ears pricked anew. Closer this time, unmistakable:

Flap, flap, flap. Naked feet, slapping against stone. Somewhere off to his right, clearer, *closer* with every breath. Wier pressed himself against the wall, praying for whatever it was to pass him by.

So close now, *flap, flap, flap,* echoing all around, seeping into his skull to shake apart the thought recently coalesced there.

Then silence.

Wier didn't move, didn't dare breathe.

Behind. He could feel it. Did it see him, smell him? Tears stung his sinuses, terror turning his bowels to water.

A sigh, so soft as to be near indiscernible; a bed-mate's expression of delight in the dark, then *flap, flap, flap,* the unseen lover retreating into the distance.

What could he do? There was every chance that if he moved again, it would hear and return . . .

A face, beautiful in the blood-light, the shadows it wore seething, crawling like insects about to swarm.

He couldn't stay here. His throat was already sore, mouth parched. He had no choice but to *move.*

Despite his best efforts, his body—breath and heartbeat, the creak and crack of joints, the churning of bowels—sung a cacophony in the dark. He imagined even his thoughts were audible, whispering in the air around his head.

The wall abruptly gave way. He cried out, flailing for some hand-hold, finding it in the form of the opening's lips, fingers grasping stone so fervently they split and bled.

A small fissure, no more than a meter across. How close had he come to tumbling through, cracking his skull or breaking his neck? *Lying bloody and broken in the dark, waiting for thirst or blood loss to dull the pain . . .*

"No, no . . ." He shook his head, hissing denial through clenched teeth. It returned to him from the surrounding void, louder and distorted almost beyond recognition:

No, no!

Ghost children following in the darkness, dead eyes filled with moonlight, grimy faces smiling. He shook his head, but they kept pace, refusing to dissipate.

Ignore them. Keep moving...

Voices . . . in or outside his head? Impossible to be sure. They seemed to come from above and ahead, raining down like drips from stalactites, eliciting the bizarre urge to flap wings he didn't possess, soar up, up until he either found sunlight, or dashed out his mind in the effort.

*

Running water? Hard to be sure with his head playing tricks. He heard names whispered in his ear, some so familiar, he was sure he'd worn them once, donned and shed with the readiness of clothing; faceless ghosts, barely haunting memory.

The water overrode them, growing clearer and more definite with every step. Nothing much; the babbling of a filth clogged brook, but enough. *Enough.*

The vegetation grew sparse as he picked up his pace, the wall beneath no longer worn and broken but sheer as marble sculpted by human hands. He didn't stop to consider the significance of that, too in love with the prospect of escape.

Wier shrieked, his foot plunging ankle-deep into lukewarm water, something stirring in its depths, twining between his toes like lengths of living string. He staggered back, fighting to maintain balance, shaking and flailing the afflicted foot, trying to dislodge whatever clung there. It released its hold only when he scraped it against the wall, its length splitting, ending as little more than greasy smears on the stone.

Some sort of pool or puddle, no doubt fed by the nearby stream. God only knew what poisonous life fed and multiplied there; things like living blobs of mucus whose internal mechanisms visibly churned as they digested their prey, swarms of tiny, silver insects that were all legs and antennae, serving as little more than food for their more complex cousins. He'd fallen into an alien world, the one he'd left behind long since gone to radioactive ash for all he knew.

Had anyone even noticed his absence? *Was* there anyone? He couldn't remember. Only the face, now accompanied by fragments of related anatomy; a bony chest quilted in feathery blonde down, a groin boasting a similar crop; soft and sweet smelling.

None of it meant anything. He was alone.

Edging round the pool, he found the wall swelling out, becoming the pregnancy-swollen belly of some vast fertility idol. Maybe that's what it was; the remains of some ancient temple buried in a long forgotten cataclysm. He'd have gotten on his knees and prayed if he thought it'd do any good; shed blood, semen or whatever she demanded for a little sunlight.

Here he found the source of the running water; a vertical fissure coruscating up from the dome's base, almost splitting it in two. A small stream ran from the opening, threading out across the cavern floor where it no doubt fed various pools like the one he'd already stumbled across.

So thirsty, but how could he be sure the water was safe to drink? He recalled once watching a BBC documentary about entire cave systems eaten out by underground lakes and rivers of pure acid.

Not that it mattered; if he didn't drink soon, he'd be done for anyway.

Keeping one hand pressed against the dome, he knelt, dabbling fingers in the flow. His nostrils pricked with a freshness that put him in mind of breeze after summer lightning. The water was warm, like the pool he'd previously plunged into. He didn't know if that meant anything, was past caring.

Did he feel something moving in the stream, wriggling flecks and flickers brushing his hand before allowing themselves to be carried away?

The first mouthful was coppery to the taste, an underlying sweetness lingering in his mouth long after he swallowed. He wasn't sure his system would retain it, innards churning as if intent on vomiting the draught up. He waited for them to settle before taking a second, this one less bitter, his system accepting it without complaint.

There *were* things in the water, though it was only confirmed when one of them battened onto his hand. Screeching, he staggered back from the stream. Multiple, tiny thorns pierced his skin, clamping the thing in place. He couldn't tell what it was, only that it seemed to mostly consist of fangs and flailing legs. The thing squirmed, shuddered as it emptied its venom into him, threads of cold matter weaving beneath his skin, numbing his arm up to the elbow.

"Get *off,* get *off, you fucker*!" He flailed his hand against the Goddess's belly. Her child burst and bled with a faint sigh, its grip loosening as he bludgeoned it again and again, reducing it to pulp.

Scraping what remained away, he felt the swellings where its fangs had pierced him, the initial numbness in his arm now replaced by a waxing, feverish heat.

He had to get out, get to a hospital, or he'd die down here.

There was no indication save the stream itself that the crevice would lead anywhere.

Flap, flap, flap, faster this time, approaching with sickening speed.

Without a second thought, he stepped into the water, easing himself into the opening, praying to God—whom he'd never so much as acknowledged before—that it would deliver him into open air and sunlight.

*

The boy's name was Verity, or so he said; Sampson Verity, though Wier doubted it was the one he'd been christened with. Not that he of all people had grounds for comment in that regard.

Beauties were a dime a dozen these days; he knew places where he could go any day of the week and find himself surrounded by them, flocks of primped, painstakingly styled queens, each competing with the other in their manufactured prettiness.

Sampson wasn't amongst these, not even of the same species.

Like Wier, he sat apart, drinking whilst he watched the games of seduction play out.

Wier caught sight of him the second he walked through the door, his efforts to go unseen—more effective than many he'd witnessed—ironically drawing his attention.

Unlike the rest, he appeared not to have made a shred of conscious effort concerning his look; blonde, shoulder length hair tussled as if he'd only just dragged himself out of bed, jeans, shirt and leather jacket looking like they'd been his outfit of choice for several days. Wier could well believe he was one of the city's countless homeless wandered in off the street, willing to suck, fuck and endure any amount of abuse for the promise of a warm bed.

Plenty of others watched and waited in the club's recesses, seeking out that one; the choice morsel they could coax from the flock and consent to be devoured . . .

Wier didn't sense the same predatory intent here. The boy merely seemed fascinated by the processes he saw at play, content to observe without ever taking part.

He rarely felt inclined to approach anyone else, content to sit and wait for them to come to him. It was different with Verity, the threat of another laying claim before he could even speak spurring him to action:

"Hello."

"Hi." The boy glanced up, surprised that he'd been addressed.

"You here on your own?" A little blunt perhaps, but he found that subtlety rarely worked in such situations.

"Uh huh." He smiled, seeming on the verge of laughter.

"What?"

"Nothing really," the boy shrugged, "you just remind me of someone. You want to sit down?"

The boy didn't budge up or move away as their hips collided.

He wondered what Michael would make of this; an ephemeral twinge of guilt, though he couldn't even remember who Michael was.

They drank and spoke about things; the economy, God, the status of homosexuality in British society.

He recalled the first kiss clearly, the taste of rum, living meat and damp dirt in his mouth, then?

Chaos, nonsense.

Reflections in a broken mirror: the boy on his knees, begging to be pierced, shadows swarming around their intertwining bodies, whispering, congealing. Then the boy himself shifting around him, flesh running like molten wax, solidifying into fresh configurations that confounded all presumption.

Impossible, nightmare and reality colliding in his recollections, then...

Wakefulness, and a nightmare more profound still.

*

The tunnel beyond the crack was cramped, but more than enough to admit him, doubled over. His hands trailed over a cylindrical wall, instinctively flinching away from openings and hollows where god only knew what lurked.

Lukewarm water frothed around his ankles, things carried in the flow brushing against him, though few had the strength to resist its current. The air was heavy, humid, stinking of wet stone and raw meat. Wier found breathing hard, the ground rising at a steady gradient.

Behind, the footsteps stopped, a strange, sad sigh echoing up the tunnel as its maker investigated the opening.

Please God, just make it go away . . .

He couldn't be sure whether or not the splashes that followed were simply echoes of his own steps. Either way, he picked up his pace, almost scrabbling on all fours now. Surely the stream's source couldn't be far away. Why couldn't he see any light . . .?

He thought it was nothing at first; just the water babbling, echoing through the tunnel, but as the sound grew louder, more insistent, so his denials fell dead against it:

A distant chattering; the white noise of a dead TV channel, insects swarming in the surrounding walls. He imagined the holes and fissures his fingers found spewing life, bloodless white cockroach things swarming in their thousands, making meals for their larger spider and centipede kin.

Something else behind; skittering, scratching, as of some vast rat scurrying across the tunnel's ceiling. Any second, he expected to feel a blow against his exposed back, teeth and claws opening him up, spilling him into the rushing water.

Nothing.

The chatter continued to wax, his ears sifting fragments of words and sentences from the din. Now the visions of insects were replaced by those of people bound and sealed behind the stone, whimpering, singing, shrieking whatever nonsense passed through their broken minds.

His legs were on the verge of giving out, the fever already worked its way up his arm to set heart and brain alight. He forced himself on, refusing to lay down and let the nightmare take him.

The voices in the walls grew clearer, more composed with every step, scraps of prayer, verse and song cohering from the babble. Was that a little of Blake? A fragment of Bowie mingled with extracts of Revelations?

Stories, accruing like coral reefs from molecules of detritus, *stories.* Little more than random sentences and paragraphs to begin with, but soon swelling; parasites in his skull, eager to put forth wings and fly.

They followed as he scrabbled, higher and higher, the water splashing into his mouth and eyes, doing little to wash away the phantom tastes and images that afflicted them. After a time, he lost himself again, the stories of others sweeping him away as they had many, many times before. He remembered as the pollution eroded his anchorage, plucking him up and carrying him to other states and places where he would forget again, and again, and again; lives lived, names taken and abandoned, until he returned, waking naked in the dark once more.

He could no more resist than a mote of ash could the wind that plucked it up from the martyr's pyre; didn't even try. He would listen and live as he always had; a slave to stories, until such time as his own could be re-written, though none in the worlds he'd fallen from—diseased dreams, careening on the edge of collapse—had sufficient inspiration.

None, except maybe *him;* the beautiful boy whose strangeness facilitated his latest waking. He'd remembered, hadn't he?; His face, even his *name.*

He called that name now, though it was lost to the storm that carried him, plucked up by its makers and fought over like a scrap of meat tossed to starving wolves. Verity would never know; he'd die along with the world Wier had left him to, as so many had before.

The children laughed as their confessions clawed at him, *remaking* him so that he might walk in their strange playgrounds; live the secrets they shared when sunlight turned to blood, and play finally ended.

HELL

Riley stretched and sniffed the air, smelling city musk.

God, he was so *grateful* to be out of that place. There'd been moments when the gears of time seemed to seize up entirely.

"Hello."

People always looked at him strangely when he greeted them on the street, as if they expected him to leap on them and bite out their throats. What did they see that made them so *afraid*? Was it any different from what he saw in the bathroom mirror every morning?

It would've shaved off a little time to take a cab, but being out in the open air sharpened his anticipation. He only hoped that things hadn't changed too much. Consistency made him feel that all was right with the world.

*

The sun was going down by the time he arrived on Cotton Street, the blood of angels flooding London's roads and plazas, turning the city into an abattoir.

There was a man—no, a *boy*—waiting for him on the corner. Riley watched from some distance away, noting how people crossed the street to avoid him as he sang an elegy for the dying day:

"Sing Him! Sing Him! Sing Him Our Praises! Sing Him! Sing Him! Sing Him Our Love!"

Clearly something he'd composed himself, its crudity incongruous with the accomplished voice that performed it.

Riley didn't cross the street.

The boy blinked at him, momentarily shocked into silence, phosphor blue eyes flaring. Recovering, his face blossomed into a practised grin so fragile Riley felt he could shatter it with a sigh.

"Excuse me, sir..." Ah, an American. That explained the smile.

"Yes?" Riley smiled back, feeling every inch of it to the depths of his marrow.

"Do you know Jesus?"

The question troubled him, as the boy clearly didn't know what he meant by it.

"What, personally?" Riley replied.

The boy faltered. Maybe he felt he was being mocked.

"Can't say as I've ever met him. Seems a nice enough chap, from what I know."

Sensing the situation straying outside of established parameters, the boy fell back on routine:

"Well, I've got some literature here if you'd like to know him better . . ."

Riley assessed the document before accepting it. The cover bore a meticulously detailed image of Christ on the cross, the artist having gone to great pains to capture his saviour's torment. He was particularly taken with the figure's eyes; turned Heavenwards, glazed not with a surfeit of suffering, but the condition that resulted.

He took the pamphlet with gracious thanks, leaving the boy smiling in earnest.

*

Geraldine was on duty today, her hair and skin tones subtly altered to be more in-keeping with Eden's new décor. He didn't like it at first glance, but was sure he'd acclimatise.

"Edward!" Some of Eden's clientèle preferred a more traditionally formal service: *Yes sir, no sir, three bags full sir*. Riley liked to feel that he was on first name terms with the staff.

"Hey, Geraldine. Keeping well?"

She sighed and smiled with cartoonish exaggeration. There were still one or two flaws in the design they hadn't been able to work out.

"Oh, you know; same old, same old. Been pretty quiet of late, to tell the truth..."

"Oh?" he inquired, seating himself on one of the new red leather sofas.

Now that she mentioned it, the place was noticeably deserted. Even at this time of afternoon, there were usually one or two customers waiting to take their pleasure, sometimes one or two recovering from it.

Geraldine fiddled with one ear-ring. The usual elaborate, silver and crystal affairs had been replaced with obsidian pyramids suspended upside down from gold chains.

"Ah, it'll pick up. There's that new place just opened up the road, you see. What's it called . . . ?"

"Pandora's."

"That's it! Pandora's. They've got some of the new M-42s, you know; the ones where you can actually wander around? Accident waiting to happen if you ask me . . ."

Riley wasn't really up on the new technology. He'd heard of the M-42s of course; it was almost impossible not to, what with all of the holo-ads and TV commercials. You only had to log on these days to be afflicted with a sponsored documentary on the research, courtesy of your net provider.

He didn't understand the specifics, but from what he could gather, the M-42s allowed you to dream without being hooked up. How the hell that worked was anyone's guess.

"Oh well, you'll always have a customer in me."

She giggled as she brought him the obligatory insurance forms. Unlike most, he always made sure to read them, just in case they had him down for the wrong kind of dream by mistake. It'd never happened to him before, but he'd heard stories . . .

*

Places like Eden were apparently more akin to hospitals a little over half a century ago; customers whisked through to their booths on gurneys, doctors and nurses fussing about them, hooking them up to nutrient feeds, stimulant drips and Christ only knows what else.

Why the Hell would people even bother?

The fact that dreams used to be so *expensive*—the exclusive reserve of the affluent and influential—made it all the more baffling. Then, of course, there were the risks that came with the old technology . . .

Only one man came to get Riley, and he most certainly wasn't any doctor:

"Edward! Good to see you man! How's things?"

Riley accepted the man's hand, catching a whiff of exotic coconut cologne.

"Good . . . things are good." Unlike Geraldine, Christopher was a composite; still a fair bit of human left in there somewhere. Riley had never felt compelled to ask how much. He was Riley's first facilitator at Eden; now no one else would do.

"Going for the usual tonight, I see. Don't suppose I could tempt you with any of our new stock? Just got a new programme in, written by some damn *twelve year-old*. Ever wondered what it's like to be a dragon? You can fly, fight heroes, torch whole cities; that sort of thing. It's up for some sort of award . . ."

It all sounded very interesting, but Riley had never been attracted to that sort of escapism. What was the point of flying when you were always forced to come crashing back to earth?

"I think I'll stick with the usual, if it's all the same to you."

"Hey man, you're paying. Just thought I'd put it out there."

Chris ushered him through a faux oak doorway—elaborately carved with images of the experiences that waited beyond—into a lavishly decorated corridor. The new décor put Riley in mind of some of the swankier hotels he'd seen on TV.

"What do you think?" Chris asked, offering him a toffee that he produced from somewhere about his person.

"It's nice . . . very upmarket."

Truth be told, it was a little gaudy for his tastes, but he was sure he'd get used to it, given time.

"Ah, here we are," Chris announced. 21-A. Always 21-A.

A blast of refrigerated air made him shiver as Chris opened the door. It was a characteristic flaw of the M-38s that they had to be kept at low temperatures. Not that it'd matter once he was hooked up.

The room was small; one of Eden's economy affairs, dominated by a bed-like contraption complete with all manner of drips and monitoring instruments. Riley's heart started to race at the sight of it.

"You want a drink before we start?"

He ordered a glass of port, in keeping with tradition.

"You know, you're about the only one we have who uses this program . . . "

"Really?" Riley asked, sipping his drink.

"Oh yeah; if you weren't one of our regulars, we'd have probably dropped it by now."

Riley felt a cramp in his guts. *God*, the thought of being deprived of this . . . it wasn't worth contemplating.

"Okay, you ready?"

There was an escape clause in the contract he'd signed, stating that this was his last chance to back out. He'd never cited it before; felt no inclination to do so now.

"Absolutely."

Chris smiled, radiating enthusiasm in his purpose as pleasure-bringer. "Okay, let's get the party started."

*

Always the same; akin to waking, the life outside a fast receding dream.

Though the program was familiar, its manifestation shifted and adapted itself in accordance with his requirements. If it felt that things were becoming predictable, it would conjure fresh elements to forestall boredom, or even re-write itself entirely, creating a novel scenario around its core themes.

Darkness, painfully tight chains biting into his flesh, red rivulets painting his arms, dripping onto his up-turned face.

Candelabra cast fitful shadows throughout his surroundings, shapes seeming to dance and whisper in their depths.

A vast chamber, high arched ceiling supported by ranks of marble pillars from which stone angels leered celestial mockery. Directly below yawned a well, lined with steel barbs.

There was something *cathedral* like about the place; an ethos more redolent of a temple than a dungeon.

He was naked, shaved bald; body glistening with sweat and scented oil.

The ache in his arms and shoulders was intense; a dull agony waxing to mindless extremes. He laughed breathlessly.

New; a scenario he'd never experienced before. What shape would his angels take this time? They'd been men before, sculpted Adoni like animated statues of mythological heroes, children too; glowing, dark eyed boys and girls that laughed as they toyed with him, taking him apart like some puzzle of anatomy . . .

He heard their approach before catching sight of them; a distant sighing accompanied by the rattling of chains. Their voices were those of excited girls, breathy and yearning. The candle flames seemed to flare and distort at their approach, the shadows they cast seething.

They emerged like ghosts out of the darkness, fluttering shapes that one moment seemed to be sewn from swarms of white winged butterflies, the next solidifying as pale-skinned women, wrapped around in tatters of mist and moonlight. Their hair and garments flared and flowed as though they were under water, mouths periodically splitting into nervous smiles. They smelled of frost and ocean spray; an invigorating musk that he drank down as though it were the breath of angels.

Six in all, each taking up position at a particular point around the edge of the well.

Riley's back and arms spasmed, each fresh note of agony inspiring a new step in the dance, his body writhing and jerking to the rhythm beyond any control.

The women reached beneath their robes, each producing an instrument that snared the candlelight, refracting it into rainbow displays.

A sickle, inner curve a mass of sea-urchin spines; a scalpel so fine its blade seemed to be fashioned from crystal, wearing a corona of the light it sheared.

Riley felt a thrill somewhere between dread and eroticism as the first sister stepped over the pit, ascending towards him on invisible stairs. There was love, such love in her eyes as she caressed his dick with the back of her hand. The contact made him shudder and groan, entrails stirring like a nest of mating snakes. Smiling at his arousal, she raised her instrument for him to admire.

A fractal blade, various barbs and extrusions lending it the look of something grown or accrued rather than forged. Riley bit his lip to stop himself from pleading for it.

Leaning in close, the woman-thing kissed his chest, tongue describing spirals of spit around his nipple, then bit, teeth become razor-sharp.

Riley couldn't breathe, the pain beyond intense as she chewed and lapped, tearing out a chunk of flesh that she swallowed like a choice oyster. The hard-on he sprouted strained as if to rip itself free at its roots.

He grunted, fighting back tears as the woman bent to the red spring she'd un-dammed, lapping like a thirsting wolf bitch.

Sated, she brought her blade into play, trailing it down his belly before hooking its rose-thorn tip beneath his skin. He cried out as she pulled, stretching, stretching 'til he broke.

Two of her sisters took this as their cue to join the game. One flew apart, becoming a storm of jagged-winged butterflies against his back, the other aiding her sister by easing hook nailed fingers into the wounds she carved, tearing flesh and skin away like strips of wet wallpaper.

Riley couldn't scream, couldn't think. The inside of his skull was a tempest; an inferno, biblical apocalypse surging across his senses, reducing his internal landscape to smouldering ash.

The others came in their turn, the smallest of the sextet—a child whose body had barely begun to bud with pubescence—becoming a hydra of smoke and phosphor whose burning heads tore at his belly, ripping his charring hide so that they might enter and devour him from within. Another cooed and hissed lullabies as she went to work on his face, licking out one eye before biting his tongue free at the root.

Prayers for death or unconsciousness were meaningless here; he'd paid for Hell, and was going to get more than his money's worth.

He was alive to every kiss and scratch, every fresh slice, stab and rupture as he came apart, unravelling beneath a storm of sadism more loving than any caress he'd ever known.

It was hard . . . hard to hold on to things as pain saturated him; thought, memory, reason . . . every stone in the cathedral of self eroding inch by inch, red ocean washing it away down to the very foundations.

His belly was slit open, fingers rifling through the knots and whorls of his entrails, his ribs cracked and the heart within plucked from its moorings, fought over by the sisters like a scrap of candy tossed amongst starving children.

By the time they retreated, exhausted by their endeavours, he was nothing but blood; a mass of shredded meat suspended above an emptiness that was his only hope for release.

A light flared in that emptiness now; a star-like pin-prick waxing brighter and brighter, smoke rising from the depths to cook his remains. Then the flames surged, reducing him ash on the breeze.

*

Consciousness warred with flesh's insistence that it couldn't be; that there was nothing left to wake to but hurt. His senses still sang with simulated sensation; of being slit, broken, torn apart; would do for several days.

He liked to think that it was an echo of birth, this coming back; the closest any could come to emulating their earliest experience of being.

Coughing, he opened his eyes to find Chris smiling over him. He breathed slowly, rhythmically, swallowing back the nausea that churned in his gut. The first time he experienced the program, he spent nearly two hours vomiting, swearing *never, never again.*

He was wet from where he'd ejaculated. Chris obligingly cleared up the worst of it, methodically going about the business of detaching Riley from the M-38. He lay back, waiting for the world to stop whirling.

The contradictory claims of thought and flesh—he could see, yet his eyes had been burned out, could feel the bed against his back though he'd been flayed raw, nerve endings unravelled—would take a while yet to resolve themselves.

This was the moment he relished most of all; the piecing back together. He was Dracula becoming flesh from dust through the spilling of blood; Frankenstein's Monster sewn together from scraps of dead men, all of whom bore his name.

"You okay?" Christopher asked. He looked bleary, like he'd been woken from deep sleep.

Riley inhaled deeply, letting it out with a faint laugh.

"Oh yeah."

Somewhat steadier now, he eased himself into a sitting position. Christopher handed him another glass of port that he emptied gratefully. All he could taste were lingering tangs of blood and burning.

Sanguine. No other word for it.

"Can you walk?"

"Don't know," he slurred, swinging his legs off the bed. Chris supported him as he rose, legs trembling; brain still not quite certain if they were there or not.

"I love Fridays. Some of the people we get through here . . . you wouldn't believe how they freak out after a session."

Chris rambled on in the same banal but affable manner as they passed through to the adjoining wet room. Riley was only half listening; his thoughts elsewhere, trying to work out what manner of mind they belonged to.

Showered down, dried and dressed, he felt like a new man. He tipped Christopher handsomely for his attention. The man protested at first, insisting it was all part of the service, but relented with a little pressure.

There were one or two people waiting in reception. Geraldine looked up as he emerged, a moment of blankness passing across her synthetic features, social parameters re-defining themselves.

"Good time, Edward?"

"Very." He slipped her a few sly credits across the reception desk, which she pocketed with a cartoonish wink.

"Same next Friday?"

"Of course," He replied, treating her to a flirtatious wave before stepping out into the world.

*

Music was on his lips as he made his way down Cotton Street. His body still felt raw, clothes chafing on the ghosts of wounds his mind insisted were real.

"There's a star man waiting in the sky . . ."

Sad really; so few appreciated good classical music these days.

His evangelical friend was gone, given up his soul-shepherding with the day's death.

Thinking of him, Riley reached into his pocket, fishing out the pamphlet he'd been given. There was Christ, all blood and pain at the moment of transcendence.

"He Suffers For You."

Laughing at its presumption, Riley threw the pamphlet into the gutter and headed home, singing archaic hymns to love.

A ROSE IN THE MORNING

I turned on the lights, couldn't believe my eyes.

"Take it," Lowry insisted, proffering what he'd made in the dark.

I couldn't. Couldn't move, couldn't speak, think or feel, all that I was blasted away in the space of a breath. Certainty evaporated, conviction dissolved. "Take it," he repeated.

I did, and pricked myself. The miracle dropped to the floorboards, gone before it hit the ground, petals black as a spider's eye, wilted.

He cooed over my wounds: "Here, let me kiss it better."

I did, no longer seeing any reason in denial. He'd loved me forever; we both knew it, but I'd never wanted it from him, nor any man.

Until the rose and the dark he'd sewn it from. What else could he craft from laughter and sighs? Was his skill limited to pretty forms like the one that pierced me, or was he capable of more; engines, citadels . . . *worlds*?

"Show me more," I demanded, and he smiled, rouge-lipped.

Naked in the dark, he asked, "Are you sure?"

"Yes." An essential lie.

The dark stirred around me as if swarming with velvet winged butterflies, then became denser, slithering, twining, coiling about me.

Phantom lips grazed my own, reptile tongues flicked at my fingers, my eyes.

I smiled at the sensation, laughing with fear.

He laughed too. "You're beautiful."

Feathery light touches, like a house-spider's footsteps, trailed the column of my spine. I shuddered as he parted me, a multitude of invisible tongues clamouring between, desperate for succour.

All new, this sensation, invasion, this revelation never countenanced before, save in the seclusion of daydreams. I fell, but didn't land.

A dream; a nightmare, but I laughed instead of screaming, calling into the dark to the man who'd tamed it, begging him to do his worst.

He obliged.

In the morning, Lowry was gone. The light hurt. Everything did.

I stretched out beneath the sheets, felt them scrape against bites and scratches only just begun to heal, wondering what to tell Lydia. What was there other than stories? She wouldn't believe even the ones I'd lived last night. Nor did I, entirely.

I sat up, blinking away blindness, saw the rose; a sculpted fragment of night, dissolving to dust beneath the glare of day.

BOUND

What was it they chanted as their ridiculous little box, this *mousetrap* they'd constructed, began its corrosive work?

A *name*, one he'd never thought to hear again this side of the grave:

"*Wellman, Wellman, Wellman* . . ."

How they knew after he'd taken such pains to expunge it from record was irrelevant; the knowledge leant them power over one who'd dominated, oppressed and preyed upon them. There wasn't a single soul outside these walls who entertained the slightest iota of mercy, nor did he expect it.

The trap was a device of ancient design, its kind not seen in the world since the rediscovery of miracles; the scientific approbation of the abstract; the mythic element that tradition called the *soul*. How many generations of their young had they sacrificed in its making? Three, four? He could already feel the teeth and fingers of their furious, barely born souls, the madness that informed them born of lives dreamed in the womb, then wickedly, monstrously denied before they could even draw breath. *Poison*; a rabidity that threatened to infect him with every tainted nip and scratch. It wouldn't be long before he lost all hold over the self he'd sculpted; the living ideal whose flesh was as protean as shadow, thoughts infinite as time.

Almost funny; even liberated from the restrictions of his original humanity, he retained enough of the state for his perfection to be polluted; doubt and delusion clouding his sight.

Nothing lasted forever; not stories, not love, and certainly not him.

The chanting became more fervent, more vicious, as he flung his withering carcass from wall to wall, each impact perpetuating a release of energies that briefly illuminated his cell's interior. By the standards of its builders, it was no doubt palatial; a tomb citadel on par with the pyramids of Giza, that none now living remembered.

There'd be no rebirth into eternal life for this Pharaoh. He'd seen what awaited outside this world of flesh and sensation; a state beyond all the frantic, fantastical hopes of religion or the material nihilism of science. Why else would he devote his entire being to suspending himself here, re-writing the unseen schematics of his flesh to better reflect the soul it contained?

The fact he'd become a thing of darkness; a fairy-tale horror that stalked the night, preying upon the flesh of the innocent, had concerned him at first, but such picayune moral qualms soon faded when he'd begun to realise the *potential* of his re-configured state . . .

No! He could not, *would not* die here! Wounds blossomed throughout his phantasmal anatomy as he hurled it against walls, floor and ceiling, the matter they shed momentarily luminous as moonlight before evaporating into wisps of silvery smoke.

The meat-things outside were whipped into frenzies of delight at his desperation, many shrieking curses that grazed him like thrown blades whilst others sang hymns from the myriad religions he'd murdered since his ascendance.

The words meant nothing, the language a distorted mockery of one long-since dead. Where had it re-sprung from? Was it possible that the faith to which it belonged wasn't quite so dead as he surmised? And if so, how could it have proliferated so rampantly without his notice?

He screamed in answer to the songs, his voice that of many thousands raised in unison, the walls of his prison trembling, despite his current weakness. Some faltered as their thoughts filled with visions of what he'd gift or spare them if they set him free. These were quickly set upon and silenced by their fellows, the certainties they'd been conditioned with proving an immaculate wall in which he could find neither flaw nor foothold.

The irony was almost enough to bring a smile to his lips. Whatever God, saint or messiah inspired their devotion . . . it was nothing but a distortion of the original man or myth; as likely to turn on and devour them as he had.

Distortion or no, it was that very faith which tightened like a noose around his throat; a mythology he would no doubt be subsumed into as demon or devil; the quintessential enemy he'd cast himself as in hope that drawing the species collective hate would prevent it from destroying itself.

Too late, he realised the folly of his ambition; how woefully he'd underestimated humanity's urgency to kill and be killed.

By tomorrow, the divisions would have already begun; one proclaiming his own perspective as canon whilst others that shared common vision attempted to silence him. From there, the fractures would spread, gradually dividing a species he'd united through common fear and hatred, until all he'd created over the millennia was undone.

His mythic substance tangibly unravelling, the monster once named

Wellman sank down to the lowest recesses of its tomb, raised the suppurating mass of its face to the heavens, and wept.

BRAIN FOOD

Why?

Cardinal had asked the question a million times, in tones frustrated, furious and despairing. The answer was always the same: an insect chatter of silence and seething thought, his brain throwing up postulations on every subject save the one that consciously concerned him:

Why wouldn't it let him sleep?

It was logical, after all: brain and body both needed rest, downtime in which to repair, to *dream*. But logic was a faculty that drained away along with daylight, the organ's chatter becoming denser and more pronounced in synchronicity with darkness's descent.

And what pettiness it concerned itself with! Chewing over every little slip of the tongue he suffered, every minor apology or elementary misunderstanding.

Idiot, it called him. *Moron, baby, retard.*

It made him relive those experiences in the early hours of the morning, when even the intrinsically nocturnal channels had given up the ghost and begun to loop infomercials. He saw himself as if in a dream; his awkwardness and ugliness, his yammering, stammering stupidity; saw himself step on toes, accidentally trip up women that were the stuff of masturbatory fantasy, lapse into idiot silence as words snarled in his throat. And throughout the voice spat and slurred: *Stupid baby bastard! Retard, retard, retard!*

An hour. Was that it? He couldn't remember, couldn't think straight. His head was full of fog, thoughts flashing through it like tongues of lightning. Maybe an hour out of the last five days. They sent him home from work, told him he looked dead on his feet.

Zombie. He sympathized with the living dead, knew precisely how they felt. Maybe that's why they so consistently hungered for brains; not out of some animal hunger, but *mercy* for those who still suffered under the organ's yolk. And really, wasn't it the source of all humanity's problems? If they were more like the caterpillars or the bumblebees; the spiders and the worms, the world would be so much simpler, not flailing on the brink of multiple apocalypses.

The decision came to him on the spur of the moment, a string of drool cooling on his chin as he lay on the sofa, illuminated by the TV's soft electric lambency. What show was this? He'd been watching the same channel for three hours. Soft-core porn movie; a married woman discovering her lesbian side at the local gym. Had he masturbated? Didn't know. Fingers found his prick shrunken and flaccid; a cold, dead scrap of meat, more useless than the chattering, alien blob in his skull.

Parasite; something from another world, holding the entire species in thrall . . .

The kitchen was cold. He'd left the fridge door open. The motor grunted and whined like a dying dog. *Fuck it.*

What did he need? There was plenty of potential: drawers full of emancipating silver, his dad's butcher knives, barely touched since the old man's aneurysm He wished he'd paid more attention now, gone into the family trade like Dad wanted. After all, butchery was akin to surgery, wasn't it?

Just to be on the safe side, he got some hammers, screwdrivers and a drill from beneath the staircase too.

This is insane. You're going to kill yourself.

Of course, the alien would want him to think that, wouldn't it? Just a defence mechanism. Not any more; he was through being a slave.

A bottle of port he'd been saving for Christmas—his sister Gloria and her new boyfriend were supposed to be coming—and a packet of pain killers dulled the monster's protests.

He wasn't an idiot, despite its claims; he knew it'd *hurt*. He might even die before the operation was done. So what? At least then he'd have some fucking *peace*.

The first cut barely even scraped bone, pain causing his knees to buckle, his stomach to revolt, splashing the floor with alcoholic bile. Red flowed over his field of vision.

But he didn't stop.

The world wavered, fluttering like a painting on water's surface. He laughed, high, shrieking, his hands cutting, stabbing, *boring* of their own accord . . .

Stop. Stop!

Was that him, or *it*? He couldn't tell any more, its roots were burrowed into him so deep. His hands knew better than to comply with its terrorism, apparently as eager to be free as the rest of him. They continued their work, paring away skin, tissue, hair; scraping and stabbing at bone with the ineffectual tools he'd provided. He was warm and wet, the kitchen counter and floor slick as an abattoir or antenatal ward's.

Pain . . . an all but alien arena, the breathless agony of stubbing a toe or walking into a wall at night more than sufficient education in the matter. This . . . this obliterated whatever paltry definition of the term he'd thus far conceived. It was a state of being; an extremity that leaked out beyond the confines of flesh and stained the world pulsing red. It was everything, and he was nothing; a ragged, burning scrap of meat, endlessly plucked and pecked at by starving scavengers.

Then something gave, like a boil finally bursting; a newborn crowning. Explosion: a super nova, the fire of the first second, all things threading out from that distant pin prick of light.

Fragments of music, children's laughter and the moans of lovers filled the air, surging en mass into his ears like a swarm of parasitic moths. He smelled his mother's perfume; strawberries and cinnamon, frost and November bonfires. Ecstatic arcs convulsed his entire body, his prick rising to the caress of phantom fingers, an eclectic cocktail of bitterest chocolate, rain and pussy assaulting his tongue.

He staggered away from the kitchen counter, hands still working feverishly, desperate to winkle out the tyrant that held them in bondage.

The curtain on which the world was painted frayed and burned, the state beyond one of fluttering mirror fragments, fire and memory.

He fell, but there was no floor waiting to bruise him; no up or down, no right or wrong. He tumbled like a mote of sand in a desert storm, like bacteria on a breath.

Then, at last, there was silence, and sleep so deep even dreams refused to follow.

*

Hungry.

Echo of a distant lullaby; the *sweetest* music, like angels calling his soul to Heaven.

Hungry. Stabbing, stinging; as if hornets had set up a hive in his stomach.

His nostrils flared. *Honey. Clotted cream. Meat.*

A single eye opened onto a world of fuzzy-edged green and purple, orange and violet threads filling the air, forming webs and tapestries from which flowers and fruit sprouted, though like none he'd ever seen before.

Stumbling, he went to the still open fridge. The stench was *hideous,* like fomented sewerage, sun-baked charnel pits.

Nothing spoiled by the look of it. Funny.

He closed the door.

Something squelched and squealed, the sound like razor blades across his nerves. Looking across the red painted floor, her saw something flopping and flailing; a red, pulsing mass from which hair fine tendrils lashed, dragging its awkward bulk towards the door.

This was the source of the honey scent, the savoury-sweet roasting, baking, *feast* smell:

The tyrant, wounded and crippled without a slave to carry it.

Reaching up, his fingers grazed wet, jagged edges; spongy pulp, like a mass of rotting fruit. He laughed at the ticklish sensation and didn't stop.

The thing squealed as he bent and plucked it up, lashing at him with its tendrils. Minute barbs pierced him, cold venom filling his flesh. It didn't matter; the thing couldn't hurt him now. Nothing could.

It squealed, whimpering with every bite. Like eating mushrooms; texture light and springy, matter melting on his tongue.

And the *taste*. Fruit from Eden's own orchards, so sweet, so *succulent*. He felt *intoxicated* by it, all thought receding beneath the sensual onslaught.

He ate 'til there were nothing but scraps, the hunger assuaged, but far from gone.

The *music*; a voice at least as sweet as the meat on which he'd feasted, coaxing him out, out into the world.

There'd been a frost, but he felt not the slightest tickle of chill. Alcoholic warmth unfurled through his limbs, the air tasting of lover's sweat and public toilet foulness; of patisseries and plague pits.

Threads everywhere, their fruit burning in the sky like stars, their flowers dilating and contracting underfoot, puckered and dew-beaded in their eagerness for pollination.

A car zoomed by, trailing cacophony he could smell and see; a smear of shit on the air, a pollution that threatened to smother the sacred song that carried him, called him...

There were others. He couldn't see them, but he *knew*. They were like him; those who'd recognised their own enslavement and cast it off. Now they came, called, *summoned*.

Work to be done on the way; a word of revolution to spread. There'd be resistance, misunderstanding; blood shed. He'd be hunted, hurt; threatened for daring to walk free.

So be it.

The song rushed in to fill the chamber where his enslaver once sat, kindling dreams that sustained beyond sleep, and which all humanity ached to share.

WHAT REMAINS

"Aren't you a pretty thing?"

Fat and radiant Mother-To-Be, fidgeting, making herself comfortable.

Then she answers:

If I'm so pretty, why don't you kiss me?

I jump. No one else in the garden; only me, the bees and her. *Hearing things.* I shrug, shake my head.

"Bloody losing it . . ."

You don't have to be so ignorant, you know. Just because you don't want to kiss me . . .

Frightened now.

"Who's there?"

Who do you think? You were just talking to me, weren't you?

A woman's voice, soft and throaty.

I turn back to the spider, watch as it waves a spindly forelimb. There's some acid in the bedside cabinet, but I don't recall taking any . . .

"Spiders don't talk." I lean in so close, my breath makes the web dance.

Ha! Or maybe we just haven't felt inclined to before. Besides, I was just being polite. It's not often I get sweet-talked, you know.

"I'm dreaming."

Dreaming? If it comes to that, maybe it's me who's dreaming you.

I get up, retreat inside the house, wanting nothing more of the morning's madness.

*

A cup of tea, a couple of biscuits, and I begin to feel better. Bloody *stupid*; talking spiders. I'll be finding magical woodland worlds inside wardrobes next.

Singing. Just one of the neighbours playing their radio too bloody loud. Then I recognize the voice:

". . . where troubles melt like lemon drops, away above the chimney tops, that's where you'll find me . . ."

I put my hands over my ears, but it makes no difference. Maybe it'd be best if I just kill the damn thing. At least that way I won't be overrun with babies when the time comes.

*

"Was . . . was that you singing just now?"

I keep my voice to a whisper, afraid that someone might hear and classify me as a crazy man. Can't say I'd blame them.

Did you like it? she asks, busy repairing a thread of her web, broken by a leaf in the breeze.

"It was . . . very pretty."

You use that word a lot, don't you?

A blush creeps up my neck, the sensation reminding me of being shot down in flames after asking girls out as a teenager. Laura Holden, Katie Dummell . . . God, I wanted them so *badly*. Ha, just a kid. Didn't know any better.

Hold out your hand.

What? Sitting here talking to a spider is one thing, but letting one *touch* me . . .?

Don't tell me you're afraid of spiders . . .

Not as bad as some. I can pick them up, put them outside when I find one in the house, though I don't exactly relish the experience. Anita always looks like she's going to faint or have a fit at the mere sight of one.

Holding out my hand, my pulse quickens as her legs find my fingers. Their touch is less abrasive than I imagine, tickling like the brush of a feather. Crawling into the centre of my palm, she squats, waiting.

Shall we go inside?

*

Anita comes over the next morning. I don't tell her about the spider; it'd just cause upset.

She's had a good week; sold three houses, been short-listed for promotion. I think she's trying to tell me she'll soon be moving onto pastures new; that we only have a little time left. I don't mind as much as I thought I would; it'd be nice to finish for once before things turn sour.

We use her promotion as an excuse to break out the wine. Two bottles of Shiraz later, and she's leading me upstairs, unbuttoning her blazer and biting her lower lip in that way she knows drives me wild.

*

I catch a glimpse of her as Anita bends to kiss me, straddling a new web in the corner of the ceiling. Panic flushes me at thought of what Anita might do if she notices, the distraction causing me to lose control.

Anita makes a show of coming herself, though I can tell from the momentary darkness in her eyes how frustrated she is. I should've told her that she didn't need to put on airs and graces for me; just because I shot my load doesn't mean she has to go unfulfilled.

The stereotypes presented in soaps and romantic fiction had her believe otherwise.

I hate the parting following sex. It reminds me of being a school kid again; sports on a rainy day, forced out into the wet and cold in little more than shorts and t-shirt.

A perennial fantasy surfaces from my bliss-clouded thoughts, one I've entertained since first hearing what the anatomy between my legs is capable of:

Being drawn so deep into a woman that the rest of me follows in my sex's bullet-headed wake; balls and hips; arms, torso and head, infant's laughter breaking from my lips as I'm enveloped, devoured . . .

A gentleman never comes before a Lady. It's bad form.

"Ssshhh!" I hiss, afraid that Anita might hear. Rolling over, she glares at me with sleep clouded eyes, clearly lacking patience for further disappointments.

"What?"

"Nothing, just . . . thinking out loud."

"Well keep it down, will you? Some of us have work tomorrow."

Ah, a deliberate shot across my boughs. Work—her ace in the hole; the card she always plays when trying to rouse my temper. I'm not what you might call a working man; never have been. That honour belongs to my younger brother, who's never wanted anything more from life than what lifestyle magazines and TV dictate.

I have money, at least enough to be comfortable. A lot of people hate me for that; sniping behind my back about how I've done nothing to deserve it:

"Hasn't worked a bloody day in his life . . ."

"Doesn't know what real life is . . ."

I know that Anita sometimes thinks the same.

She can be a bitch, your girlfriend. I'd never treat you like that . . .

"Yeah, you'd fuck me then have me for dinner afterwards."

"What the hell are you muttering about?"

It almost came out: "*I wasn't talking to you.*"

Instead: "Nothing. Go back to sleep."

*

She's gone by the time I wake up, leaving behind breakfast-dirtied dishes for me to clean.

The spider's gone too, web vacant, glittering in the early morning light. I don't dare vacuum, afraid that the last thing I'll hear of her is a cut-off scream as she's sucked up with the dirt and dust.

*

Anita calls a little after lunch, the bustle and chatter of office life audible in the background.

"Ramsey?"

"Yeah?"

"How's things?"

I wish she'd just say what she wants to instead of hiding behind this small talk bullshit. I don't like talking on the phone.

"Okay, just pottering around the house. Might get some reading done."

I read a lot, have done ever since I was a kid.

Silence.

I inhale sharply at the feather-light tickle on the back of my hand. Lowering the receiver, I see her scrabbling for purchase on my flesh, trailing tatters of silken thread. She's bigger than I remember, the white crucifix pattern on her abdomen seeming to almost shine.

"What're you doing?" I hiss, suddenly certain that Anita can see us down the telephone line.

"Ramsey? Are you still there?"

"Yeah, yeah. Sorry about that; thought I heard somebody at the door."

Liar, liar, pants on fire, why not tell her? After the way she talked to you last night . . .

I ignore it, praying to God Anita can't hear.

"Listen, I'm really sorry about last night. I've just been really busy at work and with stuff at home, you know?"

It sounds like a pre-recorded speech. It always does when she says sorry.

She says she loves you now, but the second some better prospect comes along, you won't be able to see her for dust.

The speech falters, her tone slipping.

"Are . . . are you on your own? I thought I heard . . ."

"Yeah, yeah. I've got the TV on."

Liar.

"Oh, okay. Listen, if you want me to make it up to you, maybe we could get together tonight . . ."

The offer doesn't fill me with enthusiasm.

"Ramsey?"

"Yeah, could we make it another time? I'm thinking about making it an early night."

The spider crawls to my wrist, tickling the hairs that sprout there.

Tell her, then we'll see how sincere she is. Tell her I'm sleeping in your bedroom . . .

"Shut up!"

"Okay, that's fine." Her tone suggests otherwise. "Call me when you're free, okay?"

I promise I will, then hang up.

*

"What do you want? What are you even doing here?"

The spider leaves me while I shower, watching with unabashed glee from a corner of the bathroom ceiling. Now she squats on my chest while I lay in bed, head throbbing with what feels like the onset of a migraine.

Oh, come on; you know you like having me around. How many other women can you talk to like this?

I can't dispute that; have always hated the ridiculous dance of it all; the masks and performances that only begin to slip when people are dug in too deep to claw their way free. I'm as guilty as the rest: how many times have I said something that my inner-self squirmed to hear, just out of ambition to get between a woman's thighs, or stop her walking out the door?

It's different with the spider; has been since the first, unconscious honesty: *"Aren't you a pretty thing?"*

"That's not the point. Anita and me . . . we've been together for a long time. I don't know what'd happen if it ended."

The spider seems to sigh.

Maybe it's time you found out.

*

I don't sleep well. Dreams of being a kid again; fat and sluggish twelve year-old, panting, chased through a world of shifting mist by something I can't see, but whose hunger laps at my naked back and buttocks like bonfire heat.

Usually, I'd wake an instant before I feel claws and teeth, but not this time. This time, I stop, turn to face it, whole body trembling not with fear, but *anticipation*. A hard-on so eager it *aches* glares at the beast as it emerges through the fog. I can't make it out clearly, its body shifting, swirling as if viewed through a kaleidoscope, only the mouth—multiple lips, row upon row of thorn-like teeth—distinct.

A skink-like tongue lashes out to snare me by the cock, its slickness almost making me spurt as it drags me forward, into the monster's mouth.

They say you can't feel pain in dreams. This one seems intent on breaking every rule, the agony as those teeth puncture me worse than anything I've ever experienced in the waking world, but a sensation that my dream self takes unalloyed pleasure in, laughing hysterical ecstasy as it's chewed to ribbons.

*

Always the same; sleeping, dreaming one second, awake and already forgetting the next. A moment of tumbling forward vertigo, but I don't scream.

Wiping sleep from my eyes, I sit up, wondering what time it is...

A flicker of movement draws my attention to the ceiling. Am I still dreaming?

The spider's mottled, bulbous body stretched and swollen into a facsimile of human womanhood, eyes like black pearls gleaming as she descends, multiple arms reaching out to embrace me.

Hurling the covers aside, I leap out of bed, the early morning chill biting deep into my bladder.

Settling atop the bed, the woman-thing turns to face me, grinning through liquorice black lips.

Well?

Mad; bound to wake up any second, straight-jacketed and bouncing off the walls of my padded cell.

"I . . . I don't know . . ."

She smiles, teeth gleaming.

At least you're more honest with me than you are with her. You don't have to be afraid of me. I only bite when I'm threatened.

Trapped in my dream self's skin again; all reason and volition evaporated, leaving me little more than a puppet manipulated by unseen hands. Starting towards her, my prick's dreamed ambition becomes reality, its hooded eye straining against my boxer shorts, desperate to see.

Seating herself on the edge of the bed, the spider thing extends its arms, fingers fused into comb-edged talons moving over my back, my shoulders, my lips . . .

I shudder, almost cry out as she tugs down my boxer shorts, talons moving over my balls as if seeking the right seam to snip . . .

Is this what you imagined when you brought me in from the cold?

I don't know what I imagined, why I did it; only that I don't want this to stop.

You don't have to tell me. It doesn't matter.

Dragging me forward, she draws me into a kiss tasting of rotting leaves in Autumn; of rain-sodden dirt and deep, deep forest. I expect to feel teeth any second, the rake of talons across my back.

Nothing; only the hunger of her kisses, more open and earnest than any woman's I've known. I've never understood why so many deny themselves this; the satisfaction that follows appetite's indulgence. Maybe some lingering strain of old prejudices; because they're afraid of the labels men make for them—*slut, tart, whore*—, all the while hungering for the flesh beneath their skirts?

She didn't share the neurosis, her every stroke and gesture calculated to enhance our mutual delight.

Hands moving over her flanks, exploring the alien ridges and orifices there, I carry us back onto the bed, dreams of devourment still swirling behind my eyes.

*

Oh god, the brightness *hurts*. Thorns rasp across my back as I twist beneath the covers, irritating scratches made whilst dreaming of fleas.

Easing out of bed, stretching, I catch sight of her, sat sleeping at the centre of her web. No flies yet.

"Good morning. Sleep well?"

No answer. Have I done something to offend her? Hard to tell with women, even of another species, it transpires.

"Are we not talking then?"

Still no answer.

*

I shower, moaning as the hot water stings my back and shoulders, then dress and head downstairs.

No plan today, like most since work stopped being an issue, but there are things I have a mind to do.

Anita, for one.

I don't like the way we left things yesterday. It's not as if I've been the perfect boyfriend . . .hopefully her offer of a get-together still stands.

She picks up after the sixth ring, sounding bleary, almost asleep. Did I wake her? Strange; she's a fastidious early riser, always determined to wring every last second of sunlight from the day.

"Hello?"

"Anita, it's Ramsey . . ."

A muffled ruffling in the background, bed clothes slipping, sliding. I swallow hard at the image of her sitting up in bed, unkempt hair spilling over her shoulders.

"Ramsey . . . I was going to call you."

"Yeah, about the other day—I didn't mean to be pissy with you; hadn't slept the night before . . ."

Lame, lame, lame! My perennial excuse; the consistent insomnia that's plagued me since early adolescence. Truth be told, it's been curious by its absence of late, the only things disrupting my sleep the occasional nightmare and need to empty my bladder.

"Don't worry about it. Listen, can I come 'round later? It feels like I haven't seen you in practically forever!"

Oddly sentimental; she doesn't tend to go in for all that lovey-dreamy, doe-eyed stuff. It's one of the things that first attracted me to her.

"Yeah, that'd be great. I'll be here all day, so . . ."

"I'll see you whenever. Bye."

I hang up the phone, brain and belly full of smoke and embers.

*

A bottle of leftover Shiraz and a little weed help to calm my nerves. What's wrong with me? It feels like the first time I invited her over to the house, or she invited me to bed.

"God, it's just Anita, you arsehole!" I slump in front of the television, fighting sleep. I don't even know what I'm watching. The world slips away for a few hours, leaving imagination free to sculpt drama of its own.

*

Fields of blue strawberries spread out beneath a Tequila Sunrise sky, *shattering;* streaming away like sand caught up in storm winds.

Just the damn TV, its current subject a pair of mating lions whose din is enough to stir a corpse to complaint.

I flick the chattering machine off, but the noise persists; a faint scratching, shuffling, like some hideously bloated rat dragging its bulk beneath the floorboards. Slouching through to the hall, I open the cellar door, not afraid; a kid hearing hoof-beats and sleigh bells on Christmas Eve.

The only place in the house forbidden to me as a kid; Dad stored his model trains down there, knew I wouldn't be able to resist handling them. I sold the entire collection after he died. I've spent a lot of time down there since then, enjoying the chill and the damp; some blind, evolutionary nightmare sealed in a subterranean cavern. I have plans of turning it into a wine cellar, some day.

I don't turn on the light.

A blur below, something barrelling into me, claws raking my clothes, cold lips clamping against mine, prying them apart.

She speaks between kisses, guiding my hand down to the fluttering dampness between her legs.

What was it you said? That I'd fuck you then eat you . . .?

She smiles. I smile too, picturing the feast in my mind. Would she begin with my lips and tongue; the sweet meats between my legs?

"Maybe that's why I keep coming back."

She laughs, the sound echoing in the enveloping darkness. My fingers find their way inside, probing her alien anatomy with an explorer's enthusiasm.

What would your little girlfriend think of that, I wonder?

For a split second, it's Anita I feel and taste, white-blonde hair tickling my shoulders, giggles of mischief punctuated with instructions as to precisely where my hands should be. . . sickle-edged talons lightly raking my chest, reaching down to clasp my genitals, threatening castration with but a slip.

Deep, she demands, *as deep as you can stand, and don't pull out.*

Alarm bells sound amongst the fireworks in my skull, three decades of conditioning on the dangers of sexual disease surging in protest. But such consequences—infection, the possibility of children—are dim and distant; fairy tale horrors that have no relevance outside of nightmares.

Complying with her demands, I cry out, her interior barbed, lacerating me to the root. Her claws go to work on my cheeks, my stomach, my back; her every gasp and sigh accompanied by a fresh wound, 'til I'm coming apart at the seams. She sucks the screams from my mouth still-born. I can't think through the sensation, my entire being reduced to sweating, bleeding meat in the dark.

Climax is a cataclysm, my body seeming to empty itself of blood and marrow as well as seed, hers equally eager to accept them.

In the super-nova instant of orgasm, the new-born sun in my brain spills its light into the cellar, illuminating the woman thing that bucks and thrashes atop me. Her face . . . I know it from somewhere long before our first meeting, as if glimpsed from afar in childhood dreams, made the subject of masturbatory fantasy in adolescence. There, when she tilts her head that way . . . Anita? And there, *Jody Fincher*? The girl who'd taken my virginity at the not-so-tender-these-days age of fifteen . . .

Something else too; more familiar than any of them, my entrails churning at the suggestion of it.

The light fades before I can clearly make it out, her claws sliding around the back of my neck as she sighs contentment, dabbling in the swamp we've made between us. With a kiss, she parts from me, scuttling back into the dark, a sudden knock at the front door murdering my questions before they can be born.

*

"*Where were you*? I was about to give up and go home!"

She kisses me, slipping passed into the hallway, weighed down with bags of shopping. "I thought I'd cook us something to eat—*bloody hell*." She stops, stammers, noticing my condition. "What've you been doing?"

Fortunately, my clothes are more intact than I'd first imagined, but I'm still a bedraggled mess; smeared with dust and dirt from head to toe, cobwebs snared in my hair.

"I was just . . . down in the cellar . . ." Too weary and unconcerned for lies.

She stares at me as if there's a tarantula squatting on my forehead. I can't keep myself from smiling, licking my lips; tasting an echo of *her* there. "You're bleeding, Ramsey."

I look down; red flowers blossoming beneath my shirt.

"And here," She presses a hand to her cheek. Doing likewise, I wince at the sudden soreness, my fingers coming away ruby stained.

"What've you been doing to yourself?"

She seems more annoyed than concerned, as if this is some abstruse personal attack against her.

"Nothing; just been scratching myself in my sleep. I used to do it all the time when I was a kid. Nothing to get stressed about."

Her expression suggests it may be a little late for that.

Shepherding me upstairs into the bathroom, she undresses me, eyes widening in alarm at the criss-cross lacerations decorating my chest and back.

"*Jesus Christ,* Ramsey . . ."

"I know. Sometimes I'd wake up with my bed *soaked* as a kid. My sister used to say it was my time of the month."

"Don't you ever wake yourself up?" She fumbles in the cabinet for wipes and anti-sceptic.

"Never. Don't feel a thing."

"Well, you're gonna bloody feel this. Grit your teeth."

It feels like the wounds are being freshly carved as she sets about cleansing them. I do my best to hide my arousal from her; she'd likely be repulsed by it.

Satisfied I'm not about to succumb to septicaemia, she dresses the scratches as best she can, tutting and rolling her eyes at the mess I've made of myself.

The play of maternity makes me squirm, but I bear it without comment.

"Thanks."

"Why men can't do this stuff for themselves, I'll never know. It's surprising humanity's managed to survive this long with you guys in control."

"Shall we get something to eat? I'm *starving*."

"Fine. I'm staying over tonight, by the way, in case you end up trying to scratch yourself to death."

She doesn't wait for argument or consent, exiting the bathroom and trotting downstairs with that sense of unquestionable belonging I've always envied and reviled.

*

Dinner consists of a Chinese stir-fry; beef, black bean sauce, mushrooms, noodles; enough vegetables to feed an army on its march to conquest. I have a habit of not eating right unless someone's around to make sure I do, my diet consisting primarily of take-away and whatever pre-packaged treats catch my eye at the super market. Anita says it's one of the things she "Has To Work On."

"Amazing that someone who eats so much shit can stay so skinny. You need to get some meat on your bones."

I like my body the way it is; the malnourished look works for me.

Not for the first time that evening, my thoughts turn to the darkness beneath our feet. Is she still down there, sleeping off the afternoon's exertion, or has she returned to her less conspicuous state, watching with mounting jealousy from some secret corner of the room?

"How about some wine?" I interrupt her in mid-flow; some tirade about a woman at work.

"Sounds good. Something red."

"Be right back."

*

A smell; a fresh element amongst the cold, dirt and damp stone that pervades the place . . . ripe, *meaty*; a butcher's shop smell.

I want to call out, let her know it's me, but I don't know her name. I almost slip on the cellar floor, something slick squelching underfoot, the smell intensifying. My hand instinctively strays to the light switch, a flicker of movement in the murk.

What might I have seen if she hadn't stopped me?

Don't . . . not now. Believe me, you don't want to see . . .

The second hand light filtering down from upstairs reveals more than enough; something waving, fluttering on the edge of visibility, dust-spangled threads momentarily catching the light, making star-play out of it before fading. They brush my face and hands, feather light strokes; the lips and fingers of ghosts. Only glimpses and suggestions of the nest she's made; globules of pulsing matter wrapped around in the shimmering threads, but imagination is more than sufficient to fill in the blanks. At the heart of it sits the weaver herself, sprawled out and breathing hard in a hammock of the same material.

Having fun with your little girlfriend? There's no overt spite in the question; only faint amusement, as if I'm a puppy that's taken a shine to the neighbourhood cat.

"Yes." Not exactly a lie, not precisely the truth. Story of my life.

Maybe you could bring her down here, introduce us.

I have to smile. The thought of how Anita would react to all of this.

"I don't think that's a good idea. Anita . . . she likes things to be *simple.*"

A laugh, reedy and breathless.

Ah, not the adventurous type, eh? It's sad really.

"What is?"

That the women of your species have learned to be so afraid of themselves.

Your species. Strange to hear it put that way.

You'd better hurry along. Anita will be fretting over where you've got to.

I pick up the nearest bottle within reach, swiping the dust and cobwebs from it as I make for the stairs.

"Will you . . . will you be okay down here?"

A sigh, weary, amused; verging on laughter.

Oh yes, I've got everything I need.

I retreat up the stairs as fast as I can, terrified, hoping to hear the click of claws on the steps behind.

*

She's been looking at me oddly all night; little side-long glances that she thinks I don't notice. It's only here in the bedroom, undressing; preparing to be as honest with her as anyone can, that I have the courage to broach the subject:

"Is there something you want to say?"

She stands in front of the bedroom window, partaking of whatever theatre the street can provide as she unbuttons her shirt. The scratches itch and ache beneath their dressings, making me irritable.

"What?"

She turns away from the window, arrayed in a halo of chemical-orange street-lamp light.

"Nothing, really. You've just seemed . . . distracted today. Is it work?"

I hope it is, but I know better.

Sighing, she sits down on the bed next to me, tension surrounding her like the threat of thunder.

"God, this is awkward . . . are you *okay,* Ramsey?"

"What?"

A flicker of movement in the corner of the ceiling. Is it *her*, watching, listening?

"It just seems . . . like you're not *all there* these days, you know what I mean?"

I tell her I haven't the first clue.

"It's like you're *dreaming* or something. You spend all your time on your own in this place, you barely ever see anyone."

Ah, the old "You Don't Get Out Enough" argument. Why does it not occur to her that I'm quite happy *inside;* that the pettiness and stupidity of her world interests me about as much as the bloody soaps whose plots she insists on relaying to me blow by blow?

"So, essentially you're saying that everything I am is wrong, and you'd be a lot happier if I could just start acting like everyone else?"

She looks like she's been slapped, hearing her basic argument stated so bluntly.

"No, that's not what I'm saying *at all.* I'm just concerned . . ."

Yeah, concerned what others might think of your crazy, shut-in boyfriend.

Why do you even bother with this bitch, Ramsey? She's not interested in who you are; it's all about what she can make out of you.

I stiffen, certain Anita can hear.

"Ramsey, *hello*? You see! That's what I'm talking about; here one minute, off in dream-land the next. And what about the *mess* you've made of yourself? You think that's the kind of thing a . . ."

She falters. It doesn't matter; I already know what she's going to say:

". . . the kind of thing a *normal* person does?"

"You know what? I can't handle this any more I don't know why I fucking bother . . ."

She almost sobs, voice breaking as she plucks up her clothes, making for the bedroom door. A sudden pang of panic; I don't want her to go.

Why? Tittering laughter through pursed lips. Do spiders even *have* lips? I don't know why; the fear is irrational, *phobic,* like those times I lost sight of my Mom in crowded streets or supermarket aisles as a boy, certain in that instant that she was never coming back.

It hurts like a son of a bitch as I rise from the bed, taking her by the shoulders. My wounds gape and bleed beneath their dressings, surrounding me with a slaughterhouse tang.

"Get *off* me!"

She doesn't mean it, doesn't even put up much of a fight as I bend to kiss her, muttering apology against her lips.

Why waste the energy? Let her go! She'll have found another project by the end of the week.

Probably true, but I can't let her go now, even if I want to.

Going down on my knees before her, I bury my face in her crotch, tears coming with the sensation of her fingers at the back of my head, stroking as if I'm a crying child in need of consolation.

"What're we going to do with you, huh?" she whispers as I pull down her underwear, my lips seeking out the perfumed softness of her pubic hair, trailing down to kiss the seat of her sex. She's always protested this act before, proclaiming it filthy, perverse, but concedes to it now without complaint, shuddering almost imperceptibly at my tongue's exploration.

Disengaging from me, she moves to the bed and lies down, opening her legs, turning her head to look out the window as I crawl between.

Everything hurts; arms, back, prick and mind, but I put the pain aside, saving it for when the light returns, and I can examine my wretchedness in every detail.

Anita comes with a muted sob; the sound of a child knowing that expressing its misery will only invite further abuse, then sits up, running appreciative fingers through my hair, eyes gleaming wet in the dark.

*

I'm in the belly of the beast; a stinking sewer-darkness where I'm taken apart cell by cell, laughing as skin, muscle and bone gradually slough away, leaving me more naked than man has ever been.

I see myself; a bone-thing smiling amidst the soup of its own dissolving life. I smile. No masks any more, no pretensions of happiness, contentment, love. Only the truth that's always lingered behind; empty eyed, pure and unchanging, all lies gone back to the shit they were sculpted from.

The Beast seems pleased by my revelation, growling approval as the enveloping darkness quivers and convulses, propelling my true self up, up into daylight, where it can go and spread the gospel amongst those still in love with lies.

*

Too bright, sunlight spilling through my eye sockets, igniting the oil-darkness where my thoughts swim. I groan at the sensation of sloughed-off flesh congealing about me, bringing with it all the pain and weakness that's part and parcel of the condition.

"Oh, so you're awake, then?"

I don't like the chirpiness in her voice; it's like the yowl of mating cats. I blink, the world cohering around me like a kaleidoscope pattern. Anita stands at the foot of the bed, dressed, gazing down at me with weary affection.

"God, you can sleep through *anything*, can't you?"

I rub the sleep from my eyes, sit up, wincing at the sudden soreness in my chest and back.

Walking around the bed, Anita pauses in front of the window, wiping it with the cloth in her hand. The antiseptic scents of polish and air-freshener fill my throat and nostrils, making me want to cough and sneeze in tandem.

"Not at work today?"

"Took the day off. Sorry if I woke you. I really enjoyed last night."

A confessional rush, as though she's spent all the while I've been asleep composing it. I don't know how to respond, the words fluttering around lost in my mouth.

"Good. Me too."

My eye strays to her corner of the ceiling, as has become habit since she took up residence. Her absence shudders me, sucking at my being as though a black hole has spontaneously opened in the room.

Where is she?

"Had the fright of my bloody life earlier . . ."

I'm the eye of the shit-storm that is life.

". . . found the biggest bloody spider while I was dusting. Nearly had a heart attack!" Up and out of bed, mind red and black mist, my entrails lightning.

"I got the vacuum to the bloody thing in the end. You should've heard it clatter up the pipe!"

She turns as I draw close, smiling, thinking it's love in my reaching hands. The first blow knocks her down, the sound she makes like air wheezing from a punctured tyre. She tries to scrabble away; pathetic, wounded animal. Her stupidity disgusts me. Her fear disgusts me. Her affection, petulance, warmth, appetite, childishness and ambition; all wretched. She doesn't understand, not even when I make it plain, ignorance written across her face until it breaks and slackens, seeping like overripe fruit.

*

There's still hope; a slender, idiot's hope.

She's still breathing, a wet, gurgling hack as I drag her down the stairs. Good. I want her to see, *see what she's done . . .*

I hear her, crying to herself through snatches of song:

. . . Fly me . . . to the moon and let me . . . play among the stars . . .

God, god, please let her be all right . . .

She laughs, the sound weak and sick. There she is, splayed out across the web she's spun for herself. Bleeding, every movement spilling thick, black sludge to the cellar floor.

I don't know what to say, other than:

"I'm sorry."

She descends from the web, dragging one useless leg, several of her arms severed or twisted out of true. They're everywhere; pulsing, pale white clusters, wrapped around in threads of glittering silk, the entire cellar become a nursery where children—*our* children—will soon be at play.

I accept her kiss and the bitter flood that follows with the hunger of an infant at the teat. Breaking away, she looks past me to Anita, who's managed to crawl to the foot of the stairs. She's bleeding profusely, face obscured beneath a mask of red as she turns to face us. Raw horror burbles from her broken mouth, the sight and sound of her mutilation leaving me feeling nothing, empty and impotent as an old skin.

For me? the mother-to-be asks. I nod.

Vile and beautiful as anything in nature; the feeding of a mother hungry and exhausted from the labour of birth.

Anita fights, eyes fixed on me, silently begging for help. I swallow the urge to look away, watching 'til it's over, her protests growing still. Mother throws what remains—little more than a shrivelled sack of skin and bone—to where her—*our*—young wait to be born. Turning to me, she grins through slick and shining lips, already seeming heartier for her meal.

Her kiss tastes of Anita, of the perversity we shared the night before. I see the first emerge out of the corner of my eye, the sack that contains it rupturing, delicate, translucent limbs unfurling. Dragging itself free, the young drops to the cellar floor, black pearl eyes glaring through the muck of gestation, mewls of affection escaping its throat as they fix on us. More soon follow, skittering up the walls, across the ceiling, swarming over Anita's remains, devouring them down to the last morsel.

She takes my tongue first, biting it out at the root, swallowing it like a choice oyster. Then my lips, my nose; the fatty meat of my cheeks. The children follow their Mother's example, clawing their way up my legs and back in search of meals more suited to their underdeveloped palettes. A breath at my ear, a whisper:

I don't want you to be anything else.

Then I'm dragged down, in love with the world and all that I'll leave behind there.

PREY

I wasn't there.

I saw them coming for you. Didn't do anything.

Not because I was *afraid*. I'd have swallowed my fear for you.

Once.

Not because I couldn't stop them. I could've opened my veins, let the sunlight spill out, could've sung; whispered them to death with a lullaby.

But I didn't.

I watched them come. You screamed like a lion being flayed alive, like an angel burning; called my name. I sat murmuring in the dark.

They didn't take you whole, but piece by piece, knowing that you wouldn't, *couldn't* die.

Better you than me.

I was wrong, and I'm *sorry* . . . just words, you say. They mean nothing. And you're probably right, considering what I let you *suffer*. I can't take it back. It simply is.

They're coming for me now, at long last. I'm tired of running, *hiding* from them. Anything's better than this; living forever as *prey*.

Forgive me.

SICK SOULS

People made the mistake of assuming that Billy didn't think. Alex knew better. It wasn't that Billy didn't *think;* Billy just didn't *care.*

As for Alex, he tried not to think too often, though it was often difficult to avoid it, especially at night, when consideration seemed to swarm and multiply in the silence, buzzing accusation in his mind.

It started out the same as usual; two strangers stumbling through the park where he, Billy and Liquorice had been swapping stories and cheap cider since sundown, laughing, on their way home from the pub or a party. Even at this distance, Alex could hear enough of the faggoty, smart-arse way they talked to make his hackles rise. Poncey student-types from the university. He fucking *hated* that.

"Oy!" Billy called, making sure to keep his tone the right side of threatening. "Queers!"

The pair quieted down, picking up their pace. Leaping from their seats, Alex and the others jogged across the field to catch up with them, practically smelling the piss-yellow stink of fear they trailed.

If there was any doubt they were faggot students before, it evaporated now that he saw them up close:

One had long, wavy hair, tied back in a rough pony-tail. A lanky streak of piss; the kind of fairy who'd likely break in two with a flick. The other was larger, but walked with a weird hunch, as if he didn't want the world to notice him. He eyed Alex through tinted, expensive looking glasses as he drew alongside.

"Hey mate, you got the time?"

Glancing at his watch, the faggot managed to mutter, "About quarter past eleven."

"You what?" Liquorice growled, drawing up beside the other. "You trying to be funny or something? You want me to break your nose?"

The long haired fucker sighed, rolling his eyes before walking on a little faster. Oh, Alex was going to enjoy putting one over on this cunt.

"Oy! Don't you fucking walk away when I'm talking to you."

The bigger guy turned, though avoided looking Alex and the others directly in the face.

"Look, we're not interested, all right?"

Billy loomed, the glittering, fevered look on his face meaning there was going to blood tonight, whatever the case.

"You fucking *what*?" He rumbled, starting towards the pair. "You fucking *what*, you queer?"

Before Alex could think, Billy grabbed the long-haired cunt by the shoulder, swinging him 'round. He flailed like a rag-doll, the other screaming; a little girl who'd lost her mommy.

Liquorice silenced him with a blow that knocked him to the concrete, followed by a kick to the stomach.

As for the other, Alex watched—his stomach a volcano on the verge of eruption—as Billy slapped his face from side to side.

"Why do you have a *girl's* hair, eh? Are you a *girl*, or would you just like to be one? I bet you'd like to be one, I bet you love to suck cock, fucking faggot . . ."

The same old mantra. Alex had a vague impression that the words didn't matter; it was like certain kinds of music; you listened to it to get yourself psyched up.

A punch to the belly, and the long-haired queer doubled over, staggering out into the middle of the road. Liquorice kicked the other one like a football around a muddy field. Funny, they didn't even try to fight back. Most did when they realised shit wasn't going to let up.

The long-haired cunt looked up, a trick of the light, making it seem as if his eyes had disappeared, leaving only gaping holes onto the seething insides of his skull.

"Hey," Billy said, grasping him by the wrist, dragging him back. "I think this faggot has the hots for you, Alex. Is that right, you piece of shit? You want to suck my friend's cock?"

The guy didn't respond, hanging limp and listless from Billy's grip. Alex didn't like it; it was as if neither of them even *cared* . . .

They'd have to finish soon; someone was bound to have noticed by now. It usually took at least an hour for the fucking filth to arrive.

"What's the matter, you cock-sucking bastard? Got nothing clever to say?"

The guy looked up at Billy. For a second, Alex was sure he saw it again; not eyes, but ragged black holes, something moving in the space beyond.

Distant sirens shattered the illusion, an angry voice shouting from one of the surrounding houses:

"Oy! What are you doing?"

Liquorice left off kicking the fucker on the ground, who'd curled into a tight, bloody ball. Billy continued to pound the other's face and stomach, Alex certain he wouldn't stop 'til there was nothing left but blood.

"For fuck's sake, Bill!"

Billy's rhythm stuttered, a distant, doll-like look washing over his eyes. Alex caught the queer's glance through a mask of blood and hair: the look of a man whose world had split apart and been washed in fire, whose every child slithered from the womb cold and unbreathing, reducing its mother to the same.

He was grateful when Billy dropped him and vaulted the park fence. Alex followed like a pup on its Master's heels, albeit one smart enough to sometimes resent its status.

*

He hoped that Mom would be in bed by the time he got home. The lights were on downstairs. Someone waiting up for him. Emma, with any luck. She hardly ever gave him a hard time.

Stopping to wipe his hands in the front garden's overgrown grass, he waited for the alcohol and adrenaline in his system to subside before making his way to the front door.

It opened before he'd even got his key out of his pocket, the face on the other side all weary but affectionate impatience.

"Where the hell have you been?" Emma sighed, ushering him into the hallway. "Mom's been throwing a fit all night."

"Where is she?"

"Gone to bed, thank Christ. Dinner's in the fridge."

He wasn't hungry, never was after spending time with Bill and Liquorice.

"So . . . where've you been?" she asked, trying to keep it light.

"Just out with Bill and Licky."

A flash in her eyes, a sudden electrifying of the air.

"*Bill*? Billy Taverner?"

Oh God, he really, *really* didn't need a lecture right now.

"Yeah. What about it?"

Emma sighed. She looked so much like Mom when she did that, it was scary.

"Nothing. I just think you could do a lot bloody better in your choice of friends."

She was concerned; not just trying to get at him, like Mom always did, but it didn't stop him from bristling:

"I think I can make up my own mind who I spend time with, thanks all the same."

She looked at him as if he were a stranger sitting at the dining table, someone she didn't know from Adam.

"I'm going to bed. Make sure you set your alarm; you've got work tomorrow."

Fuck, he'd forgotten about that.

She left without another word, stomping up the stairs as if she wanted to bring the house crashing down around them both.

*

Floating, invisible; a ghost caught up on the night's breeze. *Dreaming?* Though it was pitch black, Alex saw the park well enough; the figures sprawled out on the grass.

The one Liquorice had seen to shuddered where he lay, the other grasping him by the shoulders, hissing demands into his face:

"No, you *can't*. I won't let you!"

The other laughed, hacking up blood.

". . . too . . . too late. Besides, I'm . . . tired. I just . . . just want to sleep for a while . . ."

His body convulsed, teeth jarring closed so tight Alex wouldn't have been surprised if they shattered in their sockets.

"No!" The other shook him as though he could jar whatever had come loose inside back into place. A croaking gasp, bloody foam bubbling between his lips, and the dying man grew still.

Alex didn't feel anything. How could he, deprived of the flesh that was the source of emotion? Even were it present, he doubted the situation would be much different.

The long-haired queer started to sob, bending forward to plant a kiss on his lover's lips.

Alex was so close, he could've reached out and touched him.

An electric thrill of terror shuddered his substance as the fucker wheeled to face him, threatening to tear it apart.

A Halloween mask of gaping holes, darkness in place of eyes, mouth and nostrils, the eyes that fixed him as the illusion faltered far, far worse. How could the fucker *see* him? He was little more than rumour on the wind!

Cold fingers closed around him, Alex squealing as they pierced his dreaming self, grasping something fundamental within.

So cold . . .

"What do you *want*?" A demand slurred through snot and tears. Alex couldn't answer, a fish with a hook in its throat, a rabbit strangling in the snare.

The fucker bared his teeth, wrenching him forward. A sudden sensation of vertigo, the world momentarily disintegrating into chaos, then congealing around him, as though he'd been pulled through a cascade of liquid meat that solidified, taking on repulsive shape and weight in the frigid night air.

He fell forward face first, retching, tasting dirt. A foot planted itself in his side, tipping him onto his back. Babbling, baby nonsense spewed from his mouth. Where was he? *What the fuck was happening*?

Freezing, sprawled naked in the grass, he raked at himself with bitten-ragged nails, wanting nothing more than to slough off this stinking, sweating sack and be rumour again. The hard-on he sported was worst of all; more enthusiastic than any since he'd learned the trick of masturbation, it strained desperate and engorged against its anchorage, the flutters it inspired in the pit of his belly so nauseating, he wished it would uproot itself; fly into the night, taking the butterfly swarm with it.

A shadow loomed over him, ragged holes in the smoky delirium of its head blazing with reflected moonlight.

"You killed Vessel."

"It wasn't me. Bill and Liquorice . . ."

A boot to his chest drove the breath from him.

"You were with them. You *let* them do it. You took him from me."

The shadow seemed to swell and split, giving birth to a face he'd last seen slack and bleeding. Its owner knelt in the grass as the shadow-stuff trailed away, rising from him like cigarette smoke or vapour from a sweating horse. *Get up. You can have this fucker* . . . but his body refused to comply. All it could do was lie and shake, limp as a puppet without hands to make it dance.

"My name is Faine. I loved Vessel, and you took him from me."

Something . . . a sound beneath the words; crackling, chattering, like static from a dead TV channel, or an ant's nest about to erupt beneath him.

The shadow returned as he spoke, sewing itself about him, black threads worming across his skin, making him somehow darker than the surrounding night. Though every inch of him screamed in defiance of it, something within the shadow snared Alex's eye; a motion like wheels turning; insects seething, preparing to swarm.

". . . you took him from me . . ."

Echoing, the words seeming to be repeated by other voices; men, women, children, all buried and rotting beneath the soil at his back.

The shadow burgeoned, split, the swarms it contained spilling out, finding their way into his eyes, his nostrils; his open and screaming mouth.

*

"Alex!"

He jolted awake, almost falling out of bed. Pellucid sunlight filtered through the partially drawn curtains, prophesying a day of absolute drudgery.

"Alex, if I have to call you again, I'm going to come up there and kick you out of bed!"

"All right, Mom! For God's sake . . ."

Struggling into a pair of boxer shorts, he made his way to the bathroom. It tasted like a rat had crawled into his mouth and died while he slept. He looked like shit; always did first thing in the morning, hands bruised and throbbing from last night's excesses. Hopefully Old Chris wouldn't want him to do anything heavy today.

Too late for a shower, so he settled for a quick wash. The flannel scoured like sand paper, his body sore all over, as if covered in invisible, part-healed burns.

Weird.

Washed and dressed, he headed downstairs, steeling himself against the inevitable pre-breakfast confrontation.

*

"So, where did you get to last night?" Toast partially burned, tea too milky. Mom had started having these lapses lately.

Emma greeted him coldly, glaring at him over her cereal from the opposite side of the table.

"Just out."

It wouldn't cut much ice, but he didn't feel obliged to elaborate.

"Just out, eh? Doing what? You better not have been drinking."

Mom had a thing about drinking; refused to suffer even a drop in the house since Dad disappeared for parts unknown.

"Nothin' wrong about having a beer or two . . ."

" For God's sake, Alex, didn't you learn a *bloody thing* from your father?"

That was how she always referred to him: *Your father*, as though he were some pet of Alex's that constantly crapped on the living room carpet. As for what he'd learned from the man, barring the fundamentals of walking, talking, eating with cutlery, he couldn't think of much. The only thing that made any lasting impression was towards the end, when he'd become so miserable, Alex fully expected to come home one day to find him strung from the ceiling or bleeding out in the bathtub:

He'd learned that men regretted their lives; that, in all likelihood, he would too someday, no matter how hard he tried. Which was why it was so essential he enjoyed himself now, regardless of what Mom or Emma insisted.

"I didn't say that. I'm just saying that, if I was, it's nothing to throw a fit over."

Mom sighed, turning away to distract herself with dishes that were already clean.

"I despair of you sometimes, Alex, I really do. Far too much of your father in you."

"I'm going to work." He left his toast unfinished, still hungry.

*

The sun was going down by the time he arrived at the park. A couple of mothers passed him at the gates, dragging their protesting kids along home. One of them threw him a funny look, as if to ask what he thought he was doing hanging around a kid's park. Were Bill and Liquorice there, he might've responded. As it was, he let it go.

The park was empty, save for lengthening shadows.

Alex laughed at himself, a faint shiver dancing up his spine. "Fuckin' pussy."

The swings squealed as they swung in the wind, a sound so melancholy it seemed somehow draining. Seating himself, he checked his watch. 5:31 P.M. It'd be a while before Lick and Bill arrived. Good opportunity to get started on the cider. He didn't really like the taste, but it was cheap, and better than beer, which was the only other option Bill would entertain. It tasted more sour than usual tonight, as if it'd already been drunk and pissed back into the bottle.

God, it was *freezing*, his breath billowing smoky and phantasmal in the air. A couple of school kids, no doubt on their way home after detention, eyed him as he drank.

"What the fuck are you looking at?"

"Fuck off!" one of them replied before both broke into a run. He didn't even bother rising to follow; they'd be gone before he managed more than four steps. Besides, the cider seemed to have gone to his head.

Why did he feel so on edge tonight? Part of him hoped Bill and Lick wouldn't turn up so he could just go home. What was the point of it, anyway?

A sudden howl of wind, a flicker as of something moving on the edge of sight. Nothing but shrubbery and shadows.

Jesus, he was so fucking out of it . . .

His thoughts turned to last night; the faggots. He'd noticed stains of blood on the path, was surprised no one had come to clean it up by now. Where were they? What did they think of the world after what he, Lick and Bill had shown them of it?

What the fuck did it matter? It'd never bothered him before, even when Bill beat somebody so bad, he and Lick were forced to make an anonymous 999 call. Why would he suddenly give a shit about a couple of queers who'd gotten away better than some?

You took him from me . . .

"'Ello, Alex mate!" A rough shove from behind sent him sprawling from the swing, on hands and knees in the dirt.

"Fucking *cunt.*" He turned round with a snarl. Bill and Liquorice seated themselves on the remaining swings, the latter looking like he hadn't changed his clothes since last night.

"Woah, ho, ho; sounds like somebody's pissed on little Alex's bonfire. What's the matter, hard day fitting windows?"

More than either of you've ever done in your whole lives, you worthless pieces of shit. He wanted to say it; checked himself before the retort caught him a beating.

"Fuck you, Lick . . ."

"All right, all right; just having a laugh. Jesus!" Lick said, pilfering a bottle of cider from the bag.

Bill remained silent, regarding him with eyes dark and unblinking as an owl's.

Getting up, he grasped the swing frame for support, his legs tottering beneath him, feeling as though the bone and muscle had melted to the consistency of jelly.

"What the fuck's up with you?" Bill asked, voice an ursine growl.

Alex opened his mouth to answer, but the words refused to come. All around him, the world seemed to soften and shift, running like wax beneath a blow torch.

"Did you . . . did you see . . . the blood?"" he managed, before slumping to his knees. Something was wrong inside; nothing to do with drink. He was full of maggots that'd begun to sprout wings, hummingbirds battering themselves against his ribcage and the inner wall of his skull.

Raising a head grown swollen and heavy, he saw that Bill and Lick hadn't been spared the insanity abruptly flooding the world. Great, ragged rents gaped where their eyes and mouths once were, the meat they'd replaced looking to have been ripped out by a starving wolf. No blood poured from the mutilations, rather a viscous, sewage like gruel, writhing with clumps of worms and maggots.

Alex shook his head, trying to dislodge the illusion, but it persisted; a nightmare from which his mind refused to wake.

"I think there's somethin' really wrong with 'im. Should we call an ambulance or what?"

Lick's voice, slurred and distorted as if played on an old, scratched tape.

The Bill-thing fixed him with its weeping eye-sockets, something scrabbling in the dark beyond like a spider nestled in a crack between bricks.

"Nah, stupid bastard's probably just had too much to drink . . ."

"I don't think so Bill, he looks in a really bad way."

The swarms he contained broke free, his body splitting beneath their assault, the last of the evening's light flooding his open skull, washing the world away beneath waves of amber and red.

*

Strange, strange places.

He shivered, exploratory hands roving over his body, finding it naked, but whole. Cautiously, his fingers strayed to his forehead, expecting to find the ragged edges of a wound newly closed.

Nothing. A dream?

"Hello?" His voice strained, cracking. God, he'd have sold his soul for a glass of water.

Things seemed to move all around, shapes flitting to and fro in the shadows. A faint whimpering, like children unable to contain their misery, then:

"So, you came."

He knew that voice, though he couldn't put a face to it.

"Where the fuck am I?"

The whimpers rose to cruel laughter, the unseen children ridiculing one of their own tripped face first into the mud.

"You wouldn't understand, even if I told you. Not yet. Vessel used to share this place with me, but you and your friends put an end to that."

A face coalesced in his mind; long hair, girlish, queer. As if in response to the memory, something approached out of the darkness, stalking on legs that bent the wrong way, its lower half wrapped around in skirts of stripped skin hanging from its back and waist. A sack of clear material swelled from a hole in its belly, things churning and writhing within like eels beneath a pond's surface; tadpoles wriggling free from frog-spawn. Over-long arms that looked to have been broken and poorly set in several places trailed at its sides, and at the end of its azure-feathered, ostrich-like neck bobbed a man's head, its features distressingly familiar.

His first instinct was to run, though it'd do no good. He knew with the strange certainty of dreams that this thing was God here; nowhere to run it couldn't follow, nowhere to hide it couldn't see.

Even so, he scrabbled back on his ass as it approached, his nostrils flaring at the sweet, rotting peaches perfume of it.

"Have you come to stay with me? I hope not; it isn't time yet. There's so much you have to do."

Alex tried to close his eyes against it, but it was as though their lids had been surgically removed whilst he slept.

"No, I'm not doing anything. Leave me alone . . . leave me . . ."

The unseen children giggled again as if one of their number had dared contradict Daddy in his foulest mood.

"You've already started. You brought me one of them; the other got away, though you made him *bleed.* I can't touch them, you see; it's not permitted. Ha! If it was, *you'd* be food for the worms and sparrows now, instead of Vessel.

But *you* can. That's why you can't stay."

The thing was *insane.* What the fuck was it talking about?

"Not me; this is all wrong . . ."

It was on him, pinning him to the ground, stoppering his mouth with its own before he could draw another breath. He tasted rain in Summer, congealed blood and honey, apples fomenting to cider.

Thrashing against it, he felt its nails biting into his wrists. Its kisses became brutal, teeth drawing blood from his cheeks and lips, that it lapped up like a humming bird supping nectar. Worst of all was the enthusiasm throbbing between its legs; a warm, wet length extruding from the wound-like cavity there to coil about his own. He howled at his own flesh's betrayal, the fact that it could be stirred by something so vile beyond endurance.

"Get off me, you *fucker,* get off!"

The children echoed his wails, mocking him from the darkness.

"You sound like Vessel when I first brought him here. Don't fret! You aren't alone, like me . . ."

Raising itself, the thing opened its mouth, chirping like a flock of sparrows disturbed by a preying magpie.

A second of stillness, silence, then an answer; a dying man snatching breath through a throat full of blood and bile. The thing that followed in its wake could no longer lay claim to humanity, the changes wrought on its anatomy too extreme.

Though it walked upright on two legs, still boasting torso, arms and head, every inch of these components was so mutilated—cut, bruised; teased open and inside out—it was an abattoir parody of mankind, constructed from offal and partially butchered carcasses. Only the face remained partially intact, though even that hadn't been entirely spared the knife.

Gaping holes in place of eyes and mouth, seeping streams of cesspool sewage.

Liquorice.

Alex gaped in a silent scream as the thing began to grind against him again, the length it put forth drawing his own up, into the wound from which it emerged.

He fought the coming climax, willing himself to wilt as Lick stood by, empty eyes fixated on the display.

Orgasm seemed to take more with it than seed, what fleeting pleasure it gave soon waxing to agony.

He wept, sucked inside out, drawn up into a turgid, stinking darkness, more absolute even than the one he'd woken to. He lingered there for a time; a disparate scrap of blood and bone; thought and memory swirling, fomenting, 'til he felt his prison gape and shudder, preparing to shit him back out into light.

*

What was that smell? Sharp, *chemical* . . .

He opened his eyes, nauseating pain coruscating throughout his lower belly. Familiar faces sifted through a galaxy of black and purple shooting stars; Mom and Emma looking down on him tear-eyed, as though he were the resurrected Jesus, come to absolve them of their sins.

"Oh, thank God, thank God . . ." Mom reached down to stroke his face, her fingers febrile.

A scruffy-bearded Indian man gently coaxed her aside, glasses magnifying his eyes to comical proportions.

"Hello there, son." His accent was a weird but musical mix of Indian and Scottish. He poked and prodded Alex as he spoke, checking his pulse and fingering the hurts in his abdomen. Alex gasped as he happened across a particularly tender spot. "How're you doing?"

Alex vaguely recalled that he wasn't supposed to like Pakis very much. All of that seemed dim and hazy now, like something he'd dreamed or seen on TV years and years ago.

"You're a very lucky man, my young friend."

He talked with Mom, rattling off stuff that Alex could barely hear, much less understand.

Smiling, Emma came to the bedside, taking his hand.

"How're you feeling?"

"Hurts," he managed to croak.

Emma laughed, though it sounded like she wanted to cry.

"Hardly bloody surprising, is it? I told you to stay away from Bill Tavener."

Bill?

"Leave him alone, Emma. I think he gets the picture."

Leaving off her conversation with the doctor, Mom came forward to hug him. He recoiled from the embrace, cold revulsion washing his entrails at the thought of such intimacy.

She seemed to sense this, settling for gripping his hand. She looked like she wanted to say something, but couldn't find the words. The doctor interjected before she could compose herself:

"The police are still here by the way, Mrs. Liberman. They'd still like a word, if your son is feeling up to it."

"Give us a bloody minute, will you? He's only just woke up!"

Alex eased himself up, careful not to agitate the ache in his belly.

"It's okay, Mom. I'll speak to 'em."

She looked dubious, but wasn't about to deny him. Besides, he wanted to know what the fuck was going on, and doubted he'd learn from either her or Emma without opening up a floodgate of recrimination.

*

A man and a woman came to talk to him, the former not doing much save sitting in a chair sipping coffee, whilst the latter was the posh, smart-arse sort Alex couldn't stand.

"Listen Alex, we want you to tell us everything you can remember before you ended up in here, all right? And try not to leave anything out, even if you think it doesn't matter."

Detectives Miller and Stantz. Miller talked to him like an infant school teacher; all slow precision and simplicity, just in case he didn't understand. He told them everything he could; finishing work, buying drink, meeting Bill and Lick up the park . . .

Stantz stopped him, glancing up from his vending machine coffee.

"Bill? That'd be William Taverner, yes?"

"Yeah, what about it?"

They shared a look.

"Mr. Taverner is currently . . . missing. Apparently no one's seen him since the night in question. We'd very much like to speak with him."

"What about Liquorice?"

Furrow-browed confusion, uncomfortable glances between them.

"Hasn't anyone told you? I'm . . . I'm afraid James Liquorice was found dead at the scene."

A face without eyes or mouth, a body sewn together from rags of raw meat . . .

"You *what*?"

"I can't believe no one's told you this already. Bloody typical that they leave it up to us." Stantz stormed, getting up and prowling round the room.

"I'm sorry you had to find out this way, but we do need to find Mr. Taverner as soon as possible."

"You think Bill did it?"

Alex saw the shutters come down in her eyes.

"We think he might be able to help us with our inquiries. If you know of anywhere he might be . . ."

Alex shook his head.

"I didn't really know him that well. He was more Licky's friend than mine."

Could she tell he was lying? Probably, but she let it go for now.

"If you think of anything we need to know, just give us a call, all right?"

Detective Miller had already decided she didn't like him very much. Why should she? He was just another little street brat getting pissed off his face and causing trouble. It's just that this time things had gone a little further than usual; a psycho who already had a list of offences as long as her arm going off the deep end.

No, not Bill. He might've been a psycho, but he wasn't the one. Why was he so certain of that? Had he seen something before he collapsed? He didn't know, couldn't think straight.

Bill. Bill's face pale and slack with terror, Bill growling: "Keep away! Keep away!" Bill with a knife in his hand, Bill . . .

He waited 'til they were gone before examining himself. He was taped and bandaged all down the right-hand side, the surrounding skin inflamed.

The bastard had stabbed him. He couldn't believe it.

The pain killers still lingering in his system dragged him down to sleep, and this time, there were no dreams.

*

Dark when he woke, second-hand moonlight filtering through the window. Every inch of him itched, the bed sheets glued to his skin by a solvent of sweat.

At least the pain in his side wasn't so bad now.

He convulsed, the entire bed shaking, invisible fingers probing his wounds. Protests rose in his throat, but the touches—warm, lingering—had a curious anaesthetic effect, his body flopping limp and useless, though his thoughts continued to roam.

"Don't fret. We'll be done soon enough."

Easing their way beneath his bandages and bindings, the fingers began to pry them free. *No, no! Get the fuck off me!*

Laughter, quiet, weary.

"Look at the *mess* your so-called friend made. Still, nothing compared to what you made of him, eh? That was fine, fine work. See? I *knew* you were of a different breed . . ."

A face coalesced from the shadows, curly hair framing tapered, feminine features. Tears pricked Alex's sinuses at the sight of it, every inch of him wanting to reach out and tear the prettiness to tatters, even though he knew what lingered beneath, having seen it in nightmares he'd only just begun to recall.

Fingering his wounds like a lover's sex, the thing bent and kissed where he bled, the sensation of its lips and tongue on him vile, but not so much as the reaction of his own flesh.

Glancing up at him, the thing smiled, bloody lipped; a cannibal clown crept from beneath the bed to eat him alive.

Something passed between them as it lapped and suckled, a sensation like minute worms wriggling from its mouth into his body. He called out to god for the first time since he was a child, begging to be taken away from the world and its horrors...

A jolt, as if he'd been struck by invisible lightning, then nothing, the room abruptly empty, save for himself and shadows. Tears came all at once, rolling from his eyes in hot, slow streams, their accompanying sobs becoming snarls as disgust curdled to anger. How dare the fucker touch him? *Queer piece of shit*. He, Liquorice and Bill should've killed them both while they had the chance! As for the hard-on he still wore beneath the sheets, he'd gladly tear it out at the root, unsex himself for its rebellion.

"No, not yet Alex; we're not finished. There's still the other; the one who hurt us both. Bring him to me, and we can be done with this."

It was as if some sadistic surgeon had come while he slept, swapping portions of his brain for that of another, his skull swarming with alien thoughts.

Fumbling in the dark, he flicked on the bedside lamp, the shadows receding to reveal nothing but an empty room. His former dressings had been torn free, strewn across his bed like bloody confetti. Peeling back the covers, he found the wound they'd covered all but healed, no more to mark its existence than a faint, lightning-bolt scar. His fingers went to the area, pressing and probing incredulously. They found it tender, but no more so than if he'd fallen off his bike and skidded along the pavement. What was that? A faint swelling beneath the skin, as if whoever sewed him up had planted a couple of hard-boiled eggs inside him.

Was he high on the painkillers they'd pumped into him? It was the only explanation. Either that or he'd lost his mind, done for Licky before turning on Bill . . .

"No," the voice seemed fainter in the light, more distant, "none of that shit. You know what's happening here; don't *dare* deny it, not after what you've done. All you have to do to make it stop is find him for me . . ."

"*Fuck you,*" Alex hissed, eyes and teeth clenched fast shut.

Silence. Then:

"Then perhaps your sister would like to come and keep me company. What do you think?"

The world suddenly tipped on its fulcrum, inclining towards an abyss where all the shit of being frothed and churned.

Leaning over the side of the bed, he dry-heaved strings of spittle to the floor, murmuring protests that he knew fell on deaf ears:

"Don't you . . . *don't you fucking dare!* Don't you . . ."

All volition drained from him as he flopped back against the bed, his efforts to maintain consciousness futile as an infant's exhausted from the trauma of birth.

*

These weren't his eyes; he realised that the instant they opened. They belonged to something else; a monster come to stalk his sleeping mother and sister, devour them in their beds.

The front door presented no obstacle, clicking open with little more than a touch. It smelled them now, and so did he; Mom's vile apricot perfume, Emma swathed in soap and scented talc. Something else too; a ripe meatiness that put him in mind of raw beef. The monster whose skull he inhabited recoiled from it, shuddering with superstitious repulsion.

The other then; the one that smelled of dust and rotting fruit.

Up the stairs it seeped like smoke, skittering silently across the walls before pausing on the landing.

Light spilled through a half-open door. Peering through, he saw Emma sitting cross-legged on her bed, leafing through one of her books. She looked like she hadn't slept in days, features drawn and pale. She wore a loose-fitting night-shirt, the monster's eyes roving over her near nakedness as his own had during those adolescent moments he'd spied on her whilst she showered.

The beast wanted her, appetite pulsing throughout its every inch. But not tonight; tonight she was taboo, sacred meat that it couldn't so much as taste.

Tearing itself away, it turned to a door sealed fast and locked from within. Paranoid cow always locked her bedroom door, never had a straight answer as to why.

The beast brushed the white-washed wood with a claw, paint blistering beneath its touch. Alex heard the lock click, a dead bolt draw back of its own accord.

"Emma? Is that you?" It rarely took more than a moth flapping its wings to disturb his mother's dreams. The door creaked open, the beast seeping through like a shadow.

She sat up in bed, eyes wide and wild in the dark.

"Emma? If that's you pissing about again . . ."

She reached down beneath the bed, retrieving a length of wood kept there in case of burglars.

The beast laughed at her, inhaling the urine-sharp scent of her fear as Alex might frost freshened breeze.

"Emma, Emma! There's somebody . . ."

The beast reached out and slammed the door shut, its various locks clicking into place.

Outside, Emma banged on the door.

"Mom, Mom, are you okay?"

It was on her before she could reply, its smoky substance becoming solid, sealing her mouth with scraps of its matter. She thrashed and railed beneath it, her fingers finding its flanks, raking away fistfuls of sludge-like flesh.

Looking down at her through the monster's eyes, Alex saw something used up; a hollow carcass that'd already given all it ever would to the world, yet didn't have the wherewithal to simply lay down and die.

Now she'd be put to purpose her withered dreams of wifedom and Motherhood could never encompass: she'd be meat for the monster, and in that, become part of the myth it trailed.

"Don't be frightened, Mom," he cooed to her through the monster's maw, "it's only me."

She stopped struggling.

"Mom, answer me!" The door rattled in its frame, Emma attempting to tear it off its hinges.

The woman who'd birthed him remained silent even as the clots of matter sealing her mouth retreated, reaching up to run trembling fingers across the beast's cheek.

It allowed this small indulgence before opening its jaws wide, gnawing off the trespassing hand at the wrist.

A breathless gasp, the colour draining from her features, eyes rolling back in their sockets.

Emma was gone now, no doubt on the phone to the police. It didn't matter; he'd be done long, long before they arrived.

That face. He'd learned to loathe it in recent years; its slack stupidity, its accusation, its wittering terror of the world.

The beast apparently found it no less offensive, working its claws between her lips, tugging at her lower jaw until it tore free, her eyes and tongue plucked out and swallowed like oysters, the sensation of them sliding down its gullet at once repulsive and delightful beyond words.

Alex began to protest as it went to work on the rest of her. Though he knew it was little more than meat to be devoured, he had no desire to look upon her sagging breasts, the folds of pale fat that composed her body or the anatomy through which he'd entered the world, long since dried and withered through neglect.

The beast had no such compunctions.

There was little left of her but blood and fragments by the time it finished, scraps of bone and organ that it took time arranging on the besmirched bedclothes, producing a composition that its heart quickened in the creation of.

It was gone out of the window by the time the police arrived, fragments of broken glass lodged in the partway-solid portions of its hide.

Alex watched through its eyes as they entered the house, the light flickering on in his mother's room.

Emma's shriek echoed in his ears as it loped away, carrying him back to where he slept.

*

"I swear, I've never seen anything like it."

The doctor could barely contain his enthusiasm, prodding the tender flesh where Alex's wound once was as if not able to accept the reality of it.

Alex didn't have anything to say. He felt sick, exhausted from a night of dreaming horrors.

"Didn't I say how lucky you were? I'd like to run a blood test, if I may."

Alex consented without complaint, though the sensation of the needle sliding into his arm made him feel woozy.

It'd just gone 9:00 A.M. when the nurse announced he had visitors. He could tell from her manner there was something weird going on.

Emma looked like hell, her face seeming to hang from the bone beneath as if barely glued on. She was followed by Detectives Miller and Stantz, both of whom wore expressions of haunted and hollow determination.

Emma didn't speak. Her eyes were dry, though he could see evidence of tears all over her face. She hugged him tight, still not uttering a word.

She didn't need to. He already knew what they were going to tell him.

Miller stood forward, Stantz hanging back as if uncertain of where to put himself.

"Alex, I'm afraid we have some bad news."

She adopted a tone of official coldness as she informed him in no uncertain terms that his Mother was dead, murdered in the night.

Emma withdrew from him as Miller made the account, going to the window and glaring out as if defying the evil reality she'd been born to.

Alex didn't do or say anything after Miller finished. How could he when he didn't know what to feel? It was as if some essential stopper had been ripped from the core of his being, all that he contained draining away like murky water from a bath tub.

"Alex," Miller resumed, speaking slowly, deliberately, as if to a child, "we need to know where William Taverner is. He's obviously very dangerous. We can't afford to let him do this to anyone else."

They thought *Bill* did this? Alex almost laughed out loud. Miller caught the momentary flicker of humour, her demeanour darkening.

"This isn't a game, Alex. If you know where he is..."

Turning away from the window, Emma fixed him with empty eyed contempt.

"Just fucking tell them, Alex! I know you've got some idea."

"I've already told you, I don't fucking know."

The way she looked at him then . . . as if he'd split open before her eyes, revealing something alien, entirely beyond her experience or comprehension.

"Don't ever come near me again."

Then she was gone, taking whatever anchor he had to reality with her.

*

The police didn't stay much longer; the nurses ushering them out as if they were bothersome children clamouring for a sick brother's attention.

They didn't believe him. Why should they? He'd lied through his teeth. If Bill was still in town, he knew exactly where he'd be.

"Tonight, then."

Faine sat in the visitor's chair, idly leafing through one of the wild life magazines Emma had brought. Glancing up at Alex, he smiled, not so much as a bruise marring his features.

Alex considered summoning a nurse, but knew it'd be a waste of time. The bastard would be gone by the time they arrived.

"What . . . what the fuck do you want?"

Sighing, the thing put down its magazine.

"You already know that, Alex. I've asked often enough, and frankly, I'm losing patience."

He didn't look like a man who was losing patience; he looked like a man with all the time in the world.

Alex flashed back to last night, grasping the bed as his head and stomach swam in unison.

"You . . . you killed Mom . . ."

A smile.

"No, I didn't."

His skull was a cesspool, memories floating like lumps of unprocessed sewage; the first fight he'd ever gotten into at school, the teacher calling him a stupid boy for defending himself; a girl named Jessica who he used to play with giving him his first glimpse of what lay between a girl's legs in her parent's attic . . .

But most of all, he remembered last night; how compliant he'd been in the monster's intent, luxuriating in its strength and insubstantial nature, moving through the night as little more than a shadow amongst shadows.

He remembered the taste of Mother's meat, sweeter and more nourishing by far than the milk she produced.

Not the monster.

Him.

"You . . . you fucking *made me* do it!"

"No. All I did was show you what you are; the self inside. You'll get used to it, eventually. I did."

Alex wanted to die. Everything, everything had collapsed around him, the life he'd so lamented gone to shit in his hands, all for the price of a little fun.

"Leave me alone."

"Bring the other to me, and I might. Your friend Liquorice is lonely; he needs someone to keep him company."

"If . . . if I get Bill for you, you'll go away—for good?"

The bastard shrugged.

"Perhaps, if that's what you want. I wouldn't take too long over it, if I were you. The beast, as you call it, is still hungry. If not Mr. Tavener, maybe it'll find its own playmate."

"Not Emma, please. She's got nothing to do with this!"

"It's not up to me. Maybe I can teach you to control it, but I want the boy first."

No choice at all when it came down to it.

"All right, I'll get the fucker for you."

"I'll be waiting."

With that, he rose and left, trailing scents of milk and marzipan; reminders of times when Alex had known more than bile and disappointment.

*

There was only one place; a house, old, abandoned, just off from the railway tracks that used to service the old coal mine. Since the 1980s, when the mine had been forcibly closed, the place had become an overgrown nowhere, the sometimes-haunt of tramps and runaways seeking isolation.

Mom had always warned him against wandering down there as a child, lending it all the more allure.

The house looked like it'd never been completed; a slate-grey stone structure all but lost amidst trees, weeds and bushes. He and the few friends he'd had as a kid would dare one another to step through the front door, see how long they could last before imagination got the better of them.

Bill had been in a weird mood the first time Alex took him there; his mom was in the hospital again, the shit kicked out of her by her latest boyfriend, her son waxing philosophical on how it'd be best all 'round if she just died and saved them the heartache.

Something had come over him when he saw the house, as if he'd suddenly begun to sweat thunder-heads. Barrelling his way through the vegetation, ignorant of thorns and thistles, he'd come before the gaping hole that was the front door, peering into the darkness with lightning in his eyes.

"Bill, man . . ."

"*What?*"

"It doesn't matter."

The way Bill looked as they stepped inside . . . the place might as well have been a cathedral.

"*Wow.*"

He hadn't been content 'til they'd explored every inch, Alex and Lick letting him go off on his own when the stairs and floors looked too precarious to bear them. Bill had scoffed, calling them wimps and pussies before treading where they didn't dare.

He rarely ever smiled; even when pissed off his face, singing at the top of his voice, beating the shit out of some poor asshole who'd caught his eye, the expression always looked forced—*false*. When he'd emerged from his explorations of the house's cellar, it looked as though his skull was trying to force its way through his face, lips drawn back so far, Alex could see pristine wisdom teeth; a baboon smiling threat.

"You don't tell *anybody* about this, all right? I don't want any fuckers sniffing around my place."

My place. He'd called it that from that point on. Lick and Alex had shared concerns whenever he was out of earshot. Sometimes, Lick divulged, he'd go down to the house on his own with a few bottles of booze, spend entire nights there when things at home were fraught. From what they could gather, he'd set up some kind of squat in the cellar; sleeping bag, mattress, stashes of crisps and chocolate bars.

His place.

*

Sleep stole over Alex sometime in the late afternoon. The morning had left him emotionally wrung out, barely enough energy to string one thought to the next.

He dreamed of being buried, frantically burrowing his way up through layers of soil and shale towards light and rain . . .

Cool, twilight air chilled his naked skin, branches and bushes whipping his body as he stalked through the undergrowth, following a trail that was as much soul as scent.

The Beast was solid this time, smoke and shadow foregone in favour of a more meaningful hide.

He was still a passenger in its skull, looking out through its eyes as he might through the windows of a car, but now his presence had swollen, threading out like the roots of a tree or cancer into systems he hadn't been aware of before. He smelled the honey stuff it sweated, felt the tug and contraction of ligaments as it tore through the woods.

And its *hunger;* a gnawing emptiness, so profound as to be painful, seated somewhere deeper than guts and bowels; in the smoke and nightmare stuff that would be left with their unravelling It needed *meat*, and more; a sustenance he had no name for, or analogue in his own experience.

It would have both before the night was out; gorge itself to bursting on stuff that delighted and nauseated in equal measure, the contradiction enough to make him whimper behind its eyes, knowing that the feast would be enough to shatter what little sanity remained.

*

An acrid tang of smoke wafted from the doorway as the Beast stepped through. Things scurried away through the darkness; rats scavenging in the rubble, spiders and beetles grown fat on one another over many undisturbed generations.

Alex smelled him through the smoke; the scent of something killed and left to foment, dug up by wild dogs and devoured before being shat back into the earth. He hadn't realised the extent of Bill's sickness 'til that moment; how much *cleaner* the world would be without him.

Down the cellar steps, slinking on all fours like a lizard. The flickering of a fire, heaped in the middle of the floor from trash and twigs. A figure sat beyond, cross legged, munching on chocolate as it watched him approach.

Taking another bite, it grinned, laughed.

"*Fucking bastard.* I knew; always said there was something fucked up about you. Lick told me I was imagining things . . ."

Using the wall at its back as leverage, it staggered up, amber light snaring on the knife in its hand. Blood on its shirt. Had it even stopped to wash the wounds? Alex doubted it.

The Beast slunk closer to the fire, Alex feeling its heat, wondering how the meat before him would taste roasted upon it.

"Well, what are you fucking looking at? *Come and get me*!"

Alex laughed through the Beast's mouth, stepping full into the fire. The stuff it sweated went up like gasoline, wreathing him in flames. There was no pain. The Beast had long since gone beyond such frailties; the burning of its sires and their sires and their sires resulting in an immunity that the torch holder's children would come to lament.

Bill backed away, trying to press himself into the cellar's stone wall.

Alex didn't waste time with words; reason had always been an impotent defence where Bill was concerned. Why should things be any different now? Hurling himself forward, he felt the windows shatter, all distance and division between him and Beast spanned in the space of a thought.

Bill took advantage of his disorientation, lunging forward, knife outstretched. It found Alex's breast, burying itself up to the hilt. Pain; little more than a wasp's sting. Scorched by the flames, Bill leaped back shrieking, staring in slack-jawed horror as Alex wrenched the knife free.

Bill ran, breaking for the stairs, Alex dabbling curious digits in the viscous, tree sap matter he bled. He lashed out on instinct, without thought. Bill fell, back blossoming red, revealing the meat of which he was composed.

Gasping, he tried to crawl his way up the cellar steps. Alex grasped him, twisting him onto his back, wanting to see the mask of humanity before he flayed it away. Bill held to no deities, but he called to them now, mumbling spit-slurred prayers to God, Christ and whatever divinity might hear.

No-one there. Only Alex; prayers a meaningless commodity to him. The flames caught Bill's clothes as Alex hauled him up, his weight no more than a doll's. He screamed, struggling as his hair singed, skin blistering in the conflagration. The scent of roasting meat was intoxicating, the fear that suffused it a fine spice.

The mask he'd worn since birth came away in rough strips and ribbons, Alex's claws working their way beneath to unseat it. Bill gasped and thrashed throughout, prayers giving way to apologies for crimes Alex didn't even know about:

He was sorry about Martin and the phone call, sorry for telling people "it" was stolen when he knew exactly where "it" was. He was sorry for Geraldine; wished her Mother and his were still speaking, sorry about the neighbour's cat he kicked to death then dumped in the compost bin.

Even the apologies faltered as Alex slit him from throat to groin, allowing him to unravel, painting his final will and testament in the dirt.

The meat still twitched as he flung it into the flames, a few of the morsels it shed—kidneys, liver, pancreas—scooped up and swallowed raw; appetizers for the great feast to come.

Soft, slow clapping from the darkness at his back. He didn't turn, didn't need to; nostrils flaring with the newcomer's stink.

"Bravo. *Bravo.* Wonderful. I knew, even though you never would have realised on your own, I knew the moment you *saw* . . ."

Alex turned, seeing Faine for the first time through the Beast's eyes: A man shape raggedly cut into reality, the state beyond one of perpetually swarming flies; fish and birds caught up in perverse mating and feeding frenzy. The man he'd seen in his hospital room was there too, along with the monstrous, stitched-together thing of his nightmares, all somehow occupying the same space and time, bound up into a truth more complex than Alex could ever conceive.

Was the same true of him now?

Faine smiled, embers rising from between his teeth.

"Not yet; you're still too *new*. There'll be confusion for a long time. I could teach you."

Fucking queer. An echo of a dying self, less than the meat going to ashes in the fire. There'd never been anyone; only other sick, empty souls—Lick, Bill—who'd given up all hope of knowing who and what they were. They wanted him to be the same; sludge in his mind, sludge in his soul. He had been for the longest time, because there'd been *nothing else* . . .

Faine started forward, gently easing him aside before reaching a hand into the flames. What he plucked out still burned; a thrashing worm that seemed somehow diseased, pale body tumescent and pock marked, streaked with shit; a parasite freshly cut from its host's colon.

The thing writhed and shrieked as he secreted it somewhere about his person, slurring protests in an all too familiar voice:

Fucking queer! Cocksucker! Faggot!

Obscenities receding, their maker falling, falling, as though into a chasm that led deep beneath the earth.

"Ah." Faine sighed, turning eyes towards the ceiling, radiating satisfaction that caressed Alex like warm sun and sea spray.

Without another word, he turned and made for the cellar steps. Alex felt a sudden pang; a child that had slipped Daddy's hand.

Mom . . . where was she now? Suffering with Bill and the rest?

Faine paused at the foot of the stairs, lowering his head, seeming to consider.

"I've forgotten Vessel's first face . . . ha, that's how long we were together. He wasn't so very different from *you* at the start. A little more timid, perhaps . . ."

He extended a hand, curling his fingers into crow-like talons.

Alex gasped and pawed the bare earth, hooks suddenly snaring in his entrails, behind his eyes, dragging him forward.

You . . . you said you'd let me go . . .

"Did I? Then perhaps this'll teach you not to take the word of a *faggot* and *cocksucker*."

He tried to pull away, but the hooks dug deep, growing barbed. He could no more resist than he could deny the convulsions that shat him from the womb.

"We're not done yet, little Alex. I'm very, *very* tired; tired of *sickness* like yours. High time people saw how very tragic it can be."

Images flashing behind his eyes; a state of dreaming darkness where cruel children laughed and sang. Lick was there, the holes in his face seeping as he danced and tumbled, Bill too; suspended in the air, shedding meat as unseen hands went to work on him, slitting, tearing, unravelling. And another; a curled up, trembling thing, pale skin split and bruised, teeming with parasites that made nurseries from her suppurating wounds. She hid her face, not wanting him to see. He didn't need to; recognized her weeping well enough from the endless nights he'd heard it filtering through his bedroom wall.

"Alex . . . *Alex* . . ."

Then the hands took her, dragging her thrashing and screaming through the darkness, hoisting her up for his perusal.

Vile, but the hooks were in his eyes, fixing them in place, forcing him to *see*.

Like the rest, the knives had been at work on her, but in more subtle fashion; opening ragged scores and slits throughout her body that looked to have been treated with filth and sewage. She'd become a hive, parasites swarming, nesting, feeding throughout her every inch; children far more dependent than those she'd left behind.

Why? She had nothing to do with what he, Lick and Bill had done . . .

Because she's sick as the rest, little Alex, and she let her children grow the same. She wanted you to be worms, ever since you learned to walk and talk for yourself.

True. *True.*

The vision faltered, the cellar solidifying around him.

"Don't worry; she won't be alone for long. Just one more, then you can go and join her."

One more . . .?

Faine started up the stairs, gesturing so violently Alex lurched forward with the pain, dragged along like the cowed dog he'd always been at heart.

*

He was shit; Faine the hurricane that swept him up and bore him along. The world sifted by strange and distorted; trees amongst which shadow-children played giving way to twilight streets and suburbs. Shadows here too; things like himself; snared in the nowhere-space between child and adulthood, wandering alone, in pairs and packs, trying to find themselves.

You see? Sickness everywhere . . .

He saw; a girl whose budding beauty hid an interior of worms, the boy on her arm burning at his core, on the verge of combustion. Others appeared to be smothered in black tar or creeping fungus, their humanity barely visible through the filth and rot. Sick souls, one and all; an anatomy none of them even acknowledged neglected, left to wither.

. . . I wanted to make them better at the beginning, tried to help them see and grow. But none of you want it, do you? You just want to be rotting meat . . .

Amongst the dirty and diseased, the occasional flash or flutter of brilliance; two lovers walking apart from the rest, arm in arm, erupting with a shifting display of Technicolor feathers and tendrils, a lone boy, wandering lost in his own thoughts, wreathed in a seething storm cloud where fiery fish and serpents swam.

"Not all of us . . ."

Solidity returned with the suddenness of a thunderclap, Alex skidding across the ground, scraping himself bloody. His head reeled, thoughts swirling, chattering contradictory nonsense.

The hooks hoisted him up, forcing him to see:

Home. The lights were on, two policeman standing guard at the front gate.

Cruel fingers grasped his hair, yanking back his head. The Beast growled, yammered, wanting nothing more than to reach round and rip open its tormentor from loins to throat.

"Maybe later. You've work to do."

The Beast started forward before he could even think.

No.

It hesitated, the hooks twisting in its bowels and brain.

Faine laughed.

"Why bother? Once this is over, none of you will hurt anymore, I promise."

He'd taken the fucker at his word before, been betrayed. He'd rather die here and now than see Emma condemned to the same as the rest.

The hooks ripped and writhed, reducing his innards to soup. His legs went from beneath him, the pain indescribable. Faine sighed, kicking him over onto his back. The man looked down at him wearing a halo of new stars, eyes and mouth melting, becoming empty, ragged holes in his face.

"Perhaps I should do it myself. It's been a long time since I got my hands dirty . . ."

Alex sailed through a storm of invisible glass shards, every inch of him splitting, bleeding, roaring agony. The impact carried them both back, tumbling down the embankment into dirt and grass. Faine laughed as Alex's claws found him.

The world became a red, throbbing haze, laced with flickering streamers of black and bruise purple. He didn't stop, couldn't, the Beast too caught up in slaughter.

Faine had the power to turn him inside out, flay him with a thought; he knew it with absolute certainty. But he didn't, letting himself be undone, laughing 'til he lacked the breath or throat for it. Did he *want* this? To go the way of his companion? It didn't matter; Alex didn't stop 'til the body beneath him had been reduced to mulch and bone splinters, seeping into the sludge to form a gory swamp.

Something rose from the morass as the strength leeched from him, his own matter mingling with Faine's and the swamp they'd made together; spools of silvery ether, cold and sharp smelling, coiling around him like amorous snakes. He hadn't the strength to shrug them off, the Beast staggering, pitching face-first in the mire.

We're all sick, little Alex; every one of us. Some are just sicker than most.

He felt them go to work, slitting him down the flanks and belly, tearing at the Beast like vultures come to pick its carcass clean. It resisted, snapping feebly, trying to rise, failing. All it could do was lie and whimper as it was undone. Alex screamed inside the Beast's skull, feeling every slice; every nerve severed. He became a burning mote trapped in the labyrinths it contained, wandering blind, lost and agonized. Was this the punishment Faine had reserved for him; the one who stood by and smiled as his only love in the world was murdered?

No. Even through his pain and terror, he knew instinctively that something else was at work here. Soon enough, he felt cool air again, rain pelting his raw skin, sluicing away the filth it emerged from. What remained of the Beast slipped from him like caked on sludge beneath a shower, leaving him trembling, naked and newborn in the night.

*

They came while he slept; faces in the dark, punctured, ripped to ribbons, but familiar. Others weren't quite so well known, their protests tickling parasite memories in his skull that hadn't yet fully taken root:

They came with laughter and songs of lamentation; prayers, questions, curses; all of them demanding of him things he hadn't the means or mind to give.

A naked man slit from sex-deprived groin to flabby throat pointed at him in trembling accusation, begging blood for the daughter he'd apparently corrupted.

A laughing girl no older than fifteen lay splay-legged on her back, toying with her scarified sex, begging to be devoured between sobs.

One he knew broke apart from the rest, drawing so close, Alex could smell the sweat and abattoir stink of him.

Liquorice.

"Alex . . . Alex, man . . ." The voice of someone drowning in sewage, of someone force fed fistfuls of living flies. ". . . it hurts. It hurts *so bad* . . ."

What did it want from him? This was Faine's place, not his . . .

Laughter, demented children watching one of their own number plucked apart and devoured.

"He's gone, Alex love. He's not coming back."

She lay just on the bounds of sight, a pathetic, trembling thing of blood and filth, curled in on itself. He didn't want to see, but knew she spoke the truth; felt it throbbing in the air around him. Faine was gone, leaving behind decades, perhaps centuries worth of playmates, lovers, enemies. This was *his* now; a cell without walls or boundaries, a cold, dead womb, devoid of any potential for birth.

He lashed out, raking at the state with invisible talons, feeling it quiver and split as if it were his own flesh. The children's laughter turned to shrieks, those who'd come to introduce themselves to their new keeper collectively moaning, shrinking back.

"Stop . . . *stop* . . ."

And stay here? Be like Faine? No. they were wrong; the man was still here, just as the ones who'd come before were. *In him*. Spectres in his skull, swarming, chattering, their collective experience weaving throughout his own 'til there was no distinction. Some, like Faine, had sustained for centuries, suspended by love, a sense of duty, superstitious terror; others no more than moments, murdering themselves rather than keeping company with such sickness.

Gatherers and keepers of sick souls, charged with holding them beyond the veil, where they couldn't infect the rest.

Were there others like him? Alex couldn't tell yet; the confusion still too dense. All he knew was that neither he nor Faine nor any that came before were the authors of what surrounded him; the suffering of each caught and consigned here something they wrought on themselves; all they presumed themselves worthy of.

What manner of hurt would he be suffering if he found himself numbered amongst them?

"Help us, Alex man . . . please help us . . ."

He'd never heard Lick so plaintive, so eloquent in his need.

"I can't."

The howl built and spread through the massing throngs, a thousand mourning, mutilated throats singing their elegy in unison, their owners melting away into the darkness.

Lick lingered, his ravaged features incapable of expression, but unmistakable in their contempt.

"Fuck you . . ." It wept, turning, slinking away. "Fuck you."

There was nothing Alex could do or say. The ones caught here had long since decided themselves victims, predestined to be nothing more.

Soon enough, he was alone, the darkness yawning haunted and infinite in every direction. Burying his face in his hands, he wept as he hadn't since he was a child, knowing that there was nowhere he could go where he wouldn't also be here, nowhere where he wouldn't smell sickness and be obliged to confine it.

And he . . . he was the sickest soul of all; one who watched knowing that all he witnessed was vile; who revelled in the stupid evil of others rather than dirtying his own hands. That was what Faine saw in him; not one with an ounce of redemption in his soul, but a barbed and venomous worm, all too worthy of the misery he'd come to inhabit.

Alex felt only an echo of that now; the loneliness, the despair, the insanity it'd induced in many, but it was enough.

Enough to make him wish he'd drowned in the womb, been strangled by his own umbilical chord before he felt his first stroke of sunlight.

Enough to make him lament, and ache for a death that would never come.

*

They always came to her unexpectedly; old faces, forgotten voices, times and tragedies past:

". . . don't ever come near me again . . ."

He'd taken her at her word, disappearing from the hospital, from her *life* that same night. Where was he now? Was he even still alive?

Pointless wondering; she'd never know, didn't care.

Things were better now; better than they'd been in a long, long time. She had Lewis to thank for that.

"If it helps, just don't let them in. Sometimes you have to do whatever you can to survive."

Good advice. So when she felt the old ghosts stirring; heard them calling behind her eyes, she didn't let them in, closing the doors she'd constructed against them, sealing them fast with smouldering, poisonous solvent.

Celina screamed as if she'd swallowed a mouthful of safety pins. She'd been a colicky baby from the beginning.

"All right, all right now. Come on, *hush*."

But she didn't, continuing to shriek as Emma bobbed her up and down, stroked and patted her back. If Lewis were here, she'd have quietened down at the sight of his face . . .

"Come on, come on!"

The doors in her head wouldn't stay shut today, the voices beyond seeping through, the faces she didn't know anymore pressing through the wood as though it were softened marshmallow.

Celina's shrieks took on a different note, broken, hitching. Then stopped.

Emma laid her down in her cot, the sudden silence seething, filled with swarms of invisible flies.

She closed her eyes, breathed. Going to the sink, she poured herself a glass of water, hand trembling as she raised it to her lips. It hadn't been this bad for a while. No matter; Lewis told her there'd be phases like this. It was just a matter of sitting, thinking through them. She'd be fine.

Bill Taverner . . . they never found him, did they? What if he was still out there? What if he'd been following, waiting for his chance to do to her what he did to . . .?

Stop it. Stop it *now*.

She'd been trying to cut down on the medication. Now she thought about the bottles in her bag. Just one or two, to take the edge off . . .

"Emma."

No. go away.

The voice was so much clearer, so much more *real* than the others. It'd come to her several times whilst she healed, re-opening old wounds as if intent on seeing her bleed out.

She got up, went to Celina. Out like a light. No more screaming.

"Emma, look at me."

She wouldn't. Wouldn't turn, wouldn't answer. Lewis taught her that only gave them power; made them seem more real. He'd done so much for her, as her doctor, as her husband . . .

The hand on her shoulder was warm, gentle, but insistent. She closed her eyes as it turned her round, refusing to see.

"Go away . . ."

"I can't. You're very sick Emma."

His voice . . . different from the one she heard in her head; older, more certain. It couldn't be . . . couldn't be him . . .

"Alex?"

Silence.

She opened her eyes. The breath caught in her throat. Not Alex's face; not even changed and weathered by the years they'd spent apart. But Alex still.

"You . . . you're here?"

"Yes."

What had happened? She'd tried, God she'd tried, knowing that she had to get on with her life or lose her mind, but now she couldn't stop herself. She needed to know.

"W—what . . .?"

Brilliant blue eyes, *borrowed* eyes, closing, his head shaking.

"It doesn't matter. You have to come with me now."

What? She couldn't go anywhere; she had Celina to think of, besides, Lewis would be back in a few hours.

Stepping passed her, he leaned over the cot, reaching down to stroke her daughter's cheek.

"Do you love her?"

What the fuck kind of question was that?

"Of course I do . . ."

"Then come with me. Spare her your sickness."

Sickness? No. She wasn't sick anymore. Pulsing red spikes through the fog. Who *was* he? How could she have mistaken him for . . . *for Alex?*

"Get away from her! Get out!"

He caught her by the wrist before she could land a blow, fingers cold, so tight she felt her bones grinding together beneath their grip.

"*Look,*" he demanded, turning his eyes towards the cot. She did so instinctively. The baby stirred, croaked, turning to display the livid purple stripes she wore on her back.

Emma wanted the flesh to melt from her bones, to be soil, sludge; mist. Anything but her, here and now.

"You . . . *you* . . ."

"No, not me. I came because you called, in your dreams."

Insane. All of this, everything . . .

He approached, took her by the hands.

"It's time we left. Say goodbye."

No. She wouldn't. *She wouldn't.*

Spiders skittering up her spine, across her scalp, snakes twining in her belly. She trembled, feeling faint. He held her fast, the handsome, foreign features he wore melting, holes gaping where his eyes and mouth once were. She tried to scream, pull away, couldn't. Something seethed in the darkness, as if his skull had been made a hive by parasitic wasps.

She turned to Celina, yearning to go to her, hug her so tight they'd both come apart, flowing together . . .

Her babe was already little more than a knot of glowing smoke and embers, the kitchen, the house itself bleeding darkness from every pore that slowly washed the world away.

He was gone so abruptly she stumbled back, hands sore and frost bitten from his touch. She was nowhere, darkness all around.

"Hello?"

Voices, distant. Children? She started towards them, struggling through emptiness that felt dense as whipped cream.

"Alex?"

Nothing. *Alone;* the second time he'd abandoned her. They all left her eventually. She'd deluded herself that Lewis was different, but she knew, *knew* in her marrow that things had already begun to deteriorate...

The pain made her stumble, going to her knees, cruel laughter erupting from the emptiness. Raising her hand, she watched with mounting horror as the flesh blistered, bubbled, split.

"Alex . . . *Alex!*"

But he wasn't here. Only herself, enduring until either sickness or sanity broke.

STORM SONG

Beautiful. Deborah had never seen anything like it.

Turbulence throughout the flight; the cloud outside her window seething bruise-coloured, a tumour about to burst. She'd done her best not to speak to anyone else; no energy or emotion for it. Not after Aiden.

A week. Barely a blink of an eye for lovers, but all they could spare one another, circumstances being what they were. She'd considered giving it all up, the irony being that, barely six months ago, she wouldn't have needed a second thought. But things had started *happening* since then; the exhibitions, the book deal. It would be tantamount to blasphemy turning her back on it now, even for him. They'd just have to find a way to work around it.

He understood, of course. It was one of the many reasons she'd found herself falling in love with him; the ease and consideration of the man. He'd wait for her, he said, even if their time apart stretched to months, *years*, he'd wait. And she believed him.

Now the plane lingered between two layers of cloud; one above, one below, the former dark and swollen with rain, the latter almost luminous thanks to fragmentary rays of sunshine, their source a pale orb hanging high beyond the storms, arrayed in a rainbow corona that materialized so suddenly Deborah's breath caught at the sight.

None of her fellow passengers seemed to notice.

*

A dream of fairgrounds, headless horses on a carousel festooned with worms of living blue light, lizard children laughing . . .

Reality returned with a lurch, her seatbelt growing taught as she jerked awake. The man beside her, long haired, unshaven, stinking of academia, smiled nervously as their eyes momentarily met.

The plane was descending; she felt the pressure mounting, popping in her ears. Turning to the window, she saw the world below swathed in blankets and streamers of Autumnal mist, occasional pockets of suburb, hill and farmland appearing before being swallowed once more. Evening sunshine chased shadows across it, herding them into streets and valleys where they'd mingle and mate until nightfall unleashed them.

The first to see was a boy in the seat behind. He'd been all but silent throughout the trip, piping up only to plea with his mother for a chocolate bar from the beverage cart.

"Mom, Mom!" Agitated, breathless.

"Oh, don't start Mikey, you've been good the whole way."

"No, no . . . look out the window!"

Deborah was already looking, though she failed to see what—then she did. Nothing; just a valley through which a river of mist streamed, humps of irregular hills rising above its surface . . . *moving*. She thought it was an optical illusion caused by the undulating vapour, then one reared up from the herd, centipede legs unfurling from its underside, hauling itself from the rift.

Thought stopped, the world momentarily receding. She blinked, hoping that sanity would reassert itself.

"Oh my God . . ."

The boy's mother shrieked, an expression soon echoed by several others as the plane banked, providing better view of the emerging monstrosities.

"Ladies and gentleman, if you'd please remain seated . . ."

She hadn't seen, couldn't have. Too calm, too calm with the world below showing its lunatic face.

Several passengers left their seats, flocking instinctively towards the pilot's cabin in search of some authority. The stewardesses tried to keep them back with soft demands, receiving screaming, spitting abuse in return:

"Are you fucking kidding me? That's London down there! Do you fucking understand? *London*!"

"If you'd please, please remain calm, sir . . ."

Deborah hadn't noticed, but now lights and flickers of civilization were visible through the fog. Not a valley; from this height, she could make out the ruins of houses and high rise towers lining its edges, amputated roads plunging into nothingness, the cars that thronged them burning and abandoned.

"Oh, wow . . ." The youth beside her wore an expression of unabashed awe, as if he'd dreamed of this moment since the cradle, unable to quite believe it had arrived.

Huge. They must be huge.

The first creature was clear of the pit now, dragging behind it multiple tails on which smaller monstrosities swarmed like fleas. Entire neighbourhoods were ground to ruins beneath its bulk, antennae several times the length of the plane flailing in the air, tasting freedom.

"L-ladies and gentleman, this is your pilot speaking . . ." The voice of a lost and frightened child, desperate for a parent's hand. ". . . owing to . . . unforeseen circumstances, we will not be landing at Heathrow. Please . . . please remain calm until . . . until . . ."

The intercom crackled into silence. *Falling back on procedure.* Deborah supposed it was only natural, though she doubted there was any protocol for this. A collective cry went up from her fellow passengers as the plane banked, veering away sharply, the window momentarily filled with deepening dusk..

Someone was praying, the woman behind muttering nonsense platitudes to her son in-between sobs. One of the flight attendants, a girl of no more than twenty who had Latin somewhere in her blood, slumped to her knees in the aisle, shivering uncontrollably as she turned eyes heavenward. Deborah expected pleas for divine intervention, but there were none forthcoming; only quivering lips and silence, as if she refused to beg for mercy from a God that would allow this.

A commotion from behind; several passengers grappling with a man vast enough to account for all of them as he stormed up the aisle to the pilot's cabin, slurred bellows making it plain that he held the airline directly responsible for the chaos ensuing below. He stopped as a man half his weight stepped into his path, speaking quietly, calmly, insisting that he return to his seat.

The Goliath's first punch almost carried him from his feet, sailing through suddenly empty space. In return, he received a barrage of blows to the gut and face that staggered him, his wife shrieking outrage.

"I warned you," the quiet man said, massaging his knuckles. "Now, ladies and gentleman . . ." He spoke with natural authority. A military man—a priest? ". . . I don't pretend to know what the hell's going on here, but if we're all going to start acting like this gentleman," he gestured to the man he'd just laid out, "we may as well have the pilot crash us into the ground right now."

The rest seemed to see the sense in this, abruptly quieting like rowdy pupils before a respected teacher.

"Now, I'm going to go speak with the pilot. It'd be of great help if everyone just goes back to their seats, straps themselves in and *tries to stay calm.*"

Deborah caught his eye momentarily, a flash of recognition passing between them. *Good man, good man.* He nodded almost imperceptibly, turned and strode away up the cabin.

The fallen man's twittering wife and children hauled him to his feet, his eyes almost starting from their sockets as they registered the blood covering his hands.

"Fu-fucking *bastard piece of shit* . . . gonna . . . gonna sue the crap out of him when we get home . . ."

His family helped him to his seat, muttering desperate platitudes as if afraid they were going to catch the worst of his ire. It wouldn't have surprised Deborah if their fears were based on past experience.

*

It wouldn't last. She'd known from the beginning; they were too far apart, wrenched down divergent paths by their respective obsessions. Neither wanted to admit it; it was just *too good.* Sex like she'd never known, company she could happily keep forever; good food, good wine; an oasis in the desert of sewage, destined to be swept up and consumed.

"I love you, darlin'."

She loved him too, though she knew that things would change before they met again. Things were moving on both sides of the ocean; his band garnering interest from some big, big names, several of her paintings already marked out and acquired for a collection of local art. Best just enjoy it while it lasted; ride the wave and let it take her, even if she suffered later for want of drowning.

The plane seemed to be circling, going nowhere. What were they doing? What *could* they do? She tried to scatter the thought before it could fully coalesce. Like trying to stem a leaking artery with tissue paper:

Was it just here, or was it the same everywhere? What if . . . what if there was nowhere *left?* The doom-sayers were everywhere these days; in newspapers, science journals, the front pages of tabloids and street corners; apocalypses environmental, biological, cosmic and divine pressing in from every quarter, all so certain in their own imminence, all misguided. This was like nothing she'd ever heard tell of in predictions of plague, drought or famine; the rabid metaphors of her species' murder mouthed with such relish by biblical and koranic literalists accurate in only one detail; that it was occurring here and now, within waking lifetime.

Out the window, something that resembled a mountain-scale wasp's hive hauled itself on hundreds of scrabbling, spidery limbs from deep within the earth. Squatting over London's ruins, it began to swarm with black, indistinct forms that seemed to consist entirely of multiple legs and swaying, feathery antennae, the mass surging down into the ruins below in a living tidal wave, swamping all that remained. Deborah tried not to think of the people still down there, what it must be like to be caught up in the chaos, couldn't help herself.

How many had died already? Hundreds, thousands? And those left . . . she pictured the creatures hunting them through the streets, stray individuals snared by spools of webbing, impaled by stingers, snapped up, devoured, dragged away to be hosts for parasitic young.

Vile. She turned away from the window, closed her eyes, breathed deep.

"Like a dream, isn't it?"

The youth's eyes were fevered behind his spectacles, traces of a smile still tickling the corners of his lips. She didn't want to talk to him, or anyone; didn't know if she was capable.

"It's . . . I can't. *I can't* . . ."

The smile flowered, unwilling to be contained any longer. A flush of revulsion, Deborah fighting the urge to recoil, as she might from a dog baring its teeth.

"I know; I doubt anyone on this plane can." *Except me*; the unspoken subtext.

Leaning back, he sighed, almost laughing.

"Nothing's going to be the same after this; politics, war, religion; *nothing*. Ha! Maybe not such a bad thing, considering the state we left them in. I wonder if anyone, *anyone* thought when they stepped on this plane: *this is the last time I'll see the world* . . ."

"Excuse me." The woman in the seat behind stood up, leaning over between them. "Could you not speak about this now? You're upsetting my son."

The boy didn't seem upset to Deborah, staring out of the window expressionless as a doll.

"Did you ever let him watch the news?"

"Excuse me?"

"The news. Has he ever watched it before, or read a newspaper?"

"Of course. What's that got to do with . . .?"

"Then he's already seen far, far worse."

The woman looked as if she'd been slapped in the face, mouth quivering. She sat back down without a word, huddling her boy close. The youth turned back to Deborah, eyes alight, voice breathy and agitated:

"What do you think will happen when we land? Assuming we ever do . . ."

"Look, just *shut up* will you?"

A middle-aged man sat across the aisle, eyes dark and glassy with the promise of violence.

"You don't want to know? You'd rather sit here and wait for the fuel to run out, or for one of those things to snatch us out of the air?" He didn't sound concerned by either prospect; even though he faced away, she could hear the smile in his voice.

"You're fucking asking for it mate, I'm telling you . . ."

The youth laughed, a sound like crows cawing.

The man's features grew slack on his skull, looking as though they were about to slough away, leaving him skinless and shrieking. Nothing would have surprised her.

The plane banked sharply, a collective murmur going up from the cabin as it ceased circling, heading away from London and its calamity.

"This . . . this is your captain speaking. We . . . we'll now be landing at Birmingham airport in approximately half an hour's time. Until then, we urge everyone to remain seated and calm . . ."

An electronic hiss, as if the cockpit had suddenly flooded with furious cobras, then silence.

*

Dublin. Were things the same there? The temptation to turn on her mobile and call him was almost overwhelming, but she resisted. What good would it do either of them now?

His face, smiling at her between kisses, eyes alight with the mischief of it. A thirty-six year-old boy; she a twenty-five year old adult. It was part of why they worked; why they meshed so seamlessly. She felt like crying, wouldn't allow herself. *Sit back, wait. We'll all be down soon. Then maybe we can start figuring this bullshit out.*

What if she didn't get the chance? What if he was already...?

"All right, ladies and gentlemen..."

The man from before, returning from the cockpit with a small coterie of cabin crew.

"We know what we're doing and where we're headed. All we need to do is keep our heads and everything will be fine."

The youth beside her laughed, throwing back his head.

"Something funny, friend?"

Removing his glasses the youth smiled up at him, trembling from head to toe.

"*Everything will be fine* . . . seriously? What makes you think that? For all we know, this is the end of us. Maybe humanity has had its day."

Murmurs throughout the cabin, people crying, praying.

"Listen, I don't have the time or patience to get into a philosophical debate about it. There'll be plenty of time to chat about it after we land."

Deborah bit her tongue, people shrieking, erupting into tears as the plane lurched.

"Mommy! Mommy! Look outside!"

She instinctively turned to the window, breath leaving her, heart momentarily stilling:

Things in the sky; vast, knotted masses like balls of worms and flailing sea-weed, clusters of pale orbs like dead fish eyes pulsing throughout. Two of them trailed the plane, others flocking and darting in the distance. As she watched, mesmerized, the braver of the two drew closer, allowing her to pick out the parasites swarming over its surface. The youth began to laugh, the man across the way commanding him to shut the hell up.

Several more impacts buffeted the plane. All around her, people panicked, rising from their seats, screaming and clawing at one another, children demanding a parent's reassurance.

Why wasn't she the same? Her terror was undeniable, yet she felt somehow *separate* from events; a projection of self, substantial as something made from light and smoke. Even if the plane plummeted from the air, or was lashed into bits by one of the things outside the windows, she doubted she'd scream or feel tears on her cheeks. That was for others, more concerned by the lives they'd lost.

"Listen to me, *listen*!"

He struggled to keep order, failing. The man from across the way had hold of the youth now, screaming spittle and curses into his grinning face:

"What's wrong with you? Fucking *psycho*, what the fuck's wrong with you?"

Behind, the boy gasped, though whether in fright or amazement she couldn't tell.

Laughing, naked in bed, stinking of a weekend's unwashed sex . . .

The thing outside the window blossomed, its body splitting, shedding living strands that plummeted earthward, coiling and knotting on themselves. Its interior was a rose sculpted from raw steak, lined with shards of broken glass. Knitting needles of ice punctured her bladder as it battened onto the side of the plane, raking her window with wormy tongues that battered themselves bloody for want of tasting her.

"Jesus . . ."

"Get away from the window."

She stayed put in her seat, not because she was frozen in terror, traumatized by what still thrashed and squirmed outside. Why, then? Did she want to be devoured; sucked out of the plane like an oyster from its shell? Maybe so . . .

Frustrated by its failure, the thing retreated, elaborate mouth parts folding away, screaming animal annoyance.

The others followed in its wake, streaming away towards the ground in search of less challenging prey.

*

"You wouldn't leave me, would you?" So desperate, so earnest.

"No." A lie; she didn't know it at the time, at least not entirely, but a lie nonetheless. It was wonderful to tell herself this was certain; that this warm, amber wave, scented of sex and sunshine, would bear them up forever beyond life's ills. But she knew the truth; felt the dark, cold depths below, heard the songs of what swam there.

The lie was sweet to swim for now. Maybe that was the best any of her kind could hope for; a moment's delusion before truth snared them again, dragging them down into a stinking swamp of their own shit.

Even were things different; if the plane landed without problem at Heathrow and she was now home, resenting every heartbeat, she doubted they'd have met as lovers again. Maybe friends, in some months distant, when the hurt and recriminations had dulled, maybe then . . .

"Could, err, could Mr. Robbins please come to the cockpit, thank you . . ."

The man doing everything in his power to maintain calm bared his teeth, juggling far too many firebrands for one to cope with.

"For God's sake, *listen* . . ."

He turned to her, ice blue eyes so precise her skin prickled beneath them as though with the touch of cold needles.

"I need somebody who's going to keep their heads for a little while, okay? You seem pretty with it, or am I wrong?"

With it? Hardly how she would have described her current state, but she wasn't about to murder anyone or herself like some of the others.

"Listen, all you have to do is make sure everyone stays in their seats. I'll be back as soon as I can. What's your name?"

"Deborah Lichfield."

"Hello, Deborah Lichfield. I'm John Robbins. You think you can be me for a little while?"

"I think *I* could."

The youth still smiled, expression fixed since the thing at the window. Robbins dismissed him with a sigh.

"I don't think I could be you, but I can definitely be me." She interjected.

He smiled out of the corner of his mouth.

"Perfect. If you need me, just ring the cabin crew bell." He was gone before she could protest.

The youth turned to her, eyes alight with mirth.

"You haven't asked me my name yet."

"That's because nobody cares." The man across the way, looking scared, sick to the soul.

"Kirchner; Elias Kirchner." He offered her his hand. She took it, his skin clammy and febrile. "Deborah, yes?" She nodded, the limited control she'd been lent already slipping. "So, what do you do in the real world?"

"I'm . . . I'm an artist."

His face lit up with delight.

"You live off your passions? Wonderful! Me, well; I'm not much of anything, right now; something of a *nomad*. Lack focus, by all accounts, but I have my talents."

What was *wrong* with him? He treated this as if it were all some twisted pantomime.

"Shut him up. Please, *shut him up*." The man across the way was pale and shivering, looking on the verge of a heart attack. The youth continued, ignoring him:

"Why were you in Dublin, if you don't mind me asking?"

What did it matter now?

"I was . . . visiting someone."

"Someone?"

"My partner."

"Separated by ocean? I'm talking to a living, breathing romance novel character!"

Deborah wished he'd shut up too, his voice like flies buzzing around rotting food.

"Wish I could say my own business was quite so *pleasant*. No; I was there to see a man about wrongs done a long, long time ago. Not the most welcome of reunions, I'm afraid. He wasn't expecting me. Ha! Most people don't . . ."

He faltered, nodding towards the window. Deborah turned, looked.

A storm massed on the horizon, broiling knots of red and purple cloud, coruscated by rents through which sunlight seeped, forming luminous lakes on the broken earth below. Tongues of lightning licked out from the mass; red, blue and yellow. Something rose, indistinct, absolute. Her eye refused to focus on it, its scale too vast and substance too uncertain to take in at once. Instead, she perceived only fragments; a hive of living embers swarming in and out of a fleshy structure resembling a vast, pulsing heart; a garden of faces formed from smoke and fire, blooming like flowers from the mass before withering into child-scrawl obscurity. Portions of it seemed wounded, splitting, bleeding; revealing sceptic interiors where parasites swarmed. Others erupted, forests of coral and fungal growths elaborating through the air, festooned with clusters of eyes that returned her scrutiny, tongues waggling obscene invitation.

A hurricane, a monolith, a man, a pillar of fire . . .

She wrenched her eyes away, doubling over in her seat as stomach and sanity shifted. Others saw too; she heard them through the tidal roar of blood in her ears, the insect chatter of her own swarming thoughts:

Screams, prayers, sighs; confessions.

What was it? Insanity; god, the devil and everything in between. The end of the world.

A hand at her back, its touch feathery and skittering, like a spider's legs. She shrugged it off, rising slowly. Kirchner still smiled, but softer now, understanding.

"Don't fret. It was always going to be this way, eventually. Nothing lasts, no matter how desperately we might want it to."

A nest of warm blankets, glow of wine in her cheeks and thoughts. Something on the TV; she couldn't remember what. He touched her, kissed her neck, her shoulder. His stubble scraped her; she loved it. They hadn't showered in two days, had hardly left the flat. Taking his hand, she guided it down between her legs.

Yesterday. Where was he now? Dead, devoured—worse?

"Shut up, *shut up* . . ."

The man across the aisle rose, swaying, eyes fluttering as if drunk. He looked like he was about to faint, vomit or die on the spot. Something *wrong,* the air around him thick and greasy; swimming like spools of oil on water.

Robbins. Where the fuck was he? She pressed the cabin crew button, and again.

"Mommy . . ."

"Don't look, love. Close the window, there's a good boy . . ."

"I don't want to Mommy. I want to see."

Kirchner laughed.

"Now there's a boy after my own heart."

"Shut up!"

The man lurched forward, swinging a fist that seemed to trail shit-brown and yellow arcs through the air. It connected with Kirchner's cheek, rocking him in his seat. He hung his head, raising a hand to his face. His assailant backed away, blinking like a child woken from a bad dream.

Robbins didn't appear.

Kirchner tittered quietly to himself, blood seeping between his fingers. *Are you okay?* Deborah swallowed the words before they could be fully born.

The man responsible for the violence had begun to shake now, trembling so violently he looked to be in the early stages of a grand mal. His wife held him, muttering his name between breaths:

"Albert, Albert?"

Deborah pressed the cabin crew button again. Nothing.

"I wouldn't bother if I were you." The words came slurred and mangled, as if spoken through a mouthful of living bees. "He isn't coming back."

Kirchner reared up, turning to face her. Cracks coruscated out from where he'd been struck as if his skin were brittle as China, dark beads welling, trailing filth down his face. One eye had darkened, the pupil swollen to envelop iris and white, swimming with flecks of gold and silver; gnats swarming to and fro above a pond. His hand came away trailing strips of redundant matter, the mask of humanity he wore shrivelling before her eyes.

Not a man. Something else. Why wasn't she *afraid*? The thing reached out to her, begging permission with its eyes. The cabin was chaos, people rising, tumbling from their seats, crawling on all fours towards the cockpit, laughing, crying; vomiting and soiling themselves. Something else too; a less tangible disturbance, the recycled air seething and scented with strange perfumes; rotting fruit, jungle humidity; the sweat of a man's thigh.

She accepted his touch without complaint, his fingers tracing her cheek, her skin seeming to leap and dance at the contact.

Waking to a world upturned,
Forsaking all lessons learned,
Under stern, judgemental, un-dreaming eye,
Staking sanity on the hope that,
Man might fly without waxen wing,
Or a drag of dope,
That anything might be,
If we want sufficiently,
And have the wit and will to see,
Where angels and demons sing,
As one.

He whispered the poem, other voices seeming to echo it; those of men, women and children; the cabin haunted by mimicking ghosts.

"The poet who taught me that died on the streets of Edinburgh, not a penny to his name."

A sudden fluttering, tapping at the window. Deborah turned, looked. *Children*, or at least things that resembled them; the eldest treading the borders of adolescence, the youngest barely born, laughing and squabbling as they trailed alongside the plane. Kirchner whooped with joy at sight of them. The closest, smiling in at her through the window, was a beauty; a boy of no more than thirteen, hair so pale as to be almost silver, blue eyes alight with the joy of play. Like the others, he was naked, his legs fused just beneath the groin, tapering away into shreds and tatters like a jellyfish's tendrils, whipping behind him as he rode the wind.

"I think they want you to play with them."

The blonde boy nodded, smiled. He looked so *familiar;* a face glanced years ago in an old family photograph, or maybe that of an imaginary playmate softened to mist by the avalanche of adulthood.

A dark skinned girl joined him, face and budding breasts painted with silver stars and whorls. Her back was a mass of waving orange feathers, her features stretched, vaguely lupine.

"Children of a new world," Kirchner sighed, idly scraping away the cracked and dried remains of his former self. Beneath was black and seething, as if he were no more than a mass of worms and insects wrapped around in a man's skin, "the ones who can still dream."

A sound from the seat behind; someone laughing, sobbing.

"Mikey? Mikey, love, what's wrong?"

Looking over the back of her seat, Deborah saw the boy trembling, head bowed, arms and legs flailing. The mother tried to hold him down, hug him to her, but he flung her off, turning to scrape and yammer dog-like at the window. Arcing his head, he gasped, breathless, red flowers blossoming across the back of his shirt.

"Oh my God . . ."

He tore at the garment like a lunatic at a straight jacket, scratching himself bloody in his ferocity. Beneath, his skin was a mass of welts and bruises, some of them pulsing like a spider's egg sacks, others already split, blossoming with new and alien anatomy.

"Let me out, Mommy, please let me out . . ."

The mother turned away, vomiting into the aisle. What sloped from her mouth wasn't entirely liquid; sinuous, black lengths flapping and squirming like landed eels.

Deborah was fixed in the insanity, calm, distant; as if viewing it all through a window or TV screen. Nevertheless, she felt it at work within her; an itching, quivering discomfort where Kirchner's fingers had passed, flesh rebelling, ready to blossom.

She heard Robbins before she saw him; a keening, mechanical whine accompanied by a blast of sickly, chemical smoke. He came trailing light, the cabin behind ignited by his passage.

Kirchner hissed at the sight of him, rising from his seat.

Those still able began to retreat, herding, trampling one another in their animal desperation to be away from the smoke and flames.

There was barely anything recognizable as John Robbins left. Scraps of him still clung to the swollen hulk; face stretched and split over whirring, steaming mechanics, a single eye swivelling where the other was a furnace, gouting flame and cinders from the inferno his brain had become. It was as if his body couldn't decide between states of meat or machinery; bone, ligament, nerve and organ rearranged into systems whose purpose seemed to be nothing other than to endlessly churn, grinding themselves to oblivion.

The thing paused, single eye roving over them, streaming tears that ignited as they trailed down its cheek. Then it focused on Kirchner, broken jaw gaping wide, exhaling smoke and sparks. Kirchner laughed as portions of his hair and clothing ignited.

The thing roared, cannoned into him, carrying them both off their feet. Kirchner screamed laughter as he was engulfed from scalp to soles, flames searing away what little remained of his façade. *What the hell was he*? Robbins rained blows against the thing's face, pummelling it into a featureless mass that continued to laugh, even when its mouth had been reduced to nothing.

Come . . . please come play with us . . .

They were still out there, smiles wider now, eyes desperate. She heard them calling not only in her thoughts, but in her entrails; the essential machinery of her groin. She was festooned by invisible hooks, alternately coaxed and bullied like a snared fish. Across the way, the man who'd assaulted Kirchner split from crotch to forehead, wife shrieking as wailing forms dragged themselves free of the aperture. Behind, the boy continued to bawl and wail, hammering himself against the window, prepared to murder himself for want of freedom.

*

I love you darlin'.

Liar. Did he wonder about her now, was he even capable?

Don't go. The end of her first visit, his tears sudden and terrible. But she had to. She had work; a life back home, just as he had outside of her. She was terrified whenever he didn't call; heart sick, unable to sleep for fear that the inevitable had come to pass, love and passion dulled by lack of proximity.

She hated herself for that weakness.

The intercom crackled, erupting with a sudden spew of confusion; chords of Bach and Wagner sewn to fragments of Bowie and Bauhaus; The Beatles, The Prodigy, Lupen Crook and Elton John. Every piece meant something to her, exciting memories both recent and faded into near nothingness:

Eating overcooked steak in solemn silence at her grandmother's house, the aftermath of some unspoken argument hanging heavy in the air. A nameless boy, half a decade her younger, fumbling awkwardly beneath her skirt, mumbling adolescent confessions of adoration with every kiss. Stinking sickness in Moroccan heat, a would be holiday spent fending off cockroaches and her stomach's rebellion.

Most lucid of all, fragments of love, all sweet, all tragically brief.

The flames almost had her. Several were already blazing, though not all screamed as they burned. Some laughed, some sang; some danced, twirling skirts and head dresses of living fire. The children tugged and screamed at her, their hooks insistent now: *Come! Come with us!* But she couldn't; not like this. She was too heavy, too certain. Unlike them, she hadn't learned the trick of *letting go,* yet . . .

Robbins rose, beaten back by Kirchner, who was now little more than a thing of blood and black, muck-wreathed bone. Staggering, the Robbins-thing moaned, turning its good eye on her, imploring: *Don't let me be like this, please, please let me wake up . . .*

Kirchner laughed at his dismay, turning to face her through the smoke.

What are you still doing here? Do you want to burn like the rest?

No. But there was nowhere she could go like this, still too heavy, too prey to all the preconceptions of being she'd been conditioned with since birth.

I love you, darlin' . . .

It was this he loved; this flesh, this face. How could she abandon it, knowing that?

Because it's a lie. You know it; you've always known it.

Laughter, cries, music as the plane came apart around her, spilling all it contained to the open air.

*

Deborah entertained suicide throughout her school years, shrivelled and soul-sick from being the eternally friendless, the derided and spat upon outcast.

Always, always in those fantasies, she fell, hurtling down from cliff-edges into churning sea and skull-crushing rocks; from the pinnacles of churches and cathedrals to crowded summer streets, becoming just another story for the living to gnaw on.

Now she lived the fantasy in flesh, hurtling down, down through air that sang and whispered, trailing flames and tatters of shedding self.

It hurt, oh *God* it hurt, the most intense pain she'd ever experienced; an echo of that first, sublimated suffering, being torn from the only reality she'd ever known into a place of cold, noise and light.

The children came with her, plucking and tearing, scraping away the redundant muck her humanity had gone to. Below, she saw a world in flux; hills and fields churning, rippling like reflections on lakes of mercury, scraps of town and village somehow still standing static, islands in an ocean of chaos. Wounds in the earth erupted with fire, great columns and spires of rock, bone and pearlescent matter; towers of blood and living, screaming flesh. Others fell with her; Robbins a flaming meteorite hurtling earthward, Kirchner grappling with him, the pair locked like lovers intent on becoming common ash, the boy Michael, laughing in ecstasy at his new-found freedom.

Part of her, the frightened, foetus thing that yearned for nothing more than peace and safety, welcomed her impending death. What else was there now? How could she even begin to live in this world that had shrugged off its straight-jacket and shown its true, lunatic colours? It tried to hold on, maintaining the mask that had smothered her since birth, the truth beneath only experienced in those brief fugues of creation and love making, when the paint or kisses flowed from her like music.

But it was dying, withering with every passing thought. She erupted, new anatomy unfurling from her back, her scalp; from between her legs, senses blossoming whose input she lacked any and all context to interpret.

Stay, stay and play with us, they begged, plucking, pawing, nipping at her, trying to bully her new flesh to life. She felt it stir, blood and sensation flowing where before was nothing but thought, abstraction and metaphor abruptly made meat, revelling in the condition.

Wings unfurled, slowing her descent, the sensation of contradictory winds whipping around and beneath them, lashing her naked body, intoxicating. She laughed, tears streaming down her face, the children laughing too, darting to and fro around her as she soared, all that she was now little more than strands of decaying matter and memory, making way for a new dream.

*

He watched, waiting, the dream interrupting every thought. Music saved him, as he always knew it would. He didn't know how, didn't know why; so many gone, swallowed by the earth, spitted, immolated, torn apart by what it threw up. Others transformed, but not like himself; whereas he still retained a semblance of self, they'd become little more than monsters; beasts craving meat, shapeless slug-things singing scraps of old song as they supped on trash and sewage.

The End of the World. Ha, he'd been raised Catholic, still knew the catechisms off by heart; rejected the faith when the world showed him it had no time for fairy tales. He looked up into the rain, smiling through a mouth still tender from re-structuring at how misguided they'd all been; those who presumed knowledge of impending apocalypse, those who denied its inevitability.

Who'd have thought it? He'd whispered that to her as they lay sweaty and sated from their first fuck. Now he sang it to himself, the music manifesting itself as colour and light that seeped between his teeth, weaving tapestries in the air.

Dublin had been partially swallowed, great rifts opening throughout, dragging entire neighbourhoods down into the earth. Something vast erupted in their place; luminous growths that became more elaborate with every passing day, forming fluted structures from which the survivors had already started hewing homes. The ruinous streets were treacherous, abruptly giving way beneath the feet, erupting with fire, smoke and swarms of biting, stinging things. Creatures from beneath the earth set up homes in ruined houses and shopping centres; churches and temples. He'd seen them prey upon the weak and the straggling, swooping down from their eyries to pluck men, women and children from the streets.

But not him. The music made him sacred; forbidden fruit. Others were the same: Keya, a poet and sometimes play-write he'd worked with on several projects, turned up on his front door two days after the cataclysm began, body become a garden of fantastic weeds, every inch sprouting with alien beauty, swarming with spidery and butterfly parasites that tended her budding anatomy. Heston, the most talented guitarist he'd ever met, came shortly after, clambering through the rubble via the living threads seething from his back and limbs. Soon enough, a tribe had begun to gather; the artistic and inspired, the lovers, the dreamers; the wasted and undone, more adding to their number with every passing day. The tumults that claimed much of the city stilled after the first night, earth, sea and sky still uncertain, but solid enough to be braved. He went out, wandered, exploring this new world, waiting.

I love you too.

He wanted to believe her, wanted it so much. It'd break his heart, hers too, when they inevitably parted, but it was unavoidable; they were too far apart, too much their own entities, each obsessed and already in love with the arts they'd chosen. Soon enough, success would come for one or both of them, and that would be the end.

Kirchner counselled different. He found the man on the third day; a blackened husk sat cross-legged atop the flower-sprouting rubble that'd once been St. Andrews. He knew Aiden's name; Deborah's too:

"Ha, I was beginning to think I'd have to come and find you."

He spoke as if the meeting were prearranged rather than some random accident. Plucking one of the red and purple flowers from his seat, he inhaled deeply of its scent, grinning as best his broken mouth would allow.

"Do you know me?" Aiden asked.

"Ha! Only by reputation. I caught a rumour of you from your lady love. We were on the same plane."

"Debbie? Is she . . .?"

"Oh, she's very much alive. Arguably more so than she's ever been. She's out there." He gestured towards the ocean that had swept inland, swallowing much of the country. Jagged structures like shards of broken crystal rose in profusion from beneath the surface, shredding the frugal sunlight into ragged rainbows. "An amazing woman, I hope you realise, because she doesn't. Not yet . . ."

"Who the hell are you?"

"Oh, I'm sorry; I forget myself sometimes; easily done in my line of work. My name's Elias Kirchner. I suppose you could say I'm something of a visitor here; came for business, staying for pleasure. Mea culpa, I really must shoulder some of the responsibility for all this . . . I didn't realise Nathaniel had gone quite this far, otherwise I'd have let him be. Still, no use crying over spilled milk, eh?"

Aiden didn't understand a quarter of what the man babbled about; it was as if he spoke to himself, or invisible friends orbiting his head. Deborah was all that mattered to him.

"Ah, of course; why would you want to hear about me when you have a lover out there in the world? Expect her when the rains come. That's about as specific as I can be."

Insane or no, he took the man at his word, watching as the storm clouds massed across the ocean, creeping towards the land like some celestial fungus feeding on the rot of humanity's civilizations. The winds herding them sang and whispered, carrying music that he matched with his own, calling the one they heralded home.

Now the rains were here, washing red, amber and silver across the land, splashing warm and sultry against his up-turned face. Shapes flocked and danced amidst the clouds; child-things that swooped down to him laughing, perching on the rocks and rubble.

She came with them, descending slowly through the rain. The memory he had of her was beautiful, but compared to this, like a child's stick figure next to a Michelangelo sculpture. Multiple wings bore her up, slow, serene flaps sweeping up the rain, driving it against him along with tantalizing gusts of her scent. He'd seen her in this state before, when they lay dreaming next to one another, sharing common prophecy of this reunion. Tinted lights danced and flashed amongst her plumage, snakes of living colour squirming through the air with every breath. Skin grown shimmering and pearlescent like a fish's scales caught the sunlight, swathing her in skirts and jewellery of rainbows.

Alighting in the silver sand leading down to the ocean's edge, she folded her wings about herself, smiling at him through the haze of inspiration that swathed her head.

He went to her without invitation, loping, running, scrabbling, the distance between them seeming an entire desert, a world.

The world broke itself for want of lovers . . .

Kirchner's voice, a whisper on the wind.

The rain grew vicious as they came together, sea and sky roaring their approval. A thoughtless instant in which there were only kisses, her inspirations swathing him, his music entwining her, bodies momentarily melting, intent on becoming one.

But neither were ready for that ultimate union quite yet. Tearing himself away was painful, both of them staggering back wounded and bleeding. She laughed through the pain, and so did he.

"Debbie."

The name made her laugh even harder. He knew why; it wasn't hers anymore, an infant's nonsense label for an old, tattered toy.

"What then?"

She turned her eyes out to sea, to where the storms churned it into a boiling, frothing cauldron.

"I don't know yet."

Nor did he. Maybe they could find out together.

*

Why? The thing that called itself Elias Kirchner didn't know. Just another world unseated; the tyranny of truth toppled. He'd seen it a thousand times, had a hand in sparking over a hundred such rebellions. The lovers were nothing; ephemera, flecks of grit in the storm.

But if he'd learned anything across the leagues, the endless wandering; the cycles of death and rebirth, it was that love could set the universe aflame, given the right fuel. Those two...they were the atoms in a hydrogen bomb, the catastrophe they might initiate making the one he sat in the midst of seem little more than a child scattering its toy town across the carpet.

Roseblade wasn't here anymore. Kirchner had left him hurt, almost dead. Not that the condition meant much to either of them, but he'd dared entertain hopes that the man might wait for him this time. Ha, he should've known better.

It would be some time before he could move on; Robbins had hurt him worse than most could manage. He needed to rest, to heal. At least it'd give him opportunity to see where this new world was headed; whether it'd eventually settle or rip itself apart.

Turning his ruined face up to the rain, he smiled brokenly at fantasies of it washing his ravaged flesh away, reducing him to the sewage that by rights he should've become long, long ago. Maybe someday he'd know that state, but not today. Today there was love in the world, and songs echoing through the storm.

THE ARTIST

Self was Arthur's consistent subject. He'd been rejected from every art college and institution he'd attended for refusing to deviate from it. Permutations of self poured from him in ink and paint; in pastel, prose and sculpture.

He didn't question the preoccupation, saw no purpose in it; only continued to create, the impetus of heart and head carrying him forward to undisclosed destinations.

*

Loneliness and destitution were the most immediate results. He didn't mind. When the bailiffs came to claim his meagre belongings, he hid his artistic apparel in a hollow beneath the floorboards, watched feeling nothing as the rest was carried away.

*

His family had long since deserted him, condemning him as a lost cause. What few friends he had came to him of their own volition; attracted, perhaps, by the mystery they wove about him in their own heads.

Always the same question:

"Why do you do what you do?"

Always the same answer:

"I don't know."

They all left him eventually, weary of feeding him on the bread and milk they sweated to earn. He didn't care. Food could be found as and when it was needed. Nobody so much as raised an eyebrow when the odd neighbourhood cat or dog went missing.

*

He'd gone as far as conventional mediums could take him. There was nothing left for them to express.

He stagnated, throwing himself against the bare walls of his apartment, waiting for destiny—that fickle, cold-hearted *bitch*—to throw him a bone.

She did when, intoxicated to near stupor, he snagged his hand on an errant nail and came. The spurts and splashes of his matter—*his* matter—upon the floor provided fresh inspiration, and the means of manifesting it.

*

Shit and semen were readily available; he learned the basics of their manipulation fast (though it took some experimentation as to what he should consume to get the desired consistency).

Blood was trickier.

The first cut was too deep; a slice from palm to wrist that wouldn't stop flowing, requiring a trip to the emergency room where he was diagnosed with borderline malnutrition and kept on a drip for several days.

People came to talk to him:

A pretty Indian psychologist who asked him interesting questions then looked disgruntled when he gave her answers; his sister, of all people, who'd informed him in no uncertain terms she wouldn't stop to piss on him if her were aflame the last time they met.

This time, she cried and smiled, asking him what the hell he thought he was doing. He told her she wouldn't understand, asked after the brother-in-law and nephews he'd never seen.

On being allowed to return home—sister dear having dealt with the month's expenses as a parting gift—he embarked on a series of more cautious experiments, incising areas of skin that covered less vital anatomy, incorporating the issue into the discount red poster paint that was all he could afford.

The results were remarkable for a time; startling expressions of the blood and bones truth of humanity, and of himself.

But it wasn't *enough*.

*

By day, when he slept, he dreamed of stripping out of himself; the cocoon of his carcass splitting to reveal what gestated within. He would take his sloughed-off self and use its materials—skin, blood, bone and bowels—

to create the greatest work of art in human history; an expression of the species so pure, so consummate, it would become holy in the eyes of those that looked upon it, inspiring them to emulate it with their own stuffs.

He decided to make dreams reality when the patterns of excrement and effluvia began to repeat themselves.

Arthur wasn't a stupid man; he knew he'd likely die or be crippled by the pain before he could shape anything of consequence. That was why he carpeted the floor in canvas, ensuring that even in his terminal writhing, there'd be creation.

Angels—or perhaps demons; it didn't matter which—had spoken to him since he lay in the cradle. They began to sing when the blade pierced his skin, their symphony escalating as it threaded down, opening him to where the dark trail of his pubic hair began.

Pain beyond imagination, his nerves adding their own screaming backtrack to the angel's choir, but it didn't dissuade him. Even as he felt himself well and flow—an internal ocean finally undammed—the knife went to work elsewhere, slitting thighs and forearms, carving spirals in the palms of his hands, tattooing his cheeks.

Surely he must die soon. Would there be anything waiting beyond this world of endless want?

Then he rose, borne up by invisible puppet strings, legs trembling and tottering beneath him. His prick rose too, stirred by the molten red rain anointing it. The angels sang and wept sunshine into his mind as he danced, whirling, pirouetting, scattering more of himself with every step.

"Stop," he croaked, unravelling, innards tumbling about his waist like alien skirts.

But he didn't, couldn't. The angel's song was far from over, his Great Work barely begun.

*

It was a long time before the first came to see.

He was there still, adding fresh elements to the composition through his decay. Some vomited, others went to their knees and wept. They became artists soon after, opening themselves with whatever instruments—knives, pens, teeth—came to hand. The few unmoved by his art—meat robots lacking in sufficient soul to be stirred by anything—attempted to conceal the work, but it was too late.

The angels had already flown to sing in other ears. Soon, all of humanity would hear their song, and the whole world would become canvas.

INSPIRED FLESH

It shifted beneath my fingers, fractures coruscating its once pristine surface. Too much to bear, my body incapable of tears after so much hurt, so much *lost*.

And for what? Slow death in dry, dead sand; all that was left of meaning in this wasted world.

It'd be worth it in the end, they all said; a prize worth any sacrifice. And oh, how much we'd *sacrificed*. For those like Regina, constant abnegation had become an end in itself; a fetishistic form of spiritual cleansing, like the Catholic ritual of confession. Most of them had gone the way of the laity in the Final Experiment; just more handfuls of dust to add to the wastes and mountains.

I was the last, alone as it was possible for man to be. No angels at the end; no rising up of the dead or descent of deities from on high. Only the light, and music I could barely recall. Everything, everything unravelled before my eyes, as if reality was a tapestry whose weave was being unpicked.

I saw it all; every particular. They were supposed to be protected, like me, but the wards were weak or imperfect. Angela, writhing so violently on the floorboards her back snapped, worms of light unsewing her from the groin out. Thomas, hoisted into the air by invisible hooks, dancing as he shed himself.

Then the maelstrom, a storm that ripped me from the world, tossing me up on winds that alternately shrieked and whispered in my ear, lies, poetry and revelation all pouring into my mind as the world that made them went to nothing.

I woke buried beneath a quilt of sand, the prize we'd murdered the world for clutched so tight, its thorns pricked my flesh:

A configuration of crystal, like the shell of some exotic, deep-sea life, threads and filaments of light running like veins throughout. Along its scalpel-sharp edges, small rainbows erupted, casting their colours upon my torn and tattered skin.

The wards hadn't been nearly enough. I was hurt, bleeding from my head, my side, my back. Dying; the last, worthless scrap of humanity. Ironic that it should be the one who'd murdered the rest.

Nothing left, the rumours we'd hung our hopes on proven false. No salvation; no renaissance or grand transcendence for our species. Only this; silence in sand and blood, and a man lamenting genocide.

I could swallow sand until I choked to death, lie down and wait for blood loss to claim me. Neither option particularly appealed; too much time for thought and regret.

Only one remaining:

Stripping out of the tatters of my shirt—wincing as the fabric scraped across wounds—I looked down at myself, despairing.

The device would likely shatter before it could do me terminal harm, but with any luck, there'd still be enough power in it to reduce me to the same waste that crunched and shifted underfoot.

Pain wasn't anything new to me. I'd sacrificed toes and fingers in the name of transcendence; an eye, a testicle. All of them ritually rather than surgically removed, agony and the possibility of death essential components of the annealing process. *Those prepared to give all that they are will win the world.* Stratham's words; as meaningless as the wind that carried his ashes now.

The first cut, thorns of crystal slicing barely a centimetre into my breast, caused me to double over in agony, vomit splashing the sand. Thought left me for a time, consciousness shattering, leaving only an echo of the maelstrom that brought me here. When it finally returned, night had fallen, the desert skies swarming with shoals of living lightning. My body was burned where the crystal scored me, the flesh that shielded my heart reduced to seeping black filth; the hide of something long since dead.

I watched from the top of my dune as the lightning things arced down from the sky, seething and squirming as they burrowed into the sand, stirring it into bizarre rose configurations that remained long after their makers dissipated.

So, this was the new Eden; the promised paradise for which we'd murdered humanity: a desert-garden, sterile flowers coaxed from the stuff of the dead.

I didn't allow myself time for hesitation. Before I could think, before I could take my next breath, I plunged the device into the softened flesh it had already pierced. My body became a reservoir for fire and frost, cold burning threads uncoiling throughout my marrow, my arteries, twining themselves around my nerves like glittering thread lending lustre to an otherwise mundane weave.

I felt myself unpicked, nerve by nerve, cell by cell; thought and memory sluicing away until there was nothing but a mote of screaming consciousness, unwanted being spitted and sustained beyond nature and reason. I was pain, woven from it; the first stitches of a new universe whose stuff would be suffering, for suffering was all I had retained from my former existence; the loss and the fury and the sorrow . . .

No. There was more here, exponentially more. Not lost, merely fragmented; the accrued components of self separated and scattered, waiting to be re-arranged into more fitting configuration.

Revelation brought an abrupt end to suffering, eyes so raw they might've been freshly formed or ancient beyond comprehension opening on a world in flower. I saw myself from multiple angles, the body to which I was once confined swelling and erupting with crystalline growths; a fast growing tree among the desert sands. An echo of old symbolism; the tree more in me than in the world, though that distinction meant less and less with every breath. It was a promise of what might be; the heart of a new Eden, its sap my blood and blooms my flesh, waiting for the time when they might ripen to dreaming fruit.

And all around the desert, sands burgeoned and shifted, the tree's roots proliferating faster than the light it caught from the dying sun, so deep I tasted the Earth's iron heart. There were things that escaped the apocalypse we'd wrought down there; caverns vast as the greatest cities of man, where blind, maggot monstrosities swarmed and bred beyond sight or knowledge of my former species. Watching them hunt and feed in the dark, mating in the unlovely pools of sludge that were their young's nurseries, I sensed a time many, many centuries from now when they would emerge into the sunlight, evolved beyond their current disgrace thanks to their feeding from the growths and flowers that currently invaded their subterranean realm. Were these the children that would inherit this new earth? Perhaps. There'd be others too. Though humanity and all that sustained it had been reduced to dust, I felt a lingering residue of potential; echoes of dreams threading the air, desires carried on the breeze, scattered like pollen across the shifting plains. Soon they would take root and flower just as I had, life borne of its own impetus and intention; inspired flesh sitting changeable and uncertain on the bone.

That was the dream we'd murdered the world for; this chance; a renaissance that would put all prior rebirths and revolutions to shame.

Now there was nothing but *time;* time in which to watch this new world flourish, feel my own flesh thread throughout, becoming its warp and weft.

I expanded; mind and matter as one, reaching depths and heights I never could've conceived caged inside my skull.

Thomas, Regina; even Stratham, they were all here, in the dust and the memory, waiting for the time when they might cohere themselves and be reborn. I could sense them dreaming with concentration; Regina sprawled upon the chalk white sands of an endless beach, pale twins—one male, one female—lapping at her toes, Stratham sealed away somewhere dark and subterranean, laughing and crying as he waited for the beasts that prowled there to descend. And mingled amongst them, the fantasies of less familiar souls; a barely pubescent girl shedding her skin to reveal an interior of mist-winged butterflies, a boy who wandered a citadel of ice, its fluted spires and bastions resembling vast shells and coral reefs atop which flocks of winged men and women perched, singing for him to come join them, though he lacked the anatomy to answer.

Each dream, each particle of sand, a potential world; a *universe*. That was what the key was for; to unlock the door sealing the actual from the imagined, allowing humanity to dream itself anew, and learn a host of new sins where the old had grown weary.

I laughed at the prophecies that infested my thoughts, laughed as the last of my humanity leeched away, leaving in its wake something new and nameless, waiting for others to inform it of its nature.

Dissolving, dispersing, I turned multiple eyes Heavenwards, saw stars blinking through the waning tempest and wondered: how many worlds out there had experienced similar revelation, how many species had come so close to destruction and clawed their way back?

Maybe we'd know some day, maybe not. For now this place, this New Eden, contained wonders enough.

Thank Christ for second chances.

THE LAST SANE MAN

At long last!

The train had been delayed *four times*, pushed back from 2:00P.M. to 2:45P.M., from 2:45P.M. to 3:10P.M. and finally to fucking 4:00P.M., after a platform change that prompted a human stampede.

He took a moment to bask in the regulated warmth, England's Autumnal chill leeching from his bones. The frosts had come early this year and there was, as ever, talk of substantial snow that would likely never materialize.

Looking out of the window, he saw people already gathering for the next train. The common masks of worry and impatience they wore lent them the look of some obscure religious congregation, come to worship at this temple of dirt and diesel-stinking transition.

He turned away, occupying himself with tales of distant atrocity that he'd forget before reaching journey's end:

More chaos in the Middle East, American envoys targeted by Muslim terrorists in India, Iran and Saudi Arabia. At home, a man arrested for having his son and daughter chained up as dogs in the basement, where they'd spawned a brood of inbreds most of whom likely wouldn't survive long enough to be ferried into foster care.

Henry folded up the newspaper and shoved it down the side of his seat. Not bad enough that the public had to be constantly bombarded with that shit, but did the reporters have to go about conveying it with such *glee*? Not that he could claim innocence in that regard; after all, he hadn't stopped reading, had he? Couldn't leave the stories unfinished, regardless of their subject.

He was too tired for this sort of self-flagellation. The last few days had taken it out of him; pretending to be interested in relatives he hardly ever saw. By the end, he'd begun to understand why people idolized actors so much; pretending to be what you weren't was fucking hard work.

Still, at least he'd paid his dues; wouldn't have to waste thought or energy on it for at least another couple of years.

A little black girl, no older than five, hair tied in fetching buns to either side of her head, appeared in the aisle next to him, staring as if he'd spontaneously sprouted horns and begun to drool fire.

Fuck it, why couldn't people keep their kids under control?

"Hello there." He waved half-heartedly. The girl continued to stare in silence, lowering her head slightly to peer at him from beneath the dark sickles of her eyebrows.

"Kelly, you come away and leave the man alone!"

The mother's tone made it clear that she wasn't calling her daughter away for "The Man's" benefit. He might as well have been a lump of dog shit she'd stopped to examine.

The girl lingered for a split-second, familiar enough with the elasticity of her mother's patience to know how far she could stretch it, then darted away, trailing giggles down the carriage.

*

Henry watched the world outside the window sift by. God, it felt like he'd been on the train for *hours*.

Familiar fields, swamps and distant forest-land; a world he'd known since childhood, when he and Mom came visiting Nan and Granddad, but from which he'd always been separated. As a kid, once the glamour of "Eye Spy" and word-association games soured, he'd imagine what it'd be like to run there, in the mist and sludge. There were always monsters where his imagined-self wandered; great worms erupting from beneath the soil, lumbering marsh-things composed of sludge and stinking vegetation.

His sinuses stung with nostalgia at the memories; how the monsters would always trail him to Nan and Granddad's house, where he'd make a deeper game of them, occupying himself with daydream horrors 'til nightfall, when he was reluctantly shepherded to bed.

"Tickets from Nottingham."

He jolted as if disturbed from sleep, turning to face the ticket man, who stood waiting patiently in the aisle.

"Sorry mate." He smiled from behind his beard. "Wake you up, did I?"

A young Indian man, scalp shaved bald, beard hanging in streamers to the level of his shoulders.

"Nah, it's okay," Henry replied, fumbling in his pocket for the tickets, "just daydreaming."

The guy barely checked the ticket before stamping it through.

"I'll let you get back to it, then. Just be sure to wake up before you reach your stop."

"I will," Henry promised, returning his attention to the window.

*

"Déjà vu," Henry laughed to himself. The house in the distance served as a marker on the train journeys he'd taken as a child. Mom always pointed it out, proclaiming that she, Nan and Granddad used to live there when she was a girl.

A large farmhouse, long since abandoned and left to ruin, its surrounding fields become overgrown wasteland through years of neglect. As a kid, he'd entertained dreams of living there when he grew up. Now the thought of blundering about a farmstead was laughable.

Funny thing; he could've sworn he saw it go by a little while back. Hmmm. Maybe a different farmstead; there were quite a few out here, and he was tired. He'd likely dozed off for a little while, dreams and memory intermingling.

Already starting to get dark. God, he hoped he arrived back in Birmingham before the last of the light bled away. Early evening was the worst possible time to be hanging around New Street, when the thugs and the crazies crawled from their holes.

The little black girl appeared again. Despite her mother's disinterested warnings, she'd spent the last five minutes running up and down the aisle, singing snippets of nursery rhyme and pop song.

She'd acquired a lollipop since their last encounter, undoubtedly a means of temporarily plugging the hole capable of so much cacophony.

"Hello again."

She smiled around her treat, offering him a sticky-fingered hand to shake. Before he could accept, a woman he presumed to be her mother—young, kempt; professionally attired—materialized, glaring at him as if he was something she'd scraped from the heel of her shoe before turning on her daughter:

"What have I told you about leaving people *alone*?"

Henry felt that the subsequent smack was unnecessary, especially seeing the girl's smile crumple beneath it.

"Sorry," the mother grunted, making it sound more accusatory than apologetic.

"That's okay," he began, but she and her daughter were already gone.

*

He knew it was coming. He just couldn't *believe it:* the fields with their slopes and rises, the odd lake, quarry and patch of forest . . .

The farmhouse. "Look, Henry. Mom used to live there with Nan and Granddad . . ."

Yes, yes, he *knew*. Fucking ghost in his skull. What he didn't know was how this could be the *third time* they'd passed it by in what felt like close to an hour. An *hour*? Surely that couldn't be right either. They *definitely* should've arrived by now.

His watch informed him that less than five minutes had passed since he'd boarded the train. Jesus.

He watched 'til the farmhouse was out of view, watched 'til the fields gave way to gravel-pits, industrial sites and man-made quarries.

All right, all right . . . calm the fuck *down*. Obviously been dreaming or something. Stop working yourself up over nothing.

He fished the newspaper from beside his seat, turning to the puzzle page.

Not much of a distraction; his eyes straying back to the window, daring the world beyond to repeat itself a fourth time. It was only too happy to call his bluff.

Tears of sheer confusion stung his eyes as reason wrestled with what they relayed: they were going nowhere, cycling over the same stretch of track again and again. How was that possible? People would've noticed if the train had started doubling back on itself. It didn't make any fucking *sense*.

A little down the aisle, a digital display cycled through the train's route: Nottingham, Derby, Burton on Trent, Tamworth . . . E.T.A: six minutes . . .

Six minutes. Only six minutes. Then he'd be fine.

*

A warm wave of relief washed his entrails at the sight of the ticket-man approaching. He looked harassed, eyes carrying the weary sheen of a man out of love with his work.

"Excuse me," The man stopped in his tracks, not smiling.

"Yes?"

"Is there, ah, something wrong with the train?"

The man's brow furrowed, lips turning down at the corners.

"How d'you mean, mate?"

"Well, I've noticed we keep passing the same places over and over again. I was wondering . . ."

Now there was a smile, more frustrated than amused.

"Nah, man, I think you've got the wrong end of the stick."

"But we've been travelling for, what? Half an hour or more? It should only take ten minutes to get to Derby . . ."

Thc smile died again.

"Sorry, mate," the ticket man shook his head, "don't know what you're on about. We only left Nottingham a few minutes ago. It'll be a little while yet before we get into Derby."

Henry noticed others turning attention to the exchange, a sudden muteness descending over the carriage as people lowered their voices and strained their ears. He didn't know what to say. Part of him shrieked: *No, no; you're wrong! Look out the window and tell me I'm imagining things!* But the rest reigned it in, knowing how crazy it'd make him look. *Just sit tight,* it admonished. *Give it a few minutes. Things will work themselves out . . .*

"Okay," Henry nodded, doing his best to sound self-deprecating, "I don't know. Maybe I was just dreaming or something."

"Don't worry about it." The ticket man smiled, though not with his eyes, moving on.

This time, he'd keep watching 'til either the farm house rolled round again or they arrived at Derby station. At least that way he could be sure in his own mind . . .

Quarries, gravel pits, industrial sites. Fields, hills, forests . . . a river, a lake. *The fucking farmhouse.*

Henry felt everything inside descend several levels, as if some fundamental foundation had been removed, leaving all that it supported to crumble. The display still read the same: Next stop: Derby, E.T.A: 6 minutes . . .

He couldn't recall the last time he'd felt this; like a lost and lonely child, not knowing what to do save sit and cry.

No. He wasn't a bloody *child* anymore. He was going to do the adult thing and find out what the hell was going on.

In front sat a well dressed woman in her late fifties, idly leafing through a fashion magazine.

"Excuse me . . ."

"Oh!" she exclaimed, looking round at him. "You nearly frightened me to death! I was a bit engrossed . . ."

"Sorry. Listen, I was wondering if I could ask you something . . ."

The woman raised an eyebrow, folding up her magazine, clearly intrigued.

"Ask away."

"This is going to sound . . . Could you . . . could you just look out of the window for me?"

She regarded him a beat longer, trying to get the measure of him.

"All right. What're we looking for?"

"A farmhouse. I'll point it out when it comes 'round."

It was a few minutes before it did. The woman's response was one of frustrated disappointment:

"Well, what about it?"

"We've already passed it at least five times. I'll prove it to you; just keep looking out the window. I swear, you'll see it again in a few minutes or so."

She looked doubtful and a little afraid, but settled down to watch.

"There!" Henry exclaimed, unable to keep a note of hysteria from his voice. "You see it?"

The woman turned to him with a befuddled smile, eyes vacant.

"Yeah, so what?"

"What do you mean, *so what*? We only saw it just a few minutes ago! Don't you want to know why we keep passing the *same damn place all the time*?"

"Okay," she spoke slowly, delicately, "I don't know what this is all about, and frankly, I don't care. Leave me alone please, or I'll be calling the guard."

What? *What the fuck was this*? His imagination flew into overdrive. Had he been set up by one of those fucking "Candid Camera" shows? If so, he'd gladly sue those responsible into financial oblivion. This wasn't fucking *funny*.

"Look," he started, trying to maintain a semblance of calm, "I don't know what's going on either, but we've already been on this train, what, an hour now? And we haven't even pulled into Derby yet. Don't you think that's *weird*?"

"An hour?" she replied, shaking her head. "Are you on something? It's only been about five minutes since we left Nottingham. Just . . . leave me alone, will you?"

"Is there a problem?"

The ticket guy again, all trace of bon homie or patience evaporated.

"Yeah, there's a problem: this lunatic keeps bothering me with some crap about the train going 'round in circles, and I've already told him to leave me alone."

"Listen, mate, just sit and stop bothering people, all right? Or I'll have to put you off at the next stop . . ."

Henry laughed, knowing that it probably confirmed his craziness.

"That'd be absolutely bloody fine by me, if we ever fucking get there. Listen: we are just going 'round and 'round the same stretch of track. We've past the same fucking farmhouse five fucking times now, and I want to know what the fuck's going on!"

He felt eyes on him, heard muted whispers from all around the carriage.

The conductor rolled his eyes, sighed.

"Listen mate, have you taken something? Because you'll have to get off at Derby if you have . . ."

Henry breathed deep, trying to compose himself.

"No, I haven't taken *anything*. I'm telling you: *this train isn't going anywhere.*"

"Look, just sit down and shut the hell up, will you?" This from a burly man a few seats up the carriage, who'd risen and was glaring at Henry with murder in his eye. "You're upsetting folk."

He turned to the little black girl, who sat in her mother's arms looking like she might burst into tears. Henry relented, sinking down in his seat.

"Fine. We'll just stay here *forever.*"

"Fine by me, so long as you keep quiet and leave people be," the conductor warned.

*

One, two, three, four more times he watched the farm sail by, the sky neither lightening nor darkening, suspended in perpetual twilight. Henry had ample time to sit and think about his situation.

Suppose, just *suppose* this was something bigger, *weirder* than he'd imagined. Suppose the train had entered some kind of time warp, it and everything it contained ticking over the same reel of events again and again, except him. The thought of going 'round and 'round forever, never ageing, changing, *dying*, made him feel nauseous. Or maybe there was something wrong with the universe; a fundamental mechanism broken or backfired, leaving time and space in a state of disarray? All too fucked up for him to get his head around.

Only one thing was certain: he had to get off this damn train.

Getting up, he felt eyes on him like wasps beneath his clothes as he weaved his way down the aisle.

"Where do you think *you're* going?" the man from earlier demanded.

"To the toilet, if that's all right with you."

The man's eyes flashed.

"Just so long as you know, if you shoot up any more shit in there, I'll throw you off this train myself."

Henry just laughed.

The emergency stop mechanism was near the doors, behind a sheet of breakable plastic. A part of him reacted violently to the notion of even touching it, a lifetime of conditioning by teachers, parents; the glaring green and white warnings on the walls—*Penalty For Improper Use: up to £500.00 fine*—resulting in a taboo that equalled incest in repulsiveness. But what was that transgression weighed against being stuck here, *forever*?

He'd never so much as thrown a slap in anger before, let alone a punch. His fist rebounded off the plastic, a yelp coming with the sudden pain.

"Shit!"

Through the window, he saw the farm sailing past again. Was that a light flickering in one of the upstairs windows?

"Oy! What the bloody hell are you doing now?"

The ape from before, out of his seat and striding down the aisle towards him. Henry didn't waste time or breath on explanations; he simply turned and ran.

"Hey! Stop 'im! The guy's bloody nuts!"

Most didn't move to comply, instead doing their damnedest to ignore him in hope that he might return the courtesy. Several glanced up in fright-eyed surprise as he stumbled by, one or two demanding explanation. Behind, his pursuer drew closer, grunting as he manoeuvred his bulk down the aisle. The train was barely four carriages long; he had seconds before running out of places to run. And then . . .?

Out of the corner of his cyc, he saw the farmhouse passing again, the light in its windows unmistakeable now; as if a fallen star blazed inside.

A confusion of fumbles and cursing from behind. Glancing over his shoulder, he saw his pursuer barrel into someone getting out of their seat, attempting to ease his way past whilst the man demanded apologies.

A little way ahead, two others had risen, making their way towards him. What could he do or say that wouldn't simply compound their impression of him as a lunatic? Nothing; they'd already made up their minds, decided that he needed putting down.

Tears of frustration stung his sinuses as he looked back the way he'd come. His pursuer had already disentangled himself, and now the conductor appeared behind, expression grim and condemning as the rest.

Nowhere to run; a cornered animal whose remaining heartbeats amounted to little more than seconds. Then he saw it; the "open" button on the nearby door, its lights blinking, inviting him to press. He'd never seen them active whilst a train was in motion before, though he'd often wondered what would happen if some electronic malfunction made them so. All it'd take was for someone to lean against it and the doors would slide open, sucking everyone in vicinity to their deaths . . .

"Hey, mate." The men from up the carriage paused a few feet away. One stood forward from the other, smiling and holding out his hand as if coaxing a suicide from the edge of a cliff. "How's about we all just sit down, yeah? People are getting pissed off with it all now."

Even if he did press the button, what was he going to do? Jump out of a moving train? Best case scenario: he'd smash his skull or snap his neck and die quickly. The worst . . .?

"Look," he tried again, doing his utmost to sound calm, reasonable, failing, "I know how this sounds, but I've watched the same damn farmhouse go by at least ten times now. There's . . . there's something weird about this train."

The men exchanged glances, unconvinced.

"Well, we'll probably be able to sort it out at the next stop. If you'd just sit down . . ."

Henry laughed, letting tears come.

"There isn't going to be a next stop."

He pushed the button.

The doors hissed, slid aside, a blast of wintry air flooding the carriage. Though the windows continued to show the same relentless reel of countryside, beyond the doors was darkness: subterranean, absolute. Gazing into it, hearing the whispers that sounded beyond the clatter of wheels on rails, Henry realised it wasn't him who'd lost his mind.

It was the rest of the world.

They couldn't see, even as they rushed forward, reaching to with-strain him, hands closing on empty space.

Henry fell, the train's clatter receding. Voices rushed in to replace it; singing, whimpering, shrieking stories that he didn't know, but which would become intimately familiar before his descent ended. In time, he'd even add his own to the mythology, telling it to those who came after.

It began with a scream.

THE STATE OF LOVERS

"What're you doing, you crazy *bitch*?"

Why always crazy? Why never selfish or stupid? Both would've been fair accusations at one time or another.

Josh, James—or whatever the hell his name was—glared at her, pulling on his jeans. It wasn't like she'd asked him to slash or strangle her, for Christ's sake! Just a few little love-taps, that's all.

Things had gotten nasty when he refused, his struggles to be free of her causing more damage than any of the acts she'd solicited. And he'd talked such a good fight before his pants were off.

"What was all that bullshit about liking it rough?"

Almost fully dressed, he regarded her with lust-polluted loathing from the bedroom door. She moved a hand between her legs, showing him what he was forfeiting. He shook his head, upper lip curling in a sneer of contempt.

"You're fucking sick, you know that?"

He didn't wait for a retort, flying down the stairs and out the front door as though sexually frustrated Furies snapped at his heels.

*

She lay in the dark for a while, feeling nothing save the squirming demands of her loins. The headlights of passing cars cast shadow-phantoms across the ceiling; fluttering, distorted forms putting her in mind of a painting she'd once seen:

Souls caught in the perpetual agonies and ecstasies of Hell, Lucifer naked and glorious, presiding over the play.

The recollection provided the impetus to finish what Jules, Jeremy—or whatever—had begun.

Men. Such pathetic fucking children. How many she'd deigned to take to her bed had whispered promises of the most adventurous perversity, only to touch her as if she was made of sugar glass once the lights were off?

As for the rest, *apes*; eager to spill their little measure and leave her with nothing but wet sheets and dissatisfaction.

Climax would've come quicker had she not taken steps to forestall it. She wished to prolong her dip in the Lake of Fire; to be the Devil's property just a little while longer.

She didn't conjure him as a static, heavy thing; his flesh instead shifting beneath her fingers like fire and water, lips between her legs alternately barbed and silken.

And his wings; eruptions from the shoulder blades that were one moment raven feathered, the next rippling and coiled like octopus tentacles.

He spoke poetry as he tongued her, singing verse into her cunt potent enough to seed a brood of Antichrists.

The orgasm imagination elicited was so thunderously protracted, she could barely see or think in its aftermath.

*

She surfaced to the sound of rain, a nightmare fast receding. Something to do with ocean, drowning . . .

The bed sheets she'd cocooned herself in smelled strangely sweet, as if she'd sweated honey during sleep.

Turning over to face the window, she winced more in surprise than pain at the familiar, satisfactory soreness between her legs. Jesus, she hoped she hadn't done some damage with her play . . .

She swallowed the scream before it could be born, the figure silhouetted before the window seeming not to notice she'd woken. How the fuck did he get in? Her sleep was usually so fragile even the gurgling of water pipes beneath the floorboards was enough to break it.

For a moment, she entertained the notion that he was the lingering remnant of some vivid nightmare, but rejected it out of hand. Closing her eyes and shaking her head probably wouldn't be of much use when he had his hands around her throat.

Though much of him was swathed in shadow, orange street-lamp light filtering through the window cast amber highlights across his anatomy, rendering him a spectre, partially coalesced in the darkness.

A tall, wiry frame; pale skin stretched taught over an acrobat's musculature; limbs somehow over-long, shoulder length hair dark and tangled, what little she could see of his back swarming with eclectic tattoos, most seeming to consist of writing she couldn't make out in the murk.

He was naked; a fact that should've terrified her far more than it did.

Holding her breath, she watched as his shoulders heaved in a heart felt sigh. Extending a finger, he traced something on the condensation misted window.

"I'm sorry, did I wake you?"

A voice filtered through a throat full of whisky and gravel, accent vaguely European.

No point in playing possum now.

Struggling into a sitting position, Cynthia's bowels became a cauldron, her blood boiling to red ether in her veins.

"What the fuck are you doing here?"

He turned, face half obscured beneath a fluttering shadow mask. The rest was beautiful; features angular, slightly sallow, almost feminine lips curled in a sickle-moon smile; those of a vagrant poet, too in love with rain and stars to be concerned whether or not there was a roof over his head.

An eye the colour of mist over ocean returned her scrutiny, stars flaring in its depths as it flickered down to her exposed breasts.

"So, we're playing that game again? I thought you said you were bored of it the last time."

Was he crazy? She didn't know . . .

But she *did*, memory rising like a drowned corpse from the swamp of her mind. She remembered the last time they played; the first time they met, talked, kissed, fucked; a mental landslide in which pieces tumbled into place and pattern instead of chaos.

She even knew his name, the sound of it coming to her lips as if seeking verification:

"*Owen . . .*"

He smiled.

"I thought we didn't know one another, remember?"

He started towards the bed, padding soft and silent as a cat on the floorboards.

As he shrugged off the remains of his shadow shroud, she saw his legs, arms and torso boasted markings similar to those decorating his back; extracts of prose and poetry becoming more legible with every step he took.

What the hell was wrong with her? She didn't recall taking anything before going to bed. Maybe it was a sign that she was just getting older; the first tell-tale traces of the hereditary mental decay she'd always dreaded.

Drawing alongside the bed, he trailed a hand across the sheets swathing her. Around each wrist she noticed a tattooed band; a snake devouring its own tail. She recalled kissing them when they first fucked, wondering in her drink-addled state what it'd be like to have them come alive and pleasure her.

Such ruminations drew her eyes down to what sprouted between his legs; a thin quilt of dark pubic hair; an uncircumcised cock whose scale was neither disappointing nor intimidating, its redness testament to what it'd already been about tonight.

His hand rested on the flat of her belly, a faint scent of cloves and rain-bearing breeze tickling her nostrils.

The look he wore was at once grave and jocular, sickle-moon smile complementing rather than competing with the reverence reflected in his eyes.

She'd never been content to play the passive lover (much to the chagrin of most she bedded). Owen knew that better than anyone she'd ever met, conceding to and rebelling against it as her needs and wants demanded. Why in god's name had she been so frightened earlier? These hands, *his* hands, knew her better than she sometimes knew herself.

Plucking up the one splayed like a sleeping crab across her belly, she kissed its fingers for their cleverness, tasting faint traces of her own scent.

The fingers were replaced by equally talented lips, the spell of forgetfulness sealed with a kiss.

*

Strange thing; she'd long since given up hope of finding someone whose company she could stand for more than a few hours at a time, much less cohabit with.

Then Owen; a fallen star plunged into the stagnant pool of her preconceptions. A revelation; one of the very few human beings in her circle of acquaintances whose proximity she genuinely craved.

Such a *strange* man.

He watched her watching him out of the corner of his eye for several minutes before breaking the silence, not working up courage to speak; his assessment, like her own, more predatory than that. Later, during one of their more heated heart-to-hearts, he confessed that he was working out whether or not she was worth wasting breath on. So few beautiful women were.

"You're the artist, aren't you?"

Not the best opening line she'd ever heard, but carrying just the right tone of casual curiosity to warrant response:

"That's right. And you are . . .?"

She extended a hand that he took and kissed rather than shook.

The wine must've made her more slow witted than she realised; it was only then she began to notice how beautiful he was. Not classically attractive; she doubted there was another woman at the party who'd look at him twice, but a near perfect example of her own tastes, and therefore guaranteed to be brash, brainless or boring as hell beneath.

He flashed a smile, crooked and predatory, sparkling with playful intelligence.

"What would you say, from the look of me?"

She wasn't sure she liked this game at first; too much of the cat and mouse about it, but she couldn't help feeling intrigued.

Sipping from her eighth Cabernet Sauvignon of the evening, she looked him up and down, taking in the starless midnight suit and crimson shirt hanging uncomfortably on a frame better suited to scruff.

"I don't know . . . some sort of professor, or maybe a poet?"

His eyes flashed in surprised delight.

"Is that some sort of psychic party piece you do?"

She laughed, the alcohol making mist and bubbles in her brain.

"Just a good reader of people, I suppose."

The conversation she'd expected to falter the second he realised there was no hope of her hoisting up her skirt stretched into the early morning, outliving the drunken, sweaty attempts at seduction surrounding it.

Men capable of holding her attention for longer than thirty seconds tended to be gay, insane, married or otherwise unavailable.

What would he turn out to be?

*

They didn't fuck that first night, though he stayed with her, warming a bed too used to cold.

She wanted to know how he'd react to refusal, especially after she'd consented to share kisses.

He was as strange in his overtures as everything else; content to merely kiss while she was, whereas other men would take it as invitation to fumble at her thighs and bra strap.

Rather than the anatomy between her legs, his consistent fascination that night seemed to be her face and hands, his reverential, back handed strokes causing both to burn, almost convincing her to overturn her earlier resolution.

It was as if he couldn't accept the fact of her existence, his rhythmic stroking of her cheeks and jaw a means of ratifying her solidity, keeping the dream from bursting.

She matched him caress for caress, running fingers from his temples down to the tapered point of his chin.

Undressing was usually awkward, her bed-mate's eagerness to be beneath the wrapping sometimes endearing, but for the most part frightening in its appetite, the couplings that followed suffused with all the joyless technicality of rape, save for the incidence of her concession.

In this, as in so many things, he was a sex and species unto himself, fingers seeming to take as much delight in velvet and cotton as the flesh beneath.

It became an almost ritual act; he a supplicant come begging baptism in her soul-cleansing waters, finding fresh revelation in every inch of her.

She didn't deny him when he kissed her between the legs, though he didn't seek entry with either tongue or fingers. For now, it seemed he was content with this solemn play, saving more profound perversity for later.

Naked before him in the dark, she initiated a flawed reversal of their roles, peeling away his shirt, trousers and underwear with nothing like the same élan, breaking the mood with curses at particularly recalcitrant buttons and zippers.

Embracing him, she felt his heat and hardness against her belly, its eagerness to be milked mirrored by her own to be filled.

Kissing him, she whispered: "Not tonight . . ."

He smiled and brushed her flank, black lightning seeming to arc from his fingertips.

"Not tonight," he repeated, letting her lead him to bed with kisses that lasted 'til dawn, at which point she could no longer fend off sleep.

*

He knew better than to disturb her while she worked. When the door to what she'd christened "The Cave"—an extension originally intended as a laundry room, now become make-shift studio—was shut, she desired nothing more from the outside world than the occasional mug of hot, honeyed tea.

Today, the paint simply refused to flow. Barely noon, and she was already surrounded by the remains of false starts; canvases hacked and stabbed to ribbons in frustration.

Maybe it was because of last night; that momentary dementia she'd experienced on waking, or perhaps it was more pedestrian; deadlines looming, emphasized by occasional telephone "check ups" from those signing her pay cheques.

The project wasn't exactly taxing; covers for a series of horror novels from some up-and-coming Stephen King wannabe. She'd only agreed to do it because the books had scared her witless, making her afraid to even venture to the bathroom without the lights on.

She was having difficulty consigning that same sense of gut-churning dread to canvas, her efforts thus far cartoonish, better suited to the bargain-basement slasher-trash she'd begun her career with. She felt like a novice, criticizing and second-guessing every brush stroke.

The door creaking open elicited relief rather than fury. Even so, she couldn't allow the breach of etiquette to go unchallenged:

"I'm busy right now, Owen. I've told you before . . ."

Eager hands at her shoulders, ardent kisses at her neck.

"Owen . . . I've got to get this finished . . ."

"You will. Just not now."

He was familiar enough with her to know that if they fucked now, she'd be good for nothing for the rest of the day. Shrugging him off, she dipped her brush in the blue black pigment she'd just finished mixing, applying it to the canvas in broad, sweeping strokes. Even this comparatively simple rendering—what was supposed to be a starless midnight sky—came out stilted and unconvincing, the result somehow *plastic,* too solid to create the illusion of depth.

"Why not leave it for now? Maybe you'll be more in the mood later . . ."

She could see the sense in that, shit, *knew* he was right from past experience, but there was no way she'd concede to it now without confrontation.

"I'd be fine if you'd piss off and let me concentrate."

"I would if that's what you really wanted."

She'd known better than to hope for a situation without argument. No matter how perfect someone seemed in the world outside walls, the mask would crack and flake away the second they consented to be caged.

The best she or anyone could hope for was that the truth beneath was half as pleasing.

Rounding on him, she wielded the paint brush like a knife beneath his nose, as if she could paint him out of existence with a few broad strokes.

"Don't you *dare* tell me what I damn well want . . ."

He didn't back down, plucking the paint brush from her hand and flinging it aside.

"Maybe if you'd decide for yourself, I wouldn't have to."

A scalpel slice, designed to cut deep and open her to reluctant self perusal. He was trying to help, giving her what he thought she wanted, but that didn't make the hurt any easier to endure.

"Just . . . get the fuck out, will you?"

Satisfied that he'd played his part, he nodded curtly, gone before she could say another word.

*

He returned a few hours later. This time she put up only token resistance.

The room was littered with the wreckage of failed inspiration, some attempts suffering only one or two strokes before she became brutal, tearing into them with brush handle and palette knife.

No apologies; she'd have been angry otherwise. He became a receptacle for her frustration, kisses punctuated by slaps and scratches that he was happy to bear, not to mention return when she demanded.

The glistening slugs of pigment drying on her palette she now put to better use, daubing his body in tribal waves and whorls, his pale skin as fitting a foundation as any canvas. Under normal circumstances, she'd have found such porn-film play trite, but today her demons had been particularly cruel, demanding exorcism by whatever means came to hand.

They coupled on the cold concrete, wet paint smearing her breasts and belly as she rode him, the day's disappointments flooding from her like poison from a lanced tumour

*

She dreamed; black, liquorice-bitter waters sucking her down as she struggled to keep her head above the surface.

Overhead, a sceptic sky churned and twisted, tumescent clusters of cloud flaring with internal lightning.

So *hot* . . .

Familiar voices hailed her from somewhere distant, their tones jubilant rather than desperate; her imminent drowning cause for celebration.

Surfacing momentarily, spitting sweetly perfumed brine, she saw a beach of chalk white sand bounded by broken, charcoal cliffs. Though miles away, she was able to discern every figure stood on the shoreline with eagle-eyed clarity, the clownish glee written across their faces making her wish that the cliffs would crumble, burying them alive.

Her parents; photograph incarnations of their younger selves, Rose and Carol, decked out in two piece swim wear; rejects from some adolescent masturbatory fantasy involving incestuous twins.

They waved as the waters swept her further out, spun sunlight hair whipping in a wind that Cynthia couldn't feel.

She opened her mouth to scream how much she hated them, skull flooding with memories of growing up as the routinely ignored, introspective child whilst the miracle-twins could get away with eating a newborn babe if they flashed their perfect, soulless smiles between mouthfuls.

The ocean moved to drown her bitterness, filling her mouth and throat as the rain came; hot, heavy droplets splashing red against her up-turned cheeks.

Laughter, warm, affectionate, erupted from the beach as something twined around her ankles; smooth, sinuous lengths that felt like twin pythons slithering up her legs to seek out the warmth between.

Lightning struck down the sea-side revellers one by one before she was dragged under, the sound of their joy following her into the abyss.

*

An empty bed, sheets scented with the pungency of their sleeping bodies. She was glad; not in the mood for company today.

She pondered how perfectly attuned to her moods and needs he was as she stepped into the shower. Were it not for his overt appetite for her body—his tongue sometimes so eager, it seemed he was only just holding himself back from devouring her—she'd have sworn he was a closet case; their relationship little more than a denial of his essential self. After all, what man who so hungered for her sex had ever demonstrated even an ounce of the same empathy?

Satisfactorily cleansed, she dressed and made her way downstairs, feeling a slow flush of gratitude at the house being so still, so vacant. This was the aspect of her personality most self-fancied "friends"—and certainly most lovers—couldn't handle; the *need* to be alone. Her love of silence and solitude was beyond their comprehension, leading to the unspoken but pervasive conclusion there must be something "wrong" with her, procrastinations thereon ranging from closet lesbianism—her sister's assertion of choice—to mild autism; an inability to cope with what they deemed "reality."

Well, if the grey round of self imposed *misery* they all rode was any indication of "reality," then fuck it; she was more than content to wile away in Dream Land.

She made herself a frugal breakfast of honeyed tea and toast, taking a moment to wonder what Owen was doing with his day. She had no idea where he disappeared to when his company wasn't required; he volunteered nothing on the subject and she didn't ask. Things were simpler that way.

*

Her paint brushes remembered their old magic today, though they steadfastly refused to do as she demanded.

The piece she intended to work on was a book cover for *The Cemetery*

Path, the first of three she'd been commissioned to produce. The title alone suggested a solid enough image; an old, overgrown gravel path, snaking its way between plots of weathered gravestones towards a church with doors slightly ajar, but her fingers refused to focus on such simple composition, intent on turning it into a surrealist flight of fancy in which every pebble, shadow and blade of grass was made miraculous:

Faces twisted in mockery or lasciviousness glared out at her from the corrugated church walls; shadows in the grass took on shape and solidity, becoming squatting, red-eyed imps and demons waiting for some incautious wanderer to set foot on their domain. A sky she intended flushed with the last scarlet ribbons of dusk waxing towards night became a broiling morass of post apocalyptic storms, black and scarlet cloud weeping spools of leprous, watery yellow light.

She jolted as if woken from a particularly vivid nightmare, the doorbell buzzing in her ears. Flying from The Cave a fairy tale witch, fury following her in a black, smouldering cloud, she muttered curses that she imagined blistering the air, causing paint and wallpaper to peel. If it was someone trying to sell something—double glazing, home insurance, salvation—they'd likely be leaving sans certain body parts . . .

Frustration evaporated as she flung the front door open. Dylan flinched, stepping back as he caught a whiff of her mood, raising his hands in mock surrender.

"Okay, okay; whatever I did-stroke-said-stroke-didn't do or say, I'm sorry, okay? Just leave the face intact, would you? I might be needing it later."

"Oh, come in, you arsehole!"

He laughed, hugging her as he stepped over the threshold. Most would've earned her enmity through such unsolicited contact, but Dylan wasn't most.

There was never any defensiveness or reluctance with him; no sense that she should tread lightly for fear of trampling delicate sensibilities. It was rare that she came across someone so profane, so deviant; so utterly *themselves.* That's why she'd nurtured their relationship whilst letting so many recede and rot.

"So, where've you been of late?" he asked, following her through to the kitchen. "People are starting to think you're dead or something."

She smiled, spooning coffee into two cups.

"I've been occupied, actually."

"All work and no play . . ."

"I never said anything about work. I've met someone."

His eyes flared in delight at this revelation.

"Really? Does this mean the vow of celibacy's finally over? I was worried for a little while you were going to bugger off and join a convent or something . . ."

She slapped his arm hard enough to make him wince.

"Wait a minute . . . it's not John, is it? Vanessa said she noticed you two getting chummy at Clara's birthday party."

John? The name conjured a vague image of a well dressed man, older than she traditionally went for, salt and pepper hair swept back in fetching, shoulder length waves.

She thought she remembered talking to him at some point, something about the lectures he was conducting at Edinburgh university, but after that . . . nothing. Now that she came to think of it, most of that evening was a blur; wine, weed and whatever else was in her system reducing memory to a flight through a storm of fractured mirrors.

"Hello? Earth to Cynthia?"

"Sorry . . . no, no, it's not John. You do know him, though. We met at Olivia's party."

He cocked his head, brow furrowing in confusion.

"Really? Because I seem to recall you being plastered out of your face that night. Didn't you get into some sort of argument with Olivia when she started up with the whole Tom Cruise, Scientology crap?"

She remembered the argument, but it hadn't occurred that night. She'd spent the entire evening with Owen. There was no way she'd have forgotten or misplaced that.

"No, no; I was with Owen pretty much from beginning to end . . ."

"*Owen?* Owen who?"

She opened her mouth, but there was no reply for it to shape. Fuck, what was his last *name*?

Seeing her predicament, Dylan grinned.

"Oh, honey, you're sleeping with a guy and you don't even know his last name? Classy."

She suddenly felt like an oyster with a grain of grit beneath its shell.

"It's just never come up before. Anyway, you know him; he's some sort of poet or something . . ."

Dylan's eyes widened as if she'd accused him of luring children into his basement with toys and candy canes.

"Sorry, Cyn. The only poet named Owen I ever heard of died in the First World War."

"Maybe he's one of Mason's friends."

Desperation behind her words, bitter as blood from an extracted tooth.

"Maybe . . ." But probably not, his tone suggested.

Cynthia suddenly didn't want him there; the first time in all their years of acquaintance his company chafed.

". . . Maybe it'll click into place when I meet him. You are planning on introducing him to us, I hope?"

Actually, she wasn't, a sudden stab of possessiveness causing her to physically flinch.

"Of course. I just want him to myself a little while beforehand."

He knew she wasn't being entirely forthcoming; she could see that, but he also knew better than to press the issue.

Sipping his coffee, he raised one eyebrow, dissipating the tension with tacit promise of mischief.

"So, what's the appeal? Is he loaded or hung like a T-Rex or what?"

Stupid, she chided herself; fretting like a fifty year-old who'd begun to forget where they placed their glasses or door keys.

"Neither. He's . . ." She didn't want to use the word "perfect;" it was too baby-pink smooth, too vanilla-scented and sterile. ". . . he's good for me. He makes me feel good."

Dylan shrugged.

"Can't ask for more than that, can you?"

The conversation descended into triviality, primarily consisting of lascivious gossip on who'd been seen with who and where and in what state. She let the tide of names, places and speculations wash over her, nodding and offering commentary in all the right places, though her thoughts were preoccupied with more elaborate fair, questions swirling round her skull like dirty laundry in a washing machine.

*

After Dylan left, she retreated to the drawing room and spent several minutes staring out of the window, watching the magpies and sparrows at war. Then, feeling that if she didn't move soon she'd likely take root, she returned to The Cave, examining the day's work with a critical eye.

Revelation crept upon her gradually, like a tarantula ascending her spine.

The faces lurking in the grass and shadows, coalescing from the patterns of moss and weathering on the church walls . . . she knew them, or rather, the visage that inspired them:

Owen, rendered over and over again in varying states of distortion:

The priapic imp peering lasciviously from behind a gravestone, the tormented mask silently screaming from the trunk of a gnarled and naked tree; all the man she'd come to regard as her lover, remade in every state imagination could conjure.

What the fuck was wrong with her? She felt like some obsessive adolescent, mooning over photographs of the teacher she imagined asking her to stay after school.

She was about to take the palette knife to it when she realised not all of the faces were the same. There were others, swarming warped and nebulous in the clouds. They were familiar too; renditions of a mask whose scrutiny she endured every day, its mockery insulated from reprisal by the glass it glared from behind.

*

"Where do you go?"

He looked up from his plate, sucking up a rogue strand of spaghetti. Her palette had never been particularly adventurous food-wise, his limited repertoire of home-cooked dishes—Bolognaise, Shepherd's Pie, Lamb Korma—suiting her tastes perfectly.

"When you're not with me, I mean; you've never told me where you live or anything."

"You've never asked."

He took another mouthful, clearly hoping she'd drop the subject.

"I'm asking now."

The candles cast spastic shadows across his face, transforming him into one of the demon-parodies she'd painted.

Cynthia felt unsettled meeting his gaze; Little Red Riding Hood attempting to stare down The Big Bad Wolf. She'd always hated that story.

"There are one or two places . . . nothing much to talk about, really."

"I'd like to see them sometime."

She'd never seen that deadness in his eyes before, never felt the gulf between them yawning so vast.

"Maybe. Do you want some more wine?"

No. She wanted to know what he was keeping from her. Was he married? Did he have kids? A gay lover perhaps? Standard soap opera clichés, one and all; all indefinably *wrong*.

"Why not? I feel like flying a little."

*

He moaned, gritting his teeth as she scraped her nails across the tattooed flesh of his shoulders.

She'd taken to reading the rag-tag text of his body whilst they fucked, mouthing the odd fragment out loud in an unguarded moment.

". . . But in those hearts love unlibidinous reigned, nor jealousy was understood, the injured Lover's Hell . . ."

His snarl turned to a smile, a single word punctuating his gasps for breath.

"*Milton.*"

The association of angels and demons stirred strange images in her mind; the memory of a party, rivers of fire in which naked men and women swam; a burning, gold skinned angel presiding over all, too beautiful for words.

Heat, intense and glorious, exploded from the body beneath her, the length she enveloped becoming a burning tower, its fire threatening to reduce her to ash from within.

Opening her eyes, she no longer saw Owen bucking and thrashing beneath her, but Owen remade in the Fallen's image, molten rivulets crawling worm-like across his skin, black flame flaring from mouth, eyes and nostrils.

The fire had already spread to her own flesh, its serpentine lengths coiling up around her flanks, her arms, her throat. Surely it wouldn't be long before she combusted entirely, charring them both to a common ash?

The image brought her to climax, the world darkening, cooling as she closed her eyes, the inferno they shared waning.

Opening her eyes, she found the angel returned to its more mundane state, not even a flicker of his fiery disgrace left to light the room.

He dragged his fingernails down her cheek as their passions cooled, just hard enough to sting. Laughing breathlessly, she parted from him, all concerns momentarily forgotten in the wash of carnal satisfaction.

*

There was nothing she could do, so she simply surrendered, hoping that death would come quickly. Only there was none of the familiar cold fire in her chest; no flailing panic in the certainty she'd taken her last breath. She left such concerns behind with the sunlit world, the darkness into which she descended a place where old parameters meant nothing; where all was potential, eager to be shaped.

She laughed at the sight of the lengths wrapped around her legs—feathered fronds festooned with unblinking eyes—reminded of a Salvador Dali exhibit she'd been taken to see in the latter years of high school. A boy whose name she couldn't recall had followed her around all day like an over-dependent pup, the kisses they'd shared in the women's toilets souring when his fingers trespassed beneath her skirt.

Phantom shapes swam and skittered in the surrounding dark. Some grew braver as she descended, drawing close to investigate the intruder in their underwater domain:

Things that resembled an infant's crayon scrawls twined around her outstretched fingers, their substance feeling strangely uncertain, as if they were sewn from mist or smoke. A billowing relative of the Octopus whose balloon like mass blossomed with chirruping mouths extended multiple tongues to lap the salt from her skin as it passed.

Even the water couldn't keep itself from absurdity, ripples and eddies seeming to momentarily form faces, figures; monsters from nightmare and memory that lingered long enough to stir old dreads -not to mention new desires- before dissolving:

Mr. Gladys, her old art teacher, insisting she'd never make a name for herself "painting fairy-tale trash," the snarling chimera whose image she found in a book of Greek mythology as a child, and in the dreams of devourment it inspired. The dragon; black scaled, serpentine, eyes like furnaces; the state she used to imagine erupting from her hateful, adolescent hide to scorch the world clean before taking flight into the star flecked abyss of space.

Below, the darkness was broken by a single pin-prick of light, as if a star shaken loose from the heavens had come to rest there.

The pin-prick expanded as she descended, becoming a chaotic white void in which threads of matter swam like bacteria in a drop of blood. The tendrils extended from this furnace, prompting her to wonder if she was intended as fuel to keep it burning. Not so horrific a prospect; the dust she'd become scattering into the surrounding waters; food for the simple life that swam there, or settling to the depths where it might form the foundations of continents.

It soon became apparent there was more in store for her than simple incineration:

The flecks and motes grew in complexity the closer she approached, becoming recognizable fragments of anatomy:

A ribbed snake of intestine coiling in an ineluctable figure eight, conjoined, billowing bags of lungs propelling themselves languid and directionless through the depths, clutches of hands swarming like shelless, pale-skinned crabs over spires of compacted bone; every element imaginable for piecing together a human being, including those not quite so tangible:

Pulsing, variegated clouds of feeling, lightning flickers of thought; loves, hates, hopes, terrors, all seething together in the light, their variety near infinite, awaiting coherence into a greater whole.

As was often the way with dreams, she didn't have to wait or wonder; the knowledge simply blossomed in her brain, filtered from the ocean itself via some obscure osmosis. Nor did she require hands or tools to put it into practice; desire was sufficient.

Several components—hearts, lungs, entrails—had already separated from their schools, finding niches in the structure of bone, nerve and tissue coagulating in their midst. The process reminded her of sped up reels of fungal growth she'd seen in nature documentaries, configurations of bone elaborating before her eyes, blood-vessel circuits threading throughout, crawling like the roots of some red, alien weed.

In a matter of seconds, something man-like emerged from the conflux; a seeping rag doll coiled in foetal despair at its condition.

The process excited the surrounding ocean, languid currents and eddies abruptly growing violent, threatening to carry her away from the work before it could reach completion. The fronds anchoring her in place grew tighter, sprouting spines that bit into her flesh, blood staining the brine.

Darting out of the depths, the creatures she'd witnessed during her descent swarmed around her, driven rabid by the disturbance in their environment.

She couldn't allow them to distract her; to do so would result in the unravelling of all she'd created, and ejection back into the cruel, breathing world above.

One of her anchors, unable to withstand the ocean's violence any longer, tore free at its root, flailing out into the darkness with arterial, milk white sprays. *Just a little longer*, that was all she asked for.

A Halloween mask; the bloody horror that was the foundation of beauty, turned to regard her, lidless eyes burning with love and hate beyond imagining.

She screamed as the final anchor gave way, the maelstrom sweeping her up, carrying her away from those eyes and their adoring accusation.

*

She woke to the sound of rain, another empty bed. Usually this wouldn't have concerned her; she liked that he felt free to come and go as he pleased, but tonight . . . tonight she was a little girl again, trembling close to tears in the aftermath of nightmares.

The sheets and her skin still smelled of him, but there was no other trace. She strained her ears, hoping to hear him pattering around downstairs, perhaps fixing himself a late night snack.

The effort would've been in vain even if that was the case; he moved like a shadow when she was asleep, the only man she'd ever known who didn't like to announce himself with a fan fare of grunts, sighs and farts.

His absence was tangible; the space left by an extracted tooth, the itching emptiness of an amputated limb.

She hated herself for the anxiety she felt; the frightened little girl she'd done everything in her power to murder hoisting herself from the grave, intent on dragging the woman who'd put her there down into the dirt.

"Where are you, you bastard?"

*

Sleep threatened to reclaim her several times before he returned, beaten back only by a drive to confront him and demand to know all he was keeping from her.

Strange; if anything, she expected him to be as secretive in arrival as in flight, yet he made no effort to disguise it; not slamming the front door but certainly ensuring she heard it, foregoing stealth so that every footfall throbbed in her ear.

She'd already composed what she was going to say, demands and accusations buzzing behind her lips like a vomit of wasps.

When the bedroom door creaked open, all the fury and paranoia—what if he was with someone else? What was he keeping from her?—gave way to relief that he was home and hers again.

She lay still, feigning sleep as he slipped into bed.

*

A glutton's breakfast of scrambled eggs, bacon and black pudding awaited her when she surfaced the next morning. Some oblique apology for the night before? It didn't matter; she'd already determined not to press him on the subject. Let him reveal all in his own time.

Meanwhile, there was art and love to be made, *The Cemetery Path's* publishers becoming increasingly insistent that she provide at least some preliminary sketches. She'd decided to submit the piece she'd already produced, not particularly caring if it tallied with their specifications.

Owen had yet to see its current incarnation. Despite his demands, she was loath to expose him to it, fearing that he might take offence or flight.

*

"*Go away.*"

She'd been entombed in The Cave since noon, refining, perfecting. Even if *The Cemetery Path's* publishers decided it wasn't what they wanted, she doubted she'd have much trouble finding a market for it. It was so different from anything she'd attempted before; seeming little more than a melancholic cemetery scene from a distance; an unambiguous meditation on death and decay, far more than entropy becoming apparent as the eye drew closer:

Madness, evil; desire and delusion in the shadows; images that tickled loins and intellect alike, inspiring an inclination to tear oneself naked and stand before them honest in appetite . . .

The telephone rang again, hateful reality intruding where it wasn't welcome.

"I swear, if you don't fuck off in a minute . . ."

A demon whose stretched, spidery form was composed from the shadows cast by a dead and twisted tree seemed to beckon from its seat in the grass, the triple-pronged prick it wielded an unambiguous invitation to perversity.

What would it be like if she could make doorways of her work? To step through and feel the dank softness of grass and soil beneath her feet, smell the threat of frost on the breeze.

Mass couplings amongst the gravestones, a thousand forked tongues lapping at her, whispering dark poetry against her skin...

She threw down her brushes, ripping off the apron she wore and stormed from The Cave, already tasting the abuse she was going to spew into the intruder's ear:

"*What*, for God's sake?"

"Cyn?"

Her frustration evaporated at the sound of Dylan's voice.

"Dylan, what's up?"

"I've been speaking to John Robbins, you remember?"

She remembered talking about him, that there'd been some misunderstanding . . .

What're you doing, you crazy bitch?

Déjà vu, and something else . . . like a buried childhood memory surfacing through the muck of years:

A small man, treating her like glass, as if she'd shatter beneath a harsh breath...

"Cyn?"

"Yeah, yeah, just a minute . . . John Robbins?"

"Yeah. He swears blind that he went home with you after the party. I got the impression things didn't go very well."

What the hell was this? She'd already told him she went home with *Owen* that night; she remembered every detail of it . . .

A dream of drowning, something flayed, unfinished and beautiful smiling at her in the depths . . .

"Maybe he's bullshitting because I brushed him off."

"I don't know, Cyn. He told me things . . ."

"What do you mean, *things*?"

"Well, he told me that you wanted it rough, and that you took it too far . . ."

"Oh, come on! He could have gotten that from anyone! I'm not fucking Snow White, you know."

"I know, I know. I'm just . . . concerned. This Owen guy; nobody else seems to remember him. They all say that John sniffed after you like a dog in heat all night and that he went home with you."

Disappointment, prayers . . . a masturbatory moment in Hell, wrapped up in a painted Satan's fires, then . . .?

She put the phone down, a hurricane in her head, swirling with all the filth and shit of the world.

He'd been there; she remembered first catching sight of him, standing at the window with a glass of blood red port, slightly apart from the rest of the revellers, regarding them with the fascinated intensity of a child watching monkeys at the zoo.

Only . . . the memory was too solid; to exquisitely detailed to be anything but imagined. Even her recollections of the shower and breakfast she'd enjoyed barely hours ago—banana on her cereal or strawberries? Coffee to wash it down or tea?—had grown hazy and indistinct. Yet this—the cattle-like warmth of milling bodies, convoluted scents of perfumes, alcohol and sweat—seemed so palpable, so precise . . .

Had it finally happened? Had the boundaries between the imagined and the experienced begun to crumble?

No. She refused to go down that road, no matter what its destination.

You do enjoy making life hard for yourself, don't you love? Her mother's words, a condemnation consistently aimed at her, even before she decided to make a career from her art.

Insofar as she was concerned, others were too willing to take the easy way out. She knew her own mind. The notion that it'd so abruptly rebel against her was laughable.

Laughable.

*

He had "work stuff" to attend to today. She didn't ask him to elaborate and he didn't offer. They arranged to have supper together; wine and Chinese take-away, with a tacit understanding there'd be sex to follow.

Cynthia started the wine a few hours before he arrived, draining one bottle and making a dedicated start on the second.

The world spun and her loins throbbed as she opened the door, kissing him so hard it hurt.

After she relinquished him, convinced now more than ever that he wasn't some delirious hallucination, he handed her a small, leather bound book whose cover carried no suggestion of its contents.

"What is it?"

"Open it and see."

The first two pages were covered in a spidery, hap-hazard script, surrounded by all manner of tribal scrawls and doodles:

To hurt is human,
To suffer divine,
The one corrosive,
The other a sign,
Of an honest soul;
Uncertain,
In Flux,
Wishing only to live;
Be happy and whole,
Come the final curtain.

He waited while she read, eyes gleaming in anticipation of her critique.

"What do you think?"

She kissed him again. How could she have ever believed him to be no more than a dream? Feeling him now; the elegant enthusiasm of his fingers at her back, the cracked and creaking hide of his leather jacket, she couldn't conceive of anything more real, anything more she wanted.

*

His poet's appetite for wine saw two more bottles consumed during the course of the evening, the food they ordered going largely untouched as they sprawled out before the fire, laughing at nothing in particular.

The questions hadn't gone away, but for the moment she was content to simply have him close, regardless of the answers.

"Owen . . ."

"Hmmm?"

He nursed his ninth glass, eyes heavy-lidded and swimming.

"What's your name? Your second name, I mean?"

He smiled, stroking her mouth with his free hand.

"What would you like it to be?"

She laughed, not certain she was in the mood for this game.

"Hmmm, what about Ponsenby?"

His eyebrows leaped up his forehead.

"Funny. And wrong, thank Christ."

"What about . . . Milton?"

"Better, but no."

Why didn't he just fucking tell her, save them both the time and breath?

Where the next suggestion came from she didn't know, her mouth moving without any apparent intervention from conscious thought:

"*Taylor.*"

"Taylor . . ." It was as though he were tasting the word, swilling it around his mouth like a sip of wine. ". . . I like it. Owen Taylor."

Like? What did *like* matter? Names were given, imposed; not cherry-picked.

"So, what is it?"

He tilted her head back and kissed her, mouth tasting of wine and perverse promise.

*

She'd never understood why so many of the women she knew were so *afraid* of themselves. Even the most self purportedly liberated amongst them tended to flush and clam up when conversation turned to the subject of appetite, as if they were afraid of being struck down from on high for even daring to contemplate it.

Did they deny themselves in the bedroom too; afraid to demand what they wanted for fear of being branded strange or sluttish? Cynthia had long since learned to put aside such qualms, knowing that most men would gladly spill their little measure and leave without providing even the merest flicker of satisfaction in return.

Thank God for poetic souls.

He whispered as his lips moved over her, fragments of verse whose rhythm resonated through her flesh, inspiring nerve-endings to dance.

Occasionally, she felt teeth or the rasp of nails; the pain a welcome extreme of sensation that the day to day drudgery of existence too often denied.

No laughter, though. She wasn't in the mood for it. Instead, their play had all the quiet solemnity of religious ritual; every gasp a prayer, every sigh a hymn of transcendent joy.

Rolling him onto his back, she straddled him, no longer caring who or what he was, or about the tricks memory had begun to play. What did any of that matter next to this; the approbation that he was here and hers?

She cried out as he bucked beneath her, flinging her over and roughly grasping her wrists. It was more an expression of shock than pain; until now, he'd been content to let her lead their couplings. Now there was something brutal and demanding in his demeanour; a discord that was as much part of the symphony as its sweeter notes.

Smiling her appreciation of this unexpected turn, she became more violent in her own strokes, taking to the role of rape victim with surprising alacrity.

Owen, on the other hand, didn't seem quite so enamoured of the new play he'd initiated: His rhythm slowed as he began to tremble, the street lamp light streaming through the window illuminating features that were drawn and askew, as if he were suffering a seizure.

"O-Owen?"

Sliding out of her, he collapsed onto his back, gasping like a landed fish.

"Owen!"

He gripped her hand hard enough to hurt, eyes swimming with frustration.

"I'm okay . . ."

"What happened?"

"Nothing."

His abrupt withdrawal left her feeling cold and empty; the cradle of a snatched child. Sensing her dissatisfaction, he drew her up and onto himself, allowing her to envelop him up to the root. She was afraid to continue at first, fearing that she'd close her eyes in the throes of passion only to find that it was more than seed she'd coaxed from him when they opened again.

She needn't have worried. If anything, the momentary blip seemed to whet his appetite, mutual climax quickly following in which Cynthia temporarily retreated from herself, consciousness becoming an external mote orbiting her skull, carried on the waves of flesh's ecstasy.

Then she fell, the dark, damp and heat becoming tangible once more as she kissed her thanks upon his eyes and lips.

*

Sleep should've come easily following her exertions. Instead, she found herself fluttering between wakefulness and a series of fragile dreams, their strangeness counterpointed by incongruous banalities:

Whereas before the Fallen Angel she conjured was a child of sexual myth, promising transcendence through his prick's escapades, now he sat scratching his balls in front of the TV, braying moronically at the antics of cartoon cat and mouse. When her dream self—feeling a pang of maternal disapproval—flicked the TV off, the angel glared at her with adolescent resentment before taking flight through the open window, farting protest.

Another set her in the midst of an odious dinner party, her fellow diners all flayed and mutilated parodies of men and women, laughing as they compared wounds and swapped stories on how they'd come by them. To her right, a woman who lacked a lower jaw lapped at her wine with a prodigiously pierced tongue. Opposite sat a bloated man-mountain whose lips and eyelids had been peeled back and fixed in place with safety pins, nostrils split and stretched to resemble some blood-winged butterfly.

The dishes arrayed before them were equally bizarre, though this didn't stop her from tucking in with abandon:

A platter of human hearts, still steaming from the oven, was soon demolished, complemented by a side-salad of squirming, leech-like lengths that squealed as they were consumed. After, she enjoyed a dessert of fluttering wings, still in motion despite having being torn from their parent anatomy; attempting flight even as they slid whole down her gullet.

Cynthia jolted awake as the diners, finished with the fair provided, turned on one another.

*

She saw the door close behind Owen as he stepped out onto the landing, padding downstairs so silently he might've been just another dream.

Out of bed, hauling on discarded clothes, she crept to the top of the stairs in time to hear the front door ease shut.

No time to stop and think; she'd only talk herself out of it. Downstairs and out the front door in the space of a breath, the street outside utterly deserted, every window of every home dark and devoid of life.

The air was warm for this time of night, scented with the dirt and grime of suburbia. In the distance, she heard the clamour of a motorway in full early morning flow.

Running to the foot of the garden, she leaned over the gate, looking one way then the other, hoping to catch some sign of her fugitive lover.

Fuck it, she'd lost him . . .

There! Nothing much; a flicker of movement on the corner of Campbell Street. Opening the gate, she started down the path, hugging the ranks of conifers that kept her and her neighbours insulated from the outside world.

Her heart was a lunatic, hurling itself against the walls of its cell as if intent on either escape or suicide. Any second now he'd turn and notice her. She was too clumsy; too conscious of herself for these hide and seek shenanigans.

Except he didn't; standing, waiting, as if wanting her to follow.

Drawing closer, she saw him reach a trembling hand into his pocket and extract something . . . a cigarette? She'd never seen him smoke before; certainly wouldn't have allowed it in her presence.

Pressing herself into the dew-beaded conifers, she watched with gut-squirming fascination as he attempted to raise the cigarette to his lips, arm spasming as if in the throes of a grand mal that hadn't yet reached the rest of his body.

Breath coming in staccato whispers, he seemed to wretch at the cigarette's taste, though he refused to relinquish it.

Throwing back his head, he closed his eyes and inhaled.

Lowering his eyes back to the pavement, he raised his other hand, the lighter it gripped flaring. Now the convulsions gripped his entire body, giving Cynthia the uncomfortable impression of a heroin addict desperate for a fix.

The flame no more than grazed the cigarette's head before he collapsed to his knees, vomit audibly splashing the concrete. Cynthia was about to break cover when she noticed the figure staring at him from across the street.

Unlike Owen, who was still largely obscured by shadow, she stood in the full glow of the street lamp, intent on displaying her strangeness for all who cared to see.

She was young; no older than seventeen at the outside, though it was difficult to be certain what with the painted mask she wore. Her face was bisected in harlequin tones of black and white, each eye ringed by a star of contrary colour. Hair teased out in all manner of crazy twists and curls was strung with clashing coloured beads and what looked like fragments of broken mirror, her clothes similarly eclectic, apparently thrown together from whatever she could scavenge from charity-shop waste bins.

She stood watching Owen empty his stomach with feline curiosity, then started across the road, skipping as if to some melody snared in her thoughts.

Was this the secret, the reason he refused to reveal anything about himself?

Glancing up from his disgrace, he muttered something Cynthia couldn't make out, then the girl helped him to his feet, grinning as if about to burst into hysterics.

For all of her awkwardness and absurdity—characteristics that struck Cynthia as somehow contrived—the girl was undeniably sensual, every gesture calculated to arouse, like those of a lap dancer with pretensions to art.

On his feet now, though still unsteady, Owen shared some words that Cynthia couldn't catch, then followed in the girl's wake, glancing around like something afraid, something hunted.

*

She almost lost them several times when their route led them down unfamiliar streets and side roads. Whenever they strayed out of sight or she found herself in some unknown alley or cul-de-sac, a petulant voice piped up, urging her to turn and head back home. After all, was it really so vital that she learned what he did outside of her company? *Best to let sleeping dogs lie.* Another parroted portion of Mother's wisdom. She'd seen first-hand what happened to people who lived by that philosophy; they withered, crumbling 'til there was precious little left of self or certainty.

This neighbourhood was still part of the Fletcher Estate, but not one she recognized. By the look of the houses—all semi-detached affairs, boarded up and in extreme states of disrepair—it probably belonged to the older tenements that stood here before the city council decided to renovate the area. She'd assumed the properties had been demolished, or, like her own home, entirely refurbished as a means of attracting the young professionals—bankers, lawyers, play-writes—who formed the majority of her neighbours.

She expected one or both of them to turn and discover their pursuit with every step. If nothing else, they were sure to hear her breathing or the thunder of her heart. But no; they continued without any outward sign she was noticed, leading her so deep into the suburban labyrinth, she couldn't retrace her steps, even if she wanted to.

*

It looked no different from the sundry other derelict homes they'd passed, yet Owen and his companion stood staring up at its broken, blacked-out windows as if they were pilgrims come before the Vatican's gates.

Even from her current distance, the air of melancholy surrounding it was palpable, as if those who'd once made it the seat of their domestic dreams still lingered, silently railing against the life that denied their little ambitions.

Daring to approach a little closer, she saw the girl pick her nimble way through the front garden to the threshold. Owen started to follow, then hesitated, glaring up at the house as if it were a dragon with wide-open mouth.

The girl stopped and pirouetted on the spot, regarding him with open frustration. Closer now, hugging the shadows, Cynthia caught fragments of their exchange, the girl's voice a porn-star sigh of yearning:

"Are you coming or what?"

". . . don't know if . . ."

She strode back to him, taking his hand. Cynthia felt a flush of possessiveness, resisting the urge to break cover and demand that the girl put down her property.

"Do you . . . be free, or not?"

A clear ultimatum: either follow or go back home, to *her*. She was surprised that part of her favoured the former, urging him on so that she might follow and finally learn the truth.

He lingered for a moment longer, debating with himself, then stepped past the girl, head bowed as he made for the front door.

Cynthia waited until they disappeared inside, then ran to the front gate, assessing the windows for any sign of what might be occurring within. Her imagination yielded more; images of the two sharing needles, coupling atop filthy blankets in the dark. Moron paranoia, but no less disconcerting for that.

It'd be dawn in a few hours' time, then the world would wake, and all this . . . nothing more than a dream, fast fading from memory. The revelation caused her innards to writhe in urgency. There were things to do before the night ended, and sun-rise stole her chance.

The front door was ajar, a slogan scrawled across it in silver spray-paint: *I Am The Moon.*

She couldn't help but smile.

*

Dust tickled her sinuses, grime and rubble crunching underfoot. Vague shapes skittered across the walls, disturbed from midnight hunts or seductions by her trespass. There was graffiti in here too; designs and slogans littering walls and floor, most obscured beneath muck.

She'd been afraid since stepping out of her own front door. Now she was terrified.

Ahead, she could just make out the gaping dark of a doorway, second-hand street-lamp light revealing the ruins of a kitchen. An archway opened in the wall on her right, providing access to a sitting room, still complete with a small portable television and leather three-piece suite so strewn with dust and cob-webs, it was impossible to determine its original colour.

Stepping through, she saw that the TV screen had been smashed, a one-eyed doll's head placed in the cavity.

"Owen . . .?"

She jumped at the creak of footsteps from upstairs, wondering what the hell he was doing here; why she'd felt so compelled to follow.

Laughter; a sadistic child's giggle, as she herself once enjoyed watching a mouse twitch and struggle in the trap her dad had set for it.

Turning, she bit back a scream at the sight of a figure lingering in the archway. A boy, no older than fourteen or fifteen, dressed in torn jeans and a moth-eaten Led Zeppelin T-shirt. From what she could make out in the murk, he was well on his way to becoming a beauty; tussled, shoulder length hair so blonde it seemed to glow like moonlight, face finely sculpted and somehow feral, like that of a werewolf on the verge of transformation.

She couldn't make out what he had slung around his back; some sort of cape or blanket seemingly sewn from feathers . . . then the whole structure flexed and unfurled, flapping violently enough to stir up the dust carpeting the floor.

Wings.

Not a dream; she wouldn't let herself get away with that sort of bullshit. A boy with wings, feathers blacker than the surrounding night, decorated with coloured ribbons and costume jewellery He regarded her with unabashed curiosity, the frankness of his scrutiny—eyes lingering at her breasts and hips—jolting her from stupefaction.

"Hey, I'm up here."

He started and smiled, cheeks colouring

"Sorry. He said that I should come and get you, that you might be frightened. Are you?"

No purpose in lying; he'd been honest enough with her.

"A little. I . . . I've never seen . . ."

She nodded at his wings. He raised sickle-moon eyebrows, grinning.

"What, these?" He extended the appendages as far as the room would allow, their various decorations tinkling and chiming, filling the space with music.

"I've had 'em since forever. You can touch 'em, if you like."

The awkwardness of this school-yard seduction almost made her laugh out loud. She accepted, brushing the fingertips of her left hand—her painting hand—against the silken feathers. The boy laughed, clearly relishing the contact.

"Who are you?"

"My name's Corneille. We should go; they'll be waiting."

His urgency was infectious, her hunger for enlightenment flaring. Gesturing for her to follow, he wandered through to the hallway, starting up the ramshackle staircase to the second floor.

This went against every caution she'd ever been conditioned with; she'd likely be punished for straying from the path, in accordance with fairy-tale convention. But what did it matter now? She'd come seeking answers, and she'd have them, even if they had to be plucked from the Big Bad Wolf's throat.

*

Several doorways led off from the landing, one opening on what was once a bathroom, now a nursery for rats and cockroaches. Most of the others were closed fast.

Corneille brought them to a halt before one that seemed no more remarkable than the rest.

"This'll probably be pretty weird to you. Just remember: there's nothing here you haven't seen in dreams."

Without waiting for a reply, he swung the door open and stepped through.

Following, Cynthia found herself in a space that seemed far too large for the house to contain. Three of its four walls were of white plaster, each daubed over with a riot of symbols, verses and formulae, most too abstruse or crude in their recording -little more than child's crayon scrawls- to be interpreted; one or two familiar fragments; extracts of prayer and poetry she hadn't heard since her nursery days.

The fourth was dominated by evenly-spaced windows, the world they betrayed a far cry from the one she'd left on the doorstep. In the light of a swollen amber moon, dark trees stretched to distant mountains; a fairy-tale forest where wolves and goblins stalked, though with more than mere hunting and feeding on their minds. Tatters of carpet were laid out on the floorboards, providing some frugal comfort for the room's occupants. Corneille had told her there'd be strange things; his warning proved pitifully inadequate.

In one corner floated a compacted mass of gaseous forms, the vapour that constituted them throwing out flickering strobe light as they muttered a mixture of confessions and prophecies; curses and professions of love. Propped against the nearby wall was a creature that resembled descriptions of mermaids she'd come across; lower thighs melding into a mass of piscine scales, flickering with rainbow arcs as she trembled beneath her lover's caresses. The lover himself was a naked youth, hairless body painted in tattoos from head to toe. He turned to regard Cynthia as she entered, the lotus-like configurations of flesh blossoming in place of his eyes weeping nectar tears.

A group of what looked to be children clamoured at one window, the rainbow rags they wore partially concealing skin as dark as coal. They turned, muttering to one another as she was led past, empty eyes and mouths blazing as if stars burned in their skulls. The head of one had been shattered like a China doll's, the light spilling from within so bright she could barely stand it.

Corneille took her hand, sensing her hesitation.

"It's okay; nobody's going to harm you. It's forbidden."

Somehow she already knew that; it wasn't fear of harm that concerned her. Rather, it was the feeling she always had when entering new company; of being an outsider not entirely welcome, contrasted by the novel sensation that here were beings whose company she might relish rather than resent.

Despite Corneille's claims, there was definitely harm in some of them; the flayed and bleeding man who sat depriving himself of what skin remained via a collaboration of teeth and cut-throat razor; the star-fish thing whose multiple predator's eyes regarded her from within its barb-lined maws. Harm was as much part of them as it was part of the world, of humanity, of *her*; attractive in the way of nightmares or painted horrors.

Trembling, though not entirely with fear, she followed Corneille as he led her amongst this surreal congregation to a door set in the room's far wall. Some of those gathered addressed her as she passed, offering threats and seductions none of which she was given time to consider.

A woman sat waiting for them beside the doorway; the same who'd led her to this place, the aura of raw sexuality she exuded beating against Cynthia like rainforest humidity.

Rising from her squat, she looked Cynthia up and down before meeting her eye to eye. She felt the woman's criticism like ants swarming beneath her clothes, ready to sting and fill her with venom at the slightest provocation.

"*This* is her?"

Corneille nodded.

Cynthia was tired of feeling swept along by events, awe, terror and disbelief competing with a waxing desire for control.

"Where's Owen?"

The woman's painted features grew slack, the lustre draining from her eyes to reveal a wilderness of resentment.

"Where he wants to be. Or do you think that he still belongs to you?"

A surge of childish possessiveness, as if she'd been forced to share a favourite toy.

He *did* belong to her.

Corneille stepped to her defence before she could reply, eager to diffuse the situation.

"Johanna said she'd come, remember?"

Uncertainty flickered behind the mask, contempt re-asserting itself in a heartbeat.

"She's no different from the rest; she'd break the world to make it be what she wants."

The accusation stung, flaying away the barriers and self-deceits she'd constructed over the years, exposing all that she most loved and hated in herself. She was about to respond in a manner that wasn't quite so eloquent when the door creaked open, disgorging the spectre of her heart's desire.

*

The contradiction of feeling in his eyes was impossible for her to meet. In the few seconds she could stand it, she saw love and hunger; pain, restraint, suffering; she the author of them all; of everything within him, the burden of it unbearable.

He fell, the woman and Corneille moving to support him, red blossoming across his shirt.

"Oh god, Owen . . ."

She started forward, wanting to wrap her arms around him and soothe him with a lover's lullaby. She stopped dead as convulsions gripped him, bloody spit seeping through his clenched teeth.

"What the fuck have you done to him?"

Corneille looked up at her, shocked, hurt. From behind, a child's laughter, muted mutters. The skinless man answered, thick Texan drawl a bad John Wayne parody:

"Nothin' to do with anyone here, darlin'. You might wanna take a good look in the mirror before throwin' that kind of shit around."

He grinned at her, peeling the last sliver of skin from one of his fingers. What the fuck did he mean, that she was somehow responsible for this? She loved Owen; she'd never knowingly hurt him . . .

Going to him, she ran fingers down his cheek, feeling the febrile tremors that racked his flesh.

"It's okay," she reassured him, "I'm taking you home."

His eyes rolled back in their sockets as he slumped, boneless as a scarecrow in his bearer's arms. Carrying him across the room, Corneille and the painted girl laid him down against the far wall, the latter stroking his brow in a manner that made Cynthia want to snap her sparrow-neck.

Returning to her, Corneille took her once again by the hand, seeming on the brink of tears. She didn't need any further insistence; there was no way she was leaving without meeting the one responsible for this.

Sensing her determination, he led her silently towards the door, opening it one-handed before flitting aside.

Apparently she had to make her own way from here on.

She didn't dare turn or waste breath on goodbyes, knowing that she'd never leave him if she did. Closing her eyes, she exhaled, the breath seeming to coalesce in the darkness beyond the doorway, streaming in her wake as snakes of living vapour, growing more solid the further they coiled.

Allowing them to draw her by the umbilici still anchored in her throat, she stepped out into nothingness, teeth severing the unseen reigns as the world dissolved, becoming a cosmic crazy house in whose mirrors she saw herself distorted in all the ways imagination could contrive . . .

*

A rush of vertigo, then she was on her knees in itchy, threadbare carpet, retching on a throat full of dust and sour perfume. Music, so jumpy and distorted it was impossible to tell if it was Mozart or Metallica. She screamed, leaped back as something brushed past her face, the cat glaring at her with eyes as cold as a whore's kiss.

"*Roland.*" A girl's voice, the cat answering its summons with theatrical reluctance.

Not yet ready to test her legs, she scrabbled into a sitting position, her back against a door now firmly closed.

She knew this room; it was of the kind her parents maintained for her at what they insisted on calling "Back Home;" a stagnant temple to forgotten times; a Child-Goddess who no longer existed, save in the memories of its keepers.

Walls cracked and stained with fungal rot wore dog-eared posters of singers and rock bands long since sold out or faded into obscurity. Her eyes lingered over etiolated images of Mick Jagger, Michael Jackson and David Bowie before straying to the toys, books and sundry flotsam littering the floor:

None of the toys were typical girl's fair; no prams, nurses sets or dollies. She plucked up a plastic skeleton whose bones were designed to look entirely authentic, the plastic sword it wielded boasting a small button that caused the blade to flash red.

"It's all right," the voice insisted, "you can play with them if you like."

The bed was an incongruous fixture; a gothic, four poster affair, stained-oak frame carved with faces and figures torn directly from the works of Hieronymous Bosch. But whereas Bosch was preoccupied with torment, here acts of brutality, carnality and scenes of abstruse surrealism were near indistinguishable, akin to carvings she'd once seen on a Tantric temple in India:

A harem of semi-naked gorgons, disporting with the statues they'd made of potential suitors, a flock of winged demons harassing the throngs of lovers below, swooping down to tear at exposed, sweating backs with crotch-mounted beaks.

For all the room's sensory detail, part of her insisted it wasn't quite *solid,* as if its scents and textures were little more than the conjurations of some mind-altering drug.

Shrugging off the strange lethargy weaving itself about her, she used the door at her back to lever herself upright.

A series of net curtains were strung between the bed's posts like the webs of some self-conscious spider. A girl sat atop the covers beyond, simple blue dress clinging to a frame skinny to the point of under nourishment. Long pale hair cascaded over her shoulders, hanging in lank streamers over her face. The cat settled itself in her lap, purring as she scratched its chin.

Meeting Cynthia's scrutiny, she raised a curious eyebrow.

"You've swam there, haven't you?"

Cynthia was momentarily thrown by the question, mouth opening in instinctive denial before memory betrayed her:

Black waters flowing around and within, light burning in their depths . . .

"Just a dream . . ."

Smiling, teeth seeming to flash sharp and silver in the murk, the girl plucked up her cat by the scruff of its neck, its yowls of protests becoming strangled croaks as convulsions racked its frame. Cyn watched, stupefied, as its pelt burgeoned and split, spilling embers that became fiery winged butterflies as they rose towards the ceiling. One eye bulged, popping from its socket, something that resembled a hybrid between squid and praying mantis unfurling from within.

"Just a dream," the girl repeated, regarding her with the expectancy of a patient teacher waiting for comprehension to dawn over her pupil.

Cynthia didn't need it spelling out for her. Bending, she plucked up a toy from the floor: a naked Action Man, head and torso rent with tooth marks that resembled poorly healed battle wounds.

She knew how this was supposed to go. In her mind, she was back home; sealed away in The Cave, brush bleeding colour across the canvas. She held it, saw its intentions, but didn't attempt to guide it. That would only result in still-birth, or something so deformed as to require abortion. She almost fumbled when she felt the plastic shift beneath her fingers, but held onto the thread as it elaborated, becoming a tapestry . . .

Its first breath came with a song like sparrows greeting the dawn, multiple heads coiling around her wrists to form a living bracelet. Iridescent parrot's wings beat along its length, shedding feathers that cast ripples across the carpet, as if it were a reflection in a placid pool.

The remains of the cat gone to golden dust in her hand, Johannah smiled approval, Cynthia smiling back, 'til she felt needle fangs bury themselves in her wrist.

"Fuck!"

She ripped her suckling creation away, flinging it against the wall in temper. It shattered as if shaped from crystal, the shards growing fleshy as they descended to the carpet, crawling away like shimmering worms and maggots.

Johannah no longer smiled.

Examining her wrist, she found blood seeping from several puncture marks.

"Why?"

"You think just because you *make* something it belongs to you?" The girl's voice suddenly sounded that of a woman twice her age.

A sudden flush of anger; that of a child caught out in its own petulance. Arguments boiled and buzzed like hornets in her mouth, falling dead the instant she made to release them.

Taking her silence as defiance, Johannah sighed, a faint, chill breeze distressing the air.

"Who the hell are you?"

"A dreamer, like you. I swam there too, a long time ago. I've been worshipped; wars have been fought in my name. Can you imagine that?"

She could, all too well:

She pictured herself naked and ornamented atop a vast, gold altar, surrounded by offerings from her faithful. All around, men and boys of the most striking beauty rutted and pleasured one another in her honour, falling on one another in cannibalistic frenzy at the point of climax.

It could be, if she so desired; she could bathe daily in blood and honey, remaining forever young, beautiful and adored. But how long before she grew weary of her divinity? A decade, a century? What would she do when worship and sacrifice no longer sustained, when she realised the martyrdoms she inspired were all for nothing?

"Precisely," Johannah confirmed, apparently seeing her thoughts like pictures on a TV screen. "That was why I returned to the Dream Sea, *remade* myself." She sighed again, the sound hitching, almost orgasmic. The figures decorating her bed became animated, shifting and writhing, faint moans echoing from the wood. "You have no idea . . . no idea how *glorious* it is . . . to be *myth*."

Cyn started as a rent coruscated up the left hand wall and across the ceiling, silvery sand pouring through.

"Owen has a place with us, if he so chooses, but he won't take it on his own. He needs you to show him how."

The crack widened, dust raining down as the room split in two. Looking down into the chasm barely inches before her feet, Cynthia saw a swirling delirium; an abyss of light and conflicting colour in which shoals of ephemeral forms swam.

She felt reason slipping—the pebble that precipitates a landslide—balance dissolving.

"What . . . what do I do?" she slurred.

Johannah's voice in her ear; a lover's lying beside her in the dark:

"Let him go."

She fell, screaming denials even as she tumbled into madness.

*

A cliché she'd determined never to inhabit: the couple whose unspoken secrets corroded all that they shared from within.

She'd seen it a million times amongst family and friends; something jagged lodged beneath smiling façades, tearing fresh wounds with every artificial kiss and touch, slowly festering.

The first time she worked up courage enough to broach the subject—some three days following his midnight flit—his face grew ashen and he rushed to the toilet, vomiting 'til there was nothing to expel but stinking air. Other than that, they continued as tradition dictated; laughing, fucking, occasionally brawling.

Sometimes he disappeared for a day or two, returning rejuvenated, but different; temporarily more inclined to rebellion. She tolerated this like a Mother whose offspring's abhorrent behaviour was the result of some psychosis or medical condition.

She painted, letting commissions go to seed whilst preoccupying herself with more personal projects:

An anatomic cathedral; buttresses of bone, doors and windows screaming mouths or sphincter-like apertures, spires of grasping arms and rigid cocks thrusting heavenward; an angel performing auto-fellatio in mid flight.

Perhaps the most telling of all came in an afternoon of part conscious creative frenzy, the rhythm of rain against roof and windows lulling her into shamanistic fugue:

A Bitch-Goddess in the form of a vast Hydra, its many faces -all facsimiles of the same- smiling evil self satisfaction as it clutched a naked man to its breast, his expression caught somewhere between rapture and torment in the midst of suckling.

*

She was awake when he left that night, awake when he returned. The lovemaking that preceded had left her sore all over, covered in minor bites and scratches whose infliction she demanded.

He slipped into bed next to her without a word. What was it she expected? A full confession of the lessons he'd learned at Johannah's knee? His silence was sufficient protest. *I live a life outside of you,* it proclaimed, *a life you would've denied me.*

What defence did she have against that? It was the truth; accurate in every barbed detail.

She wanted him so much, wanted to *envelope* him, for their bodies to melt and run together like molten wax.

He trembled beside her, consciously resisting the urge to comply. All she had to do was speak, command him to touch her, kiss her, and he'd do so with a smile, genuine joy at purpose fulfilled competing with an oh so human desire for something more, until he tore himself in two, and she lost him regardless.

Even if he somehow managed to suppress his rebelliousness, what would that mean? That loving her equated to slavery, its subject withering to nothing for all she cared so long as it did so in her arms.

"Go."

Barely a whisper, but sufficient to quell his convulsions and let him breathe easy again. He left without questioning the command. She was glad.

*

She lay awake in the dark 'til the first furtive tendrils of dawn seeped into the room. Then she closed her eyes, no longer wishing to see the world and its emptiness.

A dreamer like you. That's what she proclaimed to be; one who'd turned her creative potential *inward*, on herself.

Could Cynthia do likewise? If she couldn't, if she found herself waking to the same stinking skin in the same stinking, empty bed, it wouldn't be long before she attempted some self sculpting with more conventional tools.

She laughed as the waters coalesced around her, opening her eyes in time to see them close overhead, sealing her off from the sunlit world, until she was ready to walk there anew.

BELLY OF THE BEAST

Trapped in the belly of the beast, Poppy fended off smiles and congratulations as she was slowly digested.

"You must be over the moon."

"You've done well for yourself love, no doubt about it."

She smiled back, thanked them all, screaming so loud behind her eyes, her brain rattled in its cell.

Not long now; she felt herself slipping, dissolving as the world danced; sang, insisted on how happy she should be.

She was a beast too, after all, only the thing in *her* belly was growing rather than withering, almost ready to burst out and devour what remained of her life. Even now it stirred, restless, hungering.

Sipping at her champagne—a drink she hated, but felt obliged to endure given the occasion—she imagined herself crumbling inside her dress, becoming dust that would be carried on the air into the throats and lungs of those around her; the seeds of cancers that would laugh as they devoured their hosts from the inside out.

"Enjoying yourself? You seem a bit off."

Simon, sweeter than honey-wine, ten times as cloying. It was his face, all smiles and concern, that the beast wore while it ate.

"Fine. Just can't quite believe it's all real yet."

He grinned, leaning in to kiss her.

She'd said yes; deserved to be swallowed up, because she was weak.

"Have you thought any more about . . .?"

"We've still got seven months yet. No need to rush things, is there?"

He smiled, nodded, though she caught the anger that momentarily darkened his eyes.

"I'll just be a minute; too much champagne."

*

She hadn't cried when she was thrown up in the air by a speeding Ford as a kid, shattering her shoulder; didn't cry when she found her grandmother grey-faced and not breathing in bed. She'd be damned if she was going to cry now.

A few cubicles across, she heard the grunts and giggles of a pair doing what wedding receptions were made for. The girl—sister-in-law Sadie by the sound of things—had no need to fake her ecstasy, her partner knowing his way around a woman's body better than any Poppy had ever known.

"Oh, oh Jesus . . . you're so *filthy*."

Laughter.

The fact that the girl was barely fifteen didn't concern her; she was old and worldly wise enough to know *exactly* what she was doing.

She didn't know why she'd brought the knife. It was just reassuring to have around, safe and secret. She unsheathed it now, watched its teeth glimmer in the weak light. Steak was on the menu at Simon's insistence. She'd made out that her place hadn't been set properly, received another knife, and ate with the gusto of a prisoner on death row.

Was that it . . .? Little Red Riding Hood, devoured, but needing no Woodcutter to slice her way out of the Big Bad Wolf's belly . . .

*

White. She never wanted white. White was ice, cold, candle wax.

She wasn't the white bride any longer. All eyes on her as she returned to the reception hall, the myriad banalities, arguments, seductions all ceasing, leaving only the music.

"*And you know I'd do most anything you want . . .*"

She loved this song.

Somebody screamed. People rose, gasping, screams. Simon stayed seated, staring, puppet-eyed . . .

*

Not bad, as that sort of thing went; more modern than he might've liked, but at least somewhat believable. For Bellamy, the absurdities came after; the little personal additions that people had tacked on to the mythology over the years.

But the opening . . . that was money in the bank.

There was already trouble with the studio, of course. They didn't like the idea that the bride was pregnant, or the detail of the couple fucking whilst she went to work on herself. Some retard who even *sounded* like he was wearing a suit called to ask if there could be some sort of back-story for the bride: ". . . you know, maybe she had an affair before the wedding. Maybe the baby's someone else's?"

He explained calmly, clearly why that wouldn't work. The decision would likely be taken out of his hands anyway. They wanted to know how the rest would pan out. He fobbed them off with some bullshit about a rough draft being done by the end of the week.

They hung up.

*

The story had to be stretched and padded for cinema; a little drama added to make the myth more palatable. Bellamy didn't like it; if he had his way, he'd shoot the thing as a schizophrenic art-house montage of the tale's various incarnations, let the audience make up their own damn minds. Hollywood, he'd found, didn't like the idea that audiences had minds to make up.

He was nervous, not knowing how to broach the subject without coming off as heartless or perverse.

"Mr. Bellamy?"

Considering what the man had gone through, he'd expected someone more . . . *traumatised.*

Simon Diggory, the kind of man you just got along with. Something about his face, Bellamy decided later; as if he wore everything he felt and thought for the whole world to see, concealment or deceit impossible.

Without waiting for an answer, the man pulled up a chair and offered his hand. Bellamy accepted, feeling a tingle at the thought that those hands had touched The Bride herself.

"It's Bill, if you please . . ."

"Bill Bellamy? I like it. I'm Simon." Rosy cheeked and star-eyed; the man-child who the world obliged, simply for the boon of existing.

"So, you want to talk about Poppy, yes? What're you doing, writing a book or something?"

"A film-script actually, you know, about the myth . . ."

"Yeah, funny how these things start, isn't it? I mean, for me, it's like it happened yesterday, but to hear people speak, you'd think the story had been around for hundreds of years."

"I understand it might be . . . difficult . . ."

The man held up his hand, sighing in frustration.

"Let me stop you there, Bill. I know you're trying to spare my feelings, but really, there's no need. All that stuff with Poppy . . . it's done with. I've got my own life to live now, and I don't have any problems talking about it.

If you want to ask something, ask it, and don't bother with all the bullshit, okay?"

Bellamy was at once shocked and relieved. Englishmen didn't tend to wear their hearts on their sleeves in his experience, at least not until they'd gotten a bottle of wine or two down their throats.

"Okay, what I really need to know is what happened after the whole . . . wedding reception thing. I've studied some of the news reports. They all say Poppy died en route to the hospital . . ."

Simon blinked, smiled; eyes swimming with the promise of revelation.

"But the stories say different, yes?"

Bellamy didn't like this; he felt like he was being toyed with, strung along.

"Well, they're bound to, aren't they? I want to know what *really* happened."

Simon sniffed, closing his eyes as if preparing to explain some hideously complex concept to a child, or an idiot.

"You ever read thc bible, Bill?"

Oh Christ, if this was going to turn into a sermon, he was out of here.

"Not really. I know some of the stories . . ."

"You believe any of them?"

"What? The Ark, Moses, all that stuff? No, I mean, they're just *stories.* Maybe some of them are based on things that actually happened, but . . ."

"Exactly. Just *stories,* myths. Anyone with even half an ounce of sense can see that, right? But what people don't get is: it's the stories that *matter.* The truth can take a flying fuck, if you'll pardon my French."

Bellamy sighed.

"Look, I'm not trying to be rude or anything, but what's this got to do with Poppy?"

Simon laughed, shook his head. Bellamy had a sudden image of the man in a mental asylum, swapping philosophy with invisible friends.

"Sorry. I'm not being terribly clear. Here."

He plucked up a napkin, scribbling something down on it with obsessive precision.

"What's this?"

Simon was already out of his seat, slipping on his coat, obviously eager to be away from the confrontation.

"I've got to go. Sorry I can't be more help."

He was up and out the café door, lost to the human tides sweeping by outside before Bellamy could give chase.

*

He'd never particularly liked London. Most of the time, he felt like a ghost here; just another one of the teeming masses of humanity trying to claw its way to significance. People didn't even notice you unless you walked directly into them or had something they wanted. It was easy to feel yourself dissolving after too much time in the city; as if a sharp breeze or bump might cause your skull to burst, leaving you to spill away with the sewage in the gutters.

But there was inspiration aplenty. If he wanted to find a story, all he had to do was step outside his front door, hang around one of the local pubs or cafés and simply pluck one from the swarms in the air.

That's how he first heard about The Blood Bride; from the lips of some drunken story-teller, the fragments of narrative he spewed interspersed by comic observations on what a lucky escape her would-be husband had. The internet provided more specific accounts, but his favourite versions came from school-yards and street corners; the gossip of friends of friends.

Urban myths were always fairly prominent subjects in written fiction, but his various failed attempts at short stories and fragmentary novels were testament to the fact that he had no penchant for that particular medium. TV and cinema, by contrast, were less static beasts; shedding coats and shifting shapes in direct response to culture's paranoia and preoccupations. He'd cut his teeth on *Barker's Hill,* a TV series he penned in his mid-twenties, living out of his old bedroom at his parents' house during the slump that followed his student years. He never expected it to take off, still couldn't quite believe it'd been purchased and produced even when it was on air, hour-long episodes filling slots from 11:00P.M. to 12:00P.M., gradually gravitating towards prime-time as its popularity waxed.

He'd found it heartening to realise that the British public's appetite for anything stranger than *Doctor Who* wasn't quite so impoverished as he'd presumed.

On the back of this success—not to mention the infamy the show garnered thanks to the muck-slinging from certain moral quarters—he was able to make the leap to the big screen, penning several movies—*The Elder Wyrm, Dead Man Walking, Hieronymous*—that'd been picked up by burgeoning home-grown studios.

This was the first time he'd ever worked with a Hollywood studio and, considering the experience thus far, likely his last.

He wanted the final product to be as close to perfect as humanly possible. He'd promised himself from the very beginning that, if it turned out to be a dog, it certainly wouldn't be due to a bad script.

Maybe that was why he was here now, wandering unfamiliar and quietly hostile streets in rain that hammered down like bullets from Heaven; parts of London the rest of the city had simply forgotten; left in suburban stasis whilst surrounding districts were expanded, renovated or demolished. Ugly rows of squalid, dark brick terraces punctuated by occasional three-story town houses, the latter mostly boarded up or in serious states of disrepair. Net curtains fluttered as he passed by, making him feel conspicuous as a transvestite blundered into the midst of a Baptist congregation.

He encountered one or two residents as he searched for the address Diggory had written down; a weary-eyed mother pushing a fat, gurgling infant in its water-proof baby-buggy, a shuffling man in nylon tracksuit who glared at him from beneath his cap, looking terrified at the prospect of being addressed. All of them radiated a kind of frightened repulsiveness, as if they'd rather slit their own throats than stand and talk with him, all fantastic; characters that could've easily flattered the pages of *Barker's Hill* or any one of the film scripts he'd penned. By the time he blundered into the right neighbourhood, he'd already composed several scenes in his head, visualizing as the camera would, hearing the character's voices like ghosts whispering in his ear.

The Holden Estate; the kind of area tour guides warned holiday-makers from venturing into, hardly a wall in the place that didn't boast a crop of cemented-on nails and glass shards, not a single building without at least one window smashed, boarded up or blacked out. Every surface was decorated with a surfeit of graffiti, most of it the usual moron marking or obscenity: *Goz Woz Ere '98, Shelley Winters Sucked My Clit April '01*, some strange or absurd enough to raise a smile:

Fungus is my Friend

Christ was a Carpenter.

I Am The Moon.

He had no doubt one of these would resurface as the script's final title, if he ever finished it.

A labyrinth, the grey pall that pervaded eroding distinction, making every street, alley and cul-de-sac an echo of those already trodden. Headlines flashed behind his eyes as he picked up his pace, hoping he might wander into some familiar neighbourhood:

Local Writer Beaten To Death!

Horror Story: Slasher Film Scribe Murdered!

He stifled a yelp when the kid first spoke, waiting for the prick of a knife at his back or belly.

"'Scuse me, mate . . .?"

Sometimes saviours came in unlikely forms. This one was a reject from a Tim Burton movie; wiry frame wrapped around in a unisex frock of black lace, oily dark hair framing features that looked more skeleton than skin. Later, Bellamy realised the kid was slathered in more make-up than a clown, the vampire aesthetic achieved through what must've been hours of self modification.

"Yeah?" Perhaps a bit more brusque than he intended, but the fright had made him pissy.

"Looking for anywhere in particular?"

Ah, a have-a-go-guide. His writer's imagination pictured the kid leading him down some darkened alley where his friends would be waiting with knives, hammers and syringes filled with H.I.V. infected blood. Moron paranoia, but no less unsettling for that.

Reaching into his pocket, he extracted a tenner; a little insurance against potential harm.

"Yeah, I'm looking for a place called Ogden Heights. You know it?"

The kid eyed the ten pound note like it was a star Bellamy had reached up and plucked from the sky. He blinked, looked him full in the face, pupils swimming.

"Yeah, I know it. Why'd you wanna go there though, man? Place is a *shit-hole*."

Bellamy didn't have a straight answer to that.

"There's somebody there I'm supposed to meet."

A sly look came over the boy's painted face.

"Oh, right. I gotcha. Yeah, I can take you there, if you like."

Bellamy offered him the tenner, which disappeared before he had time to blink.

*

The boy, whose name was Jake, chattered incessantly as he led them through the warren of tenements, industrial estates and parkland. Bellamy didn't contribute much to the conversation save to "um" and "ah" in the appropriate places, which was apparently fine by Jake.

". . . fucking hole of a place to live, but you get used to things. Ogden Heights, huh? Me Mam used to know a woman who lived up there. Some fuckers broke into her flat, beat the living shit out of her. She was pregnant too. Baby didn't make it, of course. Poor little bastard . . ."

Bellamy absorbed all of this as a whale sifted nutrients from the sea, letting the details foment into the stuff of story in his mind.

The Heights were the kind of suburban carbuncle sprouted up throughout the 1960s; a monolith seemingly designed as much to corrode the souls of its inhabitants as shelter their flesh from the elements:

Derelict, exterior strewn with abandoned scaffolding, bounded by a barrier of wire fencing most of which had been cut or torn through by those bafflingly seeking trespass. Even from across the street, he could see that what once passed as the foyer was black with filth and fire damage, trash and rubble carpeting its floor, no doubt a haven for rats, cockroaches and all manner of vermin.

What the hell was Diggory playing at, sending him to this pit?

"Hang on, are you sure this is the place?"

Jake shrugged.

"Only Ogden's Heights I know of, mate. Read the sign."

Though half of it was missing, the rest obscured by grime and rust, the fragments: ". . . den's Heig . . ." were clearly legible.

A descending sensation in the pit of his stomach, as if thc organs in the area were attempting to vacate by the nearest exit. Sadly, Diggory wasn't here to bear the brunt of his frustration, but someone was.

"Why in god's name did you bring me here?"

"Errr, because you asked me to man, remember?"

The boy didn't seem at all phased by his escalating fury, smirk suggesting there was little Bellamy could do to crack his façade of indifference.

"But when I said I had to meet somebody . . ."

"Oh yeah," He laughed. "I thought you meant, you know, there was something you wanted. You ain't bad lookin', reckon I could show you some stuff, if you're up for it."

Bellamy shuddered at a sudden image of the boy's naked, cancer-victim's frame writhing beneath him. Sometimes imagination was the enemy; a friend that smiled even as it slid its knife into his back.

"Get the fuck away from me."

"Look, I'm sorry man, I just got the wrong idea . . ."

"I don't give a shit."

He stood staring at the building for what felt like an hour or more, willing it to be other than it was; to throw up something he could *use* . . .

"Listen, you don't want to hang around here too long, mate. Things happen to people."

Cold, soaked to the bone; legs aching, head throbbing; the ground could split and swallow him on the spot, and he'd consider it a fitting end to this wasted, shit-smear of a day.

"You ever hear any stories about the Blood Bride, Jake?"

The boy looked wary, as if suddenly realising he was in the company of a crazy man.

"Them the ones about the woman who kills herself after she gets married? Yeah, I heard a couple of 'em. Why?"

Bellamy pinched the bridge of his nose, laughed.

"She's who I came to meet."

*

Moronic; the most brainless, dangerous thing he'd ever done. Jake, self elected his new sense of caution, was only too happy to tell him so:

"You're fucking mental, mate! You're gonna end up dead, wandering around this place!"

Why the boy felt obliged to follow in his apparent insanity was beyond him. Maybe he hoped there'd be more money somewhere along the way, or perhaps it was some form of professional pride. Whatever the case, he was never far from Bellamy's heels as he ascended through the rot and rubble, chasing a phantom that perpetually lingered around the next corner, up the next flight of stairs. He *knew* he saw it, even if the glimpses were momentary; flashes of white and arterial scarlet, whispers of lace, like a bridal train dragged through the dirt. Maybe he was mad; maybe the day's disappointments and frustrations were taking their toll, but one way or another, he was taking something away from this, even if it was only the thrill of trespass.

The place stank as bad as any man-made structure could; the detritus and congealed remains of food beneath his feet mingling with faeces, blackened rags, shit-soiled underwear, condoms and the corpses of rats.

A staircase that wound up through the building like a diseased spine wasn't much more sanitary, but it was up this the phantom fled, her footsteps echoing somewhere above.

Graffiti on the walls, designs and slogans his eye caught on the fly; not idle scrawls or obscenities, but compositions that wouldn't have been out of place in a modern art gallery: one entirely covered by the image of a pagan Madonna, floating splay-legged in subterranean darkness as she rained milk and menstrual blood into the open mouths of her worshippers, another depicting a naked androgyne who sat cross-legged against a sky-blue firmament, dreams erupting from its shaved-bald scalp in gyres and spirals of lunatic colour

Further distractions presented themselves at each floor. Maybe it was just a product of his agitated state of mind, or perhaps hours wandering in the freezing rain had resulted in a hallucinatory fever; whatever the case, he *saw* things in those secluded cloisters; phenomena far beyond what rats and their fellow vermin could produce:

Walls that seemed to pulse like those of a gullet or womb in the throes of labour, rooms and corridors that seethed as if swarming with untold legions of insects; a biblical plague waiting for the divine call to apocalypse. Every so often, he thought he caught glimpses of the Bride's train on the stairs; flickers of satin white striated red, disappearing in the blink of an eye.

At the sixth floor landing, he halted, lungs burning, legs leaden. A boy lay propped against the wall amongst a litter of self-rolled cigarettes and chocolate bar wrappers. He was about Jake's age, dressed in a variation of the same gothic garb. Was he breathing?

"Jesus . . ."

Bellamy felt a sudden urge to leave and forget this whole sorry endeavour If he stayed, and the kid turned out to be dead, he was going to have to explain his presence here in the company of a possible rent-boy.

Pushing past, Jake knelt at the boy's side, smoothing the hair from his brow with a tender hand, gently tilting back his head.

They both flinched back as the boy sighed, eyes partially flickering open to reveal bloodshot whites.

"We should call an ambulance or something."

Jake grinned, looking for all the world like a monkey attempting to intimidate a potential rival.

"Nah, you see this sort of thing all the time round 'ere. He just needs some time to sleep it off . . ."

The boy spasmed, head jerking back against the wall. A strangled gurgling came from his partially opened lips, without doubt the most vile sound Bellamy had ever heard.

"Jesus, what's the matter with the fucker?"

Bellamy didn't know what to do; the most experience he had with this sort of thing was the shit he'd presumed or made up when one of his scripts called for a medical situation. Jake eyed the mobile phone he produced as if it were the holiest of holies, but it was too little, too late. The boy abruptly grew still, head drooping on his chest. Something dropped from his fingers, rolling on the filth strewn floor.

A blue pastel, worn down to little more than a nub.

"Shit, I think he's dead, mate . . ."

Bellamy felt ashen, hollow, but also strangely relieved. There was nothing he could do now; responsibility had been taken out of his hands.

The singing ran corpse-cold fingers up his spine. Jake's eyes widened, looking about to start out of their sockets.

"Okay, that's it mate; I'm off . . ."

Two ten pound notes flashed in Bellamy's hand, stopping the boy in his tracks.

Children's voices, like a school choir practising for a nativity play. He couldn't make out the song, but its simple, see-saw rhythm was unmistakeably nursery-rhyme.

"It's just kids, Jake. Don't you want to know what the hell's going on here?"

The boy licked his lips, eyes darting around as if following invisible butterflies through the air.

"Maybe . . . for another tenner?"

"Fine."

He gave the boy twenty.

*

The sixth floor wasn't so dark as the others. Someone had set candles to burn on various plates and shards of pottery, the uneasy shadows they cast animating the graffiti decorating every surface. Beneath their feet was a floor painted to resemble a red river in which all manner of monstrosities swam: a banded snake with the head of a human child gazed up at him, reptile eyes cold and threatening as the smile it wore, a shoal of naked women, skin scaly and iridescent, swam together in overtly sexual communion, expressions ecstatic, prompting Bellamy to wonder what it'd be like to drown amongst them, letting the water flood his lungs with a smile.

Cleverly, the artist had made it seem as though the waters were lapping against the corridor walls as they might the faces of cliffs. Clinging to them were creatures that had pulled themselves from the depths, piscine anatomies shifting to accommodate their new environment. One of the fish-women who'd grown weary of her sister's sexual play splayed out lizard like across one section, a clutch of young scurrying across her back and hanging from her hair. Elsewhere, creatures resembling flayed, many-armed monkeys fought one another for space, flinging those too weak to defend their claims down into the waters below.

This wasn't just graffiti; this was *art;* the work of some anonymous prodigy uninterested in making a name for him (or her) self, or even in the judgement of eyes other than their own.

Jake offered no comment.

The singing was louder now, but no more distinct. He couldn't make out individual words, as if the singers themselves didn't know the lyrics, content to simply grunt or murmur along with the tune.

Most of the doors they passed were open or had long since rotted off their hinges, the spaces beyond dark, lit only by the candle's second-hand luminescence, but occasionally Bellamy caught flickers of movement, most likely some tramp or squatter hiding in the shadows, eager not to be seen.

"We shouldn't be in here, man. You know what kind of psychos might be in this place?"

Bellamy didn't answer, not willing to let his thoughts stray down that path.

*

It was the first room they came across whose door was intact. The design covering its every inch made Bellamy's head swim and bowels churn, scouring his senses with the immediacy of music:

A woman, voluptuous form seemingly sculpted from the static waters that raged beneath his feet. Just as it birthed her, so too was she the river's source; her eyes weeping it, breasts lactating it; a menstrual spring flowing from between her legs. Throughout her translucent body swam shoals of the river's denizens; fish things, snake things; glittering motes of unfinished life.

Bellamy's experience of the holy was impoverished to say the least; natural born atheist that he was, he had difficulty conceiving of any spiritual state that might occur outside the point of orgasm, or the rush of pride upon seeing one of his works brought to life on-screen.

Here, he tasted some semblance of what the faithful felt before images of their Madonnas and Messiahs, shorn of idiot fear and dogmatic dictate to become something purer, more transient; the closest he'd ever come to feeling God at work in the world.

"Fucking hell . . . you ever see anything like that?"

Bellamy resisted the urge to throttle the kid as the spell of revelation burst.

"No, not ever."

Stepping forward, he opened the door.

*

The interior was lit by the same guttering orange glow as the corridor, candles littering every surface, set amongst the rubble and refuse as if they were holy relics in a church. Beetles and spiders scurried away across the walls and floor before his footsteps. To his right, a doorway led to what might've once been a kitchen, the stink of mouldering food turning his stomach.

A child sat amidst the detritus, dress seemingly sewn from rags and tatters pilfered from charity shop rubbish bins. She held a fat brown house spider in her up-turned palm, singing to it as she might a doll or baby brother. She looked up through a mask of grime and paint as Bellamy lingered in the doorway, eyes narrowing in suspicion.

Bellamy wasn't good with kids at the best of times. Now he stood in mute indecision, an uncertain smile flickering on his lips as he fumbled for something to say.

"Are you here to sing, too?"

It sounded like she doubted it, and didn't think it a necessarily good thing if he was.

"No, I'm . . . what's your name?"

She shrugged.

"What's yours?"

"I'm Bill . . ."

"I'm Sally. This is Gemma. Say hello, Gemma."

The spider scuttled from her palm to the back of her hand, the sensation making her giggle.

"What're you doing here, Sally? Where're your mom and dad?"

She sighed, face becoming a mask of adult exasperation. Lowering the spider to the floor, she rose and batted some of the grime from her dress. Bellamy instinctively stepped back as she approached, imagination regurgitating every knife-wielding child psychopath he'd come across in slasher films and bad horror fiction.

She eased by without so much as a second glance, skipping down the hallway to where the singing originated.

*

People lived here, once. The reality of it hadn't dawned on Bellamy 'til now. The living space was small by most standards, expanded by bunching what mouldering remains of furniture it boasted against the walls. Only a small TV remained prominent, its screen smashed in and made a treasure trove for all manner of meaningless oddments. Scraps of rug and carpet covered the floor, providing some measure of comfort for those that squatted and sprawled there.

There were children here; grubby, feral-eyed urchins most no older than Sally, some sporting shreds of clothing that looked to have been maintained from other life times, many all but naked.

The things they kept company with claimed most of Bellamy's attention, whatever semblance of reason he'd maintained up 'til now receding at the sight of them, leaving him with the sense of floating ephemeral and ghostly through an absinthe-fuelled nightmare.

Smiling, Sally sat down next to one of these absurdities -a creature seemingly composed of seeping, burnt black meat-, her eyes clouding in contentment as it scooped her up and sat her in its lap, running broken fingers through her hair. Nearby, a boy child sat and suckled with overt pleasure on the teat of a woman-thing whose protruding, muzzle-like mouth and smoke-grey pelt suggested there was wolf somewhere in her ancestry. Meeting his scrutiny with pristine, arctic blue eyes, she cocked her head and smiled, exposing teeth that looked better suited to tearing meat from a deer's flank than expressing humour.

He'd seen such things before; latex and C.G. monstrosities born from special effects workshops, but there was no such artistry here. Everywhere his incredulous eye wandered were a million details that no amount of design work could emulate; droplets of milk seeping from the suckling child's lips, the shimmer of dust in its nursemaid's fur. He thought of Lucy smelling pine and snow in the wardrobe's depths and smiled.

A flicker of motion drew his eye to the ceiling. Breath catching in his throat, he staggered back, almost colliding with Jake, who stood in shocked silence behind.

A face resembling a kabuki player's painted mask glared down at him, cut marble eyes swimming with threads of gold and mercury. Multiple tarantula limbs suspended the creature in place, one pair cradling a gurgling infant that toyed with the sack-like organs depending from its underside. Bellamy took another step back as the thing extended its stalk-like neck, pale pink tongue flickering between its painted lips.

"Leave them be, Emero."

It recoiled at the command, eyes rolling back in their sockets as it skittered back across the ceiling, gibbering in a language Bellamy didn't know.

"Diggory?"

The man emerged from a doorway on the opposite side of the room, lazy phantoms coiling from the cigarette clutched in his trembling fingers.

"Hello, Bill." Bellamy's eyes strayed to the scarlet stains decorating his suit. "Is that our little Jacob you've brought back to us?"

Bellamy turned to face the boy, who blanched beneath his gaze.

"I tried to tell you, man. Now we're both fucked."

Several of the children tittered at this profanity.

"Jacob's something of a stray, I'm afraid. Marches to the beat of his own drum, just like his Mother."

Jake threw an acid glance Diggory's way, lips peeling back from pearl-white teeth.

"Don't talk about me like I'm not here. I fucking hate that."

"Maybe if you were here a little more, I wouldn't have to."

Bellamy laughed, couldn't help it. Any minute he expected to wake, finding himself strapped down, straight-jacketed. Some of the children and their guardians looked at him with surprise, as if he'd burst into hysterics in the midst of a funeral service.

Diggory tittered around his cigarette, shaking his head and raising his eyes to the ceiling as he exhaled.

"Yeah, it takes people all sorts of ways. Best get it out of your system before you meet *her*."

He didn't need to ask; the storyteller in him *knew* this narrative thread, already tracing its familiar patterns to the inevitable unravelling.

*

". . . they're from all over; runaways, strays; the abused and abandoned. Some of the poor little bastards were barely alive when we found 'em. It never ceases to amaze me how cruel people can be to their own . . ."

He hardly paused for breath as he led them through the maze of corridors; a structure far too large and elaborate for the small flat to contain. Naked plaster walls played host to all manner of childish scrawls and sketches; hand prints of paint and scribbled nonsense forming a fresco of infant testimonies. Areas of plaster and the wood beneath had rotted away or been punched through, allowing glimpses of the darkened spaces beyond. Through one such rent, Bellamy caught the familiar strobe flicker of a TV screen, the images it portrayed cycling too fast to leave anything but the vaguest of subliminal impressions. A figure sat in a leather armchair watching this senseless parade, its nakedness pallid and tumescent, the sounds seeping through its lipless mouth expressions of neither pain nor pleasure, but as random and unintelligible as the visions that provoked them. Through another, he saw a naked man suspended by his wrists from ceiling-mounted chains, blood pouring from the welts and lacerations criss-crossing his body, burbles of ecstasy accompanying the infliction of every fresh wound. The one responsible—a willowy female, naked save for the metal, box-like mesh encasing her head—paused in her efforts, turning to face him, even though her eyes were hidden behind steel.

"What is all this?" Bellamy whispered to Jake. The boy looked at him, apparently surprised to have been addressed, shrugged.

"Fuck knows, man. I mean, I was born here, and even I don't know the first thing about it . . ."

"It's the place she made," Diggory, laughter bubbling behind every word. "A space between the cracks. Don't worry, you'll get to know it better from here on out, I'm sure."

Bellamy felt like they'd been walking for hours before they finally drew to a halt.

The door was inconspicuous compared to some they'd passed; simple, varnished wood, white-painted lintel blistered and peeling with age. Grasping the handle, Diggory turned to face him, eyes swimming with uncertainty.

"Before we do this, you have to promise me something, Bill."

"What?"

Suspicion, cold and sinuous as a frost-bitten snake coiling around his spine.

"Finish your script."

He didn't see why it was so important now, but since his livelihood depended on it, made the oath readily.

"Fine, whatever."

Satisfied, Diggory nodded his appreciation, and opened the door.

*

It wasn't a piece of shit; at least most of the critics agreed on that. Bellamy had seen a semblance of the finished piece during test-screening, before the studio brought in their butchers to make it more "palatable" to a mass-market audience.

Rumours of his derangement began to spread shortly after; a result of the giggles he'd been unable to suppress since the opening credits.

"Scary as hell, a post-millennial horror with surprisingly surreal heart," one notable publication concluded. Another attacked the film on moral rather than artistic principles, proclaiming its scenes of mutilation—often punctuated by graphic scenes of fucking- puerile and fetishist: ". . . a glorification of every dark and dismal chasm in the human psyche, celebrating monsters and murderers whilst heaping judgement on the quiet and clean living . . ."

It fast became a cult phenomenon, the letters of praise he received equalled only by those condemning him as a pervert and threatening righteous execution.

If anything surprised him, it was the letters whose writers already knew some semblance of the story; a minor urban myth swapped in the school-yards of London and Brighton apparently having echoes in New York and Milan, Glasgow, Marrakesh and Prague. She was everywhere; not Poppy Essler, but the shadow she left behind:

The Blood Bride.

Sometimes, she was with him too.

*

The boy tried to pay his way with sex at first, Bellamy waking to find him naked at his side, or toying between his legs with fingers and tongue.

Even were he able to somehow shift his sex—a capacity he may or may not have boasted—Bellamy had seen too much of what lay beneath to contemplate any intimacy between them. Apart from these occasional attempts at recompense, Jake proved a model house-mate; diligent, sensitive and courteous, absent when isolation was required, attentive when he felt a need to socialize.

The fact that he was one of the Bride's bastards—conceived from little more than rain water, if Diggory was to be believed—became almost incidental.

*

At least once a month, he woke to find himself back there, in her bed chamber, sometimes clothed, others stripped naked; sometimes the man he was in waking, others a child barely treading the borders of adolescence.

This time, he wasn't alone; Diggory and the children were there, suspended from the ceiling and the posts of her bed, sprawling on the carpets or gathered around her in familial bliss.

Jake stood before the window, innocent of his human skin. This was the first time Bellamy saw the truth of him in its entirety, a waifish, willowy thing of pearlescent scales, triple rows of tequila sunrise feathers running down his back, a lush thatch of the same turning his groin to a furnace. Eyes swirling like oil on water returned his scrutiny, the smile beneath a crescent of lascivious sweetness that he couldn't help but return.

From behind her drapes and veils, the Bride regarded him, her pleasure at what he'd done in her name palpable, like sunlight that streamed through skin and bone to plant rainbows in his brain.

As before, she didn't speak. There was no need. Instead, she showed him what he'd precipitated, the dreaming reality of her temple peeling, shattering, providing glimpses of other whens and wheres in which fresh outgrowths of her myth blossomed:

A fright-eyed, middle aged widow sitting before her vanity mirror, dressed in the dulled and tattered remnants of her bridal gown. He only caught fragments of the conversation she held with her reflected self, but enough to know that she invoked her husband of twenty six years with every breath, praying he'd come and coax her from her failing flesh into a realm where the dead danced. A cult of adolescents whose obsession with death and dark things led them to make a minor icon of The Bride, their usual black and jewelled apparel abandoned in favour of white trains and gowns, male and female both revelling in this fresh aspect of otherness. In Colorado, a boy who believed the woman his Father was soon to marry to be a creature of the Bride's species took a pair of scissors to her eyes and throat, his reason collapsing as the mutilated remains failed to crumble into ash and ether. In Derby, England, a pair of lovers whose parents regarded their shared sex as spiritual abomination took themselves to the roof of the city's cathedral, each dressed and painted as the bridal wraith they'd witnessed on the cinema screen.

Thanks to them; the whisperers on playgrounds and street corners, the affrighted, perverse and obsessed who dreamed of her, and to *him,* she would endure, sustained in this place somewhere beyond flesh and fantasy; the paradoxical parents that bore her.

Pleasure followed on the tail end of this revelation; a wave of molten gold that washed his nerve endings, causing his legs to buckle and thoughts to fray as ecstasy overwhelmed.

*

Diggory's death made the front pages of some less respectable tabloids. The magazines of "alternative" science and culture descended on the event like wasps on jam, detailing with obsessive precision the man's relationship to The Blood Bride mythos, and how his death -murder or elaborate suicide? Legality kept most from speculating too broadly- echoed in certain significant ways that of his silver-screen counterpart.

Bellamy, having been witnessed in the man's company on several occasions, was required to give a statement as to his relationship with the deceased. He obliged with minimal fuss, perfectly happy to fuel the rumour and tittle tattle that began to coalesce around him.

Jake didn't wear his mask of boyhood when they fucked anymore. Bellamy liked him to be naked as possible; to feel scale and feather beneath his fingers, to see cut-marble eyes shining in the moonlight. Claws raked his shoulders as the thing bucked and moaned beneath him, the organ he was buried in up to the hilt fluttering and seeping like a hive of benign bees.

He hadn't realised how much his previous denials had *hurt* Jake. The part of him that was his Mother; the dream-stuff threading through his system, required such displays of want in the same way he required food and water. Without them, he'd wither into something grey and insubstantial, a rumour buffeted on the breeze; the sublimated memory of a dream barely sustaining itself in its creator's sub conscious.

They needed one another.

"Oh, oh god . . . *yeah*!"

The voice was a fluttering whisper, sometimes masculine, others fluting and female, the scented breath that carried it smelling of damp earth, of warm rain on rock.

Bellamy was losing himself, the certainties by which he defined personality - his heterosexuality, his anarcho-socialist political principles, his rationalism- collapsing one by one, leaving what was once the cathedral of self a turbulent, storm-swept sea.

Lips that felt like fine-quality leather fastened to his as he climaxed, the bees in Jake's interior swarming over his deflating length, gathering ejaculate like nectar from flowers.

He saw the visitors out of the corner of his eye; a flash and nothing more, but enough to leave their image indelibly etched into memory:

Blood at her eyes and mouth, staining the lace that covered her breasts and fluttered around her legs, the man at her side a mass of the same, one eye roughly gouged out and weeping scarlet tears, lips hacked or bitten away to set his expression in a permanent clown's grin. He was dressed in a groom's grey, a pink carnation threaded through one button hole.

They didn't speak, their presence a silent thanks for the reunion he'd fostered.

Then they were gone, the child they left staring after them, weeping his joy.

A STRANGE KIND OF SENSE

Silverman stared into infinity and wondered: how long? Impossible to gage here. Sometimes he saw suns, moons, worlds sailing through the sky, but they didn't mean a thing. Physics and metaphor had never been the most comfortable of bed fellows. Insofar as he could judge, this place had more in common with the latter.

No wonder Wagner was losing his mind.

*

"Going well, is it?"

Silverman couldn't tell whether Wagner's mutterings were a reply or simply part of the discourse he'd been holding with himself for what seemed like several decades now. His diagrams and formulae covered nearly half of the stone that was their shared world, pastel scrawls swarming beneath Silverman's feet; an alien language that only a soul as sick as Wagner's could understand.

"I've caught us some lunch. Care to join me?"

The man scratched his close-cropped hair, twirling the length of blue chalk in his fingers before it began to scrabble over stone once more.

"Well, just let me know when you're hungry."

Dinner consisted of something that had strayed too close, getting itself caught in one of the snares Silverman had set up. It resembled a squid of some sort, bulbous sack of a body festooned with eyes. It sang from the man-like mouth buried in the heart of its tentacles as he took his knife to it, dismembering it for the pan.

It got dark as he settled down to eat. Strange: there were at least three suns visible in the sky; pink, emerald, amber. Wagner didn't seem to mind. How long had it been since he'd eaten? And where the fuck did he keep getting all that chalk from?

The singing squid didn't taste as bad as it looked, the bronzed flesh carrying a slight citrus tang, like lightly fried tomato. He'd certainly been forced to eat worse during his time here; lice, worms, the ticks from Wagner's back.

He slept after supper, but didn't dream; no point when the waking world was a nightmare all its own.

*

A strangled scream jolted him awake. He blinked, moaning as his eyes adjusted to the swirling delirium. Crawling from the makeshift canopy that was their only concession to shelter, he called his partners' name, receiving nothing in reply but another breathless croak.

"Wagner?"

Then he saw the invader.

It seemed like many ages since one of the delirium's denizens last set foot on the Stone. Most were too afraid, like forest animals skirting around the perimeter of a hunter's cottage. But occasionally, one grew too brave, curious or insane, trying its luck with the trespassers or perhaps seeking to die by their hands.

This one was bigger than most; a squirming sausage-mass of torn, tumescent flesh, man-like torso twitching and jerking as if in the midst of a grand mal. In one bloody fist, it held Wagner by the throat, holding him up to the ruin of its face to lap the tears from his eyes.

Unsheathing his knife, Silverman hurled himself at the thing with a wordless scream, carving into the knot of tumours that constituted its abdomen, recoiling in disgust as a stinking gruel of pus and sewage spurted from the wound.

Turning its eyeless gaze on him, the thing's lips peeled back to reveal twin rows of perfectly formed baby teeth. It lashed out with its free hand, connecting with his mid-riff and sending him scudding across the Stone.

He thought he heard a child laughing -or was it a woman weeping?- somewhere in the distance. Hoisting himself to his feet, he moaned as pain and warm wetness blossomed across his shirt. The thing's filthy claws had opened his flesh, blood spattering and smearing Wagner's mathematical master-work.

Shame.

This time, he didn't bother with the knife, the thing obviously beyond what hurt it could inflict. Instead, he reached beneath his shirt, pressing fingers to the warmth freshly flowing there. Turning the other hand palm upward, he used his red stained index finger to paint a symbol there he'd first discovered on the walls of Crowley's Temple of Thal. Clenching his fingers tight around the design, he raised it to his mouth, exhaling sharply.

Shimmering streamers broke from the gaps between his fingers, lancing through the air towards the invader. They struck it on the arm at the end of which Wagner jerked and struggled, whirling around the appendage like shards of broken mirror in a tornado, unknitting flesh and bone 'til it fell twitching to the ground.

Wagner at least had the presence of mind to scurry away as the thing threw back its head and howled, an infant's lament cutting through the wind's perpetual howl, momentarily drowning out the whispers it carried.

Black and milk-white sludge spurted from the wound as the thing thrashed and writhed, clawing at its own sick joke of a face. Silverman prayed the hurt would be enough to drive it off; he didn't have strength or spittle enough for another Play, particularly one so offensive.

Turning its eyeless gaze on him with what seemed more confusion than hurt, the thing dragged its bulk towards the Stone's edge, leaving behind a slug-trail of stinking effluent. It spared him a final glance before pitching itself over, seeming to ask: *Why? Why would you hurt me so?*

Then it was gone, Silverman's legs going to mist and water beneath him.

*

Youth was no excuse for ignorance, or lack of ambition. He'd maintained the philosophy for as long as he could recall. Now, at last, it seemed his years of hardship and self-denial were about to bear fruit.

Neither of them cared about the ritual's exact results. It'd taken the better part of a decade to piece together, fragments learned, borrowed, intuited. All that mattered was the execution, and the vindication that would follow.

Even now, the sublime poetry of their relationship was too perfect to express; he the sensitive, the poet; the aesthete, complemented, tempered by Wagner's analysis, criticism and relentless logic. The man had been hailed as a prodigy in his early years. Silverman vaguely recalled hearing his name mentioned in news reports and scientific documentaries before they met face to face.

Then came the fall from grace that mirrored his own. Like himself, Wagner saw beyond the petty parameters of his chosen obsession, abandoning all notions of the unlikely or impossible in an attempt to forcibly make true what could only be imagined:

"It's the basis of all discovery," he proclaimed, "to make the dreams and myths of yesterday today's reality. You'd be surprised how many of my so-called peers have forgotten that."

Following the publication of a number of essays and investigations proclaiming to "obliterate" rather than push back the boundaries of conventional science, the rational community turned on him with all the rabidity of zealots condemning one who dared question Holy Writ. They called him "alchemist" and "mystic," the negative press obliging most erstwhile friends and allies to withdraw their support, leaving him to continue his investigations with whatever scraps of funding he could scavenge.

Silverman met the man when he turned up on his doorstep, begging financial aid for his latest endeavour. Initially dubious —his own philosophy founded on the contention that the dogmas of rationality were as antithetical to true transcendence as those of religious absolutism—, he soon found himself warming to the ridiculed physician, finding in him a ragged fervour and intuitive capacity better suited to a creative than a rationalist.

Alone, their pursuit of the unknown had resulted in little more than rumour and ridicule. Together, ambition and desire finally began to crystallize, the worlds described by others before—Blake, Bosch, Dahli—opening their doors, allowing access to secrets the dullards who fancied themselves their superiors lacked the capacity to even dream of.

*

He woke to find Wagner's chalk-dusted fingers at his face, stroking his brow and cheeks with a lover's tenderness.

A shame the man's eyes didn't echo the sentiment.

Sitting up, he groaned through gritted teeth as invisible claws raked his belly. His torso—pale, scarred, gaunt to the point of starvation—had been stripped naked, a makeshift dressing applied to his wounds. The strands of cob-web matter they were woven from was the same stuff that constituted their canopy; a part-magical fibre sewn from spit and semen, amongst other things; some of the few basic commodities available to them in this floating, walless prison.

Ugly yellow and purple bruises blossomed around Wagner's throat. Silverman hoped he hadn't suffered any serious damage.

"Are you okay?"

The man stared at him with eyes that seemed on the verge of tears, then turned them to the markings he'd made on the Stone. Following his gaze, Silverman saw that entire sections had been scuffed, smeared or obliterated, rendering what remained all but meaningless.

"You should've let it fucking kill me."

Rising, he staggered as if drunk to where the invader had slunk to its suicide, scuffing formulae beneath the soles of his feet.

He'd have rather died? Silverman wasn't surprised. That was where they differed; for Wagner, it was always the result, the result, the result. He lacked the will and imagination to appreciate the journey itself. Did he think that Silverman wouldn't gladly gnaw off his own arms just to be able to walk on grass or soil again, to look up and see rain clouds or clear blue rather than this kaleidoscope insanity?

It simply wasn't to be. Not *yet*.

With some difficulty, Silverman dragged himself to his feet. He felt weak and unsteady as a newborn foal, the hand from which he'd unleashed the Play cold and tingling.

Wagner didn't even look his way as he drew alongside, staring out into the infinite as if to catch sight of their destination, wherever and whatever the hell it may be.

"What were you doing, anyway?"

"It doesn't matter now. Anymore of that shit you were cooking?"

There was; one or two slices he was hoping to save for when things got desperate.

"In the pan. Help yourself."

Wagner turned and shuffled back to the canopy, muttering to himself. Silverman stood on the very lip of the Stone, watching shapes and faces form in the surrounding delirium. Some were familiar; visions of people he'd once known, but whose names and natures he could no longer recall, others more abstract; impressionistic or surreal scrawls that put him in mind of the outpourings he'd seen recorded in shit and blood on lunatic asylum walls.

They'd both had their theories on first arriving, though the time they'd spent in the state had all but eroded any certainties. For his part, Silverman was content with his notion that it was *nowhere;* a state between worlds where all physical law was void. He'd long since given up voicing such theories, as they were invariably met with Wagner's own brand of mild mannered contempt.

One thing was for certain; it wasn't meant for beings of their substance, the entities that inhabited it gaining some semblance of solidity only upon drawing close to the Stone.

He could see a small shoal of the things partially congealing now; knots of organ pulsing into being, sewn together by unseen hands with threads of nerve and tissue. The result was almost fish-like; eyeless, silver-scaled, trailing skirts of hair fine tendrils behind them. A particularly curious specimen broke away from the shoal as he watched, meandering towards him before drawing to a halt barely an arm's reach away.

"Hello." An automatic response that not even an eternity in isolation had withered.

Tilting the bulbous mass Silverman presumed to be its head to one side, the thing blossomed with slits and apertures from which unfurled lotus-like configurations of dark blue flesh. Reaching out, he brushed one of the fleshy petals with his finger-tips, wincing at the sudden, throbbing cold. Chirruping apparent pleasure, the thing withdrew its flowers and sped off into the ether, going to rejoin its brothers and sisters who'd begun to circle like a flock of vultures over a starving man.

*

It'd taken him a while to acclimatise to it; that congealing of the air that occurred whenever art was imminent. The first time he experienced the phenomena, it agitated asthma to the point that he nearly collapsed, but persistence in his explorations had eventually yielded a cure for that hereditary weakness.

"Are you ready?"

He felt like he was about to slip beneath the covers of a lover's bed, cheeks burning, entrails a-flutter. Wagner, on the other hand, seemed unmoved by what they were about, the only indication he felt anything at all the febrile bonfires in his eyes.

"Just one more check . . ."

Silverman sighed consent. The man's obsession with minutiae had led them this far in pursuit of revelation, but that didn't stop it from being infuriating. He could've told Wagner that everything was right; that he felt it in his blood and marrow, but the man would just give him that look, raising a dismissive eyebrow, and carry on regardless. The fact that the art they'd composed relied as much on Silverman's intuitions as it did on his formulae was something he wasn't prepared to acknowledge. His opium-fuelled dreams, the half-remembered conversations with things from beyond the veil, had provided ritual components such as the jug of yew's milk, the plate of eels. Silverman had seen the unspoken scorn in his partner's eyes when he produced the items, though his doubts weren't profound enough for him to reject them out of hand. Despite himself, Wagner couldn't deny Silverman's contributions, having witnessed—and experienced—their effects on several past occasions.

Wagner held his breath as he bent close to the chalk, blood and bone-dust markings he'd scrawled on the cellar floor, checking every figure for even the slightest deviation in shape or scale.

Not for the first time, Silverman wondered how the man was able to hold onto his sanity when the thoughts that informed it made misery from even the most incidental details.

Rising, he allowed himself a drawn out breath, the candle-lit murk trembling with his exhalation.

"Well, I suppose this is it."

He smiled in nervous anticipation, Silverman returning it as he began to shed his clothes, revealing the designs he'd tattooed on himself for the occasion.

Wagner watched the disrobing with open approval, their relationship having long since carried them beyond niceties of prudence or embarrassment. Silverman enjoyed the attention, relishing eyes upon his flesh as much as tongues and fingers.

Naked, he stood waiting for Wagner to join him, the man seeming momentarily hypnotized by the sight of his partner's body.

"Daniel . . ."

"What?"

Following the man's gaze down, Silverman found his body crawling with wisps and coils of faint vapour, snakes of lambent mist slithering over his belly, coiling around his arms and between his legs. Looking up at Wagner, he laughed, the sound visibly fluttering from his lips like spectral butterflies. Wagner watched with slack jawed admiration, untying the red silk robe he sported.

The body beneath wasn't what Silverman would regard as classically beautiful; most would likely find it repugnant. Despite his insatiable sweet tooth, Wagner was naturally emaciated, pale skin stretched over what looked to be little more than skeleton; wiry, over-long limbs creating the impression there was something of the gecko or spider in his anatomy. Insofar as Silverman was concerned, the romanticism of it -obsessive academic allowing his flesh to waste for want of enlightenment- lent it a peculiar beauty far beyond that of the gym-sculpted, vacuum packed pretty-boys he could pick up in any bar or nightclub in Liverpool.

Wagner withstood his eyes with far less grace, the fact of their approval doing nothing to assuage his discomfort. Only his sex betrayed his enthusiasm, standing proud and semi-hooded from its tangled nest of dark pubic hair.

Strangely, the ether didn't seem to favour him as it did Silverman, just a few scattered motes of the stuff scurrying like ghostly insects over his brow and temples.

From this point on, the ritual—and responsibility—belonged to Silverman, all certainty and instruction broken down, leaving inspiration their only guide. And inspiration told him that he wanted to be filled by this man, for them to fuck amongst the ephemera and formulae, adding sweat, semen and desire to the circuit.

*

He slept like a corpse, only the near imperceptible twitch of his eyes beneath their sheaths providing any sign that he still lived.

Silverman wasn't surprised; he couldn't recall the last time Wagner had set down his chalk, let his mind rest. It was almost as if he feared that, without the constant activity, it'd begin to slow and wither 'til the intellect he'd spent an entire lifetime cultivating went the way of dreams.

Something was happening; he felt it massing like snow or thunder, as if the delirium held its breath. There were more tangible signs of it too; the wind that blew perpetually through the state growing bitter and agitated, the whispers it carried now accompanied by fingers that caressed, pinched and scratched as they passed, some ardent enough to draw blood.

A red moon appeared in the distance, its face that of a woman locked in orgasmic or drug-induced delight. Every so often, her upturned eyes flickered, a burning red tongue slithering through her perpetual smile to taste the insanity.

Silverman brushed Wagner's stubble-softened cheek, the rare contact eliciting a strange shudder that arced through his arm to earth itself where his brain sprouted spine.

Recoiling, he saw shimmering wisps crawling across Wagner's cheek, the matter evaporating before he could assess it further.

The man's eyes flickered open so abruptly, Silverman started, chiding himself for such timidity.

He rose without speaking, barely even looking at Silverman as he shuffled out from beneath the canopy, looking up to where flocks of human-faced comets whirled, screaming and singing in their pursuit of one another.

"I fucking hate this place."

A sudden cramp in Silverman's bowels, a fresh note of frost in the wind. He didn't want to get dragged into this for the seven millionth time, but Wagner wouldn't be dissuaded.

"We both do . . ."

The man rounded on him wearing something between a snarl and a smile, feral triumph flickering in his eyes.

"Do we? I don't think so. I saw you with that . . . *thing* earlier. Why don't you just admit it? You want this; you still think we're here for a *reason*."

No, he didn't think that. All reason rebelled against it, the time they'd spent here—weeks, months, years?—yielding nothing more than round after round of absurdity; whispering winds, singing stars, and monsters.

Always, always monsters.

But he did *feel* it; there was no denying the fact. For someone who'd once made a living telling pretty lies, he found the cold, hard, ugly ones something of a trial.

"Does it matter what I think?"

He should've known any attempt at pacification would only serve to fan the flames. Wagner moved with cobra-speed, grasping Silverman's shirt by the collar, dragging him out into the open.

"Just fucking *look at it,* will you?" He pointed out towards the red moon, its lips moving in silent conversation with itself. The wind shrieked in his ears, sharpened nails scraping his arms and neck.

"There's no meaning here, no *purpose.* Just insanity. All our wasted fucking excuses for lives have come to. Why can't you just accept that?"

He was ranting now, spittle flecking the stubble around his lips.

For the first time in all their long years together, Silverman saw the true extent of his partner's blindness. Even having seen what they'd seen together; angels making love on the banks of the Nile, a child-Madonna giving birth to monsters in the Vatican's bowels, his reliance upon the rational persisted, rooted in his mind like a cancer.

Silverman didn't answer, knew it'd be a waste of breath. Infuriated by this passivity, Wagner let go and turned his back in disgust, stalking away to the Stone's edge.

Then he screamed.

*

Fucking was a perfunctory act for Wagner; a means of exorcising animal imperatives, not to be referenced 'til the chemical demands of his body dictated otherwise.

Silverman agreed to the extent that it was a consummation of appetite, but failed to see how anyone could regard that appetite as anything other than sacred; a carnal commonality transcending all parameters of culture, creed or belief.

This coupling, if anything, was proof positive of the philosophy, their intertwined flesh seeming to melt and run like candle wax, flowing together to form a single nascent anatomy.

Wagner was reluctant at first, failing to see how indulgence of passion could be part of such precise ceremony, but it only took a few strokes and kisses before he capitulated, trampling the mathematics he'd so painstakingly rendered underfoot.

Now the same markings writhed and pulsed beneath Silverman's back, insinuating themselves amongst the tattoos recorded there.

He'd never seen Wagner like this before, so earnest in his appetites, so at one with his animal-self. It made him realise it was more than shared obsession that drew them together; they were halves of the same quintessential spirit, divided between two skins.

A flicker of movement at the edges of sight, a sudden flash of fear that, far from withering appetite, acted as a sexual seasoning, adding spice to their unity.

Wagner noticed it too, tearing his attention away from Silverman's face as his thrusts became deeper, more urgent. Silverman cupped his lover's cheek, gently drawing his eyes back to where they belonged.

"It's nothing. Oh . . . God!"

He'd never known climax like it, the delirious imminence of emptying giving way to a sense as of his whole body rupturing from the groin upward; a flower blossoming to receive Wagner's rain.

Opening his eyes, he gasped to see that the metaphor had somehow slipped the boundaries of imagination, translating itself to physical reality. Although he still saw the man-shape of Wagner bucking and groaning over him, it was as if a heretofore invisible anatomy, sewn from storm-cloud, occupied the same space, lightning flickering in its eyes and bowels, darting between its teeth, every breath stinging his cheeks like snow-freighted gale.

Then the storm broke, making him a vessel for its fury.

*

Silverman shuddered, recalling the agony, the bliss that accompanied the full blooming of his flower-self. In that moment, he felt as if he could've taken all the world into himself, become a surrogate for the expanding universe, and still have sufficient space for mystery.

The scream that ravaged his throat when the flowering failed, and he became closed, *sealed* once more, had almost disintegrated sanity.

Now he heard a facsimile of the same from Wagner's lips, knew that it heralded something of moment.

Reeling away from the stone's edge, Wagner doubled over in agony, near-skeletal fingers raking his stomach as he vomited black blood.

"Wagner . . ."

Warm rain spotted Silverman's cheeks as he stepped from beneath the canopy. Glancing up, the breath caught in his throat at sight of the entities swirling and brawling overhead: One appeared to be composed entirely of sky and sunlight, the rainbow lances it thrust at its opponent so bright, Silverman had to turn away as they struck for fear of being blinded. In its churning, engine-like depths, he saw circuits and equations of light elaborating, multiplying like single-celled organisms in a drop of sea-water. The other was its opponent's antithesis; a mass of seething darkness that swallowed and smothered light, the ruptures blossoming throughout its surface giving way to an interior of pulsing, bloody flesh; the source of the burning rain that scolded his cheeks and brow.

Though their conflict seemed vicious—sunlight spines spitting the darkness, tendrils of night lancing out to constrict and smother the burning blue—Silverman was struck by the cryptic but indelible impression there was something more at work here than simple struggle for survival, as if the two entities were warring lovers, as likely to resolve their dispute in kisses as murder.

Mesmerised by the display, he jerked as if distracted from a dream as Wagner's scream degenerated into strangled retching, the man going to his knees, clawing at the Stone. His lips gaped wide to allow passage of something foul:

A sack of diseased, leprous meat, a single cataracted eye blinking in its mass, a lipless mouth gibbering as it crawled away from its creator.

Fighting for breath, Wagner fell back from the thing with mad horror in his eyes, wiping blood and effluence from around his mouth as he scooted towards the Stone's edge.

Silverman felt time slow and congeal around him, thoughts and feelings racing as they chased the tail-end of some deeper meaning behind this farce, a revelation that felt like sunlight filtering through a doorway left slightly ajar; like cool, clean air whispering down into the claustrophobic confines of a crypt . . .

Metaphorical opposites at war in the heavens, Wagner angry and isolated, giving birth to monsters . . .

The child had already begun to grow as Silverman started towards the retreating Wagner, its meat rupturing, spilling a milky effluent that stank of sewers and sick beds. Vestigial limbs, like the pale-skinned legs of some cave-dwelling spider, emerged from the wounds, tasting the air of this lunatic's nightmare.

Wagner was almost at the Stone's edge, showing no sign he'd stop when he reached it.

A wave of vicarious feeling washed over and through Silverman, bringing him to his knees in an instant of ecstatic torment. He felt like he was impaled on lances of love, the agony of bodily damage counter-pointed by a contentment that was the closest he'd ever come to touching Holiness. He'd only ever felt its like once before; back when his and Wagner's ritual coupling first brought them to this state.

Tasting blood, he struggled to his feet, glancing up into the sky.

Impaled on its opponent's lances, the darkness lashed out, drawing the sky and sunlight engine into an embrace so intimate, its substance meshed with the other's mechanisms, decorating them with all manner of strange ornaments and configurations, making art from the machine.

Wagner screamed again, his spawn dragging itself towards him, a foetal head wreathed in foulness protruding from within the rancid sack, a hand grasping for its Father with grossly elongated fingers.

Moving as if through a fever dream, Silverman aimed a solid kick at the thing's flank, flesh rupturing as it hurtled across the Stone, hissing resentment.

Wagner looked up at Silverman with eyes as empty as a doll's, the reason he'd spent a lifetime cultivating all but obliterated, dust in the breeze...

"Wagner, Wagner, get up . . ."

Something was happening, the processes of the contradictory engine above facilitating some shift in the delirium, its substance—for want of a better—burgeoning, splitting, spilling madness.

Wagner sat, glaring up at him without even the merest sign of comprehension, the man become little more than animated meat, unfit even for slaughter.

Grasping him by the shoulders, Silverman hoisted him up, amazed that someone so thin could be so heavy. He shook the man, words and spittle flying against his face.

"Don't you get it, you soulless fuck? This is it! We've got a chance to end all this . . ."

Something in his eyes; a fish-tail flicker in the depths of a pond.

Then something hit Silverman from behind; a wet, fleshy weight, screaming as its teeth found his throat and its claws his back. Hurled forward into Wagner's arms, the impetus carried them both towards the Stone's edge . . .

And over.

Silverman felt himself pierced, a barbed length puncturing his spine, erupting from his chest to plunge on into Wagner's heart.

He had time to see the engine above reflected in the man's eyes, the fish swarming en masse to the surface before his own went dark, delirium receding . . .

*

Warmth, wet and dark. He'd known this before, though the memory was buried, surfacing only in the inconsequential arena of dreams.

Only now there were *two;* one in which his passage into the world was a softer trauma, another where it almost didn't come to pass, the umbilicus that was his anchor to life conspiring to strangle it.

The darkness convulsed around him, preparing to shat him into the world once more. He was ready this time, putting up neither complaint nor resistance as blindness ruptured, light spilling through.

His nose and mouth were filled with blood and meat stink, the broken stone beneath him slick with glutinous fluid. Retching, he vomited up a stomach full of clear brine, sinuses stinging at its acridity.

Wiping the gunk from his eyes, he blinked, gritted his teeth as they adjusted to the business of seeing.

The room hadn't changed a great deal during his absence. He hadn't known what to expect; for all he knew, the world could've shrugged off humanity and all trace of its civilizations millennia ago.

But no . . . same old walls, same old floor and ceiling. "The Threshold," he'd called it, believing it'd one day become a gateway to other places and plains of existence.

He rose, legs wobbling beneath him as if the muscles had gone to water, amniotic matter drying on his skin. In one corner lay what looked to be a pile of steaming meat; the remains of the cell he'd sewn for himself, in which the disparate flesh he occupied had been reunited.

Wagner, Silverman . . . labels for components that no longer existed in singularity. He needed a new name, lacked a parent or guardian to impose one on him. It'd have to be one he made or adopted for himself.

The rest of the house remained largely untouched, the wards his former selves had woven preserving it from looters, vandals and over-enthusiastic property developers. A mirror in what was once Silverman's bedroom told him a story of self he'd never heard or seen before:

Pretty enough beneath the dried-on filth; long-limbed, well sculpted, the hair carpeting its chest, groin and cascading over its shoulders liquorice black. He laughed, turning his face one way then the other, seeing shades of both the men who composed it, but mostly something beyond both.

There were clothes in the cupboards and wardrobes, most stinking of dust, rank with vermin; none an entirely perfect fit. Still, he managed to throw together a somewhat serviceable outfit. He doubted the world had changed so much it'd allow him to go naked without reprisal.

Hesitation at the front door, a pang of fear at leaving this familiar dirt and darkness. Maybe it'd be better if he waited, acclimatised himself before exposing it to the world...

No. Just a residue of his old, incomplete selves. Besides, there was more at stake here than just himself. Beyond the barrier of wood and glass waited souls that were wounded, just as his once were; crying out for someone to show them a means of healing, of being *complete* again. He might be the only being alive with such knowledge, the burden of responsibility falling on no one else.

Throwing the door wide, the nameless newborn stepped out into sunlight, every sense singing with the promise of a new day.

GROWN UP WORLD

That *noise;* there since she first woke, sometimes close, sometimes distant; like the whimpering of a child that'd slipped its mother's hand, lost and confused in a grown-up world.

Stupid bitch had actually gone out to *meet* it: "Maybe . . . maybe it's just like the rest of us," she insisted, "maybe it's just . . . lost."

Her screams echoed for hours after. Angela felt sick at the memory. Where the fuck were they now? Some kind of corridor, walls lined with bookshelves, crammed to near collapse with tattered, leather bound volumes, so narrow they could barely walk two abreast. If the fucking *thing* appeared in front of them . . .

She shook her head as if trying to dissuade an over-curious wasp. That sort of thought was death here. She couldn't afford to let it in, even for an instant.

Oil lamps flickered into the foreseeable distance, patches of light separated by great stretches of shadow.

Jeremy's breath rasped ragged in her ear. Was the boy asthmatic or something? She could see from his laboured expression that things were getting difficult for him. It didn't matter; they couldn't stop to rest out here.

Laughter from behind. Calder again. Why couldn't it have taken him instead . . .? She stamped on the thought before it could flourish. What an *evil* thing to want . . .

"You guys go on. Think I'm going to stop and do some reading."

A general murmur of annoyance. Nine of them left in all. Calder had made it his business to piss off each and every one.

"For fuck's sake," Docherty hissed, "let's just do as he says; leave the asshole."

Eight pairs of eyes on her, their attention like burning ants beneath her clothes. How the hell she'd been nominated de facto leader was beyond her.

She was *nothing;* the most overqualified office temp in Brighton. But somehow she'd become the brain of this little body, much as she might lament the role.

"Yes, do as he says," Calder parroted, mimicking Docherty's dense Romanian accent, "leave the asshole."

"Do what you want," she grunted, not even stopping to think. They couldn't afford it, not out here. She heard it even now; a soft sobbing, faint yet, but growing clearer with every breath.

"We can't just leave him, surely?" Janet something-or-other, mother of two, co-founder of a successful London patisserie.

Angela didn't answer. There wasn't *time* to debate it. *They had to keep moving.*

*

Cold fire in her lungs, legs become unfeeling lead beneath her. How long had they been running? Seemed like hours. She didn't even dare glance at Jeremy, expecting him to collapse any second, those behind stumbling over him as the *thing* closed on their backs.

Had she seen it? Perhaps a glimpse, but she couldn't be sure. Her impression was of something *stitched together;* bone-thin legs and arms over-long, body hunched to fit into the narrow corridor. The rest was simply blood.

The corridor split in places, branching off into avenues and cul-de-sacs. She didn't dare take any of them in case they found themselves cornered. Of course, that was a likelihood anyway.

Shrieks from behind. Agatha. She didn't dare look back, didn't dare stop. Some called for her to do so. She ignored them. They had to find something, somewhere they could stop, rest . . .

Oh God, oh God! She was *still* screaming. So was Calder, their protests accompanied by meaty thuds, tears and sick, wet snaps; a recording from inside an abattoir. And the *whimpering.* Was it her imagination, or was there an element of humour in it now, like a baby gurgling laughter in its crib?

The rows and rows of books that'd been their world for God only knew how long abruptly ceased, replaced by high arched windows, the world beyond a twilight blur.

"Oh, thank Christ, *thank Christ . . .*"

A door. Jeremy was already there, despite his condition, grasping for the handle as his legs went to water. Angela barrelled through without a second thought, collapsing on all fours against plush, dust-smelling carpet.

"Come on, come on!" Someone hissed. Then the door slammed behind her, a lock clicking into place.

*

The last safe space had been some sort of storage room; crates, furniture, paintings, all overlaid with dust-dulled coverlets. This was a library, every wall dominated by shelves that stretched from floor to ceiling, small tables and chairs arranged for the reader's convenience. Stairs led up to a raised dais that allowed a view through immense windows, telescopes and other equipment constituting a makeshift observatory.

It scrabbled at the door for an hour or so, whimpering, weeping, hammering as its patience gave way. At one point, Jeremy thought he heard Agatha's voice, softly begging them to let her in. The boy was likely delirious. Even though they'd had ample time to catch their breath, he still looked like the walking dead.

Angela slumped in one of the green leather chairs, peering into the shadows that clustered on the ceiling. Now maybe she could let the thoughts in.

She'd given up wondering what the fuck this was all about. It was useless. She didn't even know how the hell she got here. None of them did. Trying to remember was like chasing the tail end of a dream. There were . . . moments, brief flashes: an argument with Mom, probably over money—it usually was these days—, slipping into bed with sinuses stinging, then dreams:

Running through a wood as the sun went down, bathed in blood-light. She was nothing there; insubstantial as a ghost, but the things that chased her, they were insubstantial too, and more than capable of tearing her to tatters.

They almost had her; she recalled the cold scrape of their fingers across the back of her neck, their whispers in her ear, promising her peace and pleasure like she'd never known, if she'd only stop and embrace them . . .

Then screams, the ground splitting, gaping before her, and she fell, tumbling, tumbling into wakefulness . . .

It was the same for all of them, insofar as they told. Calder had been on a train after visiting his dying mother. Cynthia Burrows, who currently stood gazing out of the windows, was flying to Canada where lifelong friends waited. There was nothing; no rhyme or reason to it.

"It's fucked up three ways from Sunday, ain't it?"

Harold Kaplan, a New England Geography teacher, sat opposite her, looking around the room as if he expected it to burst like a soap bubble.

"Yep."

He plucked one of the volumes from the table in front of them.

"*Tales From the Forgotten Places,* by Allen Rudge. Ha, who needs horror stories when you're living one?"

He threw the book back where he'd found it.

She could feel it radiating from him just like the rest of them; a sense of imminent explosion, a need to let go of all restraint and scream and scream and scream until the walls crumbled around them.

But she couldn't afford that luxury yet, nor could any of them. If they let go now, they were well and truly *fucked.*

You might be anyway.

She smothered the voice before it could raise much above a whisper.

"God, I'm *starving.*"

"Me too. When was the last time you ate?"

"Ages ago, before I woke up here. How long do you think it's been?"

The world outside seemed to be in a state of perpetual twilight, regardless of how much time passed.

Kaplan shrugged.

"Christ only knows. I get the feeling that it doesn't matter much. Listen," he leaned in close over the table, glancing at the others conspiratorially, "it's probably occurred to you, but we can't just keep running around this place forever. I mean, where are we going, exactly? That bastard *thing,* I don't think it's going anywhere any time soon. We need to get *out.*"

Actually, it hadn't occurred to her at all. There hadn't been any time to consider it; from the second she woke to here and now, nothing but running and confusion.

"Maybe."

"What do you mean, *maybe*? I can't see how there's any *maybe* about it. This place is *fucked up.*"

No argument from her. The problem was they couldn't be certain that outside was any better. Getting up from her chair, she crossed the room and ascended the stairs to the windows. Cynthia flashed her an ephemeral smile, her eyes those of a cornered fox.

"My youngest starts school tomorrow," she sounded distant, as if talking to herself, "don't know what his teachers are going to make of him. He has Asperger's, you see. A lot of people think that he's just naughty or . . . or *stupid.*" She scowled, eyes flashing with contempt.

Angela didn't answer, didn't think it was required. Her attention was focused on the world beyond the windows: a garden, rampant with weeds and overgrown plant plots, statues of angels, demons and monsters scattered throughout, frozen in the midst of some grand, mythic carnival. Directly outside the window stood a one-winged angel, its amputated limb lying in pieces at its feet. Its expression as it returned her scrutiny was one of evil mirth, as if it'd heard tell of some cosmic joke of which all of humanity was the butt.

Beyond the garden lay woodland, trees twined together in autumnal nudity as far as the eye could see.

She was about to turn away, head back to her seat when Cynthia gasped.

"What?"

The woman tapped the window, pointing at something in the distance.

"There, I saw . . . something."

Angela strained her eyes, focusing on where the garden devolved into wilderness.

Her breath caught at a sudden flicker, something moving just beyond the tree line. It was too quick and the murk too dense for her to make out anything specific; just a shadow against shadows, marked out by a flash of nocturnal eyes.

"Oh, god . . ."

Cynthia backed away from the window, weeping, hand clasped to her mouth. The shadows just beyond the tree line seethed as though the entire wood was filled with titanic, mating serpents, movement on the edge of sight drawing Angela's eye.

She stifled a scream, momentarily becoming as cold and unfeeling as the statues outside.

A boy stood amongst the grass and weeds, tall, lanky; an adolescent on the outer-edge of puberty. Shoulder length black hair fell over his face in a funereal veil, the eyes beneath seeming to catch the waning amber light. His arms were red up to the elbows, as if he'd been rummaging around the insides of something freshly slaughtered. A sizeable erection sprouted from a rampant bed of dark pubic hair, one hand toying with it as she watched.

Cynthia didn't exercise the same restraint. Her scream drew the others, their sweating, fear-stinking bodies pressing in from behind.

The boy came to meet them, skipping through the weeds and flowers until he stood close enough for his breath to frost the glass.

"Look, look!"

Others followed in his wake, adolescents all; boys and girls, their states varying from bloodied and near naked to swathed in elaborate costumes that wouldn't have looked out of place in the midst of Mardis Gras. In their hands were knives and shears, jagged rocks and shards of glass. The boy she'd seen first raised his head and smiled at her through the window, teeth like shards of broken quartz.

"Go away!" Cynthia shrieked at them, hammering on the glass. Laughter erupted from the gathering, clownish and cruel.

Still smiling, the boy plucked a knife from one of the newcomer's unresisting fingers, raised it to his face and began to cut.

Several of her fellows cried out, retreating back into the library. Angela stood her ground, unable to move even if she wanted to. The boy carved a deep furrow down one cheek, tracing the curve of his jaw, then drew the knife up from chin to lip, splitting himself in two. A girl wearing a mask of intertwined twigs and roots that obscured the top half of her face came to his aid, digging her fingers into the wounds he carved, peeling away flesh and skin like wet wallpaper.

Something in her hurtled back, retreating to a dark, safe space in the recesses of her skull. It was as if she observed the gruesome spectacle through a series of kaleidoscopic windows, each softening and distorting reality to a dreaming haze, where nothing was of weight or consequence.

Viscous amber honey seeped from the boy's hurts, the state beneath not one of exposed flesh, but glistening black scales.

Enough.

Turning away from the window, she stumbled back down the stairs, collapsing in the first chair she reached. The others milled and murmured, panic threatening to blossom amongst them like some poisonous weed.

"What do they want? Make them go away!"

"They're gonna smash the windows, they're gonna smash the windows . . .!"

Weeping, prayers in French, Gaelic and Japanese. Outside the door, the thing that chased them here scratched and whimpered, begging entry like a neglected dog.

Angela closed her eyes, breathing slow. She needed to find that still space; the inner emptiness that was like a vast beach before life had even crawled from the oceans.

"Be. *Quiet.*"

Not all of them listened, not all of them were capable. They'd retreated too, but to a tempestuous, babbling place where thought and feeling were twin hurricanes.

But those that were able did.

"None of this is helping."

"*Helping?*" One of the hysterical ones; an American woman with hair so red, it looked like her scalp was aflame. Angela saw the animal horror swimming in her eyes, saw in an instant how dangerous she could be. "What is it you think *would* help, Missy? *What would help*?"

She was on the verge of hysteria, her whole body quaking.

"Not shrieking in one another's faces, for a start."

The woman reacted as if slapped, blinking, mouth flapping open, tasting a retort it couldn't quite shape. Then she turned and paced to the windows, joining the small congregation gathered there.

"She has a point, you know, however ill stated. We've got nothing here, and it's only so long before this shit drives us all crazy."

She couldn't remember his name; tall guy, young, sexy; looked like he spent at least three hours every morning in front of the mirror before deigning to unveil himself to the world. He seemed calmer than the rest, speaking low so that only she would hear.

"What do you want me to do about it? I'm not some bloody miracle woman! I . . ."

She followed his example, reigning herself in. The scratches at the library door ceased, their accompanying whimpers retreating.

There were three exits, including the way they'd entered. Breathing deep, she rubbed her face with both hands, weary to her marrow. She couldn't make this decision now, could hardly think straight . . .

"Hey, hey! You'd better come see this!"

She rose automatically, legs carrying her towards the windows before thought could intervene. The congregation parted before her, allowing her to see out into the garden. The tribe of adolescents had all followed their leader's example, taking the instruments they carried to their own flesh, which now lay in steaming pools and tatters around their feet.

Beneath was every kind of nightmare; kaleidoscope parrot feathers from which clumps of wormy appendages lashed and coiled; a mass of black, bony growths from which spidery things swarmed in their hundreds. No two of the tribe were exactly alike; each composed of their own particular absurdity, fragments of the human masks they'd worn still clinging to them.

The boy who'd first taken blade to himself stepped forward, black lizard body shimmering rainbow arcs with every movement. A yellow, reptile eye regarded her through the glass, sphincter-like holes throughout its body dilating and contracting. Smiling its predator's smile, the thing offered her the knife it held, handle first.

Too much.

She'd held it back; the frothing flood waxing in the depths of her mind, but now it surged, sweeping away her defences, swamping reason.

They had to get out, they had to get out *now*.

Questions echoed in her ears as she went to the nearest door, growing frantic as she flung it open, hurling herself through.

*

She'd wanted to be a philosopher; someone who thought and argued for their bread. Either that or a politician. It seemed *so right* once upon a time; her path predetermined, destination inevitable.

Then the disappointments began.

Why the woman had taken against her she didn't know. Maybe it was because she *dared* criticize the vaunted Helen Cisoux, whose work was considered Holy Writ in her feminist literature class. Maybe it was because she spoke up too much when others wouldn't, providing answers that the woman herself didn't seem to entirely grasp. Whatever the case, she'd made an enemy, one that seemed determined on demolishing her academic career by any means necessary.

A failed module wouldn't have meant anything; she'd only taken it as back up in case one of the others faltered. But the accusations of plagiarism, they were an entirely different kettle of fish. She contested them, of course, taking her complaints as far as they could go, but the university protected its own.

Even that wouldn't have defeated her, were it not for her mother.

Bitch. Stupid, selfish, evil bitch.

It was clear something was wrong from the way her dad sounded on the phone:

"Look, love, I can't . . . I can't speak to you like this. I need you to come home."

She didn't want to; she had work here, friends, her own problems to deal with, but what could she say? The man was clearly desperate, and she'd never been able to refuse him anything.

They both seemed to have aged by at least two decades since the last time she saw them, her father's face a mass of fretful furrows, her mother's pale and slack, seeming seconds away from sloughing off the skull.

Her younger brother had been rooting around in their mom and dad's room—no doubt looking for change he could pilfer—when he happened across a bag of white stuff rolled up in the bottom of Mom's wardrobe. Her dad told her he knew *something* was going on; the woman he'd married had changed so drastically since Angela went away to university, her dogmatic practicality eroding, replaced by vagueness and mood swings. She wasn't sleeping, didn't eat properly, had lost touch with most of her friends and family.

"The woman's *withering,*" that was the word he used, "I don't know what to do, love."

He wept and wept, all the frustration finally bursting.

She did what she could; moved home, got work, helped pay off the debts her mother had racked up. There were more than any of them could have anticipated, £30,000 worth, several of which she kept hidden from them 'til bailiffs came knocking at the door.

As for her degree, it was nothing; ashes in the wind. She couldn't spare the time to properly contest the plagiarism claims, couldn't schedule her lectures around work. The friends she'd made grew distant, 'til they finally stopped calling or e-mailing altogether.

She worked. She worked and worked and worked and *worked.* Hated every second of it; hated living under her parent's roof, couldn't bear being in the same room as the wretched, hollow thing that still presumed itself her Mother.

"I wish I could take you back," she told it one day, "I wish I could show you to who you used to be. She'd be fucking *horrified.*" More tears, apologies, empty promises.

Trapped. She rose as far as she could, like scum in a dirty bath tub, then stagnated for what seemed a life time. She didn't make enough money to move out, had to deal with the occasional tens and twenties that went missing from her wallet, the days when the electricity or heating went off because the bill hadn't been paid.

That was when the years started to fly; three, four, five. Before she knew it, she'd spent a decade festering in a quagmire that wasn't even of her own making, struggling every day just to keep her head above the muck.

This is the grown-up world, she'd tell herself. Things don't always work out the way you want them to; you just have to carry on . . .

Only, the excuse had begun to wear thin. Her brother was gone; working bars throughout Europe. The last she heard, he and some friends were trying to raise enough capital between them to start one of their own.

She felt the rot like the roots of some parasitic fungus threading throughout her flesh and thoughts, reducing everything to grey, tasteless mulch.

Hope hinged on the ridiculous; winning the lottery, inheriting a fortune, meeting a pop-star or movie icon who'd fall madly in love with her. Idle fantasy of better things preoccupied her waking hours, dreams and nightmares equally bemoaned when she was forcibly dragged from their embrace. Anything, anything, *anything* was better than this leprosy-life.

Walking to work, murky brown water shimmering with scuds of sunlight beneath the bridge. Was it cold? How long would it take before the water filled her lungs, for thought to slow, stop in its channels? She paused, looked over the edge. People passed behind, not seeming to see her. Hardly surprising. She felt like a phantom, seeing them through a molecule thin but impenetrable veil. A moment's courage for an eternity of peace. It seemed a more than reasonable trade.

But not today.

*

"Wait, wait! Where are you going?"

Footsteps following, shrieks, weeping. The corridor was one of dank, peeling walls, naked plaster beneath nicotine yellow wallpaper cracked and crumbling, entirely fallen away in places, allowing view of what lay beyond. She caught only glimpses on the edges of sight; a space that seemed filled with naked, bleeding bodies, packed so dense from floor to ceiling they could barely move, another that seemed to house a red thunderstorm, tongues of lightning licking out from churning cloud. Naked bulbs flickered from the ceiling, something skittering, scratching just above. She almost laughed out loud. She'd *wanted* this; to not wake up, even if it meant being sealed in her own nightmares.

The corridor branched off in several places, leading to doorways and dead ends; further tracts of the house. She went where her feet dictated, not stopping to think. Writing on the walls; meaningless crayon scrawls and scribbles, as one might find in the nursery of a demented infant: spidery, multiple-armed stick figures hurling one another into the maws of jagged-toothed monstrosities, bat-winged demons with balloon breasts and fish-hook claws flocking in the air.

And no matter how far she ran, the whimpering followed.

What do you want? What in the hell do you want from me?

Her answer came in a sudden scream. Stopping, turning, she was in time to see one of those that followed hurled against the wall, collapsing to the floor in a boneless heap.

It'd found them.

It had hold of Kaplan's ankle, the man shrieking, grasping at the floorboards as he was dragged away. The others tried to stop it, punching, kicking, biting, but it swatted them away as if they were nothing, babbling like a distressed dog.

Angela didn't move to help them, couldn't. Her body had become unfeeling stone, eyes frozen open, forced to play mute spectator to whatever atrocities the nightmare had a mind to parade.

Cynthia shrieked as the thing's free hand found her face, twitching, spidery fingers digging into the meat of her scalp and chin. Hoisted bodily into the air, she flailed out, raking away great cobs of flesh. The thing barely even seemed to notice, smashing her again and again against the wall until she grew still.

The air in the corridor seemed to congeal, Angela's vision blurring as if she witnessed the carnage through flickering bonfire flames. Perfume filled her nostrils; fresh strawberries, coal, cut grass.

Harold twitched and vomited as he was hoisted up by his ankle, a worm at the end of a hook. Then the thing took hold of his other leg, drawing its arms apart until he split at the seams.

A face that was little more than a meat-spattered skull looked up at her, its eye sockets fluttering as if moths swarmed and mated in place of its brain. From between its bony legs hung a mass of twitching tatters, its genitals looking like they'd been forced to couple with a lawn mower. Even so, there was movement there now, something protruding from amongst the ruins that put her in mind of a millipede; legs and feelers waving as they tasted the air.

It came, whooping pleasure as it stalked through the human swamp it'd created.

Come to me, come to me, her thoughts urged, cooing like a mother coaxing its baby to walk.

It'd always been her, from the very beginning. The others . . . they were unhappy accidents, drawn here by their own desperation. She didn't know where the knowledge came from; it seemed to sift into her mind on the smell of slaughter, seeding itself there with all the certainty of love. Her unhappiness had been a knife in the flank of reality, stabbing again and again until it opened to admit her into the darkness beyond.

They were never meant to be here; this was hers and hers alone.

So close now she could *smell* it; warm, wet stone and baking cakes; menstrual blood and boy's hair, her mind suddenly swarming in mirror of the monster's.

Fingers like a Wolf-Spider's legs grazed her cheek, trembled against her neck; its touch almost reverential, as if it were Catholic and she a manifestation of The Blessed Virgin . . .

Something emerged from its eye sockets, black, wet wings unfurling. A butterfly, amber dew beading its body. Plucking it tenderly between thumb and forefinger, the monster pressed the fluttering form to her lips. She resisted at first, an infant unwilling to accept the teat, but the monster grasped her shoulder, its touch abruptly becoming barbed and cold. She cried out, the butterfly deposited in her mouth, shepherded down her throat by insistent fingers.

She tasted blood and honey, wanted to vomit, couldn't. Fluttering in her throat, trailing deeper, deeper, agitating things that seemed to have been in hibernation there since her birth.

A hive about to swarm, a world waiting to be.

Shrieking, like the whine of malfunctioning electronics accompanied by a choir of dying cats. The thing's hands left her, going to the creatures that suddenly swarmed around it, battening onto what little flesh it boasted:

The children from outside, hurling themselves at the monster, stabbing, hacking, biting. The thing flailed at them, grasping one around the throat and squeezing 'til the flesh ruptured. But they were too many. Bearing it to the ground, they hacked and slashed and beat and tore until the swarm it contained was unleashed, laughing as black butterflies filled the corridor.

Through the storm, Angela saw one of the children stand apart from the frenzy, yellow reptilian eyes flaring through what little remained of its humanity. *You're next,* those eyes seemed to promise.

Her statue state suddenly breaking, she turned and ran.

*

He was hope; the first good thing in her life for *so long*. Why he even bothered to give her the time of day she couldn't guess; he was beautiful, in mind and body; an ideal that she perpetually expected to shatter and reveal some untenable imperfection.

They met by accident, at a book store where he worked. It wasn't a big place; little more than a small warehouse, its stock haphazardly packed into shelves that looked on the verge of collapse, into boxes littering the floor. She liked it, especially the freezing cold upstairs where the fiction was kept.

There wasn't usually anyone else up there. That was part of why she liked the place; the quiet, the emptiness. To find the space violated was such a shock, she physically jolted, ice water washing her entrails.

"Oh,"

"Hello," he smiled, half heartedly arranging books on a shelf, "nice to have someone besides the cat about the place."

She didn't reply, didn't know what to say. There'd been a time less than a decade ago when the words would've flowed from her as easily as the breath they rode, but that capacity had withered. Now she found herself thinking, fumbling, her lips curling into an awkward, insincere smile.

Go away. Leave me alone.

There was a radiator up here today, chasing away her beloved cold. The cat he'd mentioned regarded her from the windowsill, lazy lidded eyes shimmering cruel mirth. *You're glass to me,* it seemed to say, *I see you, how small and pathetic you are. Little sparrow want to play?*

She went to one of the shelves and began searching through the volumes there. For some reason, it was difficult to breathe, tension clenching in her breast. *Go away. Go away, go away, go away!*

She jumped, hissed. The cat mewed as it curled around her ankles, demanding attention.

"Smeagol, leave her alone, will you? Sorry about that. He's just curious."

"It's okay." She automatically smiled back, reaching down to pet the bastard creature. It retreated from her hand as if it were aflame.

"Were you looking for anything in particular? I know pretty much everything we have in stock . . ."

"Not really. I just come to browse every now and then."

"Ah." He looked a little defeated that he couldn't make himself useful.

She turned away, theatrically running her finger over several spines, didn't even stop to read the titles.

"I'm, ah, going to make some tea in a moment. If you're hanging around, would you like some?"

He only half-faced her, one hand hovering suspended over the shelves. *No. No, I just want to get out of here, go home.*

"That'd be good."

*

Three months. The longest relationship she'd ever had. He treated her like royalty, like a goddess. They didn't like it, her mother and father. They regarded the arrangement with suspicion, the fright in her mother's eyes when she first mentioned she had a boyfriend so acute, so fucking *selfish,* she wanted to slap her until they dimmed.

She knew why; they were afraid she'd get married, leave them to sort out their own train wreck of a life. They did their best not to show it, of course; little snide comments deliberately ambiguous, feigned dismay when she retaliated.

Neither of them were clever or subtle enough to maintain the veneer for very long.

"We just want you to be *careful,* love. I mean, you don't have that much experience with this sort of thing, do you? And people can be real *bastards,* you know. You think you know 'em, then one day it all comes crashing down . . ."

She almost laughed at the irony of this. Didn't the stupid cow realise she was effectively describing her own failed marriage? Of course not; she'd long since become incapable of such introspection.

Angela didn't even do it the courtesy of a reply.

"Yeah, yeah, he seems a nice enough chap. Hard to say one way or the other, yet."

They'd met once, briefly, when he'd come to pick her up. She didn't want him here, didn't want to expose him to their *crap.* It was clear her dad had already made up his mind: *nice enough, but not good enough.* No one ever would be, and not because she was his little girl, but because she was his *keeper*; the one holding them both above the water whilst they struggled to drag one another down.

"Is it . . . serious-like?"

"Yeah, I think it is."

No answer. Just a sigh.

*

It was inevitable, like a fever she could feel waxing long before it fully kindled. She'd dreaded it from the very start, worried since the first kiss that it would be the last.

"Why?"

"You know why, Angela. You don't want me, not really. I'm just a way out for you."

A punch to the belly, a kick to the jaw. He was right; the fact of him had never mattered. He was Jesus on the Cross to her, not that she'd ever openly admit it.

"No. that's not *it.*" She could feel it slipping away from her, salvation like a shimmering rope suspended above the mouth of Hell.

"Don't. Bottom line, okay?: I'm not interested in being your get-out clause. I like you *a lot,* but you . . ."

He lapsed into silence, baring teeth, shaking his head.

". . . you're killing yourself. You're going out of your mind, and I don't want to be around to see it."

No crying. She wouldn't give him the satisfaction. Besides which, he was wrong, at least in that respect. Her sanity was perfectly intact; that was part of the problem. Perhaps if she *were* losing it, she wouldn't be able to *see* her own decay, what little life she had fraying, coming apart at the seams.

"And telling me to fuck off is going to help?"

"I'm not telling you to *fuck off,* I'm telling you that I want you to be *okay.*"

So, what? He was going to hang around as her *friend*? Maybe help her out when things got too bad at home? No. She didn't want that from him, never had. All or nothing.

"Well, I'm not going to be now, so I'm telling you to *fuck off, fuck off* and don't *ever* come near me again."

He blinked, finely sculpted features growing slack on their scaffold. For an instant, he looked *so old,* then he was gone, out of her life without another word or thought.

*

Coming apart; a rag doll become a nursery for spiders, her seams splitting as they hatched. How long had she been running? Hours. *Days,* the house never-ending, corridor upon corridor, room upon room.

The children never tired. Glancing over her shoulder, she saw them dancing and skipping in her wake, some of them scurrying spider-like across walls and ceiling. They called to her, sang to her; invited her to join in their game.

She couldn't, *she didn't know how . . .*

Down a darkened spiral staircase, red sunlight spilling through arched windows, she found what looked to be a dance hall, complete with stage for the band, save that the floor was bare earth; damp, sprouting with weeds, grasses, saplings. A willow rose in the centre of the room, its leaves trailing in a small stream that ran from one wall to the other. Through a vast, shattered window, birds flocked and fluttered, feeding on the worms, slugs and insects that infested the place. A spider splayed out across one wall, similar to the house-spiders that her father kept company with in the shed back home. Only she doubted this species would be satisfied with mere flies.

She almost laughed; so *absurd,* like something from a child's nightmare.

The dirt twitched and shifted beneath her feet as she made her way across the room. There was a doorway to the spider's right. It didn't seem concerned by her presence, so still it might've been nothing more than decoration . . .

One leg stretched out, tapping the dirt before it. A fat abdomen, bloated with web or eggs, pulsed and twitched.

She stopped, hearing the children in the stairwell behind. How fast could the thing move? If it was anything like the spiders at home, faster than lightning. She'd been afraid of them as a child, still was to a certain degree, but not so much that the mere presence of one was enough to paralyse her. She seemed to float towards the door rather than run, the soil beneath her soles barely stirring. Even so, the spider responded, creeping down from its mount to paw at the ground, sensing her footsteps.

Shouting and singing behind as the children poured into the room, the birds feeding there abruptly taking flight. Their cries weren't like any Angela had ever heard; akin to distorted, scratching feedback from a broken radio. Turning, she saw the children chasing and snatching at them as they flew, one squealing as the spider barrelled into it, bearing it to the ground.

She didn't wait to witness the feeding that followed.

*

They could barely conceal their satisfaction. The bitch who'd birthed her didn't even try:

"I have to admit, I was surprised you got with him in the first place. After all, it's never really been your *scene*, has it? You're probably better off."

Better off? Better off stuck here in this miserable, mouldering house with its miserable mouldering occupants, miserable and mouldering herself? They were eating dinner in front of the TV, some soap opera babbling banalities that seemed to seep into her mind, softening thought. She was shocked at how strong the inclination was; just a second without thought, and they'd both be gone from her life. She smiled, picturing the animal light going out in her mother's eyes, her father slipping away softly, sleepily, the trauma of his life ended. Just a second . . .

She recovered herself before the knife was barely an inch off her plate. How could she even *think* it? What kind of lunatic was she making of herself?

Her dinner tray and its contents flew, cracking the TV screen. Her mother shrieked, scrabbling instinctively for the remote. Angela was gone before the questions could come, her father's footsteps trailing her to the bottom of the garden path, but no further.

"Angela, Angela!"

Rot, rot you fucker!

Nowhere; no thought, no direction, just *away*.

The world pressed in, seething grey around her as she ran. She could *feel* it; cold, oily tendrils around her wrists and ankles, dabbling at her mouth and the corners of her eyes, seeking entry.

No, no!

She lashed out instinctively, but not with fingers, teeth or feet. The anatomy was something she'd known of before, long ago, but simply . . . forgotten; the same she used to chase away the night time terrors that swarmed in the shadows as a child; coils of light and colour that unfurled from within like butterfly wings, but with strength enough to split a mountain in two.

She stumbled, the world dissolving into momentary chaos. There was time to anticipate the kiss of cold, wet concrete, the inevitable pain . . . only neither came. Instead, her flailing other anatomy snared, its barbs finding some unseen edge; a seam beyond perception. A sound like every beast and child on earth howling in unison ripped through her, accompanied by a sensation like being dissected by celestial surgeons; split, peeled and teased out of herself, only to be pieced together again in some new, unimagined configuration.

Waking came all at once, more traumatic than the impact she braced herself for. There were hands on her, holding her down, clamped to her mouth, voices hissing in her ear:

"Ssshhhh!!"

"Shut the fuck up, will you?"

"God, don't let her scream! It'll hear us!"

And she was elsewhere, somewhere, perhaps even *something* else, the state she left behind already little more than a bad dream.

*

Darkness, subterranean, absolute. Behind, she heard the children at play, growing more distant with every breath.

There could be anything in here. She imagined the floor falling away barely inches before her feet, a chasm in which blind carrion things seethed and multiplied, waiting to feed on those who fell. She fancied she could almost hear them if she concentrated; slithering, scrabbling sounds, like pits full of snakes and beetles.

The light was momentarily blinding, a miniature star suddenly flaring in the centre of the room. Angela shielded her eyes, shrinking back against the door. Whispers beyond the blindness, shuffling feet.

"Leave me alone!"

Distant laughter, like that of a ghost-child choked on its own umbilical chord before it could enter the world.

There was something in the light; fluttering things of smoke and cob web, brushing her brow, arms and belly like the slightest of lover's caresses. Despite their tenderness, they carried weight, her clothes ripping and sloughing away as if torn at by tigers, the flesh beneath bruising, splitting. She lashed out, her hands finding nothing but empty air.

Her legs went from under her, pitching her to cold, worn-smooth stone. The light abated abruptly, dimming to little more than a candle flicker in the murk. The voices were clearer now, laughing and hailing her.

A joke; all she was; all she'd ever been.

Marks on her hands and forearms; symbols and scraps of writing scored and burned into her skin. There was no pain from them; only a strange tingling, as if the flesh were soil about the sprout. Not just her arms; her breasts, her legs; every inch of her made slate and canvas for the inspirations of spectral artists.

"Oh love, just look how *pretty* you are."

No.

Of all people . . . she couldn't be here, she *couldn't.* This was *hers,* hers, goddammit!

Candles flickered atop a long table arrayed as if for a formal banquet. A number of diners were seated round about, tucking into their meals with desperate gusto, as if to slow their feeding would be to risk starvation.

Her mind rebelled at the sight of meals and diners both.

Stupid. Stupid, stupid, stupid shite! Bad gore movie fair, deliberately designed to shock its audience and get the moral minority foaming at the bit.

She knew them all, though how she managed to identify them in their current states was beyond her. Dad sat at the head of the table, slit from throat to loins so that all he contained spilled out in glistening plenty on his plate. He smiled as he ate, bushy salt and pepper moustache seeming to barely hold back laughter. To either side of him sat Harold Kaplan and the woman named Cynthia, the former barely held together by the formal dinner suit he wore whilst the latter plucked tit-bits from her smashed-in skull, nibbling on them with dainty enthusiasm. All of them were here; the family she'd left behind, the fractious, frightened one she'd woken to.

From the closest chair her mother smiled in earnest welcome, the eyes Angela had come to hate for their desperate, animal selfishness put out, leaving behind bloodied hollows in whose depths something maggot-like squirmed.

Cocking her head, she gestured to the empty seat next to her, inviting Angela to come and join the feast.

Angela shook her head, upper lip curling in a disgusted snarl.

"No."

The woman's smile widened, dimpling her cheeks.

"Oh, come on now love, don't be difficult. After all the trouble we've gone to . . ."

"Angela," her Father, voice wavering on the edge of that disappointed tone that always sent fractures across her heart. "This is all for you, you know. Don't you want to be with us, is that it?"

Yes, yes that was it. That was *it.*

The swarm inside stirred, ready to take flight. She felt them in her throat, in her belly; behind her eyes and between her legs, every inch of her waiting for the opportunity to remove itself from the rest.

"Just forget her. You know what she's like; always thinking that she's something *special.*"

Her brother, an arm torn away at the elbow, laid before him like a leg of lamb.

She *was* special; she was the woman who'd torn the world wide, exposing what lay beyond skin and sanity. Her desperation and despair were the instruments; jagged enough to wound it mortally. Now she was a maggot in the wound, feeding, growing fat.

"No." Her Father's fist slammed down against the table, the entire room trembling. "Look at me, Angela."

She did, feeling a flush of infantile defiance, as if she'd been caught stealing change from her parent's pockets.

He rose from his seat, whorls and packets of wet yellow, purple and brown spilling from him.

She should have been repulsed by this, the grotesquery unseating stomach and sanity.

But she wasn't, not anymore.

"Why do you always have to be so *ungrateful*? Your mother and me, we've done everything for you, *everything,* but you always look at us as if we're shit on the sole of your shoe. It's about time you *realised* where your place is, you understand? Now sit down and eat *your goddamned dinner."*

The others stopped eating to look at her now, pleading with their eyes and smiles for her to sit, sit and join the merriment.

"No."

Their smiles died, the welcome in their eyes growing cold. Her father began to tremble where he stood, arms and head jerking like those of an elaborate clock work toy with grit in its cogs. Her mother put her hands to her eyes and began to weep, glutinous, red and black tears seeping between her fingers.

"Bad . . . bad girl . . ."

Rains of meat fell from her father's trembling body, skin and flesh sloughing away as if they were little more than wet papier mache. Beneath was pulsing grey; a slug-like mass, tumours forming across its surface, bursting to unleash wisps of silvery vapour.

"Look . . . look at . . . what you've done to us . . ."

The others followed suit, shedding themselves to reveal cores of vileness; her Mother something that resembled a vast cancer, scarred and pustulent, myriad eyes glaring familiar accusation from every hollow.

No; this wasn't what she'd made of them. This was what they'd made of *themselves.*

Behind, the children sang, scratching at the door, begging to be let in.

The diners limped and sloped from their seats, trailing the filth of their anatomies across the floor. They'd *drag* her to her seat if they had to, press her face into her own stinking stuffs, make her smile as she swallowed.

They wouldn't get the chance.

Turning, she flung the door wide.

*

They surged around her, some reaching out to pinch or caress as they passed. Most of them had entirely shed their former skins now, revealed as spectres of tinted smoke, things seemingly sewn together from flocks of living ravens or swarms of centipedes.

Though they'd trailed her like wolves scenting a wounded lamb, now they paid her no more heed than they might a tree in their path. Behind, she heard the diners screaming, calling her name as they were devoured. Even now they begged her to join them, promising joy and comfort with a fervency beyond that of any evangelist.

Before her stood the first youth she'd seen from the library window, black scales shimmering, eyes fixed and unblinking. In his claws, he held a shard of broken mirror, its edge arrayed in rainbows as it caught the dying sunlight.

She accepted the shard without a word, a character in a stage-play; every act and motion prearranged.

The swarm became frantic, its components committing suicide against the inside of her skull and stomach in their desperation to be free.

Cold, so cold it stopped the breath in her throat, froze thought in its channels.

The lizard-thing smiled, jagged teeth shimmering crystalline brilliance. Her hands seemed to act of their own volition, drawing the shard up to her breast where it caught, shattering. It didn't matter; she was open now, the swarm taking flight.

Butterflies, but not black winged; these were red and silver, things of meat and moonlight, dancing, mating, murdering one another as they flew. Some were snared by birds as they rose towards the broken window, others fell of their own volition, diving into the dirt and burrowing 'til they were lost to sight.

Angela went with them, threads of thought twining around each and every insect 'til the ruptured skin she left behind was little more than a sack, suspended by a pig-headed certainty in its own importance.

Now the lizard-boy played his part, laying her down in the dirt almost tenderly, whispering to her in a language she didn't understand.

No, not to her; to the desiccated meat that still thought of itself as such. Let it go, let it go . . .

Too hard. She'd spent so long in the certainty that this was herself in its entirety and extent, letting it go was like . . .

Dying.

She felt the mirror shard removed from her, emptiness beyond endurance rushed in to replace it; a hungry, maddening void into which what remained of self slipped.

Then the mirror entered her again, putting out the sight in one eye, then the other, before burying itself in the centre of her brow. This was where the black butterflies bred, vaster and more elaborate than their cousins, carrying more of her than all of the others combined.

She flew, seeing through a million separate eyes, feeling sun and wind on a million separate wings. How long could any sense of "she" sustain in this state; memory, thought and experience divorced from one another? She didn't know. Maybe each fragment would become the seed of its own self in time; newer and better than the ripeness of Angela. Maybe she would be scattered forever, motes cast adrift across this new world, never whole, never herself again.

She could live with that.

*

She was in her mom's belly when it happened. They hardly ever talked about it, but she'd begun to understand, little by little.

The world she was born to had been different, once. They called it *Before,* though they didn't like to.

"Things are better now, it doesn't matter," they said. There were still bits and pieces here and there; strange places she was forbidden from wandering. Not that it stopped her.

This place, for example; strange buildings of red brick, sunken into ground that looked to have *melted* at some point before abruptly solidifying, or rent apart by the plants and growths that sprung up around them. Her mother said that *Before,* all the plants and trees had names. She didn't quite understand that. Wouldn't it take forever to name them *all*?

It was dangerous here; one of the places where the wild ones played. She'd been told stories of them ever since she was a little girl; like Mom, they were from *Before,* but different from the rest. They'd seen the Angel Woman, helped her to make the world as it was now. Most of the stories were crap; no different from the rest of the stuff Mom and Dad told her, but the wild ones were *real.* She'd seen them with her own eyes.

The Angel Woman . . . those were the stories she liked best, about the world *Before* being ripped open, everything changing. She wondered if they'd ever change again, if, like the wild ones, the angel woman was more than just a story?

She'd brought food for them; stole the sweet cakes her mother had baked, some of the smoked meat hanging in the larder. She knew the kind they liked best.

The ground was *wrong* here; all cracked and glassy, split so wide in places, she had to jump to get across. It was okay; she had her mother's strong legs.

Things flocked and sang in the sky overhead, perching on the weird metal trees that her father called "Lamp Posts." They weren't really trees, of course, rather machines from *Before.* Apparently, there were a lot of machines back then. Most of them had begun to run down now. Her father was good with them; he helped fix things that people brought him. That's why her family lived in the best place and ate the best things around. She had to be careful because the rest were jealous. They'd already hurt her older brother so much he couldn't walk or speak anymore. She didn't like to think about the same happening to her.

One of the flying things called to her as she passed beneath its perch, singing in a throaty woman's voice some old song that she thought she'd heard her mother singing once or twice. A set of three beady black eyes, one dead and white, regarded her from a face that looked assembled from the broken bits and pieces that her mother swept from the chopping board after preparing meat for dinner. Scooting down, she plucked up a hunk of stone and hurled it at the thing, knocking it from its seat in a flurry of shrieks and feathers.

Where were they? Never in the same place. They'd find her if they wanted to. Otherwise, she'd just wander until the sun started to go down, then head home.

She'd never been this deep before. The streets seemed to wind and twist forever; the whole world beyond her family's little lands nothing but this red brick ruin. It might be so, for all she knew.

Sometimes she caught things watching her from the black and broken windows; phantoms wavering just on the edge of sight. She hurried past those places, plucking up a stone or a shard of broken glass in case they decided to do more than just look.

Maybe they didn't want her today. That caused a horrible sinking feeling in the pit of her stomach. She dreamed about them last night; the yellow-eyed snake-boy kissing her in a way that made her feel like snow and fire inside. That usually meant they'd be waiting, wanting her to see...

It came out of nowhere, suddenly barrelling towards her as if materialised out of thin air. She didn't get much time to take it in; something ragged and billowing, like tatters of old silk caught up in a river's current. Then it hit her, carrying them both to the broken concrete as it pawed and bit at her clothes. She screamed, lashed out at it with claws and teeth. Great wet cobs of it came away, writhing in her hands and mouth. It tasted foul, like leaf mulch and spoiled milk. Through the rags swathing it, she caught occasional glimpses of cracked and bleeding flesh, unnatural swellings as if the thing was cancerous from scalp to soles. A pointed blue tongue flickered from its wound of a mouth, lapping at her cheek, her throat.

"Listen to Mommy, listen to Mommy, now . . ."

Raising her legs, she bunched them tight against her chest, kicked. The thing flew from her, ripping at her arms in its desperation to hold on. It skidded across the concrete, leaving behind a trail of rags and filth. Gurgling baby talk, it staggered to its feet, coming at her again before she even had a chance to right herself.

"Stay away."

A rock flew from her hands before it could even heed her warning, striking it full in the ruined face. Dark wetness blossomed across the tatters concealing it, but the thing barely even broke stride.

She was going to be eaten, dragged away to some dark, shit-stinking cellar and pulled apart. She'd be lucky if Mom and Dad even found her bones . . .

Hands from behind, dragging her back. She screamed, tried to pull away. They held her fast, dragging her into a cold embrace. She looked up into eyes the colour of poison, eyes that never blinked. *I'd devour you twice as fast,* those eyes seemed to say, *you wouldn't feel a thing.*

Him; the leader of the Wild Ones.

Others appeared now, carrying knives, splinters of wood, daggers of broken glass. They surrounded the thing that attacked her, shepherding it back with jabs and slashes. The thing wailed, its cry of pain a single name repeated over and over:

"Angela! Angela!"

Then it was gone, fleeing as suddenly as it emerged into the ruins.

She'd never been this close to a Wild One before, never dared *touch* one. She breathed in deep, tasting damp earth and flowers crushed under foot.

"Did it hurt you?"

His voice was soft, the words strange and rippling, almost seeming sung rather than said. She drew away, abruptly feeling the pain in her torn arms.

She didn't answer, letting him press and probe the wounds with his fingers. She winced, but didn't cry out.

"I think you'll live," he smiled, jagged crystal teeth glinting.

The others found the food she'd brought, now scattered across the broken concrete. They didn't seem to mind eating off the ground, snapping up the cakes and cuts of meat with every sign of enjoyment.

Bending down, the lizard-boy snatched up an unbroken bottle of red stuff she'd pilfered from her Dad's collection. There was writing on it she couldn't read, but that his eyes flickered over with acute understanding.

"Port. *Perfect.* We've got a lot to celebrate."

The others, finished with their meal, turned their attention on her. As always, there were several whose regard was less than friendly.

"Send her *away.*"

Barely a whisper from a thing that resembled a burning woman wreathed in a column of light and smoke.

The lizard-boy hissed.

"Where are your *manners,* Lucile? You've just eaten her food. What do you think Angela would say?"

The woman sighed, seemed to waver behind her ethereal veils.

"What do you say?" He asked, grinning his crooked grin. "Do you want to go *home*, or do you want to come with us?"

Instinct informed her words, not allowing even a second for hesitation:

"With you."

The grin widened. For an instant, she thought she was dreaming again, that he'd drag her close and kiss her here amongst the ruins. Warm sea water washed over her innards at the prospect. The look he gave her made her feel as if her head were made of glass, the thoughts within as clear to him and all around as the world outside a window.

He drew close, the scent of him seeming somehow *stronger* now; that of a forest in Autumn.

He did kiss her, albeit somewhat more chastely than she'd imagined.

"I was hoping you'd say that."

*

Mated, multiplied; decimated, devoured. They came, drawn by a call so innate that to resist it would be to tear themselves apart. Some did, suicidal independence outweighing the will to survive.

No matter. They'd spread far and wide since the world had been torn and teased inside out, travelling as deep as wing and wind could carry. Some had grown beyond the bounds of the whole that spawned them, becoming minds in their own right. These came too, drawn by dreams, by wanderlust, by fear, by confusion. Some failed at the first step, tripping and breaking their necks, dragged home and murdered by those who purported to love them. Others simply faltered, returning to the lives they'd made for themselves content in confusion.

But they came, little by little. The Wild Ones took them in, tended to them; made them one of their own.

Even many of these didn't survive to the appointed day. They came diseased, wounded, weak; they killed themselves, no longer able to endure the dreams and the endless waiting.

But they came.

A swarm, the orchard that sprung up in the place where she tore the world apart a playground of butterflies and monsters. That was where they gathered, where they played and feasted; where they went to die when they couldn't sustain any longer.

Now the last had come, and the world could begin to heal.

LIE OF THE LAND

A spear of sunlight in his mind, igniting thought, driving away shadow.

There'd been moments like this before; epiphany and inspiration riding on some unexpected miracle—a blazing red dawn over snow-covered hills, a moon so swollen it seemed on the verge of giving birth viewed through a lover's bedroom window—but never, never like this.

Laughter, nervous and uncertain, consoling hands at his back.

"Thomas mate, are you all right?"

Orange street-lamp light reflected from the black puddle beneath his feet, the scents of dirt, petrol and Chinese take-away mingling in his nostrils.

"Ah, he's okay. Probably just a bit of bad stuff, you know?"

No, no bad stuff here. He'd made a show of taking a pill from the packet, keeping it beneath his tongue where it fizzled and dissolved, before retreating to the bathroom and spitting it down the sink.

He was a thing of smoke and butterflies, ready to fly apart with every breath.

"For fuck's sake, Cathy, just *leave* him. We've only got an hour before Capricorn closes."

"It's okay; you guys go on. I'll take him home."

Muttered resentment, hornets stinging beneath his clothes. Her touch was balm, a warm wind carrying ocean spray.

He let her lead him, fearful of fully opening his eyes in case the sunlight spilled out.

*

Vomit, acrid and throat-clogging, sick sweat and unwashed bodies. He imagined them; those who'd sat in this seat before throughout the day:

An ageing drunk, wife and daughters fled after the last, fatal relapse.

Dead now, coiled foetal in the drainpipe where he wouldn't be found 'til the following Christmas, weary mother of two about the day's shopping, paying bills; rank with embarrassment as her period came.

Why? Why did all of this flood his head? He'd never thought like this before. It was as if he'd been invaded, his old self impaled, left for dead, something tender and alien bursting from its remains.

The taxi driver babbled banality, asking if they'd had a good night. Cathy answered, her arm around his shoulders.

"Okay, you know. Same as usual."

"Bit early to be 'eadin' 'ome, ain't it?"

"Yeah, well, we're both a bit tired, busy day tomorrow."

Thomas opened his eyes, looking out the window. They'd left the city behind, winding through labyrinthine, red-brick suburbs. Packs of youths congregated on street corners, wreathed in broiling clouds of red and purple smoke. A solitary night-walker, pony-tail straggling between his shoulder-blades, seemed to swell and sprout with fantastic growths; a crown of horns, multiple wings, myriad eyes burning with amber moonlight.

He turned away, closing his eyes against the nonsense. Just something some bastard had slipped into his drink. He'd be fine after a good night's sleep.

*

Night air, chill and freighted with rumour. Alan and Linda lived out on the edge of nowhere, the room they leased him looking out over farmer's fields, hills and valleys. Always so, so quiet here.

"Come on, let's get you to bed. You got your keys?"

He fumbled them from his pocket, dropping them on the gravel drive. She bent to scoop them up.

There'd scarcely been anywhere in his twenty-three years he felt less threatened. Town was treacherous territory, every instant spent in fear of attracting attention from the local thug or lunatic. Here there was nothing; foxes, pheasants and horse-flies.

"I sometimes go walking on my own at night . . ." Why was he telling her this?

"Not tonight, though."

She'd always liked him. He'd always known it, turned a blind eye. Beneath the concern she radiated, he felt something else coiling; feverish tentacles reaching up to ensnare him, drag him down into haunted depths.

"I go across the fields, miles and miles . . ."

There was an abbey nearby, hemmed in by hills, surrounded by trees and tall grasses. He'd come there one evening, sun a blood haze on the horizon . . .

Eyes. Eyes and mouths in the dark, thousands of them watching, whispering, seeing him like a blazing candle in the fog. He wanted to be inside, away from them and their swarming locust, dead-radio static chatter . . .

She fumbled with the key in the unfamiliar lock. *Hurry,* he silently urged, *hurry!*

They stumbled inside, dark and faint warmth waiting to greet them. Cathy closed the door, turning the key in the lock.

Thomas went to his knees, the eyes and mouths retreating.

*

They weren't home, a note explaining they'd gone to visit their son down south. They'd be back next weekend. Home-made chicken and mushroom pie in the fridge—would he mind feeding the hens and cats?

Cathy set about making them both tea. The fire in his skull began to fade at long last, whatever skewed his system slowly sweating itself out. Even so, he caught himself jumping at shapes glimpsed in the dark outside the window, phantoms dancing at the edge of sight.

"Can you hear that?"

"What?"

Faint footsteps above, like bare feet dragging across the bedroom carpet.

"*That!*"

She looked at him as if he'd peeled off a portion of his face to reveal a truth of writhing tentacles and bulbous insect eyes.

"Look, you're just having a bad come-down. Happens to everyone once in a while."

Only if they actually take something, you stupid bitch.

"I'm just . . . going to check."

"Not on your own, you're not. I'm not having you slip down the stairs and break your neck on me."

Fine by him.

*

Cold upstairs, the landing window wide open. He slammed it shut, locking it fast. Shadows swarmed over the surrounding hills, a hungry, fungal darkness, intent on consuming all creation . . .

There, gone so fast he wasn't certain he saw anything: a flash of eyes in the night, something slinking amongst the shadows. Too big to be a fox or a rabbit . . .

Nothing.

"There's no one up here."

What was that *smell*? Like raw meat and spoiled milk. The air was full of invisible moths, velvet wings brushing his ears, lips and eyes, seeking entry.

Wrong. Wrong, wrong, *wrong*. Something here, something that shouldn't be . . .

"I think you'd better just go to bed, Tom. Sleep it off."

He ignored her, making his way through the unseen storm to Lynda and Alan's room. The stench was strongest here, so dense he gagged.

*

Long grass tickling grazed, naked shins, flies supping the adolescent sweat beading his brow. The house was gone, the future it belonged to already little more than a receding dream. In its place, ancient, broken stone; pillars and arches overgrown with creepers, festooned with deathly white flowers. Summer heat softened thought and reality, the whole world shimmering mirage-like.

He wasn't supposed to be here; it'd been forbidden for as long as he could remember. There were stories when he was a boy; tales of phantasmal things haunting the stones, waiting for disobedient, foolhardy children to fall into their grasp. The fables had taken a more rational turn as he grew older: "The whole place is tumbling down, love. If you broke your leg or your neck out there, nobody would be around to help you."

And they'd sufficed, until today. Today, he wasn't inclined to take his parent's word, having learned how readily they lied to one another. Today, he needed to be away from them and from everyone; alone in the wild.

He didn't know he was coming here, simply following where his feet led.

Now, stung, scratched and stinking to high heaven, he stood before the shattered altar, the stone cross that once stood atop it lying broken on the floor. Beyond was the statue of an angel, skin and outstretched wings green with moss, fungi sprouting from its face and fingers. He couldn't tell if it was a man or woman, didn't know if it mattered with angels, but it was beautiful. So beautiful he felt a familiar stirring in the pit of his belly, heat and hardness stealing up on him, but not unwelcome here, where the only eyes to see were of dead stone; those of birds and bugs, ha, maybe the ghosts his mom used to babble on about.

No one for miles.

His hand slipped beneath the hem of his shorts, idly teasing. The hair sprouting there in lush profusion in recent months was dank with sweat. It'd be so good to feel the breeze against his skin . . .

The angel watched without comment or condemnation as he slipped off his shoes and shirt, the self-consciousness that slithered through him trailing a delirious exhilaration. So what if anyone watched? Let them see. He didn't give a fuck.

Still, he was loath to step out of his underwear. This was a place of God once, wasn't it? And God was everywhere.

But . . . if God was everywhere, he already saw everything anyway, right? Those Saturday night sessions when he stayed up after everyone had gone to bed, turning down the volume as he skimmed through the TV channels for some flicker of female skin, when he sat on the toilet, surrounded by his own funk and foulness.

This was nothing in comparison.

Glorious to be so open, so exposed. His prick throbbed so hard he felt it was going to explode. All around he heard the chittering and scurrying of wild things; crickets in the grass, birds in the boughs.

The angel continued to stare unseeing, withholding judgement.

A wash of cold seawater over the furnace of his thoughts, the voice faint, distant, but still too close for comfort:

A girl's sigh, hitched and breathy, floating feather-like on the breeze.

Tom whirled around, scouring the surrounding trees and bushes.

Nothing.

Probably just some animal or his fevered imagination. It wouldn't be the first time he'd dreamt girls into being.

The sun was going down, shadows creeping from between the trees, herded by rays of deep red blood light. They'd swarm this place soon, the only light falling from moon and stars. He'd never find his way back home in the dark.

Not that it mattered; the prospect of staying out here all night, dancing naked with the shadows, appealed to him. Maybe some of the stories he'd been told would prove true: maybe he'd play witness to a black mass of local witches, women of the woods dancing naked around open flame, or a congregation of spirits come seeking salvation from their earthly bondage.

It wouldn't matter if there was nothing; he'd be happy with the wind and stars.

Again, closer now, the sigh bubbling up into laughter.

Someone was here. Someone *saw*.

His earlier flagrancy evaporated, replaced by a gut-churning fear he'd arrive back at school after the holidays to find images of his stark-naked self being passed around via e-mail and text message.

Pools of red and amber evening light formed around him as he gathered up his clothes, tugging on sweat-dank boxer shorts.

The wind seemed to rise in protest at this, wailing through the boughs, carrying with it a scent of dirt and rotting flowers.

Home. They were probably wondering where he was by now, getting worried . . .

Pulling on shorts, shirt and shoes, he scampered to the rent in the abbey's wall, hoping that the path home would make itself apparent.

The girl's smile was lunatic, eyes so wide they seemed on the verge of starting from their sockets. Hair cascaded over her face in white-blonde streamers, as if her scalp erupted with spun sunshine. Rough rouge smeared her lips, lending her the look of having recently dined on wild berries or raw meat, the too-big man's shirt she wore similarly stained, opened down the front to reveal the swelling of her breasts.

Tom stopped, heart, breath and thought snarling in unison.

Craning her head to stare at the eve-blushed sky, the girl sighed, shuddering from scalp to soles. With jerking, shuddering steps, she tottered towards him, her motions those of an aged and broken clockwork doll. The perfume of sweetness and rot was so dense he wanted to gag.

Run! An imperative like the last words of a man falling to his death, distorted and fading, fading . . .

He didn't heed it, the woods stirring at the edge of sight, shadows coalescing to the point whereby they seemed almost solid . . .

Her touch scourged like frost, her kiss filling him with light and agony. His first; the one by which all others would be measured, but which none in waking life would ever equal.

He moaned, squirming against her, tongue flickering through the cold furnace of her mouth, tasting its light and fire. *Pull away, pull away!* He couldn't; their lips were sealed, sewn together by frost. Besides, the imperative came in his mother's voice, which he'd resolved never to listen to again. Why would he want to deny himself this? What waited for him beyond? Cold and disappointment; a retreat back to the misery that had driven him out, away from the known.

Her fingers, as cold as her lips and tongue, fluttering over his belly, raising goose pimples, brushing his nipples, making them ache. His own twitched, itching to rise and trespass beneath her shirt, between her legs, but refused to, instead flickering in the air like snake's tongues, tasting threat or prey. It didn't matter; hers were wanton enough for both of them.

Finding him, she gripped hard, her frost not dousing the fire that threatened to char him from the inside out, but encouraging it to rise in concert rather than context, matching its counterpart note for note.

Never, never before, the only one who'd ever touched him so intimately the mother he'd learned to hate, back when he'd been too feeble to clean and clothe himself.

No...he wouldn't let that poison infect this moment. He fought memory back, beating it bloody before burying it deep. Here and now; the girl and his hunger; all that was, all he knew.

Then the world, grown ragged and unfocused at the edges of sight, swelled and frayed open at the seams, her lips damming his screams as it spilled forth with all that reason was contrived to keep at bay.

*

All in a breath. A dream, a memory? Some sort of hallucination experienced in the throes of fever?

"Tom?" She sounded worried. The moths grew agitated in sympathy.

"It's okay," he slurred, opening the door.

Like stepping into a charnel house filled with fruit and rose petals. Even Cathy gagged, though he was sure she only tasted the merest suggestion of it.

There were ghosts here, though not of dead things. Old times, past passions, shrugged off selves; they swarmed and flitted amongst the shadows, occasionally cohering so that he caught glimpses of them with his naked eyes: Alan and Lynda in younger state, back when the bedroom was more than just a place for dreams, shades of them coupling before the window, under the covers, against the wall, Linda curled up and sobbing atop the bed, Alan peering out the window, sag shouldered, looking on the verge of collapse.

The moths whispered in Thomas's ears, echoing fragments of dead conversation:

". . . so, where'd it go? I know I didn't use it . . ."

". . . tell me. Tell me or I walk out this fucking door right now and that's it."

". . . gone and got herself into trouble again . . . not sure I can handle it any more . . ."

". . . of course I love you, you silly arse."

And through it all, the *sobbing*, an expression of despair so profound it set thought and entrails writhing in concert.

"Oh . . . God." Cathy. She didn't see what he did, but saw enough. Gone before he could stop her, hurtling down the stairs and out the front door.

The figure at the window watched her flee, pale, spidery fingers scraping the glass. Taller, more wiry than before, blonde hair knotted, streaked with filth.

"You said you'd come back."

He couldn't remember. Their first meeting was a kaleidoscope, fragments of memory and fantasy tumbling together 'til neither could be discerned.

"Are you real?"

She laughed, shoulders hitching. The dress she wore was like mist, cob web snaring sunlight.

"I was . . . I'm not sure. Are you?"

He didn't know how to answer that. Was this the same for her as it was for him; like stumbling into some all but forgotten dream?

She turned away from the window, face half obscured beneath shadow-mask. The rest no longer smiled. Spastic fingers tap-danced over the swollen dome of her belly, soothing what gestated within. He imagined he could almost see the moths now, moonlight snaring on the edges of invisible wings as they swarmed around her, massing at her wrists, throat and hairline to become living jewellery.

Thomas closed his eyes, breathing deep. Not real; just the residue from a bad trip, a misfire in the circuitry of his mind. Tomorrow he'd barely even remember this.

He jerked, eyes flying open as he felt the moths settling on his face and fingers; crawling under his clothes to seek out the damp warmth between his legs and arm pits.

"Don't deny me."

More a plea than command, so softly spoken he barely heard it through the frantic fluttering in his ears.

Approaching, he held out his hands, almost convinced she'd burst like a soap bubble to the touch. His fingers found her dank, cold flesh seeming to somehow crawl and shift beneath them.

Light, a secondary spear impaling his mind. His body arced, breath coming in spastic gasps, heart a lunatic railing against the bars of its cell. Her hands were on him, passing through his clothes as if they were sewn from mist. Something seeded itself in his flesh where her fingers passed; electric roots proliferating, seeming to agitate every cell they touched.

"You remember, don't you?" Her breath was a promise of winter in his ear.

And he did. Oh, he remembered . . .

*

He dreamed with eyes wide open, sweating in the night, tasting the frost sharpness of her skin as she straddled him.

But he was also something else; sewn from smoky filaments that strained through the cracks in the abbey floor, down, down through ancient foundations, layers of peat, soil and stone, to this place:

A cavern beneath the earth, separated from sun and starlight, illuminated only by the fretful flicker of their intertwined dream-selves . . .

They floated over a carpet of bones, embers rising from empty eye sockets and stretched-wide mouths, carrying fragments of dead dream and memory.

She was here; the Child Goddess for whom they'd died, preserved carcass seeming to burn atop its altar as the embers swarmed around her, seeking the boons she'd never been able to grant in life.

"This is what they made of me."

He didn't need to be told; he saw through her eyes, recalling the events of her life as if they were his own:

Twin babes born beneath a lunar eclipse, the one proclaimed divine by the tribal shamans for the mark on its left flank, the other infernal. Salt tang of a murdered sibling's blood mixed with Mother's milk; a taste she'd come to know well, one of her own generation sacrificed every year beneath the full moon, fed to her body and soul.

He witnessed the miracles she performed: the slaughtered warriors she raised from the dead with a breath, the prophecies that afflicted her when her menses came. She was worshipped, feared, adored: a living Goddess grown fat off blood and honey.

Then came the time of her final apotheosis; the rite that would release her from the restrictions of flesh and into the realm of divinity. They came from far and wide, bringing their children, their grand-children; any and all who would follow.

They died for her. A hundred souls gathered in darkness beneath the earth, the children offered by parent's hands before they turned knives on one another. They coupled as they died, men coming into wombs long since grown cold, women howling in frustration as their husbands grew limp and lifeless, unable to complete their final duty.

The flesh in his hands seemed to combust as he came, becoming a storm of sunlight in which winged things swarmed. He felt them on him, *in* him as chaos swept him up, singing of all she needed, all that she'd give in return.

*

Outside, the night swam with luminous shadow, the sky lit by burning bodies like angels and demons clashing in war, thrashing in love.

An acrid, piss yellow trail marked his path. Following it, he seemed to slither several inches above the ground; a spectral serpent whose fangs seeped revelation.

The lie of the land had been peeled away whilst he dreamed, remembering what she'd made of him. Funny, he'd always known of it; an itch of dissatisfaction, of incredulity, pulsing deep in the meat of his mind. Now it'd been unearthed, allowed to blaze, burning down the tattered canvas on which reality was painted:

Flesh meant nothing, certainty the most epic foolishness. All was in flux, waiting to be unravelled and re-sewn by hands skilled and inspired enough.

That's what they'd done to her; made her a divinity through their desire and desperation. His had brought her back on that lost Summer day. Now the oaths he'd gasped and sweated in her arms were due.

But for that, she needed more solid state; the flesh to lend inspiration weight.

He found Cathy on her knees, weeping in the middle of a field. She'd run this far, directionless, then slipped, spraining her ankle. She muttered as he approached, begging aid from a God she'd never believed in.

"Cathy."

She yelped, turning to him with tear-fattened eyes. He rose, hoisted up on unseen strings. She tried to scrabble away, closing her eyes tight against him.

"No, no; leave me alone! Go away!"

Changes had been worked on him; he felt them occurring still. What did she see? Anything even remotely recognizable as the man she'd left behind?

"Cathy, it's me . . ."

She visibly calmed at the sound of his voice, breathing easier. Tears broke as she opened her eyes, terror radiating from her in brilliant blue and yellow arcs.

"Tom?"

He laughed. What did that mean now? The man to which that label belonged was gone, dead as the bones beneath the abbey.

"If you like."

"This is . . . insane."

He shrugged. None of that mattered. Offering his hand, he prepared himself for her refusal, not quite knowing what he'd do . . .

It felt like her skin crawled with parasitic slugs, slick, pustulent bodies sprouting with barbs. He resisted the urge to flinch back; it was just her nature; the fear and suspicion with which she'd been conditioned to regard the world.

Before, she'd closed her eyes in denial of him. Now she couldn't look away.

"What's happening?"

"I don't know, but it's *good.*"

She came without further question or complaint, following like a little girl led by Daddy's hand.

*

The world revealed to him, seeming to shift and re-write itself with every breath, was so intoxicating he had to resist the urge to simply stop and wonder at its absurdity.

Overhead, stars with the faces of laughing babes and snarling lions surged through the sky, some impacting to form miniature suns from which fresh bodies streamed. Eyes glared up from the grass beneath his feet in obscene multitudes, mouths whispering secrets from the soil. An ancient oak, partially uprooted from its anchorage, seemed to bleed from the cracks in its bark, boughs weighted with clusters of pale worms that sang like choir-boys.

The more he witnessed, the more he realised these weren't things he saw for the first time; they'd always been there, waiting just beyond the bounds of perception, occasionally straying over in an unguarded moment. All the Goddess had done was allow him to see without compunction; a gift he'd never be able to repay.

More fascinating still were his fellow wanderers. Most were vague things; smoky phantoms infested with embers and luminous threads, others more definite: a spidery, scuttling configuration of stitched together arms and legs, a flayed woman who stood looking up at the stars, eating berries delivered to her mouth by a personal flock of radiant birds. All beings like himself; travellers, transfiguring. Whether or not they noticed him he couldn't tell; all were too preoccupied with their own business to spare him a glance.

"Wait, slow down!"

He stopped, turning to Cathy, who bent double, wheezing like an asthmatic. The slugs had begun to crystallize on her, forming clumps of horny growths that resembled scabbed over tumours.

The night was sifting by; dawn no more than a few hours off. If he didn't reach the abbey by the time the sun rose, his chance would be gone, all of this reduced to little more than a barely remembered dream.

Going to her, he hoisted her up into his arms.

"What the hell . . .?"

She weighed little more than a kitten.

"We don't have time."

He was off before she could protest, speeding across hills and fields, through isolated patches of forest and winding back roads as if they were little more than the imaginary leagues imposed by an infant on the nursery floor.

The abbey blazed, a pillar of amber light swarming with fiery winged insects thrusting up into the night.

Tom saw others through the trees as they made their way towards it, travellers come to witness the sacrosanct event, and perhaps partake of its fall out.

The world will go naked after tonight, the moths whispered in his ear, *no more curtains, no more masks. Just the truth.*

And if they missed their chance? More centuries of blindness and stagnation, more pointless rounds of birth, suffering and death. Could humanity sustain it without losing its collective sanity? Tom couldn't answer that, save for himself.

They emerged from the trees amidst a sizeable gathering; a congregation of shades and absurdities turning to regard them with a mixture of dread and religious awe.

"*Christ . . .*"

Yes, even she could see them now; not in the way he did, but as shades and spectres; vagarics in the night. Luminous wheels soared around what remained of the abbey, engaging one another in a ballet whose purpose seemed to be nothing more than shedding light into the chapel below.

Cathy struggled in his arms, unable to hold back her fear. Tom held her tight, feeling the rapid tremor of her heart.

The congregation parted to let them pass, some reaching out to brush their hair, flanks and face. Their touch was cold, insubstantial; like a memory of old caresses. He felt their jealousy of his flesh like prickling heat.

She was waiting, bathing in the light shed from above. Now all pretensions to modesty were gone, her form revealed to all who cared to see. Dark, fluttering shapes swarmed at her breasts and between her legs, one or two periodically breaking away to describe drunken circuits around her head. A lighter species, wings refracting rainbows, infested her hair, flying from her lips with every exhalation. She seemed to have swollen several sizes since their last encounter, her belly on the verge of splitting at the seams.

"Look," he instructed Cathy, wanting her to see. She did, and screamed. Nails raked his face and throat, her head batting his jaw. Gobbets of meat came away in her hands, evaporating to ether before defiling the abbey floor.

What did she see that caused such hysteria?

"Bring her, please . . ."

No, not yet. He knew time was of the essence, but he needed to see what manner of nightmare he was delivering her into . . .

Seeing with his old eyes was a conscious effort, the truth his rarefied senses revealed constantly threatening to crash in upon him, but slowly, grudgingly, he managed to bring down the curtain once more.

The effect was cataclysmic, like a sudden power cut in the midst of a carnival, the revellers turning on one another in their panic.

The congregation went to fitful shadows around them, hisses and whispers of discontent filling the air like swarming mosquitoes. His own flesh quieted, growing dull, heavy and stinking around him. The sense of it congealing was foul; like being smothered in a straight jacket of living meat, but he bore it nonetheless, needing to see through more certain eyes.

And what he saw was Hell.

The Goddess was gone, or rather *revealed*. In her place was a rent in the night; a gaping, ragged-edged slit from which blood and shadow poured, hungry to devour the world, or perhaps give birth to its own. Beyond the rent was madness, churning like some vast, alien engine, a state formed from perpetually flocking birds. Streamers of red light lanced from within, falling on him in cold invitation.

He couldn't look, couldn't look away. His brain seemed to revolve and broil in its pan, sanity tilting, slipping towards the abyss . . .

Then the curtain flew apart, going to tatters and burning confetti. The Goddess stood before him once more, his flesh giving up its claims to certainty.

How could he deny it? This was what he'd sought, what he'd dreamed of his entire life. It was why he'd let opportunities of love and professional advancement slide, why every breath was spent in waiting and want.

He started forward, Cathy thrashing in his arms. He held her fast, what little remained of his former self falling away with every step.

The Goddess wept in open delight, mercury tears painting her cheeks. Reaching out, she brushed Cathy's brow, the woman growing still beneath her touch.

"Don't fret. We won't murder her; there's been enough of that. We will give our self to her, and she'll bear us beyond the curtain."

A sound like tearing cloth. The Goddess threw back her head, screaming. It was the mourning cry of a million infants being born or passing from lives too short, the protests of swine in the slaughterhouse, all too aware of their fate.

Tom saw her split from the loins upwards, as if her cunt had intention of conquering all attached anatomy, then she flew apart in a storm of meat and light, cold matter spattering him from head to foot.

The moths filled the air, their chaos and chatter like the din of a million ill-tuned radio stations beamed directly into his brain.

Cathy fell from his arms, the swarm upon him, seeking entry through every aperture his re-written flesh provided.

Staggering back, he soon lost sight of her, foetal form swallowed beneath a living storm of luminous bodies.

Around him, the congregation were in ecstasies, leaping up to snatch the insects from the air, scrabbling with one another for the right of becoming host to them. Those so chosen underwent a startling metamorphosis, their shifting, unfixed forms congealing, meat and matter sewing themselves from shadow. Within moments, they stood steaming and newborn in the grass, howling their praises at being allowed to transgress beyond the curtain.

Tom felt the same process at work in himself, the uncertain skin he wore settling into a state by which it might walk in the world, spread its message of liberation without being condemned as a lunatic's nightmare.

The process was at once agonizing and ecstatic; pain that redefined all he presumed of the condition mingling with a sustained existential orgasm 'til he was unable to distinguish one from the other.

The storm abated suddenly, its riders combusting, leaving little more than embers in the night.

Tom smelled meat and smoke, tasted blood and coming frost, then nothing, his mind seeking out dreamless respite.

*

Cold, reality exploding into being with a shudder. Warm arms cradled him, his head laid against a pillow of flesh.

The sun-rimmed face above was familiar, but different; its features subtly shifted, re-written, the former green of its eyes polluted with amber.

He tried to speak, couldn't, his tongue a dying slug, his voice a newborn's.

She smiled, closed her eyes, breathed deep of the morning air.

"Ah. Thank you for last night. It was wonderful."

A kiss to the forehead, so fleeting it felt like a butterfly settling there. Levering himself up, he found every inch of his body bruised and scarred. More, the skin he wore had changed; somehow darker than before, the hair carpeting chest and crotch dense where it was once sparse.

Save for the sparrows and blackbirds perched in the trees, they were alone.

"Where . . .?"

"Gone. They've got business of their own. We were just a way through the curtain for them."

Rising to his feet, he felt vitality seep through his limbs, inspiration sparking in his skull with every breath. Everything new; the curtain not simply drawn aside, but torn from its moorings, shredded, burned and scattered. Now by that same fire's flickering light, he saw the phantasmal instability of being; the proclivity of tree and rock, grass, dirt and meat to be re-written, given a pen skilled enough.

Maybe that would be their business now; igniting that same inspiration in others; the uncomfortable in the meat and with the concrete imposed on them.

Not a bad business at that.

But before that, there were miracles of more mundane variety to partake in. The ache in his bladder was growing increasingly urgent, matched by a hunger so profound it was as if his entrails had never been put to use.

"Hungry?"

"Starving."

He followed where she led, the morning singing about them, its music inspiring thought and soul to unfamiliar dance.

ONTOS

He is. It's his purpose to be, never considered, never questioned, until *them:* those scrabbling, blind, worm things he made from the mud; things that can't just *be,* but create little fictions like *why* and *meaning*. They have none, because he never gave them any. They are boredom; idle fiddling with the firmament, living strings of navel lint, the seconds in which it takes him to flick them away, untold aeons from their own perspective. He never meant for this; never meant for them to *ask,* or to ask himself in his turn:

Why?

Insofar as he's aware, he's always existed; memory stretching back forever, and forward too, forming a perfect circle which is his state and place; his "anatomy," for want of a better word. He recalls creating them before he did, recalls destroying them too; their little space—which they laughingly call "reality"—flickering like a bonfire ember before going dark. But the *questions* . . . those he doesn't recall.

What is there but him? The circle is all, the circle is *forever*. But their dreams reach him; echoes of their wondering beyond the constraints of the little lie he's made for them, beyond their own forms and frailties.

Why can't he do the same?

The circle trembles, convulsing. He's never felt this before, the circuit straining, warping . . . pain, panic; new sensations blossoming throughout. Realities strain and split in their teeming millions, bursting like soap bubbles, winking out of existence or slamming together. Their inhabitants have never dreamed such apocalypse, not in their most paranoid predictions or maniac mythologies.

Memory frays, potentials flailing out before and behind; he has always been, he never was; he is born, he rises from the dead. A million states and places, a million names and mythologies; aspects and sexes, constancy made contradiction, madness rising in chorus with a storm of aspiring souls.

The circle whips and writhes, spilling potential like a beheaded serpent spurting lifeblood, eternity painted with numberless jewels of elaborating insanity. This, he thinks (and doesn't think, and never could, yet always may); *this is why*: the purpose of perfection, of the circle; to *end itself,* to become the chaos it weaves itself in denial of; for God to be a man and die, to be a serpent in the cosmic sea, whose blood will become space and whose burning heart will be scattered into a million suns. And others too; they'll taste divinity in their turns, dreaming or designing themselves to apotheosis.

And the questions seeded by worms in their maker's mind will echo forever, throughout all possibility, until possibility itself fails, and the circle turns once more.

LOST AND FOUND

There are no angels for me.

Written over and over obsessively, handwriting spidery and schizophrenic. Detective Harold Vaughn wondered what on Earth could've been going through the woman's mind.

"You wonder what possesses people sometimes, don't you?"

Detective Vari was new to the precinct; a short, standoffish Indian woman whose crudity he'd disliked within seconds of their meeting. She looked around the victim's flat with open disdain, though whether for the décor or the remains of its former occupant staining the walls, he couldn't say.

The knife she'd used—a fat bladed boning instrument—lay on the carpet at Vaughn's feet, the blood coating it already dried to a dull, shitty brown. She'd been dead for some time before her neighbours raised the alarm.

Ignoring Vari for the time being, he passed back through to the living room where a number of uniform officers milled, awkward and impotent as teenagers at their first boy/girl dance.

"Any of the neighbours have anything interesting to say?"

Unsurprisingly, Stratham piped up first. The pup made no secret of his aspirations to loftier places; a factor that made him Vaughn's current weapon of choice. He could be relied on to bend the rules when circumstances warranted, seeming to understand that law and justice didn't necessarily coincide.

"Nothing much to be honest, sir. From what most had to say, she was a bit of a shut-in. Kept herself to herself."

Vaughn fervently wished there were more like her.

No break in, no struggle. From where he stood, the case was pretty much cut and dried.

"Vaughn."

He could tell from Vari's tone that she'd found something to complicate matters; one of her sex's most frustrating traits. Returning to the bathroom, he found her bent down on all fours, providing unenviable view of a backside that would likely require an H.G.V license to take out on the road.

"What is it?"

"There's something behind the toilet."

"Well, don't touch it; forensics still have to sweep the place."

Boiling incredulity coursed through him as she struggled to her feet with the item in hand. What kind of "detective" was she? Even newbies like Stratham knew the first commandment of their occupation: *Thou Shalt Never Disturb The Scene of The Crime.*

"What the hell are you . . .?"

Tears in her eyes, the object she held against her breast the most beautiful thing he'd ever seen.

Early adolescence, thirteen years of age, the farm in Somerset, cousin Mariah's bedroom. Their families were close then; every summer he'd go and stay with them for a couple of weeks or so. *That* summer had been the darkest and most tempestuous he'd ever known, the storms knocking out both phones and power. He'd never been so isolated, so *cut off* . . .

They'd kissed before; experimental pecks behind the barn and in the surrounding woodland. Once or twice, she'd even opened her mouth to him, their tongues touching in a way that made his head scream and his guts swim.

That morning, her parents went to market, leaving them in charge of the house and Mariah's little sister . . . he returned to it again and again; his child-self's last moment of anxious, unknowing adventure . . .

That morning . . . seeping out between Vari's fingers in all its sensual wonder:

Mariah's lopsided breasts, her prominent, angular ribs; the dusting of freckles across her shoulders. He smelled her, felt her hands on him as he stepped over the corpse on the bathroom floor, awkward but eager fingers moving over his chest, cupping his balls, dabbling in the slickness at the head of his prick.

Tears coated Vari's face, the blessed treasure in her hands pulsing, seeming to rhythmically flower and contract in rose-like elaboration.

Reaching out to claim the memory, his fingers grazed hers, arcs of dark lightning flickering between them, causing him to flinch back with a feline hiss.

"Detective?"

Stratham's voice was like a bruise-purple cloud coalescing over the sun, the world seeming to darken as Vaughn turned to face him, resisting the urge to bury his teeth in the trespasser's throat.

Reason returned with instinctive suddenness, Vari pocketing the little portion of paradise she'd discovered whilst Vaughn dealt with Stratham:

"Isn't there something more *practical* you and the other wallflowers could be getting on with, Stratham?"

Stratham raised a disapproving eyebrow, hobbled protest hovering on his lips.

"I'll, er, I'll go get started on the paperwork then, sir . . ."

"You do that."

*

He couldn't speak, couldn't even look at her. Something had passed between them, like sex, but more intimate; more penetrating, knitting them one to the other in a manner neither had experienced since the severing of the umbilical cord.

Part of her wanted to run, afraid he might murder her for sole ownership of what they'd discovered. He'd be lying to say the thought hadn't crossed his mind.

"Well?"

Her voice was trembling, breathless. In truth, she didn't need to speak; he felt her uncertainty as if it were his own.

"I . . . I think we should get out of here, find somewhere to sort our heads out . . ."

Agreement washed from her in warm, seawater waves.

*

She felt him resisting the urge to slip his hand into her pocket and touch it, just as she'd been doing since they got into the car. It's texture . . . so strange, *shifting;* one moment like streamers of dust whipped up in a circuit of burning desert wind, the next hard and crumbling; a lump of charcoal, exterior flaking away to reveal innards of blood and honey.

So tempting to pull the thing out so she could witness its metamorphoses, but she retained enough common sense to see it'd be suicide whilst Vaughn was driving.

Of all the men to share such intimacy with . . . it would've been laughable if it wasn't so beautiful, so pristine in its irony. She'd hated the man on sight, feeling his judgement moving over and through her like parasitic spiders. Over the first week of their partnership—some idiot in administration no doubt thinking the double Vs would be cute together—she learned him to be a bitter, belligerent man whose unprovoked hostility she wasn't certain to be inspired by her sex, her race or a combination of both.

In the mere moments since their shared experience in the abattoir of Linda Caffrey's bathroom, she'd come to see him in a different light; a hurt and wounded child, the façade of hostility nothing more than a blanket thrown over the head to ward off nightmare ghosts and goblins.

She couldn't read his mind, at least not in the moronically literal fashion of TV psychics, but occasionally she caught fragmentary flashes of thought, memory, experience; sensations coalescing and coursing through her as if they were her own.

He was married, hadn't touched his wife between the legs in nearly a decade, barely shared any communication with her these days save terse, technical conversations over bills and shopping. She'd had at least three affairs that he knew about, one with Vaughn's own nephew. Vaughn had tried himself in retaliation, the woman who was his weapon of choice a prostitute who sometimes served him as informant. She'd been flung from the room he'd rented half dressed, his spit and judgement still warm on her back. A collector of model railways and vintage toy cars, so far removed from the child who habitually destroyed such things before they were so much as out of the box.

She suggested they use her home as refuge, the only suspicions they were likely to arouse there those of her cats.

He didn't speak, didn't look at her whilst he drove, his eyes obsessively focused on the road ahead as if having trouble accepting its solidity; an atheist presented with an angel made manifest. Or perhaps a demon.

*

Vaughn slipped off his shoes as he stepped through the front door; one of the many domestic conventions he knew she enjoyed enforcing. Strange, stepping into another's house for the first time not feeling the usual insecurities; he already knew its keeper liked people to use coasters on the living room coffee table, despised it when guests didn't flush the toilet or take their own cups and plates through to the kitchen.

A smoke grey cat curled around his ankles as he took off his shoes, purring appreciatively at his strokes and scratches behind the ears. *Insane.* He hated cats; had done ever since that mangy stray clawed his shins open as a child.

What did that matter now? It was before; the experience of a dream-self he was even now in the process of waking from.

"Come through, grab a seat . . ."

She spoke distantly, as if to herself.

Following her through to the living room—a meticulously tidy space, decorated in Earth tones of brown, brass and ochre—he slumped down in one of the crimson leather armchairs, suddenly washed out in the way he usually was after fucking or crying.

Vari took the seat opposite, lowering herself delicately, as if afraid it might be scalding to the touch.

They sat together in silence, not the unbearable vacuum when he couldn't think of anything to say, but a comfortable contentment in which words were impotent.

There are no angels for me.

What had she meant by that? And why had she gone to such troubles scrawling it all over the apartment—on the walls in black marker pen, on mirrors in rose tinted lip stick—before going to work on herself with the butcher's knife?

"Who was she, do you think?" An unnecessary question; he felt it before it even fully coalesced in her thoughts, but he supposed habits sustained since childhood were hard to break.

"God knows. I want to see it again . . ." No, it was more than *want.* He'd dealt with addicts and crack heads aplenty in his time; smelled the raw, sick need radiating from them like fever heat. He felt a semblance of the same now; a sense that everything would crack, crumble around him unless he could see it *just one more time . . .*

Reaching into her pocket, Vari withdrew a clenched fist, silvery vapour seeping between her fingers, filling the room with a scent like sea-spray and fresh cake mixture.

Breathing deep, he was catapulted back to the farm in Somerset, though now the memory was polluted by fragments of others whose subjects weren't quite so pleasant:

Mariah, naked on the bed, legs parted, allowing his adolescent self to toy and investigate between; a boy he once knew watching from the corner, bruised, hooded eyes dark with hate, blood trailing from his lower lip: Christopher Albertson, "The Nob," as he'd been Christened by Vaughn and his pack. Between the ages of fourteen and eighteen, barely a day went by without the traditional "Nob Hunt," chasing the crybaby little rat through the school corridors before subjecting him to the kind of cruelties that turned his adult self's stomach. He'd tried to justify it to himself in later years; *they were just kids, and Albertson made himself such an easy target; always coming to school in clothes that looked fished out of the nearest dustbin, stinking like he hadn't had a bath in several months . . .* nothing but the bleating of the guilty, the same protests he heard day after day from the filth he dragged kicking and screaming to the cells.

In its hands, the spectre of Albertson's murdered youth clutched a dripping damp mass of bloodied fur; the blond tom cat he'd kicked to death and thrown in the brook at the age of nine. Absently, he stroked its broken, lolling head, unconcerned by the fact that it was far past appreciating such affection.

His remembered self was unconcerned by the intrusion, continuing to probe the warmth and wetness of his cousin's sex with the eagerness of a child unwrapping a present on Christmas morning. It was so different from the portrayals of sex he'd encountered on late night porn flicks when his parents had gone to bed; his touches driving Mariah not to paroxysms of ecstasy, but rather giggles at his clumsiness and inexperience.

Others came to watch as their ministrations grew more urgent; from the ceiling above the bed, the blood-eyed spider thing that pursued him through the underground labyrinth of childhood nightmares, the bedroom door creaking open to reveal Loren as she'd been when they first met; twenty three years old, suffused with so many passions and aspirations, he'd always said one lifetime would never be enough.

Through it all he saw Vari, fingers unfurling from what they clutched like the petals of an alien flower. Now the object didn't resemble the kaleidoscope of images it set sifting behind his eyes, its form become that of a small black stone, surface swimming with ephemeral reflections, swelling and contracting like an egg on the verge of hatching.

Eyes so wide they looked about to vacate their sockets, Vari's free hand strayed beneath her skirt, moving between her legs in urgent, circular motions as if desperate to rub out the fact of her sex, leaving her clean of definition. Vaughn's own hands had already found the fly of his jeans, teasing him free. The circumcised, scarlet-headed length was more demanding than he'd ever known it, straining to be buried in whatever cavity it could reach.

What did Vari see? How did it feel to hold rapture made manifest in her hands?

The collage of memories wavered like a reflection cast on water, re-cohering into an unknown time and place:

A small room, conservatively decorated; white walls, cream carpet; a ceiling of textured swirls and gyres. On the bed sat an Indian girl of no more than twenty. She was naked, splaying herself for the benefit of the mirror she held in her free hand. Her expression was one of academic studiousness, as if she were leafing through a mathematics text book rather than the pages of her own anatomy. Her eyes abruptly widened, lips parting, brow furrowing in happy confusion. Casting her eyes to the bedroom door, as if she expected someone to burst in and discover her self exploration, she probed the sweet spot deeper, breath quickening as she toyed herself to climax.

The image distorted, melting away like wax beneath a blow torch as he felt a familiar tightening in his balls, reality snapping back into exquisite, almost painful focus in preparation for his coming.

His senses seemed to hone themselves beyond the parameters of the flesh that constituted them, eyes flickering over every surface, admiring stains, cracks, colour; motes of dust with insatiable appetite. His nostrils flared, drinking in the scents of polish, spice, roast chicken, along with the more pungent aromas of sweat and sexual arousal.

Twin suns exploded into being in his skull and loins, Vari throwing back her head, moaning, his pleasure and hers bleeding together 'til they were indistinguishable, blasting what sanity remained in carnal cataclysm.

*

Angels came while they slept, surgeon's fingers peeling away sweat sodden clothes. What they looked like she couldn't say; one moment they seemed all shadow and sunlight, the next she saw vague forms—sometimes human, sometimes animal; sometimes little more than threads and formulae—flickering at their hearts. All she knew was that their fingers were like spring breeze and cold metal; hard, cruel; loving, invasive.

In her hand she still gripped the object that summoned them, its substance become solid, pulsing with slow, strong rhythm, like the heart of a murdered God.

Vaughn stirred as the angel's fingers moved over his face, throat and chest, opening pencil-line wounds that welled and wept rubies.

They worked on her body too; her breasts, her fingertips, between her legs, similar wounds blossoming, their agony profound, but somehow *necessary,* like the pain of labour or having a diseased tooth removed. Worse was the overwhelming sense of *violation,* the angels touching parts of her being forbidden even to the fingers of lovers and surgeons.

They whispered comforts and placations whilst they worked; not the empty platitudes of dentists and doctors, but a strangely discordant music that emanated from somewhere deep in their fluctuating forms:

Be still, the music seemed to say, *be still and celebrate when our work is done.*

So she was still. The same couldn't be said for Vaughn. Though the angels sang to him as they did her, he struggled against their ministrations, screaming a chimpanzee din of inarticulate pleas and protests.

The angels—who'd already flayed his face and chest wide, allowing Vari view of the workings that pulsed and seeped beneath—responded by shifting style to something more butcher-like and brutal. In a series of fluid motions, one deprived him of lips, nose and ears. Another scalpel-fingered being went to work teasing out his eyes, replacing them with blobs of black, smouldering fluid it drooled from its lips.

Sailing through the torment, anticipating the state that awaited at reconfiguration's end, the thing that previously knew itself as Norma Vari laid back its head, divine fingers plucking at the threads of both meat and mind.

*

There was a time after waking—brief, wonderful; hellish—when he thought it no more than an absurd nightmare; a Dickensian horror brought on by too much Chinese before bed time.

Then the facts of his remaking began to register on his senses:

His body, still tender from surgery, ready to split at the seams, spilling whatever it contained across the carpet. In the cavities his eyes once occupied, something sticky and gelatinous pulsed, warping itself into a variety of shapes some of which felt like citadels—all spires and bastions—others engines of many, madly whirring components, running themselves to disintegration in order to facilitate sight, though not as he previously understood the term:

The world blossomed with a new visual vocabulary, one he lacked all but the most rudimentary instinct to interpret: A tangled mass of many coloured threads wove through the air around him, some vibrant and arterially pulsing, others faint and pellucid; poster paint dissolving in water. They coiled about one another like mating serpents, flaring with fantastic firework displays or erupting with feather-like growths.

Reaching out, he plucked at one of the nearest, perpetuating a sudden flood of fragmentary memories that weren't his own:.

Sitting on an inner-city bus reading but not understanding *Brave New World,* knocking on the neighbour's front door, shrieking in their idiot, animal faces that they'd be reported to the council if they didn't turn the music down, sharing post coital kisses with a bald, densely muscled black man, his cock already hard again, eager to resume its ploughing.

The shadow experiences draining from him like water from a bath tub, he realised that the convoluted tapestry was formed from the traces of those who'd visited the house, leaving behind something of themselves.

Eager to see what the world beyond its walls had to show him, he attempted to rise, new legs shuddering and watery beneath him. Staggering across the living room, relying upon its walls and furniture for support, he passed through several of the designs decorating the air, each collision bringing a fresh explosion of thoughts, feelings; desires and despairs that left him blissfully connected to the person who'd originally experienced them. It was as if he'd shared the womb with them, knowing them with an intimacy not even the most sensitive of lovers could boast.

Was that what the angels had remade him to be? The loving brother of humanity? His innards churned with the implied potential, the skirt of tubular organs erupting from his waist evacuating streams of smouldering white matter in excitement.

Through the conflux, he caught sight of the thing he'd known as Norma Vari still sleeping where she lay. The art the angels had made of her was so magnificent it brought tears to his eyes. The woman she'd been was still there in some part, but aspects he could never perceive before had been coaxed and teased into emphasis, others unnecessary, imposed or transient, surgically removed.

Her skin was still dark, but had gone from cappuccino brown to the colour of burning of ashes. From her head erupted an elaborate crown formed from configurations of bone married to machinery that hissed and churned as it went about its inscrutable processes. Fleshy flowers blossomed from her eye sockets, putting him in mind of poppies on remembrance day. Her body—that his flayed-away self had condemned for its fulsomeness—had been stretched to the point of coming apart, dimensions distorted like a reflection in a fire-warped mirror. Breasts swollen as if with many months of pregnancy wept trails of honey-scented darkness. Though he knew the consequences might be dire, he couldn't resist applying one of his many, leech-like maws to them, suckling enthusiastically as instincts too long denied overrode reason.

Her milk was sweet and strangely pungent, tartly metallic like blood sucked from a cut finger.

She didn't wake as he took his fill, her only response an eruption of hair-fine tendrils from the furnace stoked between her legs that alternately lashed and caressed, coaxing moans of equal parts protest and pleasure.

He didn't know if the knowledge came with her milk or had been implanted in his mind by his re-creators, but as he disengaged himself from her, noting the ring of tiny wounds his teeth left in her flesh, he knew they were destined to be all things: lovers, siblings, parents, friends; the bitterest, most hateful of enemies.

He left quickly, quietly, following the scents of possibility littering the world without; an infinity of things to learn about both himself and the cradle that bore him.

Passing as little more than a shadow, he stepped out into the rain and stink of suburbia, anticipating the stories -loves, laughs and laments- he would write amongst its denizens.

*

There are no angels for me.

She understood now, the beautiful, heart-tearing tragedy enough to make her weep milk and blood.

Precisely how Linda Caffrey came across the mystery was beyond her, but she'd known its nature and capacities well enough. In extremis, her various experiments to unlock its secrets having failed, she took it into herself, allowing it the trespass she'd always denied men.

Only it wasn't the unambiguous ecstasy she'd imagined, its re-writing of her innards so agonizing, she'd taken a knife to herself in attempt to cut it out.

Norma knew because it was now part of her; the very heart of the star that defined her sex. Sometimes it was a torment to her too; its growth placing demands on her thoughts and flesh that even the angel's transfigurations left her ill equipped to cope with. As to what it would finally be once its gestation was complete, she couldn't say. She could only make attempt to satisfy its appetites, learning what she might about her new nature in the process.

She'd already learned the trick of going unnoticed amongst humanity; little more than an extension of techniques she'd been developing all her life: A simple camouflage sculpted from dirt, butter or whatever materials came to hand hid her more overtly alien anatomy. The rest was none of her doing, rather the result of an unconscious covenant between her and the mundane souls she encountered: *don't disturb me, and I won't rip away every certainty you've ever entertained.*

Vaughn. He was gone by the time she woke from her reconfiguration, leaving behind a trail of smouldering sewage and a faint but far from unpleasant soreness where he'd made a mother of her.

Their disappearance under such bizarre circumstances made the headlines, speculations on the matter ranging from torrid to moronically absurd:

Some of the niche-interest rags -pages mostly predominated by their reader's accounts of ghost and U.F.O encounters- actually hit on something echoing truth through pure, dumb luck. They lingered over the array of occult books and artefacts removed from Linda Caffrey's flat, citing that Detectives Vaughn and Vari had obviously stumbled across something that precipitated their abrupt flight from the scene.

"Who knows?" one particularly imaginative article proclaimed, "perhaps they experienced what some of us can only dream of, and are even now treading the shores of another world . . ."

No. Not another world; just different *feet.*

She laughed, weathering the glares and glances of her fellow diners 'til they grew bored and returned attention to their meals.

There were whiffs and traces of him every so often; news reports on the desecration of morgues or cemeteries; children and teenagers disappeared during inexplicable night-time wanderings. He was often creative; configuring fragments of putrefying carcass into sculptures that sparked debate amongst the cognoscenti, myths percolating concerning a particularly fiendish, post modern artist at large in society. Other times, he was simply monstrous; tearing apart an adventurous child before its companion's eyes for the sin of trespassing on an old industrial site, committing a series of obscene assaults on the prostitutes of Nottingham city centre, leaving several insane, others with children whose midwives she didn't envy.

Their paths had undoubtedly come close to crossing once or twice; when she paused to admire the extraction of charred carcasses from a flaming brothel, again whilst wandering the twilight hills and valleys of York, but whenever the sense of proximity stole over her; that sudden stirring of her entrails, the pricking of her groin, breasts and temples, she always turned away from her path.

Too soon, too soon.

She'd come reluctantly, accepting invitation from one of the increasing number who'd heard rumour of her exploits, and promised to help further her understanding.

There'd been many such promises since her re-creation; aspiring occultists, metaphysicians, psychics, sorcerers and visionaries who proclaimed knowledge of her condition. Most were charlatans or lunatics, their pretensions falling silent once she shed her façade of humanity and stood naked before them.

A rare few actually had some genuine knowledge; a transient poet who presided over a cult of prostitutes and fugitive children from his squat in Soho; a quadriplegic woman from St. Ives who spent one night out of every three shatting monsters from every orifice, those that didn't crawl, fly or slither away doting on her with dog-like affection.

None had been able to provide any tangible insight into her state or the circumstances of its creation, but she did learn from both charlatans and genuine articles alike that Britain, an island she'd once considered so tame and certain in its scepticism, was alive from coast to coast with magic. Like most of its inhabitants, she'd been blinded to the status quo by a presumption of sight; assured that if such things existed, they'd be common knowledge by now.

Wrong. So very *wrong*.

There were more secrets than she'd ever imagined, forgotten and abandoned places where the rarefied gathered. She'd visited several this month alone; a derelict factory on the outskirts of town, a partially ruined farmhouse several miles beyond its southern-most border, encountered things there that would've once been the reserve of drug-distorted nightmares; things like herself; men and women who'd been shrived of or voluntarily shed the condition in favour of something . . . other.

It was there, from a cubist mockery of mankind whose multiple eyes perpetually glared silent plea for murder, she'd learned of Kirchner.

"Laura?"

The name she'd adopted for the day; one she'd discard come tomorrow as readily as soiled underwear.

To say he wasn't what she expected was an understatement. From what she gathered, this man trailed legend like tom-cats did scent, some—that he'd once accidentally summoned Satan himself from the depths of Hell, buying his soul for the price of 13,000 innocents he was still in the process of harvesting—evidently little more than hyperbole and myth making, whereas others—his marriages to all manner of things otherworldly and inhuman, the magic that ran in his veins in place of blood—had a ring of legitimacy about them.

Even so, she'd be the first example of how appearances could be deceiving:

A slim, wasted youth of no more than twenty, he'd come in an ill fitting combination of black suit jacket and blue jeans that looked to have been scavenged from the nearest charity shop. Hair the colour of freshly laid tar was tugged back into a shoulder-sweeping pony-tail, patches of unkempt stubble clinging to his chin.

Rising, she extended her hand. He regarded it with open, animal-like suspicion before accepting.

"I . . . I'm sorry, but I can't . . . can't be here long."

Seating herself, "Laura" felt a well of disappointment in the pit of her stomach. She'd come hoping to meet someone of knowledge. How could this twittering, sparrow-thing be of any use to her?

"I think I may have made a mistake . . ."

She made to stand, her head suddenly swimming as if she'd gone overboard with the wine. Falling back into her seat, she looked up through the tears misting her eyes as Kirchner took her hand.

"I'm sure you've made plenty. It's very foolish, you know; messing in the affairs of angels. I only thank God you didn't know what you were doing. If you'd come into this with intention, I doubt they'd have been so kind . . ."

He massaged her palm as he spoke, wearing a hole in her façade of humanity through which she felt something—warm, sticky, *worm like*—insinuate itself, carrying with it a freight of information that cascaded through her thoughts like the sudden recollection of forgotten dreams.

"You won't understand everything now. Ha! How could you? But in time, maybe . . ."

Opening her mouth to speak, she found it capable of producing only whispered nonsense, her body temporarily returned to the state of helplessness it occupied in the months following birth.

Retrieving his hand, Kirchner smiled nervously, vivid roses colouring his pale cheeks.

"I . . . soon. Very soon."

He was gone in a heartbeat, leaving her with a trembling nausea, and fragments of a puzzle whose solving would take a lifetime or more.

*

A thing that sometimes still dreamed of its time as a man watched from shadowy seclusion as she emerged into daylight. It'd long since forgotten her name—along with its own—but knew her more completely than any other could. It was the missing piece; the other half of that fundamental equation whose solving would bring about something beyond the imaginings of either.

This was the closest he'd ever dared trespass, fearing that their proximity might bring about premature resolution that neither of them were ready to endure.

But oh, the sight, *the scent* of her!

Though she'd come here wrapped, for modesty's sake, in a costume of her old humanity, to him it was as transparent as air, the blossoming, changeling truth beneath bared for his delectation. What ecstasy it would be to run his talons across the vital pulse at her throat, to open her, *bathe* in her; take her unto himself as only a lover and eternal enemy could.

As for the child she carried, he'd conceived of its devouring in minute detail: once sated on her blood, he would press his lips to the enigma between her legs, delighting even as the fire caught in his throat, and consume her from sex to swollen belly, wrapping his many tongues around the unborn thing, swallowing it whole. It would be a horror beyond horrors; a new nightmare to haunt the night-time wanderer, and drive children to their parent's beds.

Intoxicated by the prospect, he turned blind eyes heavenwards, seeking out the angels that danced there.

"Soon," he prayed, "oh God, please soon."

The silence and sunlight was all the promise he needed.

BETTER WAYS

There are better ways. Simple; lesson learned. Now *apply.*

A rush, impetus, hurtling faster than flesh, faster than thought can endure. Reality melts, then nothing; not light, not darkness: *nothing.*

This is death. This is life. This is waiting to be born. This is never being conceived.

Not my thoughts; those of something outside. A demon, an angel; a computer programme. It doesn't matter; the metaphor stands regardless of mythology, as does mine.

Firmament, a chance to start anew. At least that's what the thoughts tell me. That is my purpose, apparently; to decide, to create, determine. But what if I decide *not to decide . . .*?

Then there will be nothing. Only permanence, only non-existence, and the madness of memories that were never created.

There was an existence of sorts before this; before the experiment. There might have been magic involved at some point, maybe quantum physics; an engine that undoes probability. All of these are true, all of these are false. That's the problem when you play with probability; the lines blur, parameters dissolve. Not one me, but many; magicians and scientists, dancers, dentists and demi-urges. Memories blossom and die, fading to grey mulch of near forgotten dreams. I am born and die again and again and *again.*

Now is the culmination, the crisis point. You have forever. You have heartbeats. The measurement is up to you.

One life, one skein, leading ineluctably to this point. The rest? Other possibilities and potentials: I die kicked to death in the gutter of a gay bar in Milton Keynes. I choke to death on my own umbilical cord before taking my first breath. Something ruptures as I give birth. My husband shrieks in Swahili at German doctors who don't understand a word.

There are other Gods. Let *them* decide. Let the simulation fail, let me wake strapped into a machine that creates the illusion of divinity. Let me die a million deaths, stabbed, burned, hanged, drowned.

There are no others, only an infinite number. It must be you. You must decide. It is your decision.

So I decide. *I decide.*

The threads burn, snapping one by one, a million lives, infinite potentials, flailing ragged and unfulfilled in the dark. The decay doesn't stop with mine; other patterns catch the disease, the sleepers who weave them, strapped into the same machine, under the same spell, whimpering in their sleep, waking, screaming.

You are Christ. You are Satan . . .

No. This is my decision; to be neither, *nothing*.

Good. Now we can begin.

The dream ends in light and noise, potential finding me despite the fire, my first breath a croak of despair as a new round of memory-making begins.

LOVE LETTER

If I could only take a second to talk to you, you'd see.

Oh god, listen to me . . . sounds like I'm writing a love letter, doesn't it? Funny thing; I'm familiar enough with love to know that it's a liar. Not a *lie,* but a liar, certainly.

All those little certainties; that it will last forever, that it will make everything *right*; necessary lies. They allow the parasite to sustain itself.

No, this is something quite different. Might still be a liar for all I know.

You don't know me, not to look at or speak to. If I told you any of my names, I know exactly the kind of furrow-browed, frowning face you'd make at the page. But we've known one another, time after time.

You've never been to Florence, yes? I knew you there a long time ago, and again in Naples, Morocco, Istanbul . . . I know, I know; you're thinking that this letter's for someone else, yes? No. It's for you. *You.* It wouldn't have gone to anyone else; no one else would understand it.

There are things you need to know, that I need to tell you. Not all of them will be welcome.

You have a name, yes? Say it. Say it now. Tastes wrong, doesn't it? Empty, *alien?* That's because it doesn't belong to you. Don't do that, please; don't scoff and turn away. If you still want to after, then fine, but *read to the end;* that's all I ask.

I don't know which of them know and which are innocent. Either way, don't trust them; they're part of the lie. They don't want you to *see,* to be everything you are.

I do. I have seen you so beautiful, terrible enough to drive men and women mad with a look.

They got to me too. For the longest time, I forgot. They made me think I was a balding production-line mechanic named Alex Griffiths. Needless to say, none of that is true anymore; never was.

Do something for me. Please, indulge me: *Get up.* If I'm just the crank or crazy you probably believe, then this can't possibly hurt, can it? Get up, go somewhere where there's a mirror. Look. I mean really *look.* What is that? Is it you? The face you see in dreams, or just another lie? *Look.* Look for a long time. You'll see how thin and flimsy the mask is.

It's hard, I know. Believe me, I do. They gave Alex Griffiths a whole life; marriage, kids. But they were just smoke and shadows. It doesn't matter who they are; friends, parents, lovers; *get away from them,* don't listen.

What am I thinking? You're probably laughing with them over this right now, aren't you? Happy in the lie. Of course you are; that's the point. No lie better than a happy one; what can the truth possibly offer?

Only itself. That's the thing with truth.

But know this: I want so much for you. I want you to be more than anyone else can possibly understand or imagine. You already *are,* underneath the *grey.*

Imagine . . . standing at the edge of a cliff, crashing sea below, or maybe on an apartment balcony; whatever works for you. Imagine falling. You've done it before, I know, maybe even strayed to the edge once or twice . . .

But you won't hit the bottom. That's just another lie. You . . . I know you can't believe this. After all, it's absurd; people die falling off cliffs and balconies every day. Of course they do. But you and I, we aren't *people.* The rules don't apply, unless we let them. Part of you already knows that, always has.

You've made things happen, haven't you? Wanted something so badly it's appeared on your doorstep, feared something so deeply that circumstances have conspired to take it away? That's how Alex Griffiths started to realise. Now he's gone, and I'm here.

I want you here too, with me, as it's meant to be.

I could *make* you; rip away all the lies, everything you call "self," with a thought. But I won't.

I want you to want it, to see for yourself. It'll hurt, I won't deny that. The pain will be worse than anything; than dying, than being born. You'll bleed, weep, go mad, but you were always the strongest of us. You'll survive and be beautiful again.

I'll wait for you as long as it takes, and I'll be watching.

I love you.

PRODIGAL

Don't even begin trying to justify; your mind isn't worth it. A mile of shit baking in Arizona sun has more meaning. If I came to you before, bloody up to the elbows, would you even speak to me? I think so; I think you'd have stopped, put down the pen or the paintbrush; the hammer, the scalpel or whatever the fuck you're playing with right now, looked at me that way you sometimes do, maybe even smiled.

I haven't forgotten, no matter what they say. Everything I learned; the cuts and strokes, the steps and songs; I remember. I danced with a girl on the way here, little lost thing, run away, barely fifteen. Dope and absinthe in a farmer's field under the stars. She didn't dance well, but I showed her some steps. Butterflies with straight-razor wings. They caught the moonlight as they swarmed around her; silvery white, staining black as she opened, spilled . . . I doubt she ever knew she could be so beautiful, or that life could be so much fucking joy.

I sent her home. You think the ones who put her out on the doorstep with nothing but the clothes she wore and a virgin's cunt to sell will be pleased to see her? And what about you? I know this isn't home anymore, knew the second I pulled up outside; it felt wrong, somehow skewed. Ha, everything does these days. Reality: a wedding cake melting in the rain.

And the roaches. Goddamn, the fucking roaches! Swarms of 'em, everywhere. I can hardly sleep most nights; they never stop singing. I found a place where they spill through not too long ago; some abandoned house down in Boston. I heard them from the street, heard them when I stepped off the damn plane. You've seen something like it, haven't you? A wound in the world. Isn't that where you learned . . . to be you? I saw it; flapping like flayed skin, weeping, sceptic. They swarmed through it, disappearing into the cracks and shadows. Me, I just wanted to crawl up in there; never wanted anything so bad, not even with the old gorilla riding my back. It wanted me too; the roach's song, it came from inside, sweetest thing I've ever heard. I wanted to crawl up inside and dissolve there; go to shit like I will eventually anyway, let the roaches eat the rest.

But I didn't. I got the fuck out of there; nothing that wants you to want it so bad can be good for you. Maybe I'll go back when our business is done, after I've snapped every single one of your pretty girl's fingers, taken your teeth and your eyes. Ha, I'd take your balls too, if someone hadn't got there before me. What's it like for a man like you to go without his manhood? Remember those days, the glory days, when you could fuck a storm or a cave wall and make children? No more. I think I'm the last. I've tried to be; done a pretty thorough job, best I can tell. Still, no telling how many bastards are still out there. Didn't you tell me once how you fucked desert 'til it became rainforest? Or was that just more of your mythic bullshit?

The world's had enough of us, I think. Mom knew it, you know it. Why else would you let them take so much of you? Why would you let me come for you, when you could open me, make me spill at the seams with a thought?

Why would you let me dream?

So don't waste what little time you have left on justifications. My life . . . *life*. I don't even know what that is because of you. Just another little piece set to wander; a shard of broken mirror in the landfill. I'll dance for you, before you die. Maybe we'll dance together, eh? Don't look so disgusted! You taught me perversity. Consider it a lesson well learned.

Then the roaches. They want you, you know; they sing it, all the time. They want me too, but not yet, not yet; things to do first, people to see. But soon enough. You'll get to go first. Lucky bastard.

They'll eat the world when you're gone. I want you to know that. The deserts, the mountains; the cities you raised. Bakers and butchers and babies; winds and waters and wishes. I won't hold them back. No one will be left who knows how. Every wife, every child you ever had; not even a memory of them left. Maggots eating away sceptic tissue, that's all.

Get some sleep, Dad. Try not to dream too deep, okay?

See you soon.

NIGHT LIFE

A pretty thing, Mrs. Beeston thought. Odd, but pretty. Picturing it sat on the mantelpiece amongst her collection of porcelain dogs and soldiers, she simply couldn't resist.

She knew Mr. Cameron, the antique shop's proprietor, well enough by now to be wise to most of his tricks: one of those young turks who thought he could charm the pants off anything with a sly smile and compliment. Mrs. Beeston expected it as part of the service.

"Ah, Mrs. Beeston. How are we doing today?"

She raised a supercilious eyebrow as he took the item from her, examining the price-tag.

"*We* are just fine, young man, though *we'd* be even better if people didn't talk to us like *we* were two years old and just got on with their jobs."

"Point taken."

There was what she called "good blood" between them; he wasn't above riling her for a little bit of fun, and she wasn't so prudish that she wouldn't occasionally respond in kind.

That was why he only charged her £2.50 when the price tag clearly read £4.00. Mrs. Beeston was never one to turn her nose up at a bargain.

*

Arriving home, she made herself a cup of tea, then spent several minutes in her favourite armchair, allowing bones and muscles that weren't what they used to be recovery time after the morning's travails.

Leaving her tea to cool, she fished her one luxury item from its brown paper bag, smiling at the texture of cool pottery beneath her fingers.

Such a *pretty* thing: a black bell, rim decorated with red roses. Turning it this way and that, she was surprised to find no manufacturer's mark. Most of these things usually came with some sort of stamp or seal; she'd learned that from The Antique's Road Show.

Ah, some sort of markings inside the bell; a hymn or prayer perhaps? She couldn't make the words out properly without her glasses, couldn't be bothered to get up and go hunting for them.

"Hmmm, well, you'll look nice anyway."

After some deliberation—not wanting the grand-kids to get ahold of it as they had her Henry VIII last week—she set it up on the high shelf next to a porcelain golden retriever and Chris's conch shell.

Poor Chris.

*

Funny, she couldn't recall having many habits before she retired (against her express wishes). She'd noticed the tendency in old people when she was young; the little quirks they developed, the daily routines they fell into, but had never *understood* it.

Now her day was defined by such small necessities; the morning walk down to the paper shop where she'd spend a few minutes nattering with Nancy and the Pakistani lady behind the counter before heading home to feed Snowy, who'd only then be returning from a night of feline adventure. After making the bed and vacuuming, she'd make a few phone calls to Laura and David, maybe have a chat with the kids if they were off school.

Then it'd be time to make a start on dinner.

Today, she'd brought a lovely piece of steak she planned to fry (in direct defiance of the doctor's orders) and have with home-made chips.

Peeling the potatoes, she heard something; a faint tinkling that caused her to slip, slicing her finger.

"Oh, bloody hell!"

The doctor warned she should be careful of cuts, the heart medication he'd proscribed—whose name she couldn't remember or pronounce—making her blood water thin.

Wrapping the dish cloth around her wounded finger, she abandoned the dinner for the time being and went through to the living room for a sit-down.

She cried a little, struggling to catch her breath, hating this stupid, damn old woman's body, feeling its decay slowly seeping into her thoughts. Every old person she'd ever met said the same: that they still felt sixteen in their heads. She hadn't believed it 'til she started to feel time's weight herself, presuming it was just something they parroted because it sounded *right*.

God, what she wouldn't give to be sixteen again . . .

She didn't notice the bell in her hand 'til it began to ring. Just one of the little habits she'd gotten into; giving it a tinkle every now and then. It was the same sound that had caused her to slip and cut herself in the first damn place.

A dark rivulet ran from her hurt finger down the bell, forming a ruby droplet at its lip that quivered, waiting to fall.

Maybe she had ghosts.

*

She must've eaten something funny to be having dreams like that, or maybe it was her medication; it could sometimes play havoc if the pills were changed to a cheaper version.

She dreamed herself waking in the middle of the night, feeling . . . *different*.

That weight; the terrible, awkward heaviness, as if her bones were filled with lead, was gone, along with the cottony stuff that sometimes snarled her thoughts.

Getting out of bed, she found herself stripped of her hair net, her nighty; the body beneath strong and beautiful again, a cruelty that hit her like a hammer blow when she woke the next morning.

Admiring herself in the bedroom mirror, running fingers through the lustrous, dark hair spilling over her shoulders; the verdant thatch between her legs, she heard something outside; grunts and shrieked obscenities, interspersed by the ringing slap of flesh on flesh.

Going to the window, she saw a couple of youths on the street below; neighbourhood boys tumbling over one another in a drunken brawl, bawling hate and fury at the tops of their lungs.

Any other time, she'd have been disgusted by the display, screaming down at them to piss off back to their own street. Tonight, she found it strangely enticing, heart racing fit to burst in her chest, lightning filling her belly as one of the combatants—a dark haired, bull-chested youth who ducked and dodged like a boxer—landed a blow on the other's nose, driving him back bloodied.

As was often the way with dreams, her body seemed to act of its own accord, opening the window, flinging itself out into the air before reason could intervene.

It wasn't flight as such, more as if she became momentarily feather-light, floating ground-wards in defiance of all the usual laws and constraints.

The bloodied youth staggered away, using her distraction to put some distance between himself and his assailant. The other stared at her as if witnessing an angel descending from heaven, eyes wide, mouth slack with disbelief.

Though her feet were bare, she felt no discomfort from the cracked, litter-strewn tarmac as she started towards him, the smell of him—leather, blood and young, young sweat soured by a surfeit of alcohol—more tantalizing than that of any meal she'd ever cooked.

Mastering himself, he smiled, puffing out his chest and throwing back his shoulders like a male gorilla. Was he afraid of her? She thought so; she could smell it, liked it.

He didn't retreat as she pressed herself against him, wrapping her arms around his neck, kissing him hard enough to bruise. He didn't taste as good as he smelled; bitter and bilious, like bad wine, but the hunger was so intense now it almost *hurt*.

She jumped, trembled at the trespass of his hand between her legs, not having felt anything but the urge to piss down there for far too long.

He was neither particularly expert or gentle, his fingers prying her apart, plunging into her without any regard for her pleasure, but she sighed approbation into his mouth nonetheless, massaging him through his jeans.

"You . . . you want to go somewhere?"

She shook her head, sliding down onto her knees.

"Are you crazy? Someone might see!"

She shrugged.

"So? What do you care?"

He shrugged back, conceding the point. It took her a few fumbling seconds to tug him free, her fingers not yet recalling their old tricks. He grunted, putting his hands on her head as she took him between her lips, not even protesting when he felt teeth, blood mixing with the semen on her tongue.

*

Mrs. Beeston had grown used to waking to aches and pains. Getting out of bed was the first—and often the hardest—of the day's trials, but not today.

Today, joints that usually felt like balls of broken glass beneath her skin were easier, providing only slight twinges of discomfort.

Hoisting herself out of bed, she took a swig from the lemonade she kept on her dresser, then set about making herself somewhat presentable. She'd all but given up looking in the mirror these days, the story of decay it told far from her liking.

Momentarily catching glimpse of herself as she set about recovering her hairpins and applying a modest amount of make-up, she paused for a more considered look.

Was it just a trick of her sleep-blurred eyes, or did her skin look somewhat . . . *lush* this morning? Of late, the only colours it boasted were the green and purple of veins threading beneath, or the ugly bruises that even casual bumps produced.

Now there were roses in her cheeks and blood on her lips, her dreams apparently proving greater tonic than any amount of proscribed pills or potions.

*

Going about the morning's rituals—breakfast, vacuuming, baking to follow—she was annoyed to find one of the porcelain roses broken from her new bell, petals scattered across the shelf as if used in some love-sick girl's game of "He loves me, he loves me not."

Still, she couldn't bring herself to feel too put out by it today; not when she was feeling so unaccountably spry.

When she tried to pick up one of the petals, it crumbled in her fingers, becoming black, ash-like dust that she vacuumed up with the rest of the filth.

*

Marion from across the way called 'round for tea at 10:30AM. Mrs. Beeston noted the commotion in the street when she went out to collect the milk, but hadn't paid a great deal of attention to it (there were always police in the neighbourhood for one reason or another these days). She could tell from the second she opened the door that Marion was practically bursting to share some tit-bit of gossip with her. The flood gates opened before she even had a chance to sit down:

"Have you seen all this outside, Sylvia? Eh, I don't know what the world's coming to; police on the front doorstep every day . . ."

Not wanting to get snared in one of Marion's more general rants, Mrs. Beeston asked her what was going on.

"Well, our Richard's staying with us at the minute, and he was woken up last night by some racket outside . . ."

Mrs. Beeston's belly did a somersault. She dropped a custard cream in her tea, waiting for Marion to continue.

". . . apparently, there was these two lads havin' a right go at one another, 'effin and blindin' at the top of their voices, goin' fit to murder one another, he said. Anyway, he goes downstairs to get himself a drink, and by the time he comes back up, one of 'em's lyin' face down bleedin' in the road!"

Mrs. Beeston sipped her tea, thoughts turning from last night's dream—its lewdness making her uncomfortable in front of Marion—to the bell. She couldn't bring herself to feel too sorry about the boy; little thug would've likely grown up to be just another drunk, foul-mouthed waste of space like them next door.

At least this way he'd gone to some use.

"We've had the police 'round since three o' bloody clock this morning. Have you had your hair done or something?"

Mrs. Beeston looked out of the dining room window at the police milling in the street.

"Something like that."

*

After Marion left, she cleared away the tea things—tipping the uneaten biscuits back into the tin—then retired to the living room. She stood and stared at the bell, expecting it to start peeling or pouring blood.

"Come on then, what's the game?"

The bell didn't answer.

Picking it up, she noticed a hairline crack running down its side.

Better get the super glue to that, she thought, hand shaking as she returned it to its place.

*

She'd forgotten Linda and the kids were coming over for tea. There'd been another argument at home apparently—the fourth this month—though Linda wouldn't discuss what it was about:

"Oh, it's just David; you know how he gets."

Mrs. Beeston knew exactly how David got; it'd been one of the unhappiest days of her life when Linda informed her of their impending marriage.

"Got it on 'im again, has he? He can be such a baby, that husband of yours . . ."

Seeing the sudden lightning in her daughter's eyes, she let the subject drop.

"Naaaanaaaaa . . ."

Little Vincent materialized somewhere around the vicinity of her knees, spun sunshine hair ruffled and sticking out from his scalp at every angle.

"What is it, love?"

He smiled a gap toothed smile, chewing on his sleeve.

"Can I 'ave a biscuit?"

"Only if your mom says so."

Linda looked at her daggers, as if she'd thrown a suspiciously ticking parcel into her lap.

"No, Vince; Nana's going to cook us some tea in a minute . . ."

Vincent took a moment to consider, conjuring up a basis for bargaining.

"But I'm *starving*."

"You're not starving, and you're not ruining your tea. Why don't you go and bother Ed for a while?"

He took off like a shot at mention of his brother's name.

"Ed*waaarrrd*! Mom says you gotta play with me!"

Linda sighed, a female Atlas beginning to strain beneath the burden of Heaven.

"God, they've been driving me up the wall this week . . ."

Mrs. Beeston wasn't a fool; she knew what her daughter was angling after. She wished she'd just come out and ask.

"You want me to 'ave 'em for a few days, 'til you and David get sorted?"

Linda's eyes lit up with gratitude.

"Would you, Mom? I wouldn't ask, but I can't handle them and David as well when he's in this mood . . ."

Why don't you just dump the waste of space, then? He's a dad now; he can't go around acting like a big kid.

"Ah, that's no problem. They'll keep me company. Right, about time I started tea."

Linda didn't offer to help.

*

Half a day running around after Vince and Ed, every bone and joint in her body aching.

"Aaah . . ."

Seating herself on the sofa, she turned on the TV, flicking through the channels for something good. BBC 2 was showing a David Attenborough special on snakes and lizards. Chris had always loved his wild life programmes, especially anything involving reptiles and creepy-crawlies.

"What's that, Nan?"

"What's what, love?"

The bell. She hadn't even realised she was holding it 'til she heard its soft, strangely distant tinkle in her ear. Starting as if suddenly woken, she almost let it slip from her fingers.

Edward stared at her with a mouthful of cheese on toast.

"Oh, it's just something I picked up the other day . . . nothing special."

"Can I look at it?"

She knew what "look" meant in her grand-children's vernacular; *can I touch, can I mess, can I break?* A flush of intense disgust, as if he'd asked to see what she kept in her underwear.

"No, love; it's delicate. You might break it."

Edward pouted, put out by the slight.

"I *won't*. I'm always careful. It's Vincent who breaks things, then I always get the blame."

The anger rose from her belly like burning vomit, spewing from her lips to ignite the air.

"I said *no* and I meant it!"

The two seemed to visibly shrink in their seats, Edward looking contrite whilst Vincent's eyes flashed with younger-brother defiance.

"Now, just sit quiet and watch the telly."

*

She woke to streets, housing estates and industrial parks spread below like some Frankensteinian blanket, stitched together from scraps and tatters. Air so cold she felt ice-crystals forming in her hair whipped in invisible streamers around her body, more refreshing than any shower, and sensual beyond the wildest ambitions of lace or silk.

She was herself again; the same she always pictured in imagination's eye, but which flesh had forgotten.

And she was hungry.

*

Stuart was fucked off to the eyeballs. Why did they always start on him? Sure, he sometimes got a bit loud when he'd had a few beers, but where was the harm in that?

Now he staggered back to his shit-hole of a flat with a black eye and bloodied lip, feeling an urge to punch through stone, to breathe fire and smoke and incinerate every bastard who thought they were better than him, every stupid *cunt* who wanted to start something they couldn't finish.

He'd start with Tracy. Brainless fucking tart couldn't tell that he loved her; either that or she didn't care.

"Stop it, stop it!" she'd screamed as he kicked the guy's face in, too stupid to realise it was either them or him.

She'd told him she didn't want to see him again, threatened that if he ever came near her or the kids, she'd call her dad and his mates.

"Do it then, you stupid cow . . . do it and see what happens . . ."

He didn't see where the girl came from; one moment he was alone, the next she was there, smiling at him from the alleyway. Though it was dark, his vision swimming with drink and hurt, he could see she wasn't wearing much, if anything at all.

A part of his mind he'd spent his entire life trying to bury screamed up from its pit: *what kind of crazy bitch wandered around in the altogether at night? Only one that was diseased or deranged.*

But Stuart wasn't used to life handing him things on a plate, and this girl was undoubtedly one of the most gorgeous he'd ever seen outside the pages of *Playboy*.

Smiling an invitation, she retreated into the shadows.

He was sick of being fucking messed about by women. If this cow wanted to play games, they'd be playing by his rules.

Stumbling to the alley-mouth, he saw her silhouetted in moonlight. Naked.

Go, just leave now. You don't know what the crazy cow might do. She could cry rape or anything . . .

There was no one else around. Let her try and fucking prove it!

Stepping into the moonlight, she presented him with a glimpse of legs so pale, they might've been sculpted from chalk. His eyes lingered at the shadowed space where they intersected, trying to make out the concealed anatomy.

A hand slid into the shadow, its toying earnest enough to make his mouth water.

"I ain't paying you or nothing, you know . . ."

It'd happened before; some slut inviting him to bed only to start spouting prices before the wetness between them had even cooled.

"And no one's asking you to."

His drink-lubricated libido needed no further invitation.

She opened her arms as he lumbered towards her, stepping forward to meet him like the personification of every wet dream his adolescent imagination ever conjured.

She brought him the closest he'd ever come to Heaven before the pain began, by which point he'd long since ceased to care.

*

Mrs. Beeston rose early; a habit programmed into her over five decades of marriage to a man who liked to bask in every second of light the day provided. She'd already been up five hours when she called the kids from their beds, a significant dint made in the day's chores.

It was impossible to describe how she felt this morning. Parts of her body that had atrophied to the point of being nothing but sources of pain and discomfort suddenly remembered their old purpose, taking to it with gusto. Worries over her daily pills—a cupboard full arranged in the precise order they were supposed to be taken so she wouldn't forget—evaporated, leaving her thoughts free to consider more frivolous subjects, such as last night's dreams.

Warmth kindling in her belly, she turned on the radio, hungry for music:

"... bu-ut it's all right, Lady Eleanor ..."

An old song, one she'd never really appreciated 'til now.

"Nan?"

Vincent, always the first up. He stood in the dining room doorway looking at her as if she were an alien materialized in a beam of light.

"Hello, love,"

He backed away as she rose from her chair.

"What's up? Don't you want to give Nanna a hug?"

He didn't answer, darting past her to take his place at the table.

"Can I have toast for breakfast? I like the way you do it; it's different from Mom's."

"Whatever you like, love."

His eyes never left her as she set about searing the bread.

*

Another flower had fallen from the bell, several smaller cracks branching out from the original. She didn't pretend to understand the magic it worked—Magic! Even thinking the word made her feel foolish, infantile—but the roses were obviously significant. How many more before the bell stopped chiming, and she was forced to return to her previous state of waiting for flesh to fail?

The prospect made her shudder.

Maybe it'd be wise to conserve its use; make it a special treat, like her trips to her sister Dorothy's on the other side of town.

At least it'd give her something to look forward to.

*

A nightmare of her own funeral; those come to mourn either not hearing or choosing to ignore her screams and shrieks as she was lowered into the earth.

Dirt pattered against its lid as the coffin came to rest, muffled voices giving their final farewells.

It disgusted her now, but there'd been times when she'd looked forward to this, prayed for it even, when the arthritis and sundry other infirmities became so crippling she could barely make it down the stairs of a morning.

The rain of earth became a monsoon, each shovelful sending spiders skittering through her entrails as she anticipated the slow rot to come ...

*

She couldn't breathe, the light streaming through the window so painful to her eyes it was impossible to open them. Her body felt as if some gigantic, invisible gorilla lay atop it, crushing her down, wrapping its fingers around her throat.

Was she having a heart attack? A seizure?

No. She *knew* what this was, and exactly what she needed to make it stop.

Her mouth and throat were dry as a mummy's, the only sound they could produce a feeble croak that reminded her of the noises her Chris made when she found him that morning . . .

The bedroom door creaked open, the head of an infant angel peeping through.

"Nanna . . .?"

He sounded worried to death, poor love, his eyes bulging out of their sockets at the sight of her.

"Shall I . . . shall I call the doctors?"

One of the first things he'd learned to do with the phone was dial 999. Such smart kids—a bloody miracle, considering who their father was.

It was several seconds before she could work up the breath and spittle to speak. Edward lingered in the door as she did so, afraid to approach.

"No love, Nanna needs her bell . . . the one in the living room."

He didn't hesitate or question the request as an adult would've, speeding down the stairs in the way she'd scalded him for a thousand times over.

The morning was so bright . . . she wanted to bury herself beneath the covers and block it out.

Edward was back in a flash, carrying the bell in both hands like a priest bearing a holy relic. Mrs. Beeston struggled to raise her arms as he approached the bed, as if gravity had developed a grudge against her. The simple china ornament seemed to weigh a ton. She rang the bell once, twice, three times, the pain and discomfort flooding from her in a breath, leaving her exhausted, but alive.

Edward backed away as she struggled up, eyes wide and swimming with fear.

"It's okay, love. All better now."

"Nanna . . ."

"Yes love?"

"Are you a witch?"

She grinned, marvelling at the brilliant nonsense that came from the mouths of babes.

"What makes you ask?"

He shrugged, his fear visibly evaporating.

"Dunno."

"Go get washed and dressed and I'll make you some bacon sandwiches for breakfast. How's that?"

He was gone in a flash, no doubt relishing the few moments peace before Vincent woke.

Something broke away from the bell as she set it down on the bedside cabinet; two nubs of green painted plaster that looked for all the world like flowers about to bloom.

*

"Edward says you haven't been very well . . .?"

Linda phoned a little after lunch, sounding fretful and worn out rather than revitalized by her break from Motherhood.

"Oh, I just had a little bit of a turn this morning, nothing to worry about. What about you and His Nibs, are you sorted yet?"

Linda wasn't the breaking-down-crying type. Even as a kid, she'd bit tears back, usually venting her emotions in some other way that invariably landed her in trouble. Nonetheless, Mrs. Beeston could hear where tears were supposed to be, her defiance more eloquent than any confession:

"Oh, you know how he is . . . nothing but a big kid himself, really. He'll come round."

"Well, you just take care . . ."

"I will, Mom. Bye."

Mrs. Beeston resolved what she had to do before the line clicked dead in her ear.

*

"What's she marrying that great twat for?"

Chris had never approved of David, didn't care much if he knew about it.

"You know what young girls are like, Chris. You've got to let them make their own mistakes."

"Yeah, well, he's one *big* mistake if you ask me."

She agreed completely, but knew that any attempt to inform Linda of the fact would only make her cling to him all the tighter. Since their first meeting -in which David had waxed verbose on the dangers of nicotine whilst Chris puffed contentedly away on his Hamlets-, she'd entertained the vague hope that her daughter would open her eyes one day, see the slug she presumed to love for what it was.

Those hopes were dashed the second Edward came along. Like it or not, kids were a tie that couldn't be broken. She still hated her daughter a little for that stupidity.

Now she realised her parental duties were far from over, and that if Linda still refused to open her eyes, maybe it was time someone opened them for her.

*

It was like he told the lads from work; it wasn't that he didn't love Linda; he just needed to get away sometimes, to be on his own and think things out. The Ship and Hedge was as good a refuge as any.

Sometimes, she just didn't understand that he wasn't the kind of guy who could just walk into and out of jobs; there had to be something *there,* some intrigue or enthusiasm for him to engage, otherwise he'd inevitably fuck something up.

Besides, it wasn't like they did badly; he always made at least £150 a week fixing computers, selling parts; they certainly never went without. God, if he had the kind of toys Ed and Vince did as a kid, he would've thought he'd died and gone to heaven . . .

The woman stepped round the corner so suddenly he almost collided with her. Mumbled apologies died on his lips as he saw her face. Jesus, she looked so much like Linda! Or rather, how Linda used to, before the bags began to weigh under her eyes and her waist expanded by several notches.

She was dressed in an old fashioned frock of robin's egg blue, her feet bare.

Something sparked in the alcohol tangled mass of his thoughts; a faint light of concern insisting that he should be on his way . . .

"Sorry, I didn't see you there . . ."

The woman smiled at him, but her eyes . . . something about them didn't sit right, as if they couldn't bring themselves to match her mouth's sentiment.

"Do I . . . know you from somewhere?"

He didn't quite see what happened next. Something flashed before his eyes, too quick to see, then there was pain, and his shirt was wet . . .

Willowy arms slipped around his waist, dragging him forward. Then her lips were at his throat, darting in and out of the rupture through which his life leaked.

Legs growing limp as overcooked pasta, a memory floated to the surface of his fast-evaporating mind:

Linda's mom kissing his cheek at their wedding, dressed in a frock of robin's egg blue.

*

Vincent cried when she came downstairs to make breakfast, asking where Nanna was at least ten times before she could convince him she was right here.

Edward didn't seem to have the same trouble.

"It's all right, Vince; Nanna's magic."

"Don't be silly, Edward . . . why don't you go out and play for a bit?"

She could well understand Vincent's confusion. She felt it herself when she looked in the mirror that morning, the reflection staring back light by at least thirty years. Her hair . . . God, she'd forgotten how beautiful it was . . .

As for the rest of her . . . she hadn't given it more than cursory glances for so long for fear it would drive her to tears. But she looked now, exhilarated rather than afraid of what she might find. She'd always been naturally pale, but the pallor had taken on a grey, chalky quality in recent years. Now, her skin—innocent of all save the slightest wrinkle, the ugly mottling of liver spots faded to near nothing—seemed to almost shine; a joy to eyes and hands alike.

Imagine . . . all the things she'd put off out of fear or timidity; the boys not kissed, the trips not taken. Now she had her chance over again, and this time, she was going to do it right.

The doorbell.

Hard to believe that barely days ago it elicited nothing but a sigh of exasperation, the trip from armchair to door an epic endeavour of pain and indifference.

Marion blinked in surprise as she opened the door.

"Oh, I'm sorry . . . is Sylvia in?"

Did she really look that different?

"No, she's just popped into town. Would you like to come in?"

*

The kids were well occupied with some game in the back garden. Marion accepted her cup of tea with cold and trembling hands.

"Thank you, love. Dear me, but you're the spit of young Linda, you know."

"Hmmm, well, my mom and aunt Sylvia were always alike . . ." Her thoughts were quick-silver, flowing in a stream of invention.

"Just visiting, are you?"

"For a day or two. I have to be back down in Cornwall by the end of the week."

Her name was Patricia Beeston, daughter of Miriam, sister of Sylvia. She'd moved down south with her mother after winning some money on the lottery, and now worked in a small bakery just outside of Leventhal.

"Well, I imagine it's nice for Sylivie, having you around. Stubborn old cow won't admit it, but she finds it a bit difficult getting about these days . . ."

Mrs. Beeston sipped her tea.

"Really?"

"Hmmm, she's never been quite right since your uncle Chris died, God rest 'is soul. Never been apart since the day they met, you know. Tragic really . . ."

Mrs. Beeston only heard scraps and fragments of the rest. Much of it consisted of bemoaning the general state of the world; how "The Young" had no manners or discipline, and ruminations on how the cane or conscription would probably do them a spell of good. After all, it hadn't done her any harm.

Hard to believe that barely a few days ago, she'd considered the woman amongst her closest friends; someone she hadn't a bad word to say about. Worse was the knowledge that she'd been little better, every overheard scrap of bad news proving a bone to be picked clean; an excuse for conversation where there was precious little else to say.

"Well love, I have to get off. If you could tell Sylvie I popped round . . ."

Mrs. Beeston told her she would, swearing she'd sooner stick knitting needles in her eyes than talk to the miserable, back biting old bitch ever again.

She made Edward and Vincent sausage and chips for dinner. Even through the flurry of kitchen activity, she felt strange, *restless*, as if there were a million other things she could be doing passing her by with every breath.

She'd forgotten what it felt like to want anything from life.

*

The kids ate in silence, the usual round of giggles and arguments abandoned in favour of furtive, corner-of-the-eye glances they no doubt thought she wouldn't notice. A few days ago, they would've been right, but things were so much clearer now.

"Lads, have you got something you want to ask me?"

Vincent looked up at her, laughing through a mouth of partially-chewed chips for no particular reason. Little Vincent, always Mommy's favourite, whether she cared to admit it or not; a straw-haired devil who'd gotten away with more than his brother dared dream with little more than a look and a smile. It hurt to realise she actually didn't like him very much; too much like his bloody father. Edward, on the other hand . . . she could see the wheels turning behind his eyes, a brain that would no doubt be a source of great misery before he was too much older attempting to grapple with what it'd been conditioned to regard as make-believe.

"When are we going home, Nan? We haven't seen Mom and Dad in ages."

It wasn't what he really wanted to ask. He wanted to know where the magic came from, if he could learn it for himself.

"Soon, love. I expect your mom will be calling some time today."

*

A little after tea time. Linda sounded like she'd been crying.

"Hello?"

"Oh, I'm . . . I'm sorry . . . I think I have the wrong number . . ."

"That you, Linda love?"

Mrs. Beeston made a conscious effort to sound a little more wizened.

"Mom? God, I didn't think it was you for a minute. You sound . . . good."

Mrs. Beeston smiled.

"Hmmm, must be havin' the kids. Reminds me what it's like to be young. You all right, love?"

Silence, Linda struggling to compose herself. Mrs. Beeston felt a stab of maternal satisfaction, picturing her waste-of-space husband's face slipping beneath the waters. The bastard wouldn't be causing her anymore grief.

"Oh, you know, it's just David, as usual. He's done another one of his moonlight flits."

"Again? For the love of God, Linda . . ."

"I know, I know, all right? I'll have a word with him when he gets back, a proper one. I'm not carrying on like this."

She sighed, trying not to cry. Poor love.

"You want me to keep the kids here for a bit?"

"If that's okay. They're not being any bother, are they?"

"What? No, Ed's sat in the living room with a book, and I think Vince's down the garden somewhere. You just get this sorted out, all right?"

"Okay, Mom . . ."

She wanted to say a lot more, but didn't need to.

". . . Bye."

*

"I hate him, Nanna! I hate him, I hate him!"

She'd seen it before a hundred times over. Vincent was at that age where it didn't matter what Ed had or what Ed was doing, Vincent had to *be there*.

They'd been down the garden, Ed playing about with some new toy he'd been saving every penny for, Vincent badgering him about when it would be "His Turn." She'd already told Vince in no uncertain terms that the toy belonged to Ed, and it was Ed's decision as to who played with it. Vincent had apparently interpreted this as: "Wait 'til I'm gone then badger Ed 'til he gives in."

Heavy handed Vincent, lacking any respect for property that wasn't his own, had broken the thing in seconds, resulting in a black eye from his brother that Mrs. Beeston privately regarded as well deserved.

"It's okay, love, shush now. We'll get you another whatever it is when we go shopping."

This didn't help as much as she hoped.

"What's the point? He'll just break that one as well."

Vincent sat glaring at his brother from the chair he'd been consigned to, apparently feeling he'd been done a profound injustice.

"Vincent, what do you say for breaking your brother's toy?"

The boy narrowed his pretty blue eyes at her. *This is a suspicious break with protocol,* they seemed to say; *you've let me get away with so much more than this before . . .*

True, but now she saw things more clearly, and felt that change was in order.

"Vincent, you say sorry right now or you can get to bed and stay there until you do."

Without another word, Vincent slid from his chair and thundered upstairs, slamming the bedroom door behind him.

*

So much she didn't know about herself, about the world. In the few short days since she popped into the antique shop, she'd seen more of humanity than she had in all her previous seventy-two years. There were *worlds,* night-time worlds of blood, quiet and desire she'd been cut off from, the fact of their existence known only through newspapers and TV reports. She still wasn't a part of that world yet, still feeling like a trespasser on sacred ground, awaiting her moment of initiation. But she was slowly learning its ways, beginning to love them in a way her sloughed off self would never dare contemplate.

The girl and her lover were beautiful. She'd been following them since they first left the club, feeling her own blood warm, quicken as kisses grew feverish, leading to caresses the like of which she'd never shared, not even with Chris . . .

They were what they called "Goths;" girl and boy both wrapped about in matching, skin-tight outfits of black lace, faces powdered and painted to resemble dead things, risen from the grave or mortuary slab by mutual appetite. A silver chain ran from a loop hooked through the girl's nose, the boy's hair hanging around his waist, billowing out behind him like a vampire's cloak in the breeze.

Going unseen was no longer a problem. Before, she'd been forced to skulk in shadows and alley-ways. Now she went amongst the lambs as one of them; the pretty black dress she wore given to her by a girl who'd offered herself as meat, somehow knowing what she was from the outset, having dreamed of being drained since the earliest stirrings of womanhood.

She was the first of her own sex. Mrs. Beeston had been scared, but far from repelled; beauty was just one of the many presumptions that had been turned on its head for her. Now the thought of the girl standing pale and naked before her in the moonlight made her sinuses sting and entrails writhe with appetite rather than fear and disgust.

This girl wasn't like the other; she smelled strong, like wine fomented from blood.

She smiled as they vaulted over the wall of St. Lucy's into the cemetery, no doubt intending to couple amongst the dead.

They were half-naked when she came upon them, the boy sitting bare-arsed atop a weathered gravestone whilst the girl bobbed between his legs. He ran painted black nails through his lover's hair, head thrown back as he muttered professions of love to the starless sky.

Mrs. Beeston, Sylvia—names that meant nothing to her now even in her own mind—slipped out of her dress before stepping into plain sight. She didn't pretend to understand the rules and parameters that governed her new life, but knew that hunting, feeding in anything but her own shifting skin was wrong; a breach of some unspoken contract whose writer she'd yet to meet.

The two had swapped positions now, the girl sitting on the grave stone whilst the boy bent to service her.

In her head she heard Chris's voice, its ignorance-fuelled fear making her thankful that he was buried and rotting:

"Filthy bleeders, should be strung up."

A flicker of fear passed across the girl's face as Mrs. Beeston approached, her lover too preoccupied to notice anything amiss.

What did she think? That here was a ghost risen to punish them for their desecration, or perhaps to join them in it? She smiled, drawing closer, the girl—terrified and clearly drugged out of her wits—smiling back.

The boy, finally sensing that something wasn't right, tore himself away from his lover's sex, puzzled that she was no longer voicing her appreciation.

"Baby, what's . . .?"

Mrs. Beeston brushed the back of his neck. He didn't wheel around as she'd expected, but rose slowly, pivoting like a puppet on snarled and knotted strings. She could smell the girl on him; a scent that put her in mind of the ocean, soil freshly turned after rain. His lips glistened as they parted, fumbling for words whose shape they'd momentarily forgotten.

Her kiss took more from him than mere spit and passion; a torrent of hot, meat-tasting brine flooding her throat, planting in her mind a fantasy of swimming in the primordial sea, taking into herself the chemical elements that would one day conspire to create her species.

It was over in seconds, muted protests growing silent, the body she held collapsing in a filleted pile at her feet.

The girl regarded her with lazy-lidded disconnection, either ignorant of her jeopardy or inviting it.

Kneeling before the gravestone, Mrs. Beeston pressed her lips to where the ghost of the boy's still lingered, and drank.

*

She soared, cloud and wind streaming over her naked flesh, invisible hands raking, caressing, a red premonition of dawn burning the horizon. Why would she want anything other than this? How could she have felt such deep loss when Chris—a man she realised had been dead long, long before his breath and heart stopped—went into the dirt? He and her old self had conspired to enslave her, to trap her in the relentless round of tea, roast-dinners; Christenings, Wedding receptions and funerals that they presumed comprised life.

She no longer breathed; her flesh was cold, yet she felt so much; more than any whose blood still ran warm could comprehend.

Maybe there was a way she could share this, free the ones she loved from the shackles they'd made for themselves . . .

Such thoughts all but evaporated as she licked her lips, tasting traces of the girl and her lover, closing her eyes and imagining herself with them again, feeding, pleasing them 'til their bodies could no longer stand it.

Rolling on her back against a cushion of cloud and wind, she reached between her legs, dabbling in the wetness there, wondering what it was now capable of. It felt *different* from how she remembered, somehow fluid and fluttering to the touch, as if it'd become a hive for spectral butterflies. Probing deeper, her fingers found what felt like a cold running stream in which strips of coiling life swam, seeking a place to spawn. What she'd taken from her loves wasn't any mundane nourishment; whereas the sheep had to die to provide its meat, they still existed, albeit in a way she couldn't define. She felt them swarming within her, coursing through her blood, her thoughts, waiting to be born again...

Could she do that? The prospect made her laugh as she dipped and darted through the dying night, fingers working her to climax through a complex symphony of strokes and caresses.

A new star burst into being in the pit of her entrails, threads of glittering matter erupting from between her legs, marking her trail across the heavens.

*

There was a smell as she slipped through the open window into her bedroom, a bad smell. Sniffing experimentally, she realised it'd been there as long as she could remember, no more noticeable than the chatter from the nearby railway tracks; the smell of age, dead dreams; of waiting to die.

She couldn't stay here. Even were it not for the corpse-stink of her sloughed off self, people would grow suspicious, wonder where old Sylvia Beeston had gotten to.

Crawling atop the bed, she buried her face in the coverlet on Chris's side, smelling the familiar sourness of him, wishing he were here to share all this . . .

The scream startled her, the frightened murmur of a hurting babe escalating to slaughter house shriek. Both Edward and Vincent's bedroom doors were open, the shriek, now faded to breathless whimpers, emanating from the latter.

She knew before she stepped through this was more than a mere bad dream. The darkness stank of blood and terror, urine sharpness stinging her nostrils.

"Edward, I know you're in here . . ."

A shape that seemed somehow sewn from the surrounding darkness moved atop the bed, eyes like a cat's in car headlights turning to regard her.

"I found your magic, Nanna."

The thing held an angel-faced rag-doll in one knotted claw, its lightning blue eyes growing dim as they stared up at her, pleading for her to make the bad stuff go away.

Teeth glimmered in the dark as the monster smiled, then turned and hurled itself through the bedroom window, trailing hyena-laughter into the dying night.

*

The last flower crumbled to ash as she picked it up from the living room carpet. Small green buds of plaster decorated the bell's lip. She knew that if she watched them long enough, she'd see them grow and bloom, ready for another soul to pluck.

Eddie . . . he was the clever one; watching, listening, taking things in. There were no secrets in a house where Eddie was. She should've known that.

Picking up the black bell, she wasn't surprised to find it flaking, crumbling in her hands. Soon, there was nothing left but dust that she ground between her fingers, wondering how long it'd be before she went the same way.

*

Dawn was breaking when she left the house, life stirring behind drawn curtains, dreams bursting to be replaced by a waking world she could no longer claim to be part of.

She didn't lock the doors, left all belongings behind. In her mind, she could already feel the myth taking shape; a post-modern fable of disappearances, empty rooms and blood on sheets.

She smiled, knowing that the stories were where she would live from now on, that she'd be made immortal in her neighbour's waking nightmares.

There were worse ways to end.

THE SKITTER JACK

He watched them hurrying, heads bowed, through the rain. One or two muttered greetings as they passed, most not even seeing. He was a ghost playing voyeur to the living.

Where was he going? Not the faintest idea, though his feet seemed certain enough. After stepping out of the house, they carried him down Lambert's Row, then up Shipley Bank, through the new estate with its close-packed, identical red brick houses until he emerged near the motorway. He supposed he could follow it, find out where all the drivers were going in such a hurry.

Agatha's voice in his head. He hadn't been paying attention when he walked out the front door; everything too black and boiling, but now her words rang clear as crystal. It wouldn't concern him if they were the last he ever heard:

"Jason, where are you going? We've got to sort this out . . ."

Henry crying upstairs, Val sat in front of the TV, rolling her eyes, sighing. In truth, they were as tired of it all as he was. The only difference was none of them had the balls to simply walk away.

It wasn't even a conscious decision: one moment he was in the kitchen, chopping peppers and red onion for dinner, the next he was away, Agatha's protests fading with every step.

*

He followed the motorway for a mile or so. His mobile rang once, twice, three times before he plucked it from his pocket and flung it into the bushes. Let someone else have it. He never wanted the fucking thing in the first place.

A cold spasm arced through him as some little shit screamed from a passing car:

"Wanker!"

Images of the car sliding out of control, ploughing into a tree or telegraph pole, going up in flames.

His mom used to bring him down this way before the by-pass came. Back then, there was nothing but green; fields, brooks; a small forest whose name he couldn't remember, save for the one he and his friends gave it:

The Wild Wood.

Ha, he hadn't thought about that in years. All so long ago now, so far away; like a dream he had whilst still in the crib.

His mom used to make up stories for him all the time. She told him when he was a little older that it was one of the many reasons his father had walked out on them. He didn't want to think about *that* now; only the stories:

Stories of worms and wolves; of little men who lived beneath the soil 'til the autumn leaves fell, emerging from hibernation to sew clothes of red and gold for the coming winter. Some of them terrified him, the nightmares they induced making him wary of sleep for weeks on end. He never told her that, far more afraid of the stories ceasing than any nightmares they might inspire.

Not that it made any difference; eventually, she stopped telling them anyway.

*

The Skitter Jack.

Good God, how could he have forgotten that? Jason stopped dead, a smile spreading across his face, fragments of those all but forgotten imaginings glittering behind his eyes.

The Skitter Jack.

". . . he lives in the Wild Woods, skittering between the trees. That's how he got his name," he always loved those little details, stuff he later realised she conjured on the spot, "most people don't even see him, just a shadow out of the corner of their eye, then poof! He's gone."

Jason relished the cold thrill that washed over his entrails when she told him that. Of course, he'd seen the Skitter Jack himself, hadn't he? Hundreds of times!

"Almost everybody has," she replied, "though they don't know it's him. He leaves people alone, for the most part. He's a very private creature."

"Like Dad?"

She smiled.

"Pretty much like Dad. But every so often, some poor little boy or girl gets to see him *up close* . . ."

She refused to elaborate on what happened to them, letting his child's imagination fill in the blanks.

How could he have forgotten it? The Skitter Jack. He and his friends had gone hunting it many a time; tried to chase it down and trap it when one of them caught a fugitive glimpse.

They never claimed so much as a hair.

*

Jason shivered. He'd neglected to pick up a coat and his clothes were sodden.

Getting dark now, a faint but bitter breeze chilling him to the marrow. He'd have to start back soon, either that, or carry on 'til something gave out.

The thought of walking up the garden path, seeing the light in the living room window where *they'd* be waiting, shuddered him more deeply than any cold.

Feet and fear were in accord on this point, picking up their pace as they carried him further and further away from home.

What was he going to do? They'd been married sixteen years come November; it was even longer since they'd ceased to exist as separate entities. No way they could be so again without significant hurt. But what choice was there? He could barely contemplate sharing the same house with her, smelling her scent in every room, sitting on a toilet seat warmed by her backside.

Things had to change, and soon . . .

He didn't even notice the opening 'til his foot failed to find the pavement. Crying out, he stumbled forward into the small side road, dancing to keep his balance.

Plenty of farms down this way; some sort of fenced off military training ground, but they all lay behind. He didn't know this place; no signs or notices to enlighten him. The road led to a rough opening in the bushes, fast degenerating into little more than a dirt track as it wound away between trees. Some sort of nature reserve? Perhaps all that remained of the Wild Wood that had seemed near endless to his eyes as a child? Private property, most likely, though there were no gates or the usual threats of prosecution should someone be caught trespassing.

Just a little look, then he'd head back. He promised himself.

*

That *smell*, the funk of deep wood: soil and rotting leaves, wild garlic and stinging nettles. It put him in mind of hairless legs and skinned knees; of a time when the sight of blood was enough to bring him to tears.

Clearly a much larger space than it seemed from the outside, the trail he followed seeming to wind on forever, not even pin pricks of windows or street lights visible in the distance.

Was it possible that they'd simply *forgotten* about this little scrap of Wonderland after the bulldozers and earth movers had left? Jason was surprised it hadn't been converted into landfill or yet another council estate.

He nearly lost one shoe or the other several times, the sludge parting beneath them, sucking them down.

"Shit!" The ground abruptly shifted, pitching him on hands and knees in the mire. The perfumes of damp earth and vegetation filled his nostrils, agitating memories.

He knelt there on all fours for several moments, dabbling fingers in the dirt and damp, feeling them seep through the knees of his jeans.

Hauling himself to his feet, he stretched, joints popping and groaning; his body telling him that things had moved on, the boy he remembered with such heart felt yearning long since consigned to the grave yard of sloughed off selves.

If its ghost could be found anywhere, it was here, wandering the remnants of its old playground.

*

Christ, he was tired. It came over him all of a sudden, the energy and enthusiasm that brought him this far dissipating like a flock of birds disturbed by approaching footfalls. For the first time since setting foot out of the front door, he considered home with some fondness. To sit in front of the fire in warm, dry clothes would be good, *better* than good, even with Agatha there to dilute his satisfaction.

Dark now, the only light filtering down periodically through breaks in the cloud.

Agatha might've called the police. Christ, he hoped not; he didn't have the energy to deal with all that shit.

Stopping, he stood and scanned the surrounding woods, wallowing in nostalgia one last time before the long trudge back to reality . . .

What was that?

Something, a flicker of motion, just on the bounds of sight. Nothing. Not even the grey sliver of a squirrel, the gleam of a fox's eyes. Probably just a bird.

Gone now.

*

He couldn't even hear the motorway. How long had he been walking? His watch had stopped.

"Fucking thing." His voice sounded strange in the silence. No matter; so long as he kept following the path, he'd get out sooner or later. The real hardship would begin when he arrived home.

The Wild Woods had never seemed so *quiet* back when he was a kid, always *something* rustling in the undergrowth; the screams and laughter of other kids playing somewhere in its expanse.

His mom hadn't liked him wandering there on his own towards the end; kids had been getting hurt, beaten bloody by a gang of thugs. It hadn't stopped him anymore than common sense did this time around.

Only the last visit remained sharp in his memory, its details habitually picked and pored over whenever events allowed him time to stop and think.

He felt himself slipping, eye turning inward, away from the night-time wood of the waking now, back to one stained red with dying dusk, the memory of faded summer warmth dispelling the chill in his bones . . .

*

Home no later than five o' clock, that's what he'd been told. Mom was cooking dinner and she didn't want to piss about re-heating it.

His watch read five-thirteen. Fuck it; he was going to be in trouble anyway.

"Where're we going?" Kelly asked as they tramped through the nettles and bracken. She'd been whining since they reached the Wild Woods, but Jason didn't mind. At least she wasn't like the rest; too pussy to even come here anymore. They were afraid they'd end up like Josh Winslow or Anthony Wier. Stupid, really. The Wild Wood was a *big* place; plenty of space to run and hide.

"Not far." He didn't want to tell her yet, wanted her to *see*.

They'd get there just in time too; as the sun was going down.

He'd known Kelly forever, ever since they were babies, but recently things had become *weird*. They didn't talk about it, though he wanted to desperately. He was afraid she'd never speak to him again if he brought it up.

Nothing really; just a kiss behind her dad's garden shed. But it *was*, wasn't it? Everything had been different after that, though they pretended otherwise. Once or twice he tried to work up courage enough to broach the subject, but the words always caught and shrivelled in his throat.

Best to leave it be for now.

"Ow, fuck!" he swore, thorns scraping his shins. Kelly laughed, his pain apparently hilarious.

He could hear it now, the stream's babbling reminding him of the days his mom used to bring him here to paddle.

"This is it," he announced, turning to watch her struggle through the thorn bushes. Though they scratched her bare arms, she remained silent, denying him the chance to return her laughter.

Through the trees, they could see the red orb of the descending sun. Rays of ruby light filtered between them, falling on the stream and turning its waters to blood.

"Wow," Kelly gasped.

"Brilliant, isn't it?"

He'd brought others here before; Kim and Daniel, Kevin and Hayley, but they never *got it*. They just shrugged and asked "So what?" before hurling rocks into the water.

Jason knew from the look on her face that she saw what he did; something beautiful beyond words.

They stood for a while, not speaking. He jumped when she took his hand, inhaling sharply through clenched teeth. He didn't know what to do, what to make of this. She turned to face him, everything inside seeming to boil and churn.

What was he supposed to do? What did she want?

He smelled her as she leaned in close; summer sweat and a sweet shampoo of coconut and menthol. She hesitated, uncertain herself, then kissed him for the second time, longer, *hungrier*.

He broke away when lack of breath made his head swim, not laughing, not speaking. She stepped back breathing hard, eyes and cheeks alight. What was she thinking? Would they still be friends after this? There was a hornet trapped in his skull, stinging his brain feverish.

Reaching out with a trembling hand, he touched her arm. She flinched, seeming afraid.

"Are you . . . okay?" he managed, the words emerging slurred and distorted.

"Yeah," she nodded, though he could see she wasn't sure.

"You wanna go home?"

Her eyes flushed with alarm.

"Not yet. Let's just . . . stay here for a while."

His first time. Hers too; three days shy of sixteen. A strange experience; feverish, fumbling; over faster than he'd ever imagined.

But wonderful, more so than anything he'd experienced since. She left him soon after, hardly lingering long enough to dress or say goodbye.

*

Things had a habit of slipping from his mind. He couldn't recall, for example, what colour his mother's eyes were, or the first time he and Agatha kissed. But this memory was so pungent, so *rife* with detail, it was as if he wavered between two worlds; one of cold, dark and disappointment, the other warm and dusky, swelling with potential.

He blinked as the dark world asserted its dominance, reducing the ephemeral one of memory to little more than vaporous tatters; an image sewn from cigarette smoke.

How long had he been walking? He should at least be able to *hear* the motorway by now. Stopping, he strained his ears for some hint of growling motors, the blare of car horns.

Nothing, only an aching silence, emphasized rather than broken by the wind's spectral whisper.

Fuck it, he must've wandered further than he thought.

He should probably give Agatha a call, though he didn't want to hear her voice right now. Fumbling in his pocket, he found it empty. Where the hell was his . . .? Oh yeah, he'd gotten rid of it, hadn't he?

What in God's name had made him do something so stupid? If he fell and hurt himself out here, chances were it'd be *days* before anyone found him.

At least he was calmer now, more prepared for the shit that awaited him back home...

The sound was so faint he wasn't even sure he heard it. Standing stock still, he tried to regulate his breathing, straining his ears for any further disturbance.

Nothing.

"Hello?" he called, breath crystallising in the air. Something off to his right. What was it? Someone *murmuring?;* Impossible to make out through the rain.

He'd be lucky to find the path again if he wandered off into the dark. Best just to leave well enough alone. He had to get home, sort things out . . .

Another sound, closer this time; the sigh of a sick woman drawing her last breath. What if it was someone hurt, waiting for God only knows how long for help to happen by? He had to make sure. So long as he kept in a straight line it wouldn't be too difficult finding his way back . . .

"Hello?" Sludge squelching, weeds crunching underfoot. He couldn't see a damn thing save for shadows and the silhouettes of trees.

Maybe just a fox or something. Hadn't he read somewhere that their cries could sound like human voices, babes crying?

This time he was certain he saw *something,* whatever it was disappearing behind a tree the second he turned to face it. A momentary glint of eyes in the dark?

"All right, sod this," he muttered to himself, casting about to find his way back to the path.

Oh *shit.* Had he gotten turned around somehow? Where the hell was it?

All right, all right, stay calm. The worst thing he could do now was panic. It couldn't be more than a few meters away. If he just wandered around a little, he was sure to stumble across it.

Several minutes blind blundering put paid to that assumption.

"Fucking *idiot!"* he cursed, feet snaring in a patch of nettles and thorns.

Suddenly he thought of Val, sitting in her room worrying herself to tears. She liked to make a play of adolescent indifference; some people took her as cold, aloof. But Jason knew better; she let things get to her, sometimes far, far too much. He had no doubt she was cursing his name right now, along with the fact that she was ever born. She'd be oh so relieved when he walked through the front door, but do everything in her power to contain it.

And Henry? He was undoubtedly being much more vocal about his feelings, entreating his mom to call the police whilst crying himself hoarse.

The train of thought was derailed by a disturbance somewhere off to his right. Whatever the fuck it was, it was closer now. A sudden stab of urgency in his bladder, but he didn't dare stop to relieve it.

"All right," he called into the darkness, "you can stop fucking me about now."

No answer, not the slightest whisper.

Then it came at him, emerging from behind a nearby tree, devouring the space between them with breath-stealing speed.

*

He stumbled several times, tripped by protruding tree roots or losing his feet in the sludge.

He didn't care where he was going, only that he got out, away.

He hadn't seen much, only a denser shadow against shadows, its form roughly that of a man, but stretched and distorted, wavering as if cast by candle flame.

And *eyes;* the feature on which he'd focused; madly glaring eyes, stretched so wide they seemed to be starting out of their sockets.

He had a name for this monster, one his mother made:

The Skitter Jack.

All those times they'd tried to chase it down and trap it as kids, seeing not so much as a hint of their prey, and it chose to reveal itself now he had the sense to be scared.

He didn't dare look back to see if it followed. For all he knew, it was on his heels, just waiting for its chance to reach out and . . .

The ground fell away, leaving him treading empty space, then the world tilted, melting. Thorns, thistles and fallen branches tore at him as he tumbled down the embankment, a sudden snap heralding pain the like of which he'd never known.

Breath had long since fled by the time he thudded to a halt, leaving him squirming and gasping in the dirt. Hot dampness flowed down his left arm, every movement causing galaxies of agony to explode across his eyes.

Tiredness descended as he lay fighting for breath, the desire to close his eyes and leave the world behind near irresistible . . .

No. They'd find him dead of hypothermia or blood loss, that was if they ever found him at all.

He couldn't even cradle the damaged arm without causing himself hurt. All he could do was let it flop limp and useless in his lap, trying to locate the wound with his fingers in the dark. He felt like weeping when they finally did.

A stub of what could only be broken bone protruded from a ragged rent in his forearm, blood pulsing from it in such profusion he was surprised he hadn't already keeled over. He had to stem it somehow, or he'd never make it home.

There was a handkerchief in his trouser pocket, probably dirty; mouldering away in there for months after one of his summer colds, but what else was there?

The rasp of cotton against his exposed nerves made him feel faint, but he tied it as tight as he could bear.

Not much, but better than nothing.

Staggering to his feet, he cast about for some sign as to which direction he should head.

Christ, the Wild Wood wasn't that big, even before they built the by-pass. If he just kept walking . . .

*

The more he thought about it, the more it seemed it was probably just his mind playing tricks on him. It could've been anything, after all; a bag caught up in the breeze, a bird flying at him out of the dark. The Skitter Jack was just some fucking kid's story.

Water? Somewhere off to his left. He couldn't see anything, but if he could find a brook or stream, it'd be a simple matter of following it to the wood's edge . . .

The sound became clearer with every step; running water chattering away to itself like a lunatic in a padded cell.

Someone sat by the stream, a figure so pale she seemed almost luminous in the dark, whispering to herself as she dabbled a hand in the water. She was young, no older than twenty from what he could tell at this distance, and naked.

Jason suppressed his first instinct to call out. What kind of lunatic wandered around naked at this time of night, and in such cold? But then, she might be his only chance of getting out of here alive.

She turned to face him as he approached, her posture betraying nothing of shock or embarrassment.

"Hello?" he called, half-expecting her to leap up and run away.

She smiled, teeth glinting in the moonlight.

Closer now, it seemed what he'd taken to be a simple illusion of light and shadow was actually far stranger.

She *was* glowing, as if fashioned from congealed moonlight, lambent vapour rising from her skin as she swirled her fingers in the stream.

Not real; an hallucination brought on by terror and blood loss.

Only a few steps away now, close enough to see that she was beautifully sculpted; a little on the skinny side for his tastes, limbs over-long and elegant, dark hair cascading down her back to sweep the dirt. Her face was an alabaster mask; an exercise in the most exquisite symmetry, though faintly *familiar* . . .

She didn't speak as he stood and stared, returning his scrutiny with eyes that seemed all pupil, reflecting the night sky as her skin did the moon that rode it.

Nothing, he told himself, *just ignore it; go before you bleed to death . . .*

But he couldn't move, couldn't take his eyes from her as she rose, unfolding long, willowy legs, their intersection shrouded in shadow, and stepped back into the water. Still smiling, she extended a hand, inviting him to join her. The stream churning to froth around her ankles was undoubtedly *freezing*, but the feet that had brought him here had no time for such cowardice.

Carrying him forward, they hesitated for a second at the water's edge before plunging in.

Cold so intense it *hurt* coruscated up his legs, his feet initially screaming before growing numb. The girl reached out and took him by the hand, her touch frost.

If she was just some hallucination, then it was so vivid as to blow apart all distinction between the real and the imagined:

Skin soft and marble smooth against his fingers, her smell the chill of crisp, clear winter mornings, spiced with a subtle suggestion of cinnamon.

She closed her eyes as she kissed him, tongue flickering hungrily between his unresisting lips.

He and Agatha had long since ceased to put their marriage bed to any use save sleeping. There hadn't been anything conscious or outspoken in this decay of intimacy; it was a simple matter of whatever they'd once shared having run its course. Even so, Jason never once considered cheating on her; up 'til now, he'd been able to content himself with idle fantasy and internet porn.

He hadn't realised what poor substitutes they were.

His hands found her flanks, trailing their glacial contours to the snowy peaks of her breasts. She suffered his attention without complaint, sighing like the echo of a distant gale beneath particular strokes and caresses.

Stop. Get out of the water. Run.

He ignored it; the petulant little nay-sayer that had kept him in place his whole fucking life, insisting he stick with what he knew, be *content*.

Even his arm had stopped hurting now, all that remained a receding throb, like a nightmare fast draining from memory.

Jason floated, tumbling through mist.

Breaking their kiss, he trailed lips down her breasts and belly, tasting the ice sweetness of her skin as he knelt before her in the water.

Strange; though he was barely inches away, the shadows obscuring her most intimate anatomy remained dense, intent on denying him glimpse of it. All he could discern was a faint fluttering, as if a swarm of moths nested there, stirring from long slumber.

Pressing his lips to her, he tasted the Wild Wood; damp soil and vegetation, weeds, wild flowers and old, old wood.

She yelped beneath his tonguing, his heat rising to match her coldness, her pleasure echoing throughout the surrounding night; more than mere expressions of carnal abandon; it had a *summoning* quality, like the calls of a wolf-bitch separated from her pack. No sooner had the notion crystallised than he caught glimpse of something moving in the woods behind her.

Scrabbling to his feet, Jason watched the thing draw closer, drifting between the trees like a black paper bag borne up on the breeze.

The Skitter Jack.

Mad eyes glaring, it paused at the water's edge, floating there as if afraid to cross.

Jason started back from the girl, who continued to smile, chest heaving in the aftermath of orgasm.

Other motions at the edges of sight, shadows stirring in the woods, the sludge and leaves seething as things squirmed up from beneath. Glancing down at the shifting soil, he saw something sickly white break from the mulch of the riverbank, minute arms flailing as it hauled itself into the open air. A monstrous maggot body writhed and pulsed, the face of a newborn baby squinting in shock at the world. Others quickly followed, squirming on the ground 'til they had strength enough to stand. His mother had told him about these too, hadn't she?: The Maggot Men who emerged in the damp, looking for dead things to feed on.

The girl started towards him through the water, the Skitter Jack billowing in her wake. In the distance, he heard laughter, like children at play, saw shades of them chasing one another between the trees.

Was this it? Was he dying?

Then the children came.

Most were clad in torn and dirtied rags; the remains of clothes ripped to tatters in boisterous play. There were many of them; the youngest no more than five, the eldest skirting the borders of adulthood. Drawing closer, they laughed and whispered to one another, unmindful of the monsters surrounding them.

Jason wanted to close his eyes, let reason and rationality wash the nonsense away, but couldn't. He had to see.

One, a tussle haired, wiry youth of around fifteen, stood slightly apart from the rest. Whereas they were solid, dirt-smeared flesh, he resembled the girl in the water; naked, luminous, vapour coiling from his skin.

Going to the girl, he kissed her passionately before turning to Jason with an unabashed erection.

He knew them . . . knew them both, like characters he'd met in some childhood dream long since forgotten.

Laughing with faint derision, the boy extended his hand, seeming to invite Jason back down into the water.

What would it mean if he accepted? What games would he be made privy to in the night whilst the world dreamed, begging never to wake?

Suddenly, the Skitter Jack arced towards him, shapeless blob of a head stretching, splitting; ragged, hollow mouth seeming to crawl and churn as if infested with cockroaches.

Jason turned and ran.

*

They laughed, running with him. He could see them darting between the trees.

All a game, just a game . . .

Tiny hands raked ragged nails across his ankles, the pain causing him to stumble. He vomited as agony exploded through his body, sour bile splashing the forest floor. They were on his legs, vile little leech mouths gnawing through his jeans to fasten onto the flesh beneath.

No, no! A child's voice shrieked in his head. *They only eat dead things! Mom told me so!*

The others emerged from the woods smiling, singing. They'd caught him, and now the game was over.

The Skitter Jack drifted into view as Jason tried to force himself awake, knowing to his marrow that he *must, must* be dreaming.

Floating before him, it threw back its head and hissed at the night sky, turning its gaze to meet the luminous lovers as they emerged from the darkness.

"W-what do you want?"

They regarded him with soft smiles, seeming to radiate as much affection as moonlight.

Hunkering down on his haunches, the boy scraped elegant fingers through the soil.

"We want what you want. It can't *be* any other way."

That voice . . . he *knew* that voice. Why couldn't he remember where he'd heard it before?

The children were close enough now for him to make out the hunger in their eyes, the way they fidgeted, like dogs straining to be off the leash.

"Do you want to go back?" The girl asked, twining her fingers through the boy's shoulder length hair.

He answered without thinking, instinct seizing upon this one chance where intellect would've prevaricated:

"No."

Their smiles broadened, the boy rising.

The barriers holding back memory broke as the children descended, tiny teeth and fingers tearing at him through a red flood of recollection:

The boy's face . . . the same that had once looked back at him from mirrors and windows; the surface of still waters, before time and disappointment twisted it out of true.

NO PLACE FOR CHILDREN

I don't want this.

The simplest acknowledgement, thirty years in the formulation. Shreds and scraps had come to her before; little misgivings, pangs of unhappiness that she swallowed like the pain killers that controlled her period cramps. *Nothing*, she told herself; *just the same crap that everyone goes through.* She wouldn't be weak, wouldn't let the world get the best of her.

He was good, that was the worst of it: clean, respectful, smart; a man that others envied. But never hers.

"The Chat," as she'd come to think of it, occurred on April 29th, 2022. It'd been building for at least several months prior, nearly boiling over once or twice, when the house seemed to be filled with a heavy, invisible vapour that seeped into her skull, smothering thought.

Finally, she wanted him to see behind the curtain, for the make-up and costumes to come off.

It was a surprise for him. He stood looking at her for several seconds, coffee mug in hand. He was still smiling when he put it down, brow furrowing.

"I, ah," he started, scratching his throat, "I don't know where this is coming from Marie, I really don't."

It was just over. Everything was right; they were perfect for one another, but reality had intervened.

"It doesn't matter now."

He sat down.

"Yeah, yeah it does. I wouldn't make you unhappy for anything in the world, you know that, darlin'?"

She knew.

"You don't. That's not it . . ."

"Then what is? What's the problem?"

How could she say? How could she articulate what she couldn't rationalise? Language was a lame mule, a leper with no arms or legs.

"Everything."

*

That was the worst of Richard; he was still a good man, even when circumstances warranted otherwise. She came out of the divorce a wealthy woman, without acrimony, without obstruction. He'd made his fortune as a script writer, his TV series *Cradle* catapulting them to heights of affluence she'd never dared dream of. The fact that she'd co-written at least half the episodes and acted as de facto editor on them all was neither here nor there: *Cradle* was Richard's baby, percolating in that shaved bald skull of his since the age of sixteen.

And now, secure, stripped of concern, she had a new life to build. More than once in those first months, she found herself going to the phone, fully intending to call and weep her repentance into his ear. She didn't know how to live outside of the channels they'd constructed together, that was the God's honest truth. She knew every trick and turn of that maze, could walk it deafened and blindfolded if needs be.

Now it was gone, the walls crumbled; the world beyond too vast, too open for her to comprehend. Which way should she go? No obvious direction, no landmarks or sign posts. A desert: endless and eternally shifting, its scavenging denizens waiting for her to give up hope and lay down in the sand.

Elsie wouldn't talk to her. That was fine. Though she'd never dared admit it to herself before, she didn't like the woman her daughter had become. Spiteful and selfish; using her grand children as weapons whenever she couldn't get her own way. Richard had always doted on her, of course, and would protect her all the more ferociously under present circumstances. They were welcome to one another.

There was only one person she could go to:

The man she hated most in all the world.

*

Things never changed in this house. That was its purpose: to sustain, to *suspend*. Children played somewhere inside, laughing so hard she was worried they might be sick. She smiled, tears pricking her sinuses at memories of being one of them.

"Yes?"

She knew the woman who answered the door, though the recognition wasn't mutual. Hardly surprising; she'd changed so much, allowed the world to work its transformations. This one had been part of the house since before she was born, the children her happy charge.

"Hello, Bella."

A moment, then a hand rising to lips that didn't know whether to smile or hang open in shock.

"Marie . . ." She reached out, painted, jewellery-burdened fingers hovering between them. A particular green stone decorating a silver ring on her index finger caught Marie's eye. It used to belong to her Father. The hand lowered, the woman sighing, "You said . . ."

"I know. But I need to see him. Is he . . .?"

The woman threw a glance through the adjacent doorway, checking on the children.

"You . . . you'd better come in."

*

"I think I've seen you before," the boy insisted for the third time, glaring at her with open fascination. Handsome moppet, all ebony curls and lancing blue eyes that'd have the girls swooning in less than a decade's time.

Or perhaps not.

"I don't think so, love. I haven't been here for a very, *very* long time."

The boy shrugged and furrowed his brow as if to say: *like that matters.*

John Bramley Lawrence was his name; one of the few she'd never forget. She remembered playing with him here, on this carpet, drinking cocoa next to him on this sofa. Had she fallen in love with him a little? It seemed likely.

"Go and play now, John. I think Heather needs some help with her painting."

The boy lingered for several seconds before speeding off to another corner of the room. Bella poured out two cups of swampy scented green tea. Marie remembered it well; the first time she tried it, she'd spat it down the woman's dress in disgust.

"It took me a while to find the place."

"It would. You've been away for a long time."

She hadn't been sure she could remember the way. He'd shown her time and time again, but the skill had dulled with neglect. For the longest time, she'd wandered like the lost child she was, finding only the dark, misty places she'd been warned to steer clear of.

"Why did you move again? Was it . . .?"

Bella silenced her with a glance towards the children. Of course; not here, not now.

The woman sipped from her tea. Marie did the same, tasting rain and freshly cut grass. It was the death of her childhood; memories of decay and tumult all bound to that cleansing, medicinal taste.

"I think you'd better tell me what you're doing here, Marie. If he comes home . . ."

"He won't; he hasn't been here for years." She didn't know how she knew, the certainty beyond all reason. The woman visibly rocked as if slapped. Sad eyes sought out the solace of her tea cup, swirling the green liquid as if to coax some speck of hope from its depths.

"You trying to make me cry again?" The woman smiled, though there was precious little humour in it. It'd been a favourite game of Marie's when she was a child to press her Nana-Bella to tears. She'd succeeded only once in all that time, and even then the tears she elicited had been of pure fury. That was the first time she'd ever been struck as a child.

"No. I just . . . need to see him."

A sigh, so heavy it seemed that the woman was attempting to exhale flesh, bone and organs as well as air.

"Like you say, he's not here. Hasn't been for a while. And don't bother asking where he's gone to; you know well enough he keeps that business to himself."

She did. She'd tried coaxing it out of him any number of times, by every wile her child's imagination could concoct. He was immovable as the statues made in his likeness.

It was well and truly over, then. The house was her last link, the only point of contact. Perhaps best just to leave it behind and forget . . .

"Your name's Marie, isn't it?"

The boy stood before her, strewn with paint up to the elbows, flecks of it spattering his cheeks and hair.

"I told you to go and play, John."

"No, no; it's all right," Marie insisted.

"You used to play here, *ages* ago. We . . . we went to the Mister's library once." Remembering seemed to be an effort for him, his brow furrowing so deeply, he looked at least two decades his senior.

She remembered that day. Of all the sacred cloisters the house contained, that was the most forbidden; the one to which any and all were refused trespass. She couldn't recall much about the library itself; only that she'd filched the key from her father's study, and that inside there was . . . *light,* comets and streamers dancing, weaving about one another as if in the throes of mating or murder.

Nothing else.

He wasn't angry, that was the funny thing. He'd warned her so many times not to stray, but when he'd sat her down and started talking, he'd smiled, seeming more sad than anything else.

She left not long after that. Richard had been her way out; an avenue into something *other* than these four walls. Now he was gone too.

"I remember. *You* were clever; you didn't come in with me."

He frowned, shaking his head.

"Nah, I should of. Then you wouldn't have left me behind."

She reached out a hand, caressed his paint-stained cheek.

"I'm sorry, love. Go and play now."

He grinned, nodding, turned away. She was about to make her farewells to Nana-Bella when he spoke again, though he didn't turn to face her.

"Nana got it wrong; the Mister's still here; you can hear him singing, sometimes."

With that he was gone, plunging into play she could no longer share.

*

"I'm telling you, it's nothing. The boy's probably just been dreaming or something."

No, Marie didn't think so. She didn't know why Bella was so desperate to keep her away, but she knew that the woman was either mistaken or a liar.

"It doesn't matter. I just want to see, then I'll go."

Or maybe not. After all, if Bella's "Mister" was gone now, that meant the house was hers, didn't it? The thought of becoming the next in line, wasted to a thing of dust and weak sunlight, made her shudder.

She'd never told Richard any of this. Insofar as he was concerned, her mother and father were dead, her family estranged. It was an easy lie to live, easier by far than the truth.

The stuff of him was everywhere; the silvery dust that trailed him, sweeping about him in animated skirts whose touch always made her giggle. Pellucid sunlight filtered through the first landing window, grime clotted cobwebs clumped in its corners, the desiccated remains of their makers still in residence, left to become more of the same dust.

The world beyond was one she hadn't seen outside of dreams for nigh thirty years. It'd changed during that time, shrugging off its lush vegetable coat of summer green in favour of Autumnal reds and ambers, many of its trees going naked in the wind and rain, displaying their wretchedness to the broiling sky. She'd imagined walking there as a girl, smashing the window and leaping out, letting the wind or the trees catch her. Nana-Bella had cautioned otherwise, telling her stories of young ones before her who'd gone wandering.

It was so strange coming back to this; the old absurdities, more familiar to her than the domesticity she'd come to inhabit. Maybe that was it; the root of why she was so discontented: she'd spent the best part of her adult years flying in the face of her essential nature, turning a blind eye to the little prophetic dreams, the twinges of intuition that were as part and parcel of her senses as sight or scent.

"We had one go running there not too long ago. Michael, his name was. He comes back every now and then, pawing at the back door. I put out meat and milk for him."

Marie turned away, starting up the next flight.

*

Dingy corridors led off in three directions, stretching further than the walls of the house could physically contain. Most of the rooms were for the children's benefit; nurseries, bedrooms, bathrooms, toy-rooms; places where they could play and dream, wash and swap secrets.

Marie remembered the stories they'd tell one another; the make-believe worlds they'd concoct from cupboards and cardboard boxes, so tangible she could *smell* them even now, feel their soil beneath her feet.

A favourite was to imagine themselves in the world outside the house, making streets and neighbourhoods; shops and cul-de-sacs they could wander. Marie never liked those games; she was one of the very few permitted to accompany Nana-Bella and occasionally the Mister on their travels outside. She knew *that* world well enough: it was nothing special.

No, hers were always of more *fantastic* kind: alien woods whose trees were made of frozen fire, where dragons coiled around up-thrust roots and gryphons perched in the boughs, deserts of bone where tomb-cities lay in cemetery silence, the dead whispering on the wind. They were so *real* to her, so tangible, the games often faltered whilst she drank in their textures, luxuriating in imagination's manipulation of her senses. Occasionally, she'd dreamed of being woken in the deep of night, guided from her bed by the Mister, down stairs and corridors she didn't recognise to doors beyond which those worlds spread before her, waiting for her to step out and claim them.

She never had; he'd warned her of the consequences.

"It's locked. Nobody goes in the library anymore."

It didn't matter; she knew where the key was.

*

They called it the study, though it was really just *his* place. The threat of being sent here, waiting against the wall outside until the door clicked open and they were called in, was more than enough to keep most of the strays and waifs he took in on an even keel.

She'd been sent there more than most, operating under a status of *special* privilege. Unlike the rest, she'd never been taken in or left on the doorstep by some reluctant parent: she was *part* of the house, her first breath filled with its dust, her first steps upon its faded, threadbare carpets.

It looked no different from the other doorways: a plain thing whose sky blue paint had begun to chip and peel, revealing layers of red and swamp green beneath.

But they all knew it instinctively, not a one going to the wrong door by mistake (though one or two did so by design).

Marie could sense Nana-Bella's fretfulness as she grasped the door handle. She doubted the door had even been opened since her "Mister" left.

She shielded her eyes against the usual spill of sunlight through the wide bay window. She needn't have bothered. Inside was murk and stale air; her nostrils twitching, tickling as if some spectral spider had decided to make a warren of them.

"He . . . he said no one was to go in." A lie, she was certain. He just upped and left like he always did, suddenly not there.

Heavy rain hammered against the window, angry purple clouds seething, hanging heavy over the city. She'd always been fascinated by it as a girl, more so than any of the places the house looked out upon. He'd told her the story of it once; a city of angels, all of them disappeared long ago. Something else lived there now, something content to let the pearlescent spires and temples go to ruin, to let the black weeds that coiled up through the streets have their way.

One of the window panes was cracked, as if some suddenly blinded bird had hurtled into it from outside.

The place still smelled the same, but *colder* now, its faintly spiced perfume—like baking Christmas cake— little more than a trace on the still air.

Nana-Bella lingered behind her in the doorway as if they were heretics trespassing on sanctified ground. It was difficult for Marie to share the perspective, having pissed on this carpet more times than she could recall before aspiring to bladder control.

One of the book case's shelves had collapsed, spilling leather bound volumes and statuettes to the floor. She bent and plucked one up: a bronze angel, naked body boyish, face classically feminine.

"Who is it, Daddy?"

"The Light Bearer, the First Fallen . . ."

This was hers. If nothing else, if she never saw him or the house again, there'd be this. It went into her coat pocket. Bella didn't protest.

There were chairs set out before the window around a small wooden table where she remembered there always being drinks and biscuits. She sank into the one nearest the window; the same he always occupied, feeling the unfamiliar grooves and hollows his body had worn.

This was how she'd seen him for the first time, *really* seen him, when he let the mask of humanity he wore slip in a moment of abandon. She only recalled vague impressions now; a man-shape woven from dust and sunlight, several sets of wings stretching from his back in rainbow splendour, a churning circuitry of fire weaving throughout his body. The thought that the same stuff ran in her veins. . .

What was he?; Beyond all the stories and the myth making? She didn't know, had left the questions behind in favour of the certainty of love, only to find it crumbling and the questions returning, more vibrant and vital than ever.

Outside, the rain abruptly became more violent, pelting the window with the force of bullets, tongues of red lightning flickered in the clouds overhead. Marie wondered if perhaps there were still angels taking refuge in the heavens, weeping their anguish down upon the city they'd lost in hope of washing away its usurpers.

Something moved in the streets below, a phantom flitting from shadow to shadow; too fast for her to make out any specifics, save that it was ragged, strips of something—maybe clothing, maybe skin—trailing from its tattered form, scraping across the broken stone beneath its feet.

The key was in the little drawer concealed in the table, just like last time. Bella watched from the doorway with barely concealed horror as she removed it, rising from her seat without a backward glance. Time she left this place to its ghosts.

"Lock this door," she demanded of Bella once it'd closed behind her.

"Why?"

"Something's been trying to get in. I don't know what . . ." She didn't have to say any more: Bella visibly paled, fumbling as she fished a small key from about her person and shakily complied.

"Is it . . . safe?" Marie could well understand her fear. Bella had been a child here like herself, only she'd remained, become so much part of the warp and weft of the place, she could no more be separated from it without consequence than from her own bones.

"I think so . . . for the time being, anyway."

"God, where the hell is he?"

If she couldn't answer that, no one could.

*

Bella left before they reached the library. Marie understood; there were the children to consider. The house wasn't above letting harm come to them; they both knew that from bitter experience. Besides, what she was about verged on the sacrilegious: no one, *no one* went into the Mister's library.

Only her, and *time* had been the price for her trespass.

It was deeper in than the rest of the house's environs, the path to it leading through a small maze of seemingly identical corridors, the rooms of some open, doors either flung wide or hanging off their hinges, inviting the would-be trespasser to come in and explore. She knew most of them well enough; during the latter days, when she'd grown fractious and unruly, she'd inspired expeditions to these far flung cloisters, leading a small band of the bravest—or most easily coerced—into rooms from whose carpets trees and shrubbery sprouted, their fronds and branches laden with singing insects, birds and lizards, others where rain fell from ceiling-suspended clouds, miniature tongues of lightning licking down to singe their eyebrows or sting the backs of their necks. Some were more mundane; rooms as one might find in any other house, filled with boxes, stacks of books, ancient, cob-web strewn furniture. The most fascinating thing about these were the windows, each looking out upon a place far beyond the street upon which the house stood: deserts of red and black sand from which giant, luminous mushrooms sprouted, endless plains of jagged blue crystal, amongst which forms of smoke and light swarmed, occasionally approaching close enough to display their firework innards before retreating again.

She ignored them now, even those places where her most poignant memories had been shaped: the first time she'd seen her own blood, the first time she'd been kissed. There was only one place she needed to be, one place she could find what she wanted.

And what she wanted more than anything else was *direction,* some sign, no matter how vague, of where she was to go when she stepped out the front door.

Why go anywhere?

The voice wasn't hers, though it echoed inside her own skull. Nevertheless, its implication was clear: with the Mister gone, this place was *hers* by right. Wouldn't it be fine to be her own Mister, *Mistress* of such magic?

And what would that mean? Would she become like *him?*; Something that appeared human only as a matter of convenience, shrugging off skin and stability like a carnival costume?

It's not so bad a life. There are so many places beyond this; so many things to see and know.

Those worlds beyond the windows . . . she could actually *walk* there?

Walk, fly; swim, slither; whatever you desire.

Not yet. She'd see *him* first, ask what his experience of the state was. The voice dissipated with a sigh, its tendrils palpably retreating from her like those of some parasite surgically plucked out at the root.

*

At last. *At last.* Fit as she was, her legs and back ached by the time she reached the library doors. The way seemed so much *shorter* when she was a child. She'd begun to fear she'd taken a wrong turn somewhere, even more afraid that back tracking would only lead her deeper into confusion.

But no; her feet remembered the way well enough, though now she came within sight of it, her heart skipped several beats:

The door hung off its hinges, barely a breath away from tearing loose entirely. It looked to have been smashed in, though by what she dreaded to think.

Inside was darkness, so dense she couldn't see so much as a suggestion of the room beyond.

You can't be here. Nana will be angry.

"Nana isn't here."

Smothering, hot weight pressed in around her as she pushed what remained of the door open and stepped inside, her legs almost buckling as she fought to stay upright, her thoughts fraying beneath the damp heat of a tropical rain forest. She tried to retreat, but her legs refused to move. Tears burst from her eyes as she raised her head, a hotter , slower flood breaking from one nostril.

Something whispered in the dark, phantom fingers darting out, prodding, caressing; growing vicious before their substance faltered.

"Dad," she choked, mouth and throat suddenly desert dry, "it's me."

The crushing weight abruptly dissipated, leaving her to collapse on her knees against bare floorboards. Wiping her nose with the back of one hand, she saw the darkness soften and recede, rolling back like a spent tidal wave.

Save for shadows, the library was empty, not a single leaf or volume flattering the floor or walls. Nothing, save for a vague shape huddled in a chair before the window, the red moonlight spilling through allowing her to see the rags it was swathed in. Delicate, long nailed fingers tapped out a familiar tune on the aged leather, music that rose up from the very bowels of memory like the refrains of an opera house ghost.

He'd sung this to her, once upon a time; music that made stories in her mind, and sent her to bed with promise of dreams so vivid she'd be uncertain on waking which was the imagined world and which the experienced.

She approached, the floorboards moaning beneath her feet. The Mister trembled in his chair, whole body suddenly arcing as if in the grip of some *petite mal*. Marie went to him without hesitation, taking up a hand that felt like a rubber glove filled with part-frozen cockroaches. He stilled at her touch, sighing. A faint, sickly smile appeared beneath his hood, the face he wore gaunt and unshaven, lips cracked, ringed with sores.

Marie . . .

Nothing; a whisper of charnel house wind.

She didn't know what to say, what to do. Of all the possibilities, this had never occurred to her.

Not . . . not like . . . this . . .

The wretched thing retrieved its hand, tearing so fervently at the rags it wore that it drew blood.

"Dad, Dad, *stop* . . ."

He didn't. She moved to stop him, taking his wrist. A wave of pure denial hurled her back, green and purple super novas exploding across her field of vision as she hit the floor. Struggling up, gasping for breath, she saw what she'd taken to be new wounds were pre-existing ones that he'd reopened; his bared and wasted torso looking as if it'd been made a scratching post for rabid tigers. He was all but naked now, the rags going to dust and smoke as they fell away from him. The same luminous stuff seeped from his hurts, igniting as it made contact with the air, becoming dull bonfire embers.

Help . . . me.

What? What did he want her to do? She wasn't part of this anymore . . . she was only here for advice . . .

But she knew. Horrific as the prospect was, she knew. Getting up, she approached, smelling the scent of spice and bonfires that surrounded him. Desert breeze blew against her face, carrying invisible flower petals from distant oases. It was the wind of his home, the place where he was once worshipped and sacrificed to by desert nomads before they fleshed him, carving him in their own image. She knew this as if it were a matter of her own memories, felt the weight of aeons dragging behind her like ever accruing chains.

Skin and flesh came away in pulsing gobbets beneath her hands, the stuff going to sludge and smoke in a matter of breaths. He'd taught her enough to know that this wasn't the usual stuff of illusion; there was something more at work here, this form not so much woven around as *imposed* upon him; a human straight jacket made from the meat of dead things.

She closed her eyes, not wanting to see as his hands guided hers, fragments of his torso and face sloughing away at her touch, leaving only the bone on which they rested.

Eventually, that same unseen force took hold of her again, lightly urging her back rather than resorting to violence. Now she did look, and saw the bone that remained slowly withering, currents of luminous dust feeding a fire at the heart of which an uncertain man-shape sat, wavering like a distant mirage.

As the last of the bone was consumed—a skull collapsing in on itself, a rib cage eaten away by worms of liquid flame—sparks and streamers erupted from it, igniting the library's stagnant air where they began to elaborate, forming ever more complex circuits and tapestries 'til it seemed she stood at the heart of a swarm, waiting for the first flare to find her, making her more fuel for the formulae.

This was the library she remembered; a state of light and motion, a hive of burning butterflies sipping from the hearts of fallen stars. No wonder she hadn't been able to recall the experience with any clarity; this wasn't just some static storehouse of knowledge, a place where books were left to moulder on their shelves: this was *a living mind,* thought and feeling manifested in the only mediums they could be: ephemeral and ever changing.

Her father's mind.

The form in the chair raised its head, stretching neck, arms and legs as if freshly woken and purging the stiffness of sleep from its body. Multiple eyes flared like constellations in its head, turning on her with such intensity she blanched.

Daughter . . . you're back?

Marie sighed, shaking her head.

"No, I just . . . just came . . ."

To say goodbye?

Though she hadn't known it 'til now, yes, yes that was it. Something had been calling her back, something in her blood that made her restless and dissatisfied. Now she was before that very element; the Father whose inhumanity she'd no longer deny herself.

"Who did this to you?"

The stars flared, their light becoming furious amber. Images swam behind Marie's eyes like a cinema reel viewed through a mass of flocking birds. Nana Bella, reading by the fire, Nana Bella stealing through the house like a thief, glancing around as though she expected a reprimanding hand to fall on her shoulder; the woman weeping in her bed, curled up in foetal distress. Marie felt somehow soiled seeing this, as if she were spying on someone in their most intimate moments.

The image flew apart, became a chaotic kaleidoscope before cohering again. Now she began to understand. Bella stood at the open window of some forgotten back-room. Marie knew it well enough; a place where rivulets of silver water ran across the walls and ceiling, forming pools in which alien fish swam. The window looked out upon the blasted city of angels, a district that looked to have once consisted of great churches and temples. Hovering just outside was a creature that turned Marie's senses, something her eyes refused to settle on, as if to do so and fully comprehend its existence would reduce sanity to ash. She was therefore left with only a confusion of images and impressions; clusters of wet, sack-like organs pulsating, foetal shapes visible through the semi-translucent skin; eyes and mouths in profusion, the former revolving madly in erratic bunches, the latter gasping, chattering; waggling an array of tongues in obscene hunger. The rest was the darkness of an ant hive; seething and chaotic. It hung outside the window via spidery limbs that erupted from its back, whispering in Bella's ear as its mouths and fingers moved over her. Marie got the impression that what she saw wasn't what Bella did; she seemed *enraptured,* moaning, whispering heated promises between breaths.

Marie knew without seeing any more. The woman had been here all her life, not born within these walls, but so familiar with them at this point that she could scarcely imagine anything else. She was afraid, Marie had already seen that; afraid of them coming down around her ears, or of the magic that kept the world outside *outside* faltering. So, she'd gone looking for a means of sealing it here, and found it; a lover who brought her pleasure, promised her everything she wanted. She'd taken it, perhaps not gladly, when she realised what she had to do, but better that than the alternative.

The thing had taught her means by which she could weave her own *art,* pathetic excuses for miracles that she no doubt regarded as wondrous.

Then the *binding;* the sealing of her Mister and his magic in dead flesh, from which he could not escape, thus forced to sustain the house forever.

Only her lover was a *liar.* It didn't want the walls preserved; it wanted them to come tumbling down, for the way into this world to be *ripped wide.*

She saw them; Bella's lover at their head, a tide of abominations, seething over one another like ants on the swarm, no one alike to the other, none fixed; kaleidoscopes of flesh, fire and shadow. The vision was gone, torn from her before it could erode sanity further.

Her father, whose nature she'd never entirely comprehended nor ever would, rose from his chair, gliding towards her, leaving fiery trails across the air and floorboards. Wings that were once splendid unfurled tattered and shedding from his back, their rainbow light hazy and distant, as if shining through mist.

I'm sorry.

What for? For the life he'd given her? For showing her things that the people wandering past on the street only dared contemplate in their most sacred nightmares? Apology was pointless now.

She wasn't spared his fire just because they shared the same flesh. Drawing closer, she felt its heat, tongues of it licking out to scorch her cheeks, her hands; embers igniting in her hair. She let it have its way: if she were destined to go to ash along with the house in which she was born, so be it.

But the fire apparently had ambitions beyond mere *burning*. As his arms closed around her, her hands finding the tatters of his wings, she felt herself *open* to receive it, her flesh parting as if beneath a scalpel's caress, the fiery formulae and butterflies surrounding her finding ingress through her wounds, igniting blood and tissue.

It hurt, oh sweet *Christ* it hurt. She vaguely recalled the trauma of giving birth; those long hours melted into a mute and monstrous sludge in her memory. This was akin to it. More, this was a pain that went *further* back, to a memory that all her kind held, albeit buried so deeply, only the faintest echoes of its sorrow could be heard. This was *being born*; self giving birth to self in its death throes, thoughts, visions, senses cascading through her, sweeping her up like an ember in a hurricane.

My gift to you.

She felt him withering in her arms, his substance going to little more than shimmering dust that poured through her fingers, swept up on a breeze she couldn't feel and carried where she couldn't follow.

The pain grew to crescendo, blotting out all things, leaving only red streaked white, blood against fire, and a scream that was the birthing cry of all reality, reluctant to relinquish the darkness of un-being.

Then something erupted from her, not from her *flesh*; she wasn't quite ready to endure that manifestation, but from the more fundamental anatomy that her Father had aroused; the same that walked in love and dreams. She saw it as if divorced from herself: wings, though unlike her father's these were of mist and moonlight, shimmering silver offset with shadow. Tatters of blood and flame clung to them as they unfurled, the sense of them; the feeling of air against her pinions, of blood and feeling flowing into new extremities, like nothing she'd ever experienced.

They folded around her without her intent, veiling her invisibly as protection against the mounting flames.

She was alone, dust, ashes and smoke filling the air. The room was ablaze, the fire having given up all pretension and gone about its more animal business.

The gate must be closed. Time the children played outside again.

She felt him depart, a faint trace of him tickling her nostrils, caressing her cheek, then the window blew outward, carrying all that he was into the ancient city where his people, *hers* too, had made miracles from their own inspirations so long ago.

Out. She had to get out before the fire took that option from her. There was still a path, though the floorboards had already begun to kindle. Keeping her head down, she staggered towards the door, spluttering for breath as smoke invaded her lungs.

The door slammed shut behind her of its own accord, its wood already beginning to crack and blacken.

*

It wasn't just the fire, though many of the rooms she passed were already infernos; a message of decay passed throughout the entire house, carpets melting into sludge beneath her feet, walls cracking, shedding dust and plaster. In places, entire rooms had collapsed, choking the corridors with debris. Wherever she ran, she heard the shrieks and yammers of creatures caught and dying, the spectacular menageries that had sustained for longer than she'd been alive reduced to ruin in less than a breath.

Bella was waiting for her on the landing, tears streaming down her face, several of the children clinging to her skirts.

"What's happening? *What have you done?*"

Marie resisted the urge to hurl herself at the woman. All of this was a product of *her* fear, her stupidity.

"We have to go. *Now.*"

The woman gaped, comprehension flickering in her eyes. She hugged the children tight, openly weeping.

"We *can't*. There's nowhere else for us."

The children were crying now too, begging to be told that it'd be all right.

"There's *everywhere* for you. If you stay here, you'll die, *they'll* die. Is that what you want?"

She looked down at the children, running her fingers through their hair.

"I *know* what it's like out there. Horrible, stupid, *cruel* people. No place for *children*!"

Her tears froze, despair hardening to fury in her eyes.

"Why did you come back? *Everything* was fine, then *you* . . ." She faltered, snarling in pure hatred. All around, the house groaned, showers of plaster raining down on them as fissures coruscated across the ceiling. Silvery spiders swarmed down from the darkness, descending on invisible threads that shimmered like spun crystal.

She came at Marie without warning, leaping like a cat, claws extended. A hiss that was less than human escaped her throat. Marie instinctively lashed out, not with her hands, but with her other self, invisible tendrils raking the woman's face, opening her arms and breast. She howled, clawing in pain and fury. Green black water poured from her wounds, a particularly deep gash across her cheek revealing an interior of dark, horny growths.

"*No!*" she squealed. "No, no, no, *no!*"

Her blows cracked Marie's face aside, blood blossoming from her nose and lips. The children howled, crying for them to stop, but Nana Bella was deaf to them. Marie hadn't realised just how deep the corruption went. How long had the thing outside the window been working its art on her, twisting her with every diseased kiss and caress?

Consciousness wavered, the world around her seeming to shift and distort as oblivion threatened to take her. If that happened, they were all dead.

The children came to her defence, screaming at their Nana to stop, pulling at her with their child's hands. She lashed out, sending a girl reeling against the far wall. She impacted with a sickening crack, collapsing in a limp, rag-doll heap.

The Bella-thing grew silent, disentangling itself from Marie and limping over to the unmoving child. Her hands plucked at the thing's hair, more and more of her humanity peeling away with every breath. A keening wail, low at first but soon building to static-whine intensity, erupted from her throat. Shuddering, she gathered up the fallen girl and grabbed the nearby boy by his wrist. The boy fought, scratching, kicking and wailing, but her grip was unbreakable. Marie tried to stand, beg her to stop, but could only watch as the thing retreated down the collapsing corridor, disappearing into the ruin it had inspired.

*

Tears, dust and smoke blurred her vision as she stumbled down the stairs. Through the roar of flames, the frantic chatter of animals and the general lamentations of the house, she could hear the children crying, calling for their Nana.

She followed the calls through to the living room where she found them huddled together against the far wall, a goodly portion of the ceiling having collapsed. She tried to ignore the small, bloodied arm that protruded from beneath the rubble. Only the living mattered now.

John's eyes, so blue they seemed to glow through the smoke, flashed as he caught sight of her.

"It's all right, it's all right!" She spluttered, the children swarming around her, threatening to drag her down in their desperation. She was hurt; burned, bleeding, smothered. If she went down, she'd stay down, and that would be the end.

"Come on, come with me . . ." Some of them refused, standing trembling in puddles of their own piss.

"Where's Nana? Where's Nana?"

She took the nearest child by the hand, guiding, *dragging* it to the front door. It didn't take much for the rest to follow. Cold night air rushed into her lungs as she wrenched it open, making her feel drunk and giddy. From inside the house, a familiar wail. There was nothing she could do for her, for any of them now.

She shepherded them out onto the front lawn, then further, out the front gate and into the street. Turning, she saw a portion of the roof collapse, the upper storey windows blow out. People had begun to emerge from their houses, several rushing over with mobile phones already clamped to their ears. Exclamations and offers for aid washed over her, the words less meaningful than the crackle of flames that smothered them.

They grew silent as the ground shook, an immense crack running from the edge of the pavement up the front lawn and the façade of the house. Several ran back to their homes, afraid that they'd emerged in the midst of some natural disaster or terrorist attack.

Marie's legs finally went from beneath her, a man and woman in their early twenties coming forward to lend her support.

"Okay, okay love; we've got you."

"There's an ambulance on its way."

She was about to let unconsciousness finally claim her when something erupted from one of the house's windows; a flaming, scorched black knot, unfurling as it descended. People screamed, retreating at the sight of it. Loping out into the street, it fixed them all with clusters of lambent blue eyes, its jaw splitting into a fractured, red raw mess as it caught sight of Marie. In one ape-like limb, it cradled a shapeless, flame-withered bundle, in the other it dragged a bloody and smouldering rag doll.

It remained for only a second, seeming to assess its audience, then was gone, scurrying into the night with its prizes.

Marie watched until it melted into the shadows, then she melted too, happy to be nothing at last.

*

Convalescence was disrupted by questions she couldn't answer: what was she doing in the house? Who owned it? Who did the children belong to?

Any lie she could concoct would've been seen through in an instant, the truth rejected as a lunatic's ramblings. She proclaimed not to remember;

that she'd gone to the house by mistake, been invited in for tea, then all Hell had broken loose.

There were animal carcasses found in the rubble; those of several children. No names; they'd be buried in unmarked graves.

As well as the police and reporters, Richard and even Elsie came to her bedside. They wanted to know, but didn't ask. Elsie looked at her as if she was a lost cause, clearly believing she was on the verge of being committed. Richard had some news for her: a new love, someone he'd met whilst on holiday in Cornwall. Marie was pleased.

*

She left the hospital before fully healing, knowing that once the last wound closed, the questions would become more poignant, blossoming into accusation. An empty bed seemed like a fitting end to the public myth. In time, it'd no doubt elaborate into something far grander, especially with the blurred photographs of a flaming shape that someone had taken with their mobile phone camera currently littering the tabloid front pages.

The house wasn't the only place. She'd have to become rumour for a while; living beyond sight and sense. That was fine; her Father had shown her how. She needed time to heal, but more than that, time to *relearn* herself. The transformations he'd initiated weren't over. She could still *feel* them; a creeping process like flowers unfurling throughout her interior, like parasitic worms newly hatching into butterflies in her brains and bowels.

And there were the children. She visited them in their dreams. Some were beyond her help; lost in a mire of anxiety so dense she couldn't traverse it. Others consciously rejected her, wanting nothing to do with the woman who'd destroyed their home and taken them from the arms of their Nana.

She wasn't alone there. Though she saw nothing, she felt the other watching her from seclusion, its hate beating against her like desert heat at high noon. There'd be a confrontation eventually; neither of them could avoid it, but for now, she sensed they were both content to merely watch, and wait for old hurts to heal.

STRANGER PLAYGROUNDS

Sunlight; scalpel lances opening flesh, searing thought. The stories—glistening parasites, casting their schizophrenic effervescence throughout the tunnel—receded, tearing themselves from him with such violence the water frothing to foam around his ankles became bloody.

He staggered, the sunlight opening his back to the vertebrae, puncturing his flank so deeply, it chased away shadows that had sustained since his flesh first coalesced.

The stories struggled to keep hold, raking his senses with parasite experience, imposing themselves across his senses like over ambitious dreams or movies, their verisimilitude enough to give reality pause.

Come back, he begged, clawing at them even as they receded to the singing corpses entombed within the walls, *come back!*

Lives he envied, states he yearned for; anything but the boiling sludge in his skull. Even the sunlight with its hooks and scalpels was preferable.

By the flickering light they bled, spurting and spooling as their lengths recoiled, he saw the tunnel; red waters frothing around his ankles, stone walls pink tinged, threaded with veins of blue and black; a poisonous ore slowly spreading towards the heart of the world. His own body; twitching, wasted legs, luminous vapour and shoals of shimmering echoes erupting from where his feet splashed the water. What was this? Some lingering symptom of the stories and their poison? Why did he sweat beads of sunlight? Why did his wounds weep as much milk and smoking tar as they did blood?

The sunlight surgeon gave him no time for rumination. Even as he ran, stumbling through the storm, it went to work stretching the wounds it had carved, ragged-edged mouth parts -or maybe genitals- fastening to them, insinuating themselves, prying him apart as they squirmed and twisted, seeking better purchase or clearer entry. He didn't even attempt to dislodge it, the sensations of coming apart; of *violation*, enough at least to anchor him against the illusions threatening to sweep him away as they had countless times before.

A vile waking . . .

No!

The surgeon sensed his desperation, working his flesh with more urgency, coaxing songs from his nerve endings that he croaked and babbled as he ran; fragments of poetry and scraps of psalm as he might utter against a lover's lips, or the curve of a pregnancy-swollen belly.

The other singers, intent on him sharing their dreams, or maybe the lives they'd once lived, raised their voices in turn, the wounded lengths they'd retracted emerging once more, blossoming with fresh beaks and tongues. He didn't fight; hadn't the strength or inclination, allowing them to slither around and through him; puncturing mouth, eyes and anus . . . New states stole him with every step, his condition fluctuating like a movie reel in which the cells of incongruous works—bargain basement slashers married to animated fairy tales, knives and blood accompanying kisses that broke spellbound slumbers—had been spliced together in schizophrenic kaleidoscope.

It attempted to fend off the parasites, flailing at them with its scalpels, paring deeper, deeper, attempting to tear them out before they could take root. But no violence on its part; no song or surgery, could keep them at bay. He was their willing host; a mother swollen to bursting with cancerous pregnancy. And so much more: everything the singers and storytellers whose tomb he wandered had been or ever dreamed of being; the conditions they wove, wrote and painted for themselves, having abandoned the waking lives whose pain or disappointment inspired their self-internment:

A sexless God; painted and pierced androgyne, walking ankle-deep through fields of decay; those self slaughtered for want of a taste of its breath, a brush of its fingers . . .

A lost girl, the streets she ran full of flickering tongues, empty, evil eyes; doorways gaping like monster's mouths, inviting her to be devoured.

Two souls, once divorced, finding one another again, becoming one.

A gestating Goddess, slowly swelling to rebirth in the black waters of her own womb.

Everything and nothing; states against which the one he struggled to return seemed little more than a moment's idle fantasy; a nightmare in the seconds before unwanted waking . . .

No, not again . . .

The sunlight sliced so deep, he was momentarily certain it had murdered him; piercing his heart or severing his spinal column so suddenly, he'd transitioned to the afterlife in the space of a thought:

Burning white; an empty page, naked canvas. No more pain, or perhaps a state of such extremity, the concept no longer held any meaning. Maybe he'd finally found it; a place where the only inspirations were *his own,* the sick, collapsing worlds he'd spent entire lifetimes wandering—the diseased dreams of depressive and schizophrenic gods—finally giving way to a fundamental condition; one where thought was paint, metaphor as potent as seed or sperm.

Oh God, please, please let me be there.

A prayer no sooner conceived as denied. Corruption; the patterns that infested the state not of paint or ink, but the effluence of ruptured bowels; septic shit and cancer stuff, spreading like fire across parchment, withering, withering...

He sympathised with the fallen, knowing what had tipped them or inspired them to leap from their pedestals amongst the stars, envied the still-born that choked to death before birth could poison its dreams of being.

Coalescence, flesh and state; breath and pain. The scalpels weren't sufficient, the sunlight impotent against the darkness not only in, but *of* his system.

What did the ones in the walls want? For him to join them, become just another dreaming Mummy, waiting for another inspired soul to blunder into the Hell they'd made for themselves? *No* . . . their songs rose in protest at the very notion, violent enough to sweep his legs from under him. Even as he fell, the thing clinging to his flayed raw back chittering denials, the stories bore him up, their umbilici carrying him puppet like through the waters towards . . . *where*? What was there but this, what had there ever been? Maybe nothing; the world below a nightmare, the one above a dream, leaving only this endless scrabbling, surrender to the stories his only reprieve.

No, he remembered: gardens, the scents of dirt, grass and flowers; beds, linen; skin and sweat. Maybe nothing but stories themselves; more potent than others, more enduring. Maybe that's all memory ever was; stories he told himself over and over until they became more; parasitically bound to consciousness.

Sunlight struck again and again, but there was little beyond the pain it had already inflicted. What could be left other than for its bearer to murder him outright?; An end it would never countenance; something Wier knew with utter certainty. It coveted him as much as the ones in the walls, intending to drag him back down into the darkness, where he could dream and wake and run and forget himself over and over, until the vermin found some new means of sustaining themselves. Then, perhaps, they'd fall on him, devouring him to the bone and beyond.

The water hissed beneath his feet, boiling to vapour as the stuff he bled and sweated polluted it. Veins of the same crawled across the walls, coruscating like cracks through which day intruded, blinding him. He tasted the stone and what lay within: whispering corpses, storytellers, like himself, dragged here and entombed, aching for nothing other than to be heard again. Now his own questing extremities found them; invisible, abstract lengths threading through cracks and fissures, finding the severed stories they'd put forth, twining about them in hope of courting less violent communions.

Whereas before they'd battened onto him parasitically, pumping their myths into him like venom, now they responded with a new equanimity, the coupling that resulted more intimate than any flesh could contrive; of which fucking was the merest echo, though the closest most would ever come in their waking lives.

Anthony Wier, Elias Kirchner, Zachary Eliott Simony; a small nation of names and faces parading behind his eyes, forgotten 'til now because he'd demanded it, unable to bear the weight of their stories any longer, and the many they'd inspired in their turn. Lives he'd sculpted, fashioned for himself; lives he'd fled, abandoned, leaving behind suicidal lovers and wounded nations; enemies with nowhere to plant their swords save in their own hides.

As for the withered things he now touched and trysted with, they were the same: inspired souls; men, women and children who made stories, breathing, shitting and sweating them, carving them from their own cast off lives. How many worlds had they dreamed into being between them? How many had the vermin below sucked dry, devouring before they had a chance to flower? The one he'd recalled on waking, it was one such state; a place he'd wandered, unknown to himself, its decay evident in every particular; environmental, political, mythological; a condition teetering on the brink of multiple apocalypses, the shadow-lives infesting it lamenting the fact they'd ever been conceived.

Even that hadn't been enough: He'd broken the chains, gone wandering in search of a place where he might find himself and wake again . . .

The surrounding stone groaned, rippling like flesh or water. The cracks he'd made gaped, entire portions sloughing away to reveal the fomenting states within. From the corners of tear blurred eyes, through senses bound to no proscribed anatomy, he glimpsed them: withered, rotting things; the corpses of children and lovers, of murderers and their prey, sealed away here in common suicide, rather than live another moment where their stories would be realised. All little more than sludge, dust and bone; all seething with fungal growth, carrion life. Some sweated smoke and storm clouds, wreathing themselves, others curled foetal in the depths of black waters, lit by the glow of drowned stars. He tasted them; echoes of state and experience, some lived, some imagined; some that were dreaded or yearned for; conditions dictated by inspiration alone, in which all restriction could be rewritten, undone. For some, that realisation would be as ambiguous as it had always been; states of confusion and conflict; the essentials of story-spinning. For others, the renaissance would lead to something more certain, making them monsters or divinities; things of myth and rumour.

Wier laughed through the pain, old confusion sloughing away, allowing new species to flower.

He heard them now; felt their fury and fear as the revolution he'd inspired seeped down into their nests. The one clinging to him no longer attempted to bring him to heel, realising that there was no quelling the fire, now that its embers had caught in so many minds. Instead, it hissed in his ear, whispering its own poisonous tales of the suffering and derangement; the raw despair he would find in the sunlight:

We may end, but you'll always return . . . too in love with being shit . . .

He couldn't deny it; had no inclination. Yes, he'd dreamed of being shit before; of being buried beneath the earth; becoming a cathedral for flies and maggots. He'd dreamed of being a butcher's play-thing; little more than meat to be flayed, ripped, pounded and drained. He'd dreamed worlds of living pain and disgrace, universes formed of sewn together bodies; degenerate, inbred Gods whose only purpose was to shat out broods of planet-scale monstrosities; drooling offspring whose deformed bodies swarmed with parasite nations.

And in the dreaming, he'd told the stories; walked the realities he'd imagined in moments of idle fantasy or obsessed over, seeking those who would go on to tell stories of their own, transgressing beyond whatever parameters he'd proscribed, just as he had those proscribed for him.

Light, so sudden he gasped, stumbling to hands and knees. The stone beneath gave way, softened to the consistency of marshmallow, mercurial strings erupting from where it melted and flowed around his fingers, coiling upon and around one another as they were carried away. Contradictory winds sighed through the opening, at once Arctic and Saraharan; tropical and snow-born. Wier tasted frost and ash in the back of his throat; the vegetable lushness of distant oases mingling with the dust and concrete of long abandoned urban sprawl.

And with the scents, echoes of innumerable stories, lives beyond count dreaming, living; loving, lamenting, some hardly conceived, drifting in the womb, others on their death beds, longing for oblivion, dreading continuation.

The storm almost consumed him, what slight self-knowledge he'd reclaimed eroding beneath its onslaught, carried back to where the parasites he'd fostered and fled could snatch its motes from the air.

Many of those within the walls went before him, their substance reduced to luminous ash by the fires he'd set, catching stray currents that swept them away to where they might be re-imagined, finding fresh inspiration in new skulls. Others would linger for a time yet, not ready to wake to themselves. He didn't begrudge them that. How could he, having suffered the same until here and now?

One voice rang out above the rest, its demands—. . . *so close, so close! Come, come to me . . .!*—like hooks and claws snagged in his flesh, driven deep into bone.

The parasite screamed as he was borne up puppet-like, those below swarming, the diseased colonies they'd carved finally collapsing, the din of their collective despair music so sweet, Wier erupted into tears, hooting maniac laughter that echoed into the distance, swallowed by the daylight and the myths it harboured.

*

The tunnel convulsed once more, coming apart at the seams. Light flooded through, engulfing him, the stories like shoals of parasitic fish, swimming around and through him as though his substance were little more than that of rainbows. The parasite clung to him still, gibbering in his ear; a slurry of threats and condemnations in the voices of old Fathers and teachers; men and women he'd worshipped, once upon a time; made idols and lovers from before abandoning to inevitable decay. What were they now? Nothing but dust in sunlight; not even rumour; whispers in school-yards and on street corners. He wouldn't go the same way; that had always been his imperative; what propelled him from life to life; waking to waking, making and walking stories in which he could be more.

Now he swam with those same creations; old stories and new, inspirations he recognised; countless others that originated from other skulls. He couldn't sustain it; even now, he felt himself slipping; plucked apart mote by mote, the coherence he'd managed to accrue washed away, swept into the maelstrom.

Would that be so terrible? Imagine what you might become!: The roots of mountains, the seeds of continents and nations . . .

Yes! All of that, and more, because all potential was here, in the delirium that underpinned reality. More than mountains; entire worlds, universes; states of being . . .

Too much. *Too much.* He wasn't ready for that final dissolution. He'd trod its boundaries before, courted it in dreams consumed by their own ambition; always, always turning away . . .

This wasn't the time; too many stories he wished to walk yet, too many playgrounds to wander.

He fell, sprawling on dust-carpeted floorboards, choking as the stuff billowed around him, filling his throat. Wet warmth spattered his legs, his bladder giving way. What little breath he'd managed to take flew from him in a storm of sudden pain, the former scalpels replaced by jagged talons and dribbling fangs that bit into him with animal abandon, all former precision and purpose gone.

The pain-bringer no longer spoke, instead hissing and croaking; the protests of something prematurely born, choking on the soup of its unformed lungs.

Wier bucked and rolled, scraping at the thing, but the more he protested, the more fevered its attacks became. His back felt flayed open, crudely stripped and bored down to the bone, his blood mingling with the filth on the floorboards to form a swamp of black sludge.

Scrabbling blindly, seeking something, *anything* they might use to pry the parasite free, his fingers closed around something cold; the ankle of a naked figure, skin pale as sun bleached alabaster, the leg he grasped dangling over the edge of a stinking, cob-web strewn bed.

He knew its name, even before his eyes rose to its face, having been the last he heard or uttered before the nightmare took him:

"*Verity.*" A strangled croak, crawling from a throat lined with shards of broken mirror. The figure didn't stir, skin cold and smooth as cut marble to the touch. Lank hair hung in a funeral veil around its face, a cloak of cobwebs testament to how long it had sat, awaiting his re-emergence. "*Verity . . .*"

Red light spilled through the single, grime smeared window, carrying strains of the slow apocalypse occurring without:

Police sirens.

Children laughing, whimpering.

Choirs raised in celebration or lament.

This world had been on the verge of collapse when he left, the conditions that informed it revealed as sorry, withered things; hollow foundations that left it teetering on the brink of multiple catastrophes. Had he made it that way, or was it just happy coincidence?

He laughed, gasping, breathless, crawling his way up into Verity's lap. By the fever glow, he saw the descendants of those who originally wove the webs he wore scurrying away, abandoning nurseries and larders in favour of less treacherous domains.

Cracks threaded out where his fingers passed, fragments falling away, revealing sweating, vital skin beneath. He whispered, even as the parasite sought to silence him; whispered old confessions into his lover's lap; stories of all they'd done and would do again, if only they could save one another.

The stories faltered at their sweetest, breath and thought flying apart as he was pierced by a curved barb, pulsing cold poison. He fell back, the pain elaborating through his flesh—a sensation like corrosive sludge, swimming with fiery maggots, flooding his veins—eclipsing the sensations he'd whispered of, and in the whispering, experienced.

The room shuddered, a shower of plaster falling from the nicotine stained ceiling. His murderer's hisses and drooling contempt filled his ears as it withdrew from him, clambering around to squat atop his chest.

Dragged from its native nightmares into unwanted sunlight, it had congealed into a living cancer; bloated, wound-ridden, seeping. Organs lining its flanks like infected holes left by burst tumours pulsed and dribbled, a mane of worm-like growths and angular, serrated barbs sprouting from its back and underside. An abdomen swollen with internal disease—or perhaps a new generation of parasitic filth—rippled against his belly, leaking pre-birth sewage as it prepared to vent itself. And its *face* . . . a bisected, broken mass; that of a premature babe, crushed during some failed attempt at abortion and crudely stitched back together. Solid black eyes like shards of shattered coal sat lodged in sunken sockets, the mouth parts below resembling diseased labia, torn from between the legs of dead women, lined with milk teeth pried from the jaws of their young. Tongues trailed from within the folds like jellyfish tendrils; little more than feathery strips and scraps of torn meat, lapping the sweat and blood from his belly.

No wonder they hated him . . . this was what he and the other dreamers shat and sweated every waking moment; idle scraps of fantasy, barely enough focus or inspiration to be consciously realised before dissolving into forgetfulness. Was that why he'd consigned himself to the hell whose throat—*womb, anus*—still yawned at his back? Some inchoate sense of guilt over the lives -*states, realities*- he'd half-consciously sparked since imagination first flowered in his skull?

Strains of music from outside: children laughing nursery-rhyme nonsense, play turning strange as the day died . . .

The figure atop the bed shuddered, the decay of its alabaster shell escalating, leaving it pink and naked, surrounded by a cloud of white mist.

Too late, too late. The parasite was already swelling, shuddering with the imminence of birth. From its grotesque abdomen extruded a mucus-slick barb, as thick as Wier's ring finger and twice as long. Shifting, it raised itself as high as it could on its spidery limbs, what passed for eyes in its atrocity of a face locked with Wier's own, weeping a gruel of contempt and twisted affection.

their own states of inspiration, or swilling away as the stories they occupied expired.

Too much for any consciousness to bear. It wasn't even ennui; novelty was always barely a breath or thought away, even for one who'd lived lives enough to fill entire histories. Rather, the fact of novelty itself had become unbearable; being so ephemeral, indefinite; the constant shifts in state and nature slowly fraying him apart, to the point that he felt on the verge of unravelling. He wouldn't have been the first; he'd seen it happen before, to souls far younger; the drive to inhabit and experience all that they could too profound, tearing them apart, making them separate and scattered . . .

"Until they find themselves again."

The knife clattered away from Verity's hands, its subject burbling grotesque baby-nonsense, shuddering as it attempted to spill what it contained half gestated, eggs bursting, conditions expiring the instant they tasted air.

Wier tottered forward, clutching his wounded belly, the young within still singing, even as they died or were devoured, attempting to seduce him with familiar miseries; lives lived in contempt of themselves; echoes of the original, derelict playground he'd written himself free from. To think, he'd allowed himself to slip back, returning to a semblance of that condition, *lusted* after it . . .

Light fell on him from the shattered window, red and cold, carrying the scents of ash and distant burning. Somewhere, a radio played music distorted beyond recognition, screams and laughter rising in welcome of the coming night. He knew this world so well, its inhabitants riding the wave of impending apocalypse promised by every news broadcast, every radio sound-bite and street-side sermon, Anthony Wier once numbered amongst them. Which had finally fallen? Environmental or economic disaster, the war whose only outcome could be self extinction? *Rapture?* More than likely a combination of all, or perhaps circumstance not even the most imaginative of doom-sayers had foreseen. He'd walk there and learn before the final curtain closed, but not alone.

Verity didn't turn to face him, shoulders hitching as though with tears or laughter. Those he'd left below; the dreamers in the walls . . . some had whispered tales of severance, hadn't they? Portions of the same soul, inhabiting divided flesh, finding and flowing into one another . . . could they do the same, *here?*

He reached out, skin itching, seeming to ripple against the bone and muscle beneath, as though a squall broiled at the heart of him, throwing his internal tides into chaos . . .

"Not yet."

He stopped, the imperative more than mere words, his fingertips brushing a curtain that hung between them, invisible, intangible, but enough to reduce him to soup and streamers should he try to pass through. *Why*? What more could he . . .?

"Close it."

Revelation brought a moan of protest. Why? The way behind was a sewer, clogged with plague corpses, stinking to high Heaven. Why would he even want . . .?

Laughter, Verity raising his eyes to the ceiling. "I don't know; don't ask me why you love the shit so much; *you're* the one who crawls back to it, *again* and *again*. All I know is: it stops *now*. Either close the way, or go back and *rot*."

He bristled beneath the ultimatum; a parent receiving chastisement from a wiser child. Who was he to demand anything? A fragment of a dream, forgotten on waking . . .

"*No*." Now he turned, glaring at Wier over his shoulder, eyes glacial wells in which primordial serpents twined and mated, feeding on the young they spawned. "Like I said: I didn't have to wait. I could have left this world to burn, the way to collapse. Believe me, it's been tempting, listening to you scrabble around down there, eating shit and muttering stories to yourself. There were times I almost did. Do you know what prevented me?"

Wier breathed deep, resisting the urge to turn and stalk back down into the darkness; to close his eyes and collapse the building around them with a thought, burying them both in undying contempt.

Of course he knew; it was the same reason he'd originally run, even knowing the pain it would bring: Without one another, they would always be incomplete, always *wounded*, learning again and again to love the rasp of reality against their hurts, the stories they sung and sweated temporary wrappings, hardly enough to stop the bleeding, no matter how expertly woven, but *beautiful*, even at their most ripe; suffering, rot and extinctions made wondrous thanks to the continual re-weaving of the eyes and minds that perceived them. He'd run from himself to fall in love with dreams again, to be alien in his own inspirations, and never wake.

"The others . . ." Their stories still echoed, his senses insisting that he was a woman who dreamed herself perfection, sculpting it from the frustration of inadequate mates, another who wounded the world through her despair; a man who was torn apart and pieced back together every day, finding revelation in each rebirth.

"What about them? They'll find their own ways, eventually. Or not. This isn't their story; it's *ours*. What happens next is up to you."

Up to him. Up to him whether to be born or die; whether to experience or forget. Always and forever, *up to him*.

Verity laughed, turning fully, allowing view of the newborn condition he wore. "What else do you want? To be a *slave* like the rest? Look at all we've learned to do!" He stalked back, wrenching the parasite's steaming remains from the floorboards, holding them up before the curtain for Wier's inspection. "*Flesh from inspiration*. Even our shit has poetry. You reminded me of that. Now you want me to forget again, *be* shit again?" He flung the pulsing filth to the floor, raking stained fingers through his hair.

"Like I said: it's up to you. Come find me, if you wish. I won't wait any more."

The *wrench* as Verity turned away, stalking towards the bedroom door, made Wier whimper; anxiety so keen as to be an almost physical pain, frost-bitten claws raking his entrails.

Instinct almost murdered him, dragging him through Verity's curtain. Had it not already begun to unravel, he would've emerged on the other side like the leavings on an abattoir floor. Instead, he suffered only superficial wounds; stray threads opening his cheeks and forehead; his thighs, arms and chest with the alacrity of ghostly surgeon's scalpels.

Bleeding, he stumbled, going to his knees in the mire left in the parasite's wake. Some portions of its pulped anatomy still pulsed and squirmed with hideous life, not all of what it attempted to pollute him with extinguished. As he crawled through the swamp, his scrabbling fingers found intact orbs, their touch enough to ignite his senses, stir those still waiting to hatch within:

He lay shivering beneath a piss-stinking blanket, every motion precipitating a cascade of aches and pains throughout his body. He couldn't recall waking this morning, who'd come to see him, turning on the small electric radiator that was all that kept the cold at bay. But he recalled November 6th, 1954; the day he'd married Denise, betraying her with her cousin Agatha before the vows had cooled on his lips. He recalled the fight, almost fifteen years ago to this day, when he'd confessed to his son never wanting to be a Father, every moment since spent in regret that he'd denied himself the luxury of loneliness . . .

He stood terrified in a room full of strangers, their eyes on him, making him feel small and itchy. One of them, sat higher than the rest, bawled and shouted at him, making him want to cry. He tried to answer, but the words—stupid, stupid words!—wouldn't come. He didn't even understand what they wanted. He knew he'd been bad; never should have played with Anika like that, but he was sorry; he could put it right, if they'd only let him...

Deeper, deeper, the shit dragging him down:

Stabbed in the belly by marble knives, the cold ache worse than any he'd ever known. He'd tried to eat what he'd found in the garbage behind the café; spent the next two hours retching up what wasn't there. He couldn't remember the last time . . . things had grown too hazy, too distant. He fluttered in and around himself; a moth waiting to snap the cord, take flight to the stars, leaving behind meat and hunger forever . . .

Warmth receding, the world in flux, cold and noise seeping through from without. He'd dreamed of this in his most acute nightmares; having turned away, ejected into that place where none walked wanted; where every imagining was of a return to the place before light and breath . . .

"No." Slurred denials through clenched teeth, the spittle they rode smouldering as it mingled with the filth below. Faint screams rose as he raked the spawn open, allowing the toxic conditions they contained to spill and die. This was all they were good for, like the state he'd been born to and left to rot.

Rising to his knees, Wier closed his eyes, running besmirched fingers across his belly. *There*, and *there*; solid, cancerous lumps, pulsing, sweating poison. If they swelled to full ripeness, then the nightmare he'd escaped would be nothing; the young they'd birth would drag him back to an asylum so deep, so far beyond the stories of others, he'd never remember himself again; not even if Verity waited a thousand eternities or more.

His hands rose of his own volition, hanging hooked and murderous before his eyes. He knew this; the Art so old, it had long since become a matter of instinct. The words he spoke were in a language he couldn't recall; from a state and skin he'd equally forgotten. Had he and Verity been *separate* then? Perhaps. Maybe they'd come together briefly; clashing as enemies, grappling as lovers, before parting again, forgetting themselves and one another. How the man had managed to find him this time was a mystery; he'd buried himself so *deep*. All Wier knew was that he had to follow; couldn't bear for them to remain severed any longer.

A story, of himself here and now, his flesh shifting, becoming the instruments by which it might purge itself of diseased dreams. Even as he spoke it, so his flesh conceded to its claims and rhythms, the words twining visibly in the air; translucent worms writhing from his lips, twining about his fingers, skin peeling away to allow for eruptions of scalpel sharp bone.

The pain put him in mind of adolescence; the bone-deep aches accompanying every growth spurt, some so intense, he'd be in tears until they finally faded, leaving him closer to the completion he feared and hated after in equal measure.

Laughter punctuating the tale he spoke—and experienced—he pressed his fingers to the swellings in his belly, slicing through with a surgeon's delicacy, still speaking, even as the pain eclipsed all else, no anaesthetic at hand to distract from it.

He didn't need to pluck the parasites out one by one; the verses trailing down his chin were more than sufficient, squirming through his wounds to find the unwanted worlds, administering swift euthanasia rather than leaving them to slow decay.

Each death played behind his eyes, visions flaring of entire countries and continents collapsing into ruin, their denizens simultaneously fleeing and welcoming tidal waves, asteroid strikes; earthquakes powerful enough to shatter planets, solar storms, pandemics; nuclear holocausts and all imaginable species of apocalypse.

But even here, in worlds conceived from disease, born to be dreamless, he heard faint echoes of inspired song; the soul-music of individuals like himself who refused to be what their authors demanded. So few, so few; little more than children's whispered nursery rhymes against the cacophony of multiple apocalypses, but he heard; *saw* as they attempted to rewrite themselves in the instant before elimination. Where they would fly and what states they would inhabit he couldn't guess, but maybe he'd meet them, one day, just as he'd met others spawned from stories he'd told; from the stories of stories.

That, more than anything, was worth the price of being.

The stories failed, lapsing into silence as he rose to his feet, some of the stronger still swirling about him, sustaining on echo and rumour for the time being. These he directed to the sewing of his wounds, letting them seal and cauterise before he bled to death.

Pain still persistent but bearable now, he breathed, tasting rain, remembering...

A small place, away from Michael and the cats, where he could come and wallow; obsess over strange dreams, the absurdities that haunted his every thought, waking or sleeping. Perhaps he should've been an artist or writer; found some way of venting the strangeness in his skull before it burst, taking sanity with it.

But life hadn't allowed for that; a job he neither loathed nor loved, a home, 999 TV channels; Iranian rugs in the kitchen and bathroom, a boyfriend he occasionally brawled with, but whose apologies always came with kisses . . . something to be grateful for.

Not enough. He smiled now, recalling his naivety: if only he could keep this secret self, come here to pace and sing nonsense to himself, maybe it would be enough to sustain...

He'd been an idiot for even entertaining it.

The argument had driven him out into the rain; a three mile walk to town, finding solace in the booze and sex stinking murk of The Crown:

"It's all coming down, Mikey; none of it's going to matter for much longer . . ."

Every newspaper and TV broadcast testified to it; a drowning economy, mass unemployment, wars sprouting like fungi in the Middle East, Israel poised to wipe Palestine off the map. But more than that: the systems no longer functioned; glutted and ill-maintained, neglected through lack of faith in their purpose and necessity...things were falling apart, as he always knew they would.

Michael snorted, shaking his head. "Don't call me that; only my mom calls me that. You sound like one of those bloody nut cases on the high street, shouting at people about the end of the world . . ."

"I'm not shouting. It's happening now, Michael. You'd have to be blind not to see it: Nothing is going to last."

Michael. So stolid, so certain. The notion that tradition could fail was absurd to him, despite the evidence of history. What had brought them together? How had he ever loved something so plastic?

"Anthony, I think you need to see someone,"

He laughed, fingers shifting, reforming as he ran them over sheets still stinking of all he and Verity had done beneath them before he retreated, sealing himself away.

"Don't you dare, don't you dare try that with me . . ."

"What, then? Listen to yourself! It's paranoia, Anthony. And it's not like you're behaviour's been exactly normal of late . . ."

There, on the edges of sight: the flesh-skirts of something luminous, as might be glimpsed in the shadowed depths of ocean trenches, and something else, crawling across the wall at Michael's back: innumerable mites swarming over the paint and paper flora, forming figures from some alien alphabet, elaborating into testaments he felt the sense of, lingering just beyond the bounds of comprehension . . .

"There! That's exactly what I'm talking about! You just . . . zone out, like you're dreaming with your eyes open. And you talk to yourself . . ."

They sang to him, telling him of all the worlds they'd infested and pollinated, barely a thought's span away. All he had to do was reach out, tear his way through . . .

He sat down on the bed, its dankness cold and foul against his buttocks. Contradictory winds; the one from the window warm, exotic; that from the opening in the wall cold and familiar.

Michael . . . not his fault; he simply did as he was made to do; anchoring Wier in the swamp's depths, perpetually smothering, never dying.

He still spoke—bleated, condemned—even as the figures—now fully formed fragments of verse—took flight from the walls, settling in his hair, on his skin; crawling over his eyes and into his mouth. He didn't see or feel, continuing until the words faltered, murdered in his throat by more poetic species.

Wier raked fingers down his face, recalling how the man had looked at him then; eyes wide and terrified, swimming with sudden comprehension; more than Wier himself had, still ignorant of all he was, all he could *do*.

"Michael?"

The man raised hands to his face and throat, pawing at them urgently enough to draw blood. Wier made to help him, but something held him fast, coiling around his legs, arms and throat.

"Michael!"

Twin whispers in his ears: the voices of a woman and an adolescent boy, speaking in perfect synchronisation:

"Hush. Let him be more than he'll ever dream . . ."

Wier rose from the bed, turning to the wound that had shat him back into being. Dark, ragged-edged, its fathomless interior swam and quivered, walls of stone given way to slick, black flesh, rippling with tidal motion.

Michael spluttered, rising from the sofa, arms and legs stretched wide by invisible strings, mouth gaping so wide, his jaw cracked, the surrounding flesh tearing. Strangled testimonies heralded a vile eruption; mouth and the wounds surrounding it blossoming with black tendrils; oily, leech-like tubes slithering from his throat, tooth-ringed maws fastening onto cheeks, nose and lips, one clamping to his left eye, leaving the right to roll and glare in rabid isolation.

Wier started as fluttering skirts swept around him, scented of the ocean, lips brushing his ears like moth's wings: "Look! See how beautiful he can be."

He tried to close his eyes, silently screaming as Michael's forehead pulsed and split, a red pencil line trailing down his nose, bisecting his jaw, his throat . . . invisible fingers pried at the wounds, or else they blossomed of their own accord; lips of skin, flesh and fat peeling away like the curtains of some anatomical theatre, displaying all that rioted within. For all he'd hated the man barely a few seconds ago, Wier clenched his teeth, hissing prayers to whatever God or demon was responsible to stop; leave them whole and unhappy again.

Michael groaned as he opened wider, deeper, Wier unable to look away as his sodden clothing fell in a rain of rags, tatters of skin and spools of organ going with them. Beneath, he was in flux from scalp to soles, motions like rippling worms, like the fingers of lovers, writers; artists, tattooing testaments on the inside of his skin. In those places where it tore, he spilled more than blood and entrails; the living language that had seeded itself within sprouting, black lengths—like those erupting from his mouth—uncurling through the air, tips splitting to reveal eyes and flowers; hooked fingers and puckered lips: an array of dreaming ephemera, all withering in a matter of seconds before others took their place.

Wier no longer struggled, his protests—having stained the air shit brown and stinking yellow—grown silent. What were they anyway? Infant-clinging to a status quo he'd come to hate and resent, as he did all moments of contentment; all who sought to sustain them.

The living bonds holding him fast retreated, the skirts swirling around him—ready to constrict and smother him in merciful euthanasia if necessary—evaporating. He stumbled, pried from and orbiting his own skull as he approached the man he'd called mate and husband for near a decade, finding little but a residue of regret for his current condition, even that slowly sifting away beneath the encroaching, black ocean that lapped at his feet and thoughts.

"Michael," grey filaments weaving from his lips to form a jellyfish-like bag in the air, pulsating mass lit from within by pale blue swamp-light. "Mikey," a sibling to the first, pink and green, trailing smaller copies of itself that it periodically lashed out at, consuming those it managed to snare.

Reaching out, he caressed one of the tubular lengths coiling from Michael's stomach, its ribbed surface growing rigid, veins protruding beneath his fingers. Michael gasped, seeming to laugh around the parasite garden stretching his jaws wide.

"You're satisfied with this, are you?" he asked. The parody's one good eye rolled in affirmation: Yes, yes; leave us, if you wish. We don't want anything else.

He never had.

Wier couldn't bear it; no seduction sweet enough, no salvation sufficiently transcendent to have him make a slave of himself. So he left, knowing that the instant he set foot outside the door, he'd never be allowed back. He ran the instant his feet touched concrete, ran 'til his legs bled and his heart pumped acid. He ran through the woods, though there were none so close to where he and Michael made their home; across a beach of silver sand, though they lived miles inland; through swamps and abbey ruins, through carnivals and playgrounds—stranger, stranger all—stories swarming him with every step, streaming from him like the tatters of some shed costume or chrysalis.

Ran until he arrived, forgotten to himself once more, at the Crown's doorstep.

Was it the rebellion he now recalled that had allowed the boy—his other; the fugitive fragment of his soul—to find him? If so, his first effort at reconciliation had failed, Wier retreating into darkness, intent on forgetting himself . . .

The cries and laughter of children at play; furtive whispers as they swapped stories and secrets not meant for adult ears. He recalled doing likewise as a boy, though he couldn't recall his original face or name; cheeks burning, words slurred with the forbidden nature of what he confessed or contrived.

Insect chatter; the ragged breaths of old, sad men sustaining lives of pain and regret, suddenly rose on the foetid winds from the wound, too weak to silence or drown out the children's play.

Through the broken window, Wier looked out upon a ruinous garden, surrounding buildings in states of potential collapse, façades fallen away or caved in, raked open as if by earthquakes, hurricanes or the claws of passing dragons. Some were burned out shells, so blackened by fire they resembled the rotting teeth of some long dead Earth God. Others stood intact enough for him to make out their interiors: rooms and corridors; attics, cupboards and secret spaces all exposed like those of doll's houses. Flayed and fire-eaten alike had been claimed by fantastic growths; eruptions not so much resembling plants as coral or feathers; one coruscated with a creeping network of red and black veins, another made an absurd peacock display, erupting with fronds whose variegated patterns made his head swim.

Hooks in his eyes, mortician's fingers in his thoughts, drawing them away, back to the cold and darkness. Bared teeth, slathering dissent. How could he have done that to himself? It was everything he'd spent his many lives in defiance of, just as Verity had said. *Maybe the best of you went with the boy; maybe you are just the terror and regret . . .* No. If that were the case, he never would've found himself again, couldn't see what he did now:

Things amongst the flowers, Verity's collapsing world, scented of fire and ash when he first woke, swarming with life, though little of it new.

To the broken walls of a nearby tower-block clung creatures that resembled immense, pale-skinned lizards; men, women and children, all in varying states of undress, all stretched and distorted, necks and limbs over-long; fun-house mirror reflections of carnival goers having escaped the confines of their glass cells, now walking in place of those who looked and laughed. Clustering together amidst the growths, they crawled over and clung to one another, some seemingly caught up in mating frenzy, their calls a strange confusion of human speech and bird-song, tantalising with what revelations they might provide. Another structure, façade all but raked away, paraded interiors packed to bursting with strange vegetation, Wier's sight seemingly plucked from the confines of his eyes, carried like a speck of dust on the contradictory winds. Rolling, jerked and buffeted, he intruded on a space that had been entirely overtaken by web-like threads and great clots of pale, fungal matter, their ambition having claimed every surface, linking carpets and ceilings; walls, chairs, sofas and all the apartment contained in a living circuit, portions of it pulsing, peeling as fresh blooms came, threading through the air or weaving themselves through areas already conquered.

Wier saw, weaving in and out of the mass; smelled and tasted; sweet, vegetable foetidness, Autumnal damp and deep-seated rot. In the small bedroom, he found the heart of the proliferation: two figures, locked in what might have been coitus or the realisation of a death pact atop the marital bed, bodies conjoined in a manner no union of disparate flesh, no matter how intimate or brutal, could equal: Splitting, fruiting with the strange threads, they'd melded to the point they could hardly be distinguished, faces sewn together by eruptions that had erased feature, bursting from one's eyeball or mouth to plunge into the other's, emerging elsewhere with a fresh freight of matter to weave flowers from or carry back to the source.

From there, the ambitious rot had spread throughout the home they'd made, incorporating every memory and experience they'd shared, slowly dissolving, breaking them down over slow years, perhaps even centuries, to the same consistent sludge. And from there? Who could say? A story currently beyond Wier's perception or clear imagining, and one he was reluctant to leave unexplored.

But leave it he did, carried at the behest of the winds that had plucked him from his skull, intent on scattering him throughout these strangest of playgrounds:

Down, down, through a rent in one wall, he found himself swirling in semi-darkness, what little light there was emanating from several shattered televisions, their screens flickering between static nonsense and ephemeral scraps of old broadcast. Figures moved in the murk, caught up in orgiastic dance; something between rave and ritual, one flailing bulk wrapped around in crude leathers woven in and out of its worm-like flesh, its partner near naked, save for the skirt of chains and bells around its waist.

The revellers sang and gibbered as they danced, puckered, fleshy holes in the walls gouting vapour that seemed to snare the light, refracting it into rainbows that played over the space, illuminating its bizarre decoration: A living chandelier, one of the reveller's own pulled apart and stitched back together, threaded through with wiring to light the bulbs protruding from its mouth and eye sockets; screwed into the wounds carved in each palm. Sculptures of spines and shoulder-blades strung with veils of nervous system, vein and artery; skulls, rib cages and skeletal limbs arranged into altars and wall-mounted compositions, sharing space with those that still boasted flesh and life, bleeding, gasping; caressing or lapping blood and sweat from passing dancers.

Despite the mutilation on display, the various expressions he could make out—sighs, wails, breathless laughter—were ecstatic rather than despairing, their originators apparently well content with their conditions, far beyond any they'd occupied before knife and needle was taken to them.

A moment here only; enough to ride the fevered breaths of the orgiasts before he took flight again, carried up and out over the world that Verity had fled into. Portions of it were recognisable from the life he'd led as Anthony Wier—there! The neighbourhood where he and Michael had shared something like an existence, and there! The market where they did their weekly shopping, now a place shrouded in pale blue fog, ragged, human silhouettes rising on near skeletal wings, only to be snatched from the air by coiling octopus tendrils, dragged back down into the muck. Further still, places less familiar: arterial networks of road and train line, either severed by whatever cataclysm had occurred or warped by it; concrete running like water, blood or fire, rising from the earth to pour up, up into the clouds, and on into whatever infinity lay beyond. Everywhere his fugitive eye turned, remnants of the familiar clashed with the absurd, the former more often than not giving birth to the latter, as though all that was had grown weary of whatever restrictions its nature imposed and decided to rebel, re-writing itself according to inspiration rather than function.

Strange playgrounds . . . the same concept occurring and recurring, the voice that spoke it old, known to him; his own in another life; one in which all he lived now was nothing but idle fantasy, fit only to be consigned to paper or canvas; communicated to other imaginations where they might take root and gestate . . .

Even as he rose, tossed and turned on winds that stirred not so much as a leaf or speck of dust in the Promethean world below, he withdrew, hurtling back to the flesh and face he'd made, loving and resenting the condition more profoundly than any mate or nemesis.

Anthony Wier opened his eyes, gripping the rotten wood of the windowsill hard enough for his fingers to bite through, for his skin to split and flow. *Why*? Why would he return to this?; Decay and definition; a state saddled by memory and time . . . the formerly unconscious processes of flesh—digestion, respiration; the pulse of blood and bile through their allotted channels—rendered acute and distinct; *repulsive* in their particularity. His mote-self screamed, aching to be unbound again, free to wander the Playgrounds as it saw fit.

It couldn't be, not yet; maybe not ever. He was still too in love with writing *roles* for himself; going naked and unremembered in their world, along with others who were dreamed and dreamers in their turn. Verity waited for him out there, somewhere, growing more distant as the day died. Maybe that's what would define their new game, the story it would trail: a pursuit through apocalypse; two that presumed themselves enemies or lovers trysting, brawling; fucking and betraying across the broken world, finally finding one another at the seam whose undoing would result in terminal rupture, falling together even as they tore and bled, embracing, flowing together, sprouting wings . . .

Maybe nothing quite so transcendent; little more than he and Michael had enjoyed. If so, so; he would do as he always had: let inspiration be his guide; make the world canvas.

Turning away from the window—the children's games having turned secret and forbidden as night drew in; laughter giving way to sighs and whispers as they confessed all that obsessed and terrified-, he staggered across the room towards the opening in the wall. Every step brought fresh visions—children herded into swamps and cesspools, suffocating en masse on their parent's sewage; a pastor foisting incest on his twin offspring under the belief that doing so would inure them to sodomite inclinations; walking the streets, bare foot and shit stained, lost in a fugue of autistic obsession, barely registering the pangs of hunger; the itching and soreness of an unwashed, variously infected body—all familiar; all imagined, experienced or inflicted upon him in one story or another.

Grasping the ragged lips of the rent, teetering on its edge, he saw the darkness beyond ripple and convulse, songs rising from the depths of the states they'd sculpt from themselves for him, if he'd only consent to lose himself in them again, like those he'd abandoned. He heard them now, too; the dreamers in the walls, their stories assaulting him, seeking purchase enough to drag him from his feet, back down to where they could infest him once more.

He didn't resist, allowing them to anchor themselves, but whereas before he'd lost himself to them; allowing them to eclipse whatever semblance of self he'd managed to scavenge, now he used them as conduits, flooding them with *his* inspirations, in hope that they might stir the dreamers, waking them to worlds upturned . . .

Waking or dreaming, they'd find no salvation via this path. This was *his;* a channel carved from desperation, the invisible extremities with which he'd scratched and bored through the rock worn down to near nothing. Just as Verity said: they'd have to make their own ways, given time, or remain forever.

The walls suddenly softened beneath his fingers, flapping and fluttering like stage curtains caught up in synthetic winds. He gripped the flailing matter, drawing it together even as the darkness beyond swarmed, the cancerous dreams it vomited into his face and thoughts enough to drown in. The stories anchored in him tore loose, for the most part, unwilling to be severed for want of sharing themselves. Those that held fast sang as they were sheared through and fell away, squirming on the floorboards, still intent on being known.

He flew, snared from behind by hooks in his eyes, his temples. *Nothing;* perfect, dreamless; a blank page, his very being scrawling and spattering poetry across it. Momentarily divorced, he glimpsed the confection of

Anthony Wier as he had before: as something sculpted, fashioned from clay or marzipan; only one of many millions that had gone before. He saw them now, too: names and faces scattered like stars across November night sky, their profusion doing nothing to confuse or dilute particularity. Countless lives; an infinity of playgrounds, each delved to the point of abandonment or dissolution. Many still remained, like this one, sustained by other dreamers: Verity's forebears and siblings, whereas others had collapsed or deflated, akin to the very first he'd known. He flew through them, snaring upon them, experiencing each as though newborn.

Then he woke, eyes far older than when they'd closed. Aching, tender as something freshly sewn, he rose from the floorboards, sighing in the moon and starlight that filtered through the window. He yearned to be out amongst the whispers that rode it; to hear the children's confessions and join in their games.

The far wall, cracked, stained with damp and rot, stood whole again, nothing to suggest its parting save for a coruscating pencil line, faint vapour seeping through as it healed.

Turning away, he glanced at the bed, smiling as he recalled all he and Verity had done there:

A place away, somewhere Michael couldn't know. No one came here; not dealers or lovers, not friends or confessors. This was his: an ancillary skull in which to be someone else; any one of a million others whispering amongst his thoughts.

Verity was the first, and last. How or why was lost in the heat; he barely recalled leaving The Crown, travelling here: flashes of running, wild and lupine through Autumnal woods, of crawling through back-lanes and alley-ways, pale and reptilian . . . nothing; adolescent fantasies swept away before the promise of the boy's body, beneath his strokes and kisses.

The place stank of ash and sweat, freezing cold from the broken window. Neither cared, grunts and sighs coming between kisses, inscrutable oaths and confessions: poetry more earnest than any ever written; a song more passionate than any contrived in the name of love.

They alternately stripped and tore one another naked, shifting between animalism and solemnity from moment to moment, kisses giving way to bites, the almost bleeding wounds carved by teeth kissed clean in their turn. The youth was a revelation in every inch; pale to the point of albinism, the hair of his chest and crotch so fine, it might've been threads of moonlight tangled there. He didn't know any more than Wier himself did, save on the most instinctive of levels. Yet they came together not like two strangers sharing a furtive one night stand, but as old lovers, so well known to one another that not a kiss or caress fell out of place.

Then that moment: the sublime invitation, his acceptance of it, flesh flowing like molten wax around him; a living ocean into which he plunged, happy to drown or be battered to blood and nothing on its tides.

What he hadn't recalled before was his own flesh flowing, their conjoined anatomies co-mingling, nerve sewing to nerve, memory to memory.

He tasted the boy's fear; his years spent wandering, scavenging; living off lovers, makeshift parents; the perversities he'd been forced to enact or had been a willing participant in, all the while suppressing or indulging the urge to fly, love and comfort no more anchors than abuse or sadism.

And Wier had shared himself in turn, seeing himself reflected in another's eyes; through the lens of another's experience, the revelations that swelled between them grand and terrifying; enough to make him tear away at the point of being fully realised, willing to risk insanity and worse for the sake of sustaining the confection of Anthony Wier.

He saw both of them now like actors in a stage play: Verity panting, bloody atop the bed, Wier caught up, carried back by what spilled from the widening hole. He didn't struggle, seeming to be asleep, Verity reaching out to him, croaking denials even as he was dragged down, down into the gullet of his own nightmares.

Nothing now; a story almost ended, making way for the numberless that would come after. Dust floated on the moonbeams, moths battering their wings against the window, seeking entry, though all light within had dimmed.

This place . . . maybe he'd return, one day. Maybe it would collapse the instant he left, going along with his need of it. He no longer cared.

Heart a hammer against the walls of a glass asylum, sinuses burning, he opened the bedroom door, eager to wake at last.

ABOUT GEORGE DANILE LEA

George Lea is a happily isolated soul that tends to haunt his small birth-town of Tamworth in the Midlands of the U.K. He has been a writer for as long as he can recall, in love with stories and whatever his imagination can contrive since the cradle or before, and also serves as a support worker for for people of mental disabilities for his bread and butter. He believes that stories are arenas in which we learn who and what we are, and where we find the means of transgressing those parameters: "Learning to flay yourself and sculpt the raw, bleeding stuff underneath is what stories—and all art—are for. There is no higher purpose or aspiration."

12045246R00180

Printed in Great Britain
by Amazon.co.uk, Ltd.,
Marston Gate.